This tender story will pull at your heartstrings from the very first page to its last. Once again, Roemer weaves the timeless truths of God's provision and faithfulness into the lives of her characters. Despite the hardships they face, Daniel and Maggie discover the glorious joy that comes in the morning (Psalm 30:5). I rejoiced with them and so will you.

— SAVANNA KAISER, GENESIS AWARD-WINNING AUTHOR AND REVIEWER

"A Lasting Legacy" is a skillfully written, well-researched historical with a tender, yet raw faith thread that leaves you heart-warmed and satisfied. Poignant historical romance at its finest.

— CARA GRANDLE, AUTHOR OF THE ROCK AND THE RIBBON

Any Cynthia Roemer story guarantees readers an authentic and inspiring journey into the historic times and settings being explored. Her newest title, "A Lasting Legacy" in the *Chiseled on the Heart* Novella Collection, fulfills our expectations perfectly. Daniel's devastating loss in battle connects him to a blessed legacy. When he and Maggie are snowed in and helpless on Christmas Eve, God gives them the tremendous gift of becoming a living nativity. Read, enjoy, and prepare to have your heart warmed.

— DELORES TOPLIFF, AUTHOR OF WILDERNESS WIFE

I'm a huge fan of Kelly Goshorn's books, and *The Christmas Carving* has become another favorite! This delightful novella is a poignant reminder of the enduring power of faith, the healing potential of love, and the transformative magic of Christmas. I highly recommend it!

— MISTY M. BELLER, *USA TODAY* BESTSELLING AUTHOR OF THE BROTHERS OF SAPPHIRE RANCH SERIES

Goshorn weaves a deeply beautiful story of love, community, and reconciliation set within the folds of Christmas hope. Readers will ache for the characters, sigh in contentment at its conclusion, and leave pondering how they might grow into Christmas. This is a Christmas story to be read over and over again and should not be missed.

— CRYSTAL CAUDILL, AUTHOR OF *COUNTERFEIT FAITH*

"The Christmas Carving" is the perfect historical holiday read, with relatable characters, misunderstandings and themes of forgiveness, and all the feels. Enjoy with a mug of hot chocolate as you cheer Maddy and Wyatt on to reclaiming faith, hope, and finding love at Christmas.

— CAROLYN MILLER, BESTSELLING AUTHOR OF THE REGENCY BRIDES AND ORIGINAL SIX ROMANCE SERIES.

Sublime. A journey of hope deep into the hearts of two people caught up in the wrong circumstances and God's marvelous path to redemption. Triumphant.

— KATHLEEN L. MAHER, AWARD-WINNING
AUTHOR OF THE SONS OF THE SHENANDOAH
SERIES

Three years ago, he broke her heart, but this Christmas she has returned to help him find peace. "The Christmas Carving" is a heartwarming, hopeful walk through the aftermath of the Civil War while a lone woman tries to reignite the spirit of forgiveness and unity in a broken community, and broken lives. Rich with heart, symbols, and the spirit of Christmas, Kelly Goshorn has woven a story that stirs the soul.

— ANGELA K COUCH, AUTHOR OF *A ROSE FOR
THE RESISTANCE* AND *WHERE WILD ROSES
BLOOM*

Candace West weaves a tale of loss, forgiveness, and sacrificial love—I devoured Nathaniel and Delia's story! "Healing Within the Pieces" has left an indelible mark on my heart and will stay with me for years to come.

— TARA JOHNSON, AUTHOR OF *ENGRAVED ON
THE HEART, WHERE DANDELIONS BLOOM,*
AND *ALL THROUGH THE NIGHT*

As Christmas approaches, we are reminded of the unmerited grace God extended us when He sent His only Son into our world. This book begins with characters who are confronted with unexpected kindness. As the story continues, they help each other accept the fact that God's love is offered freely, even when it is not deserved. Beautifully written, this story will stay with you into the new year.

— JENNY CARLISLE, AUTHOR OF *HOPE TAKES THE REINS* AND *FAITH MOVES MOUNTAINS*

This story of two orphaned children, who have to relocate to Connecticut amidst the beginnings of the American Revolutionary War, puts a personal face on the hardships our early settlers experienced. Cooper's fine research and storytelling ability bring the Revolutionary War to life. Her plot, filled with excitement and danger, loyalty and love, allows the reader to experience American's birthing as seen through the eyes of young Elias

— CAROL STRATTON, AUTHOR OF *THE LITTLEST BELL RINGER*; MEMBER OF ADVANCED WRITERS AND SPEAKERS; MEMBER OF CHRISTIAN WOMEN SPEAKERS

Elaine Cooper's novella, "The Gift of a Lamb," is a must-read for those who want to escape the hustle and bustle of the holiday season and take stock of the things that are truly important. I instantly fell in love with Elias and Charlotte. Their journey to their new home in the midst of their grief and America's fight for independence helped me remember the high price paid for my freedom. And the love they shared with the people they met along the way, inspired me to hold those I love a little closer and treasure God's blessings even more.

— ANNETTE MARIE GRIFFIN, AWARD-WINNING AUTHOR AND SPEAKER

Chiseled ON THE Heart

Elaine Marie Cooper

Kelly Goshorn

Cynthia Roemer

Candace West

Scrivenings PRESS

Quench your thirst for story.

www.ScriveningsPress.com

THE *Gift* OF A *Lamb*

Elaine Marie Cooper

This story is dedicated to my husband Steve.

One

28 June 1776, Taylorstown, Virginia

Elias Hawkins kicked hard at the rock on the ground, sending it through the air and several rods toward the large horse barn. The distance was his best yet. Papa would be …

Tears filled the ten-year-old's eyes at the thought. Papa and Mama were no longer there to share such triumphs.

It still did not seem real. One day, Papa seemed as well as ever. The next day, fever overtook him, and then the dreaded smallpox. Elias's beautiful mother insisted on nursing her husband back to health. But she fell victim to the dreaded plague.

Elias wasn't supposed to stand outside her sickroom door, but he longed to see his mother. When he stared at her face with the disfiguring pustules, he nearly vomited. His Aunt Margaret placed her hands on his shoulders and forced him down the hallway toward his room. "Stay there until you can follow orders," she said with a stern voice.

He threw himself on his bed that day and never wanted to get out from under the covers. It was only his fourteen-year-old sister Charlotte who managed to persuade him to get dressed and walk arm-in-arm with her as the siblings strode behind their parents' caskets. They were transported on a wagon to their place of burial. He barely remembered the event, just a lot of tears and whisperings of "poor children."

By that time, Elias's tears had mostly dried, but they were replaced by moments of intense rage. Why did God not save his parents? He knew that Jesus had healed many when He walked on the earth. Couldn't He have reached down from heaven and healed his mama and papa? Did God not love them? Did God love him?

These questions went unanswered, and he dared not ask his Aunt Margaret. She seemed to be angry all the time anyway. *Is that how God is?*

Elias sighed and ambled back to the house, hands in his pockets. Charlotte came out the front door of their Virginia home. He could tell she'd been crying. "What's wrong, Char?"

She crossed her arms tightly across her chest and, with lips trembling, said the words that would change their lives forever. "Mama and Papa arranged for us to go live with our aunt and uncle in Connecticut. Wherever that is."

Frozen in his tracks, Elias tried to speak, but the words caught in his throat. Charlotte grabbed him in her arms and wept uncontrollably. Despite her sobs, he heard Uncle Silas yelling inside. "I told you to wait until we'd had a chance to speak to them together. And in a week or two, not so soon after the burial!"

Looking up at the open front door, Elias noticed Solomon, the black servant, staring at him and Charlotte. Were those tears he wiped away? Solomon seemed as wise to Elias as the king in the Bible with the same name. The servant spoke few words to the children, but the things he did say seemed to carry much truth. Elias often pondered his words as he lay in bed at night. He would miss Solomon almost as much as he would miss Uncle Silas.

Aunt Margaret's voice was as harsh as her manner. "Well, if you and I were not good enough to raise them, they might as well leave for Connecticut."

There was a pause, and Elias imagined Uncle Silas staring at his wife the way he often did. "Have you no sympathy for these children, Margaret?" Elias heard a door inside slam.

Charlotte looked down at Elias and wiped her tears on her apron. "I can see why Mama and Papa decided we should not stay with them."

"But we have to leave Virginia. And all our friends. Besides, I love Uncle Silas."

"I know. I do as well. He is so much like Papa." Charlotte turned and slowly walked toward the front steps. She entered the doorway, and Elias heard her speaking quietly to Uncle Silas. Then, silence.

At least it will be Uncle Silas who brings us to Connecticut. I could not bear the thought of a long journey with Aunt Margaret.

AT DINNER THAT EVENING, the atmosphere chilled each word spoken between their aunt and uncle.

"I suppose you heard of the events on Sullivan's Island?" Aunt Margaret's mouth drew taut as she sipped her coffee.

Anger glared from Uncle Silas's eyes. "Perhaps it would be best to speak of happier things here at table."

"Where is Sullivan's Island?" Elias stabbed his fork into the sweet potatoes.

"'Tis far away, in South Carolina." Uncle Silas looked with tender eyes at Elias and smiled. "No need to worry about such things that need not trouble us."

"So, 'tis not near Connecticut?" Charlotte lifted her fear-filled eyes toward their uncle.

"Nay, child, we shall be safe on our journey." Uncle Silas grinned.

Aunt Margaret stood up and announced she'd be retiring early. No one said anything as she left the room.

There was a moment of silence. "Try not to judge Aunt Margaret too harshly. She has had many a heartache in her life." Uncle Silas rose and thanked Solomon for pulling out his chair.

Their papa's brother kissed them each on the cheek then retired upstairs.

Elias looked at Charlotte. "I don't care about Aunt Margaret's heartaches. She could still be nicer."

Solomon did not speak but gently placed comforting hands on their shoulders.

"Thank you, Solomon. I shall miss you greatly." Charlotte's lips trembled, and she hurried upstairs.

Elias looked at their friend and hugged him briefly before running up the steps.

Two

Elias tried to scream, but no sound emerged. Waking up in a drenching sweat, he gasped for breath, horrified at what he'd seen in his mind's eye.

He'd dreamed that his parents were both alive. Aunt Margaret grabbed his mother and threw her down a deep crevice into a hole in the ground. Father ran after Mother, but Aunt Margaret grabbed him by the shoulders and threw Father down the wretched hole as well.

When she came toward him, Elias knew he would be next. That was when he woke up.

As his surroundings became clearer and his heart slowed to a normal rhythm, he remembered that his mother and father were indeed gone on to eternity. Salty tears joined the sweat on his face, and he tried to smother his sobs with the feather pillow on his narrow cot.

His life had become a living nightmare.

He took slow, deep breaths, the kind Mother had taught him to do when he was upset. His parents had always shown him what to do. Who would show him now?

Probably Char. Char? Was that her sobbing in the next room?

He threw the sheet off and stumbled over toy soldiers on the floor as he hurried out his door. Placing his ear against Char's portal, he could hear her cries. They threatened to break Elias' heart anew.

Elias carefully tugged on the door handle, and the creaking hinge prompted him to wince. "Char?"

If she heard him, she did not acknowledge his voice but persisted in wailing. "Char? Char, please tell me what's wrong."

No response.

Fear gripped Elias. He'd never seen his sister cry so much that she ignored him. He ran out the open door to search for Uncle Silas.

Despite several pleas for his uncle, Elias heard nothing. Except Aunt Margaret walking toward the bottom of the wooden steps. "What is all that commotion?"

He covered his mouth and peered around the stair landing. "Sorry, Aunt Margaret. I was looking for Uncle Silas."

"Well, you won't find him here." Her voice held an edgy tone —almost as sharp as Uncle Silas's straight razor.

Elias swallowed. "Do you know when he'll be back?"

"Don't know. He's gone to Farmer McDuff's to borrow his Conestoga wagon." Aunt Margaret's eyes squinted with suspicion. "Why?"

He hoped Char would forgive him for telling Aunt Margaret about her sobs. Elias didn't know what else to do.

"Aunt Margaret, Charlotte is crying something fierce. I think she may be sick. Or dying or something." Elias hadn't realized how upset he was until now. "Can you help her?"

His aunt exhaled loudly, grabbed the handrail, and made her way upstairs.

I sure hope Char forgives me.

❀

WHEN UNCLE SILAS returned later that morning, Elias hurried toward the wagon. "Can you see if Charlotte is well, Uncle? I fear she may be ill."

"Ill?" His uncle's eyes narrowed and he set the brake on the wagon. "Margaret? Is Charlotte well?"

Elias hadn't noticed his aunt emerging from the house. He stared at the ground, then lifted his gaze to look at her.

Aunt Margaret's smile was unexpected. "She'll be fine, Silas. We had a talk. I think she's feeling a bit better."

I don't think I'd be feeling better if Aunt Margaret had a talk with me.

Then his uncle reached out to his wife and held her close. He pulled back and stroked her hair that had come undone. "You should smile more, my dear."

Elias's skin crawled, like it had the time he sat on an ant's nest. He ran up the front steps as fast as he could and nearly bumped into Charlotte. "Are you all right, Char? You're not mad at me, are you?"

"Mad at you? Why?"

"For sending Aunt Margaret in to you. I thought you'd be mad as a hornet."

"No. She helped me."

Elias squinted. "Helped you? That old bat?"

"Hush, Elias. You're bein' mean—mean as a hornet." She turned and hurried outside to greet Uncle Silas.

Elias stood there and scratched his head. *Girls. I'll never understand 'em.*

Uncle Silas called him. "You 'bout ready to load up the wagon?"

"Yessir."

"Good. The sooner we get packed up, the sooner I can come home to my wife."

Elias didn't think he'd ever understand some things. Like why his uncle was anxious to return to his mean wife.

Elias ran upstairs to make sure he'd not forgotten anything.

When he realized he'd nearly left behind the wooden sheep carved by his father, he inhaled with relief. It was all he had left of Papa. Holding it close to his heart, he then stuffed it inside his bag and ran downstairs. He stopped briefly to say farewell to Aunt Margaret.

Instead of a curt goodbye, Aunt Margaret pulled him close and hugged him so tight he thought he might stop breathing then and there. She released him just in time, before he thought he could have joined his parents in the cemetery. He nearly fell over from shock when he noticed Aunt Margaret flick away tears from her cheeks. "You go on now, Elias. Don't you make your uncle wait."

He gaped at his tall aunt, and her face turned sterner. "Go on now." She pointed toward the wagon.

Unable to find his voice, he did an about-face and raced to the wagon. Her voice rang out behind him. "You children don't forget to wash your face and hands every morning. You don't want your Aunt Lizbeth and Uncle Samuel to think we didn't teach you manners."

Without thinking, he turned toward her. "We won't." He waved goodbye to Aunt Margaret and discovered tears on his own cheeks. Was it saying goodbye to her that prompted his emotions, or was it leaving the only home he'd ever known? He and Charlotte had grown up in this house with his parents and aunt and uncle. So many memories—both good and heartbreaking.

"Come on, Elias. Time to go." His uncle's softly spoken words prompted him to quickly climb aboard the Conestoga. He plopped into the well of the wagon and sat next to Charlotte. "Are you all right, Char?"

She nodded, her eyes red with shed tears. "It's really sad leaving this home though."

"You'll get right used to your new home in Connecticut. You'll have your other aunt and uncle and two cousins to grow up with." Uncle Silas sped the horses up, since they had reached the main road.

Elias pondered that thought. "How old are they?"

"Let's see, Abigail must be about Char's age, and the little one is just two."

Charlotte and Elias stared at each other. "So, there were twelve years between them? With no babies?" Charlotte spoke louder so Uncle Silas could hear her.

Uncle Silas didn't speak for a moment. "They had other babies, but they didn't survive."

Elias started to speak but Charlotte hushed him. She whispered, "That means they died."

"Well, why didn't he just say that?"

"He did ... oh never mind. You're such a child." Charlotte turned away with a disgusted look on her face.

Elias tried to swallow the hurt away, but he turned his head to the side so Char would not see the tears welling in his eyes. What was wrong with her? She never used to be so ... so ... prissy. He wished there was a boy in Connecticut his age, so they could fish and look for frogs together. All he needed was another prissy cousin.

The warm air made him sleepy, and though he tried to stay awake, his head jerked downward once or twice. He finally gave in and laid his head on the canvas bag. He felt the wooden sheep underneath his forehead and drew it out to place it close to his heart. Maybe if he slept, he wouldn't miss Mama and Papa so much.

WHEN HE WOKE UP, the wagon was still, but the town they were in was anything but quiet. Elias pushed himself up to a sitting position and yawned. He peeked out the opening in the canvas and gasped at the number of people he saw. Even if they stood still, he doubted he could count all of them. The wagon had stopped in front of a large building with a sign that read "INN."

He looked around, worried until he saw Uncle Silas speaking with two men. Both of them chewed on something that they then spit onto the ground. Charlotte awoke and pushed herself next to Elias.

"Ewww, that's disgusting! What are those men spitting out of their mouths?" She clapped her hand over her mouth, her eyes widening in surprise. She whispered, "Oh no ..."

Uncle Silas had heard her. He walked toward the wagon, his brows lowered. "Charlotte, did your parents not teach you any manners atall? Your voice carried clear over to those men, and your words smacked of rudeness."

Char swept her gaze downward, and tears flowed from her eyes. "I'm sorry, Uncle Silas." Her silent tears progressed to loud sobs.

Uncle Silas appeared to be at a loss for what to do. He awkwardly patted her on her back and then cleared his throat. He spoke quietly. "Charlotte, I'm truly sorry I was so harsh with you. It's been a long few weeks, and I am missing my brother somethin' fierce." He adjusted his hat, wiping sweat from his forehead. "You know how some men put tobacco in pipes? Well, these men—and others—prefer to chew it up. Then they spit it out."

Charlotte pulled her head up and whispered. "But it looks so ugly when that brown juice rolls on their chin."

Uncle Silas put his hands on his hips and looked at the ground while smirking. He looked much younger with his tricorn hat tipped back and a grin on his face. "You've got that right, Charlotte. But now that you're older, folks expect you to treat them with courtesy. Understand?"

She rolled her eyes. "I guess so."

Why was his uncle saying things like "Now that you're older?" *She seems like the same Charlotte to me. Maybe just a bit grumpier.*

~

LATER ON, when Uncle Silas tucked him into bed, Elias asked him about it.

Uncle Silas cleared his throat, opened his mouth, and then stopped again. He seemed to struggle for his words. Finally, he breathed in deeply and began.

"When girls reach a certain age, they start to change."

"You mean get bigger? But that's what we all do." Elias scratched his head.

"Well, other things happen too." Uncle Silas tugged at his ear, and Elias could see red coming up from his collar. He was surely embarrassed about something.

Elias sat up abruptly. "She's not dying, is she?"

"Nay, nay, Elias, Charlotte's fine. She's growing up, becoming a young woman."

"A woman?" Elias narrowed his eyes. "She doesn't look like a woman to me." Elias stared at his uncle.

Uncle Silas closed his eyes on a deep breath and held his forehead. "Elias, my head hurts. Let's get some sleep."

"But, I have more questions ..."

Uncle Silas held up his hands to stop him. "Not tonight, Elias. I'm plum worn out from this conversation. Night."

"Night." Elias rolled onto his side. Sometimes Uncle Silas confused him. He couldn't imagine that saying a couple of sentences would wear a grown man out.

Three

The trip to Philadelphia seemed like it'd never end. The mosquitoes feasted on all of them, and the main sound heard in the wagon was hands slapping on flesh. Elias started to count the dead bugs to while away the time.

When they finally rolled into the city, he gasped at the crowds. Never before had he seen this many people. There seemed to be a huge gathering in front of a grand building.

Elias pushed himself up to his uncle's shoulder. "What are all these people doing out here in the middle of the day? It's so very hot."

Uncle Silas's mouth opened, and Elias wondered if a mosquito might fly inside. After a long moment, his uncle responded. "I know not, Elias." He pulled off to the side of the road and pulled the lock on the wagon. He jumped down and tugged on a passerby's sleeve. "I say, can you tell me what's happening?"

The finely dressed gentleman in a brown suit and white cravat looked at Silas from head to toe. "I see ye are not from here. They are preparing to read from the Declaration."

Uncle Silas's eyes drew together. "Declaration?"

"Are ye so daft, man, ye do not know what has occurred here

in Philadelphia?" He shook his head in disgust and moved with the crowd toward the grand brick building.

The man's rudeness stiffened Uncle Silas's jaw. "Come with me, children."

Charlotte and Elias climbed out of the wagon, and Uncle Silas held their hands tightly. "Stay with me. I've no wish to lose you in this crowd."

He pushed his way through the throng. Uncle Silas spoke under his breath, but Elias could hear him. "I'm a citizen of Virginia, and I have every right to be treated an equal by these fellow colonists."

They stopped at a place where he could observe a man in uniform standing on the steps with a scroll. Uncle Silas drew Elias and Charlotte in front of himself and clasped their shoulders. They waited and waited. Elias heard whispers from nearby.

"What do ye s'pose that Congress came up with, Mabel?" one man said.

"I've no idea, Jacob. But I hope they get on with this readin', as I'm about to die of this heat in my corset."

Elias grew fascinated by how fast Mabel could fan herself, struggling not to laugh as he imagined the corset. He was amazed at this stranger speaking of an undergarment so freely when out in public.

He watched a line of soldiers in white and blue uniforms line up in front of the steps. Some of them carried flags that read "Live Free or Die."

Elias glanced upward at Uncle Silas. "What does that mean, "Live Free or Die?"

Uncle Silas shook his head slowly. "Not certain, Elias. But I think we're about to find out."

"In Congress ... this eighth day of July, 1776 ..."

Elias listened in awe as the words were read slowly and loudly. It reminded him of when Aunt Margaret would scold him for acting naughty.

"When, in the course of human events, it becomes necessary for one people to dissolve the political bands which have connected them ..."

What did those fancy words mean? He looked up at Uncle Silas and almost asked him. But his uncle had grown pale and visibly swallowed as if he had a chunk of potato stuck in his throat.

"We hold these truths to be self-evident, that all men are created equal ..."

The reading lost Elias at the word "self-evident." He knew he could never keep up and busied his foot moving a twig around the brick street. A crying baby caught his attention, and he wondered why someone would bring an infant to this boring gathering. Elias glanced at Charlotte, whose gaze was riveted on the speaker. He guessed she knew what "self-evident" meant. It must be boring to be an adult.

This "Declaration" went on and on. He grew warmer in the blazing sun and thought about asking Mabel if he could borrow her fan. But when he looked at her, he feared she might faint, as her cheeks grew redder and sweat dripped from her face. *That corset must be really tight.*

Suddenly the speaker rolled up the parchment scroll and all remained totally quiet—until the drums began. They played a steady beat that prompted the soldiers on horseback to turn and head down the road. The clip-clop of the horseshoes on the bricks was loud. Louder than on dirt.

He glanced at Charlotte, who looked frozen in place despite the heat. Uncle Silas shook her shoulders gently. "Time to go, Charlotte."

For the first time, Elias saw some tears on her cheeks. Come to think of it, Mabel might have been crying instead of sweating. What was this Declaration? It must be important to evoke such emotion in so many people, including his sister.

Uncle Silas grabbed Elias's hand tightly but placed his arm tenderly around Charlotte's shoulders.

Elias knew this was likely not the time to ask questions. There were a few things even a ten-year-old boy understood.

CHARLOTTE HADN'T SPOKEN a word to him all night, ever since they left that reading. Even when they checked into the inn that evening, she was so quiet it made Elias nervous.

"Char, are you all right?"

There was a long pause. "I s'pose so."

Uncle Silas had been quieter than usual too. He inhaled deeply then spoke. "I think Charlotte is a bit disturbed by the reading of that Declaration."

Elias shrugged his shoulders. "Why? I didn't even understand it."

Uncle Silas tousled his hair. "There were some mighty big words in there. Mostly, they declared that the colonies were going to no longer be under the rule of Mother England."

"Is that all?" Elias was even more confused. "That's no big problem. Is it?" He looked from his uncle to his sister, then back again. He'd never been to "Mother England." Virginia was his home, and now, it seemed, Connecticut.

Charlotte lashed out at him. "You are such a child! Don't you know that will mean war?" She threw her head back on the pillow and turned herself toward the wall.

"Is that so, Uncle Silas?" Elias understood all of this less and less.

"That is likely what will happen, Elias." Uncle Silas lay down on the bed next to him. His eyes had dark circles beneath them. "That Declaration was a bold statement by our Congress. 'Twill undoubtedly lead to war."

Elias contemplated what he said. "Is war very terrible?"

Uncle Silas rolled onto his back and placed the back of his arm across his forehead. "Aye, Elias. Terrible indeed."

"You fought in the French War, did you not, Uncle Silas?"

There was a moment of silence. "Aye. I did."

"My papa told me. But, you never speak of it." Elias narrowed his eyes.

Was that a tear rolling down his uncle's cheek?

"Good night, Elias." His uncle leaned toward the candle on the bedside table and blew it out.

"Good night."

Four

They did not travel the next day, nor the day after that. Uncle Silas spent much time speaking with the local officials about the situation in New York, their next intended stop before arriving in Connecticut.

"Char, why do ya s'pose New York is different? Uncle Silas sure looks worried." Elias placed his book facedown on the floor then rested his chin on both palms while sitting cross-legged on the floor. There was little to do in the inn, but it was good to rest from riding in a bumpy wagon.

"Because, silly, we're at war, and these are dangerous times. And Uncle Silas says the Regulars are in charge in New York." Char twisted her mouth and shook her head. "Go back to your book."

He picked up the primer he'd been reading, but soon his eyes were drawn toward the window. He set the book down again, pushed himself up off the floor, and sauntered toward the window. The streets seemed the same, except there were many groups of American soldiers nearby, guarding the grand building. His uncle had told him it was called the Pennsylvania Statehouse.

Just then, Uncle Silas returned. His face still carried a worried expression.

"We leave in the morning, early." He plopped down on the bed and exhaled loudly. Charlotte arose from the floor and crossed the room toward Uncle Silas.

"Is all well, Uncle?"

His grin seemed less than genuine. "Of course, Charlotte." He turned away and stared at the window.

Elias turned away from the window abruptly. "'Tis not all well, Uncle Silas. Mother taught us to never lie, and you are lying." He burst into tears.

"Elias! You apologize at once to Uncle Silas."

Their uncle stood and approached the window. "It's all right, Charlotte." He scanned the outdoors briefly and turned toward the children. "You are correct, Elias. All is not well. Ever since news of the Declaration of Independence went out, traveling has become more dangerous. I've asked two young soldiers to accompany us to Connecticut."

Neither Elias nor Charlotte spoke a word. Charlotte's lips trembled, and sobs burst from her lips. She threw herself onto her mattress and buried her face in a pillow. Uncle Silas went over and patted her back. "There, there, Charlotte. We'll be safe with these armed men beside us."

Elias strode toward his sister and perched on the edge of her bed. "Please don't cry, Char. Uncle Silas is watching out for us. And so is God."

His uncle looked at him and grinned. "True enough, Elias. True enough."

～

"Elias. Elias! Wake up!" Uncle Silas shook his shoulders.

Elias barely opened his eyes and pushed himself upright. "'Tis still dark." He threw his head back onto the pillow. As he rolled onto his side, he heard his sister speaking softly.

"Uncle Silas, these pants look ridiculous on me!"

That woke him. His sister wearing pants? This he had to see!

He sat up, all sweaty from the heat. Sure enough, there was Charlotte, dressed like a boy. Only, the breeches fit her sort of funny.

"What are you doing, Char?" He rubbed the sleep from his eyes. Her mouth firmed so tightly he knew he'd said the wrong thing. He'd be lucky if she spoke to him all day.

"Elias, mind your manners. I told your sister to wear them."

As he pulled on his own breeches, Elias scrutinized his sister's "new" apparel. They were too small to be his uncle's, but too large to be his. "Where'd you get those breeches?"

His uncle continued packing. "They were loaned to us by one of the soldiers. Let's hurry now. We need to leave before dawn. Charlotte, be sure your hair does not fall out from the tricorne."

As they loaded the wagon, Elias tugged on his uncle's sleeve. He kept his voice low. "Why is Char dressed like a boy?"

"I'll explain later. Now get in the wagon."

He saw the look of intensity in Uncle Silas's eyes and obeyed without question. He sat next to Charlotte and made sure he was more visible from the opening in the canvas than she was. He suddenly felt as if he needed to protect her, although he didn't know why.

"Are the soldiers nearby, Uncle Silas?" He swallowed past the lump in his throat.

"Aye. They be guardin' us."

Although Elias could not see them, he trusted his uncle. He closed his eyes and drifted off.

Five

Elias had no idea how long he'd slept. But an odd bird call woke him from a deep slumber. He tapped Uncle Silas's back. "What was that, Uncle Silas?"

Rather than answer him, Silas held a finger up as if to shush him and made a similar sound toward the woods. When he did so, two uniformed riders guided their horses through the trees and approached the Conestoga.

"Are they our friends, Uncle Silas?" Elias clung to his uncle's back.

"Aye, they are. They are guarding us on our trip. Greetings, Alexander and Thaddeus!"

"Greetings Mr. Hawkins." The two soldiers doffed their hats.

Elias had never met a soldier before. He never knew soldiers could look so young before, either. They looked to be no more than sixteen years old.

"Good day," Elias said.

They grinned at him. "And good day to you as well."

The nearest one said, "Do na' tell me my breeches fit you, young man!"

Elias scrunched his face. "Nay. My sister is wearing them. But they fit a bit strange on her." He shrugged his shoulders.

Alexander and Thaddeus looked at each other and grinned. "I s'pose that's to be expected." The one called Alexander turned redder in the face. Perhaps he was hot from the ride.

The soldiers looked at Uncle Silas, serious expressions on their faces. Thaddeus spoke.

"Mr. Hawkins, there is a guard on the road into New York. I suggest you come up with a reasonable explanation for driving into the city. And we also suggest you allow us to take the children on horseback through the woods. We can meet you on ahead, well past the sentries."

Silas was quiet for a moment. "Aye, that is likely the safest way. Elias. Charlotte. Come quickly."

Elias happily scampered out of the wagon and ran over to Thaddeus' horse. "May I ride with you?"

"Aye, lad." Thaddeus climbed down and hiked Elias onto the saddle. He climbed up behind him.

Charlotte looked terrified. "It's all right, Char. You'll be safe." Elias looked at her with pity.

"He's right you know. I'll not let any harm come to you, miss." Alexander seemed very kind. It seemed odd to Elias, considering his occupation.

Char looked amusing in breeches, stepping down from the wagon with dainty foot falls.

When she reached the ground, she turned toward Uncle Silas in the wagon. Her lips trembled as she spoke. "Uncle Silas, will you be safe?"

For the first time, Elias understood that they might all be in danger. What would they do if anything happened to their uncle? "Uncle Silas?"

"Aye, lad?"

Elias could not speak, as fear robbed his voice. His unspoken questions seemed to hang in the air like the dense smoke of battle.

Uncle Silas addressed both children. "I'll be safe, do not fear. And you will be safe as well. I shall see you both very soon."

With that declaration, Uncle Silas clicked his tongue, encouraging the horses to get moving.

Elias waved slowly at him as the wagon disappeared down the road.

Neither Elias nor Char spoke a word as fear gripped them.

"Well, time to get moving." Thaddeus brought reassurance in his voice and a commanding presence.

Charlotte looked up at Alexander and blushed as he lifted her up onto his saddle, then climbed up behind her. "Following you, Thad." The two horses with four riders soon entered into the thick woods.

"Remember to stay quiet," Thad said to Elias.

He doubted he could say a word anyway. His throat was so dry, and terror overwhelmed him.

At one point, Thad held his hand up, signaling the riders behind them to stop. Elias had to relieve himself so badly, he prayed he'd not wet the saddle. That would be too embarrassing.

Finally, Thad relaxed behind him, and they pushed onward.

"Please, Thad, I must relieve myself," he whispered.

Thad halted his horse again and dismounted. He lifted Elias from the saddle. No sooner did he reach the ground then he ran behind a tree for privacy. When Elias finished, Thad hurried him toward him by waving his hand. Just as Elias reached the horse, he heard the click of a pistol.

The four riders froze in place.

"Well, well. What have we here?" Two redcoats on foot held pistols aimed at the group. "And where might ye be traveling to, ye rebels?"

"Nowhere to coocern you." Alex stared at the enemy. "After all, we be taking a stroll with these lads and minding our own business. Our little brothers are bored of stayin' home. And what might be your business, lobsterbacks?"

At that insult, the soldiers began firing, and Alex and Thad returned fire.

Elias searched frantically for Charlotte but she was not in the saddle. Where was she? "Char! Char!"

He finally saw her, peeking out from behind a tree. She waved her hand for him to join her. He fell to the ground and crawled toward her. She pulled him behind the tree the last few inches, and they clung to each other. Her hat had fallen off, and her long hair draped down her back. Elias wanted to tell her to get it back on, but the gunfire was too much.

Just as quickly as it started, it ceased. The siblings continued to hold on to one another until a lobsterback's gaiters appeared in front of them. As one, Char and Elias looked up at the terrifying sight.

"Well, this is a pleasant surprise. Not two lads atall, but one sweet miss with hair the color of flax."

Elias prepared to punch the man, but before he could, Charlotte withdrew a small pistol from her pants and fired at the man's forehead. He fell backward with a thud.

Charlotte screamed, and Elias held her. Crying hysterically, she shouted, "I killed a man!"

"It's all right, miss. 'Twas a just killing." They both looked up at Alex, whose arm was coated with blood. He held a pistol in his other hand. His face appeared pale, and he plopped onto the ground in a sitting position.

"Where ... where's Thad?" Elias' voice trembled.

A moment of silence ensued. "He's gone." Alex lay down on the ground, his good arm covering his face as he wept.

Char released her grip on Elias and hurried toward Alex. "Elias, get a canteen. And something to bandage him."

He paused, still stunned, then thrust himself upright and searched for the items Char requested. In the meantime, she knelt, cradling the soldier in her arms, having torn Alex's shirt so she could reach his wound. Elias's legs weakened when he saw the hole in Alex's arm, which still oozed blood.

"Elias. Elias! Hand me the water and the linen." His sister didn't even seem bothered by the blood. After drenching the wound in fresh water, she gestured toward the soldier's arm. "Hold it up." Her voice commanded Elias as an adult might have.

He didn't mind her bossiness, but was fascinated by how quickly she wrapped Alex's arm tightly in several layers. Where did she learn that?

Elias noticed Alex did not stir. "Is he dead too?"

"Nay. See? He still breathes."

Scrunching his face, Elias asked, "How do you know all this stuff?"

Char's eyes glanced downward. "Mama taught me."

Before he wept at her words, he decided it was his turn to be brave. She was his sister. He had to protect her, somehow. "Drink some water, Char."

She grasped the canteen in her bloodied hands and drank several gulps. "Here. Your turn."

He did likewise then noticed Alex's eyes open. "Alex! You're awake! Please drink some water."

Char helped Alex upward, so he could drink without discomfort.

"Thanks." Alex rested his head back again.

"What should we do, Char?" Elias kept his voice steady, hoping she didn't notice his shaking hands.

"I think ... I think we need to pray."

The two closed their eyes and sought God's wisdom. They both knew they needed His guidance. And badly.

After their pleas to heaven—whispered lest anyone else hear them—Char inhaled deeply. "First we need to secure the horses. Elias, get some rope from the satchel and tie them to separate trees. Then ... I think we need to wait until it's dark to travel. "

Elias wanted to object. They were afraid enough without having to travel after nightfall. But something stopped him. She was the older one and had to make hard decisions. He would help her in whatever way he could. He stood up and grasped the leather bag on the horse's saddle. Searching inside he found the ropes and carefully looped each one through a bridle. All the while, he kept watch for anyone who might be nearby. After securing the mounts to separate trees, he slowly stepped towards the grassy plot of ground where Char held the wounded Alex.

In order to remain as quiet as possible, they stayed sitting on the ground. Whenever Alex awoke, they gave him more water. As soon as it was dark, Elias would go get pemmican, their travel food, from the haversacks. He could barely keep his eyes open, and Char encouraged him to sleep. "It's all right Elias. I reloaded the pistol Uncle Silas gave me. I'll keep watch."

When had Charlotte grown up so much? It must have been when he wasn't looking. That's what Papa used to always say.

Papa.

Elias had never missed him so much. He felt the wooden sheep inside his shirt, pushed it up and over his heart, and lay down to sleep.

Six

The crickets chirped, signaling nighttime. Elias awoke, sat up, and rubbed his eyes.

Char looked half asleep as she continued to cradle the wounded soldier.

"Char, I'm goin' to get the pemmican."

He crawled ever so slowly toward the nearest horse. He paused, then reached up to the haversack tied to the saddle and withdrew a bundle of the dried meat and fruit. Placing it inside his shirt next to the wooden lamb, he slowly crawled back to Char and Alex. "Here, Char. See if you can get Alex to eat some."

He devoured the piece in his hand while watching Char attempt to awaken the wounded man.

"Please, Alex, you must regain your strength." The man sat up slowly. Char handed him the canteen first, then the food.

Once he tasted the dried food, he chewed and swallowed it, obviously hungry. Char took a few bites, then handed him some more.

Now that the soldier had awakened, Elias was happy to defer to his instructions, despite Alex's weakness. When Alex appeared satiated, he looked around, more alert than he had been since he was wounded. "'Tis wise you waited till darkness. If you can help me stand, we must get to New York, posthaste. Your uncle will be frantic with worry."

Both Elias and Char helped the soldier stand. Elias lifted on one side, and Char placed her arm around his waist to help him upward. Although they avoided his injury, he still groaned in obvious pain.

"I'm so sorry, Alex." Char looked to be near tears.

The wounded man breathed with difficulty then spoke with a half grin. "'Tis all right. I'll be fit as a fiddle soon enough."

Elias observed the bloodied body of Thad on the ground. A sick pang, like a searing bayonet, thrust itself through his belly. He held on to the second horse's saddle and leaned his forehead against it.

"Are you well, Elias?" Char placed her arm around his shoulder.

I must be brave.

"Aye. I be fine, Char." Standing up straight, Elias turned toward Alex. "What shall we do with Thad?"

Alex looked downward then lifted his gaze, his jaw set. "We take him with us."

All three picked up the limp body of Thad and laid him across the saddle. Despite his wound, Alex did the major portion of the lifting. Elias grew in his amazement at the young man's strength. Alex brought a blanket over to throw across Thad's still form.

"I'll lead the horse," Elias said.

Alex nodded. "If we walk fairly slow, he'll not move too much." He tenderly touched Thad's bloodied hair and then walked toward his own mount. He began to lift Char upward into the saddle, but she backed away.

"Nay, my friend. I'll climb on myself." She set her borrowed boy's shoe into the stirrup, but her foot started to slip out until Alex caught her. Getting her grip, she pulled herself onto the leather saddle. This time, Alex had to push her backside to give her enough bounce in her efforts to mount the tall animal.

Elias started to grin but looked away so he would not cause offense.

"Miss, I sincerely apologize ..."

Char looked away. "No matter, 'twas necessary. What's done is done. Let's move on."

Alex climbed up onto the saddle behind her. Elias grew amazed at the young man's stamina. As weak as he was, and with just one useable arm, he managed to climb that tall horse and sit behind Char. Elias did notice that Alex clung to Char's waist rather tightly. Whether 'twas from weakness or something else, he could not tell. But he would not tell Uncle Silas. Just in case 'twas something else.

ELIAS LED Thad's horse behind Alex and Char, so exhausted he likely walked in his sleep. Alex pulled up and stopped. The soldier slid off his mount and quickly removed his soldier's jacket and anything else that identified his position in the Continental Army. He came prepared and unfurled a flannel coat he carried in his knapsack.

They were, unfortunately, in the Crown's territory now. Alex folded everything else into a tight wad and pushed it all into a canvas bag. He went to Thad's body to be certain nothing showed of his army affiliation.

Alex mounted his horse again, and they resumed their journey to New York. Finally, the sounds of men singing in a tavern greeted their ears.

Elias worried they'd never find Uncle Silas in this huge place with people milling everywhere. Alex did not seem concerned, as he headed in one direction without even looking around. They approached a quieter street, and Alex paused, slid off his horse, nearly falling this time, then he helped Char off the huge animal.

He tied his mount to a post then tied the horse led by Elias to another one.

He beckoned to Elias to follow him, then he stumbled toward the door of a much smaller tavern. Alex leaned down to whisper to the siblings. "I'm rather weak. Please pretend I've been drinking." He placed his arm around Charlotte's shoulders, and Elias fit himself around his other side, holding on to his waist.

Elias wanted to find Uncle Silas as soon as possible. His uncle would know what to do. Although Elias had been braver than he'd ever been before, he was ready to hand over the reins to a real adult. He'd gladly remain a child for now.

Inside the small establishment, he nearly shouted with relief to see Uncle Silas sitting at a table. Instinct prompted him to hold his tongue and let Alex lead the conversation.

Alex transformed in front of his eyes. First, he changed his speech to a slur, then a ridiculous grin spread across his face. "Silas, you blaggart, where've you been, old friend?"

Char joined in the deception. "Uncle Silas, Alex has been drinking—again." She rolled her eyes. "Please help me get him to bed to sleep it off."

By Uncle Silas's expression, Elias knew he perceived a problem and played along. His smile upon seeing them changed to a frown. "So this is how you thank me for taking you in off the streets?" He took over assisting Alex from Charlotte and Elias. Half dragging, half walking Alex to a back room, he kicked the door open, and Elias and Char followed them inside. Charlotte closed the door and locked it. When she turned around, tears were pouring down her cheeks.

"Oh, Uncle Silas!" She hurried to help him place Alex on a bed. "He was shot here in his arm, and he bled so very much." She attempted to smother her sobs as she helped her uncle remove Alex's boots.

"What happened?" He gathered Elias and Charlotte in his

arms and hugged them tightly. "I feared the worst when there was no sign of you for hours on end."

A weak voice behind the huddled group spoke. "They were very brave, Mr. Hawkins, in spite of it all."

Silas turned toward Alex. "Where is Thaddeus, son?"

Tears emerged from Alex's eyes. Before he was forced to answer, Elias tugged on his uncle's sleeve. "Come, I'll show you."

He led Uncle Silas to the door and unlocked it. "Char, lock this door behind us."

Walking past the few remaining tavern guests, the two exited and strode toward the horse with Thad's body upon it. When Uncle Silas lifted the blanket and saw the body covered with dried blood, he wept and shook his head back and forth. "'Tis a miracle you children are safe!"

"Thanks to Alex and Char. And God."

Uncle Silas stroked Elias's hair. "And thanks to this young soldier who gave his life protecting you."

"Aye." Tears rolled down Elias's cheeks. "I'll help you bury him in the woods."

Together they lifted the stiffening body off the horse and carried it into the forest behind the tavern.

Seven

Elias woke in the middle of the night to see Char and Uncle Silas applying wet cloths to Alex's brow. The soldier mumbled strange words and moved restlessly on the bed.

"Uncle Silas?"

"Elias. Please go look for the taverner and tell him we need a doctor. Quickly!"

He needed no further prompting, and he jumped out of bed before putting on his clothes.

"And only speak to the taverner. He can be trusted." Uncle Silas returned to tending Alex.

Char followed the boy to the door. "Stay alert, dear brother." She closed the door behind him, and he heard her bolt it.

The tavern was quiet. Where would he find the man who worked behind the bar? Elias needn't have worried, since the busy taverner was still up, drying beer steins.

"Ah. I thought you might be needing a doctor. Seen this aplenty." The taverner dried off his hands and came out from behind the bar.

Elias's eyes widened. "Sir, you will na' turn my friend in, will ye?"

The taverner placed both hands on Elias's shoulders. "Lad, the day I turn Tory will be a frozen day in hell." The man grinned. "The sooner we get those blaggart lobsterbacks out of America, the better. I'll fetch Dr. Ennis right quick for ye. Now, you wait here."

The man glanced both ways before scurrying out the door.

All Elias could do was wait. If he went into the room where Alex was tended, he'd wait and worry even more. Best to "wait here," as the man said.

The cricket song outdoors lulled Elias into a sleepy state. He finally gave in and laid his head on a table that smelled like ale. He could not have been asleep for long when voices outside woke him. Instinctively, Elias found a dark hiding place in a corner. He squatted down and held his breath.

Three men in the king's regimentals pushed open the door and began to shout for service. Obviously drunk, the men pounded on a table with their fists.

"Well, then, since the fellow canna' see fit to serve us, we'll just serve ourselves!" They must have thought this amusing as they all burst out in laughter. Elias hugged his legs tightly and barely breathed.

They grabbed three newly cleaned mugs and filled them to overflowing with ale from a spigot on a barrel. In between gorging themselves on excessive amounts of the brew, they carried on a loud conversation that alarmed Elias.

"These colonials are a pathetic lot. 'Tis a wonder the king tolerates their treasonous behavior. Did you hear the reading of that wretched document?" The speaker belched loudly.

"Aye, I did. But ya gotta admit, the colonial lasses provide much comfort to all of us." The men laughed raucously.

It was all Elias could do not to scream at these soldiers. Enraged by their words, he was ready to punch the horrid creatures but dared not. It was too risky. He kept his hands plastered across his lips lest he lose resolve.

After several more minutes of colonial insults, the men at last staggered out the tavern door, singing and holding their stolen steins.

For the first time, Elias understood why Americans could no longer tolerate the monarchy being in charge. The British cared nothing for the people of America. They just used the back-breaking labor of colonials to serve their purposes. Americans were little more than slaves of the king.

ELIAS FEARED EMERGING from his hiding place until he heard the taverner return. "Is all well, young lad?"

"Three soldiers of the king came and took your mugs. They drank your ale and didna leave so much as a ha'penny. They said terrible things about Americans. And some other things about ladies that I am not allowed to say." Elias placed his hands on his hips defiantly. "I know now why we must fight them."

The taverner tousled his hair. "Well, fortunately for your family, no need for you to join the army just yet." He looked at the opening door. "Ah, here is Dr. Ennis. Why do ya not show him the wounded man?"

The young doctor carried a leather haversack with him and had a serious bearing. "Please, show me the patient."

"Right this way, sir."

Dr. Ennis followed him down the hallway. Elias knocked on the door, and Char said, "Who is it?"

"It's me," Elias said. "I have the doctor with me."

She unbolted the door and opened it wide to allow for entrance. Dr. Ennis walked directly to Alex and examined him forthwith.

A look of concern crossed his face. "I believe the ball is still within the wound. I must remove it, lest infection set in." He began setting up his equipment.

"Uncle Silas?" Char approached him.

"You and Elias wait outside," their uncle said.

She shook her head. "Nay! I shall stay with him and help Dr. Ennis."

The doctor narrowed his eyes. "Are you certain, miss? There will be much blood. And pain."

Uncle Silas did not look pleased. "Charlotte, really this is …"

"I'm staying, Uncle Silas." Her adamant voice shocked Elias.

No one questioned her further, and Uncle Silas guided Elias out the door. They both walked out front as the first hints of dawn were etching streaks of color in the sky. Uncle Silas viewed the numerous regiments of king's soldiers unloading guns and cannons off ships in the harbor.

"Let's return inside, Elias. I've no stomach for this."

Eight

Elias awoke once again with his head lying on a table in the tavern. The morning birds sang in the trees outside, and he worried they all might leave if war started.

Sitting next to him, Uncle Silas ate breakfast provided by the taverner, who had generously heaped eggs, bacon, and fried cakes onto a pewter plate. He pushed his plate close enough to Elias so he could share in the bounty. Elias grabbed a crisp slice of bacon and devoured it, along with some fried cakes.

Dr. Ennis approached the table and plopped onto a chair. He exhaled loudly and removed his tricorn hat. He turned toward the taverner. "Any chance ye might have more breakfast, my friend?"

"Coming up forthwith, Dr. Ennis."

Elias paused in his eating, remembering Char. She must be hungry as well. "How is Alex, Dr. Ennis?"

"Sleeping soundly, lad. Your sister has done an excellent job tending his wound."

"Should I take her some food?"

"I imagine she'd be grateful." The doctor yawned then grinned at him.

Elias walked to the taverner. "Might I take some food to my sister, please?"

The taverner leaned down onto his elbows and grinned at Elias. "You can take her as much food as she wants." Smiling, the taverner stood up and filled another plate with enough food for a huge family.

Elias's eyes widened. "Thank you, sir."

He carried the food down the hall. Afraid he might drop something, he held tightly to the plate and whispered next to the door. "Char, let me in. I have breakfast for you."

The bolt was shifted, and Char opened the heavy door. "Thank you."

Elias stared at Alex's quiet form on the bed. He no longer appeared to be sweaty, and although pale, he no longer mumbled strange words.

"He's doing better?"

"Aye." Char's eyes riveted on the food. "I'm starving. Thank you, brother."

They sat side by side on an empty bed and ate the generous breakfast. It was such a relief not to feel in danger. At least for the moment.

"Char?'

"Um-hum?"

"Do you feel different after the last few days?"

"Aye. I somehow feel like I spent five years of growing up in five days."

"I feel the same. 'Tis strange, is it not?"

"Very."

They sat silently until Alex awoke. When Charlotte spoke to him, her voice soft and soothing, she sounded strange, almost like a grown-up.

Maybe she *had* grown up five years.

～

ALTHOUGH ALEX WAS STILL RECOVERING and likely would need many days in bed resting, Uncle Silas grew anxious to be on their way. The taverner agreed. "Those lobsterbacks might close up the city, and ye'd be stranded here. Best to be safe and head out."

Elias sensed danger in remaining in New York, and he hurried Charlotte along. "Come on. We must pack quickly."

"I will, but these intolerable breeches are so hard to put on. And that hat keeps falling off. My toes are cramped in these shoes ..."

"Char, let's be grateful. We're alive. But if we don't get a move on, we might not stay alive."

She said no more as she threw the last of her clothes into her satchel. Elias watched her approach Alex.

"You will come with us, will you not?"

"Aye. I've no family left in New York, thanks to the king's wretched soldiers."

Charlotte's eyes widened. "I'm so sorry. Are they all ..."

"Dead? Aye." Alex slowly sat up and ran one hand through his long hair. "My head be poundin'."

"Dr. Ennis said that's from losing so much blood. Can I get you anything?"

"You've done so much for me already, you and your family. I'm so grateful."

Charlotte grinned. "I believe we owe you our lives. The favor has been returned and then some."

Alex smiled and gazed at Charlotte. "I wish you could leave your flaxen hair down, but 'tis safer to pin it up and hide it beneath that hat."

Char stared back at him, an odd look on her face. Even her voice seemed different when she finally spoke. "I'll take the hat off once we get to Connecticut."

"Good."

"Are we ready, Uncle Silas?" Elias picked up his bag and stood.

"Aye, Elias. Alex, you rest in the back of the wagon. Dr. Ennis hoped you could recover here a bit longer, but I am persuaded we must hasten on our way."

Alex stood on unsteady legs. Uncle Silas helped him walk to the door. The tavern had become busier in the last hour, so the four hurried to the back, where the wagon had been left when Silas arrived. After helping Alex into the Conestoga, he helped Charlotte climb aboard. Elias noticed the two extra horses were already tied behind the wagon. Uncle Silas thought of everything.

They were leaving. Finally.

"Will we encounter trouble leaving New York, Uncle Silas?"

"Nay, Elias. So far, they've not stopped those who want to leave. So far."

Elias glanced sideways at all the lobsterbacks in the street and all the weapons of war meant to be used against the colonists. He decided then and there, he'd ne'er return to that city.

Nine

E lias could not wait to put New York behind him. The sentries on the road checked the identity of those entering the city but ignored those leaving. Why would anyone want to go there?

He breathed with ease when Uncle Silas's shoulders relaxed and he began conversing with Elias.

"One more day of travel and we'll be there, Lord willing." He actually smiled. Elias had not seen his uncle smile in several days.

Elias broached a topic he'd been hesitant to bring up before. "Uncle Silas, tell me about the French War."

Silence. "Not much to tell, really. Lots of marching, lots of shooting, lots of blood."

"Did you kill anyone?"

"Aye. Many."

Elias thought for a moment. "How old were you when you went a-soldierin'?"

"Eighteen."

"Did Papa go?"

"Nay. He'd just got wed, and yer Mama was expectin' Charlotte."

"Do you s'pose you'll go a-soldierin' again?"

"I pray I ne'er have to again."

Elias started to ask another question but Uncle Silas held his hand up. "No more questions, Elias. I'm weary of war already, and this one's just started."

❧

I T   W A S after dark when Uncle Silas pulled up the horses. He locked the brake, then called to the three in the back, before he jumped off the standing board. Elias was the only one awake and he scrambled to get out of the Conestoga. "Where are we, Uncle Silas?"

"This is your new home." A big hunting dog greeted them and barked just once. "Hey there, Ranger, how are ya?"

"I didn't know you liked dogs. Why didn't we have one in Taylorstown?" Elias reached out to Ranger, and the dog sniffed him then licked his hand.

"Your Aunt Margaret did not wish to keep a dog." His voice wasn't bitter about it. He just sounded sad.

A very sleepy Charlotte emerged from the wagon. "Uncle Silas, can you help Alex? I've not a bit of strength left to help him."

"Of course, Charlotte." Uncle Silas sauntered back to the Conestoga, stretching his arms as he went.

A tall man, a combination of Uncle Silas and their Papa, emerged from the front door.

"Welcome! Praise to the Lord of heaven, you've arrived safely. We worried and prayed, then prayed some more for your safe travels." He approached Elias. "You must be Elias. We're so blessed to have you here."

"Thank you, sir."

"Enough of that 'sir.' Call me Uncle Samuel." He wrapped his long arms around Elias and gave him a big hug. "And you must be Charlotte. My Abigail is so anxious to meet you! Ever since she found out you were coming, she's spoken of little else."

Charlotte curtsied. Then Uncle Samuel wrapped her in a bear hug as well. "No need to be so formal with us, my dear. We are family." He kissed the top of her head and placed his arms around each child. "Silas, so good to see you, brother."

Uncle Samuel let go of Charlotte and Elias then hugged his sibling. "You look weary to the bone, Silas. Come within for some victuals."

"Aye, Soon as I can help our soldier out of the wagon."

Samuel's eyes narrowed. "Soldier?"

"Aye. He's been wounded and is recovering. Do ya have a bed for him? I can sleep on the floor."

"Nonsense. We have sufficient accommodations for all. There will always be room for American soldiers here in our home. Charlotte and Elias, please go within and greet your Aunt Lizbeth. There are bedrooms off the hallway. Ask your Aunt to prepare a bed for a wounded man." Charlotte followed Uncle Samuel's instructions and walked silently inside the cabin.

"Aye, sir. I mean ... Uncle Samuel." Elias leaped up the three steps to the porch and approached the open door. He walked inside, the smell of ham and baked pies drawing him in and causing his mouth to water. "Aunt Lizbeth?" He looked around for Charlotte and saw her walking down a hallway. She appeared to be so sleepy that her steps dragged against the wood floor.

Aunt Lizbeth, busy in the kitchen, turned and a wide grin spread across her face. "You must be Elias." Wiping her hands on a towel, she hurried toward him and hugged him tightly. Letting him go, she said, "Let me look at you! We are so blessed to have you here. Thank the Lord, you arrived safely. Did the journey cause any difficulties?"

"Just a bit." He didn't have the stomach to speak about New York.

Uncle Silas assisted Alex through the door.

"Oh no, I was supposed to ask you to prepare a bed for Alex! He's been wounded."

"Wounded?" The smile left Aunt Lizbeth's face. "I believe

your journey must have been more dangerous than you said, Elias. Come with me, gentlemen."

She led them to one of the bedchambers off the hallway and pulled a blanket down for the patient. Alex plopped onto the mattress and moaned.

"Let me get you some wine for the pain, Mr. ..."

"Private Alex Popkins, ma'am."

Alex's eyes closed, and Aunt Lizbeth motioned for Uncle Silas and Elias to come with her to the kitchen.

Her brow furrowed. "He's terribly pale. What happened?"

"He was shot in the arm and bled much. Our brave Charlotte tended his wound. Then she and Elias transported him and his dead friend to the inn where they knew to meet me. The doctor already removed the lead ball, so he needs rest and good victuals to recover. I'll fill you in on the rest later." Uncle Silas looked around. "Where is Charlotte?"

"I saw her walking down the hallway. She seemed so tired I'm sure she found a bed to fall in." Elias yawned and rubbed his eyes.

Aunt Lizbeth sat on a chair, her mouth dropping open. Then she stood abruptly. "I nearly forgot the wine!" She grabbed a bottle and poured a glass. "I'll return forthwith."

When she returned to the kitchen, Aunt Lizbeth shook her head. "He's just a boy. Says he's only sixteen."

"That is the age they can sign on, Lizbeth." Uncle Samuel poured some cider for Silas. "Most boys that age have been hunting and firing a gun for many a year."

"Hunting for game is one thing." She shook her head slowly. "Shooting at a person is entirely different."

"Charlotte had to. She killed a lobsterback." All eyes turned to Elias. He shrugged. "What? Alex said 'twas a just killing."

"I'm just astonished." Aunt Lizbeth held her hand to her head and rubbed it. "What war does to us all."

"I gave her the pistol." Uncle Silas sat down and drank a large gulp of the cider. "I'm so glad I thought of it, for it saved her life. And her virtue."

"What's that?" Elias yawned.

"Never mind, Elias. You seem to need a bed. Would you like to sleep in Alex's room so you can tell us if he needs anything?"

"Aye. I'd like that."

After the long journey to Connecticut, Elias wished he could sleep for two days. He was so tired, even food could not tempt him.

Lying on the large mattress next to Alex, he listened to the adults talking in the other room. Then Alex's breathing lulled him to close his eyes.

Ten

Elias awoke to the farm rooster declaring it was daylight. He placed a pillow over his head to muffle the sound, but someone took it off. "Hey!" he objected in a groggy voice.

"Hey, Sleepyhead. Can you get me some victuals?" Alex sat up in bed, propped by pillows.

Pushing himself up to a sitting position, Elias groaned. "'Tis so early. But I'll go."

"There's a brave man." Alex grinned at him.

Grabbing his breeches, Elias nearly lost his footing pulling on his clothes.

"Careful now. We don't need two patients in here."

Elias, too tired to respond, walked with unsteady steps toward the door. He turned to Alex. "How hungry be you? Full trencher hungry or baby bowl hungry? I saw my aunt has small bowls for my little cousin."

"If you bring me a small bowlful, I'll have to eat the entire bowl along with the spoon." Alex threw a pillow at Elias.

"Missed!" Elias escaped out the door, grinning. When he caught the scent of food from the kitchen, his stomach growled with a loud groan.

"Aunt Lizbeth? Sorry I was too tired to eat your victuals last night. But I sure could use a heaping trencher of something. Oh, and Alex is mighty hungry as well."

"Well, it just so happens I have a 'heaping' lot of food for everyone." When she grinned, Lizbeth looked much younger than Aunt Margaret. And prettier, for certain.

She filled a trencher with gruel and fruit, then smothered it in maple syrup. "Take this to Alex, and I'll get yours ready."

Steam rose from the gruel, and Elias took care not to spill it. He pushed open the door. "Best not throw anything at me as I'm holding your victuals."

"That looks *so* good. Thanks, Elias."

"Welcome." His stomach growled again.

"You'd best go get your own victuals. Sounds like your stomach be screamin' at you." Alex grinned then took a spoonful of the gruel.

"No argument from me." Elias scurried out the door and down the hall to the kitchen. He heard a little voice crying.

"Go ahead and start, Elias. I'm going to get the baby."

Aunt Lizbeth passed him with hurried steps and opened the little one's door down the hallway.

Elias licked his lips when he sat at the tableboard. One bite of that gruel, fruit, and maple syrup prompted an audible moan of pleasure.

"Aunt Lizbeth makes some good victuals, aye?" Uncle Samuel fixed his own bowl and sat near Elias.

"So good. Almost as good as my ma's." Elias lowered his eyes. "I hope 'twas not an offense to say so."

"Elias, I expect your ma was a great cook. And no one is offended if you say she was the best."

"I'm glad. Some days I miss her and Papa so much. It hurts right here." Elias pointed to his chest.

"That's because that's where your heart is, and your heart is hurting when you lose someone you love."

"You remind me of my Papa. So does Uncle Silas, but you seem even more like him."

"Well, I am honored that you think so. Your Papa was a fine man. And I think you and Charlotte take after him."

"You do?"

"Aye. Especially when I hear about your bravery on the trip to New York. You both showed incredible courage in a frightening situation."

"We did?" Elias scratched his head. "I was really scared."

"Being scared doesn't mean you're not brave. Courage bathed in fear that one can overcome, despite being frightened—now that is true bravery."

Elias considered this for a moment then returned to his gruel. He would need to think about that.

ABIGAIL CAME into the kitchen shortly after Elias began eating and strode quietly into the kitchen. "Abigail, this is your cousin, Elias. They arrived late last night." Uncle Samuel put his hand tenderly on his daughter's back. "Won't you say, good day?"

"Good day." Her voice was so soft Elias could barely hear her.

"Good day, Abigail. Nice to meet you."

She slipped into a chair next to her father and occasionally glanced up and smiled.

"Our Abigail is somewhat shy." Her father pulled lightly on her hair.

"I was the same way, as a girl. Poor Samuel. He thought I didn't like him because I was too afraid to speak." Aunt Lizbeth giggled.

"How old are you, Abigail? My sister Charlotte is fourteen."

"I'm thirteen. But my birthday will be soon." Abigail spoke a little bit louder than before.

"Really? When is it, so I can make you something?"

Abigail grinned with her mouth closed. "That would be

lovely. My birthday is August seventeenth. It's rather nice having cousins here."

Uncle Silas grew serious. "Aye' tis a blessing to have family. I'm afraid my wife and I have never been able to provide cousins for Charlotte and Elias."

"I'm so sorry. Perhaps someday God will send you some." Abigail reached out and patted her uncle's arm.

"Abigail, you are a tender lass, full of love and mercy." Her mother squeezed her arm gently and grinned.

Gabriel had already joined the group at table. The two-year-old had gruel all over his face and played happily with the remainder in his bowl.

"Gabriel will hardly remember a time when Elias and Charlotte were not part of our family. I'm so happy he will look upon you both as another sister and brother." Aunt Lizbeth found a piece of linen and cleaned Gabriel's face.

"Down." The toddler pointed to the floor. When his mother had lifted him down, he walked over to Elias, who held his hands out to the toddler. Gabriel crawled onto his lap.

"I'm pretty happy to have a brother—even if he's truly my cousin." Elias giggled when Gabriel touched his face and patted his cheek.

"Gabriel, that is your cousin, Elias," Uncle Samuel said.

"E-why-us."

"Very good!" Uncle Samuel reached over and patted the top of his blond hair.

Just then, Charlotte came into the room.

"Look, Char," Elias said. "This is Gabriel. And Abigail here is our cousin too. She's thirteen."

"Hi, Charlotte. So glad to meet you." Abigail gave her a timid smile.

"Char are you all right?" Elias had never seen her so pale.

"I'll be fine. Abigail, so pleased to meet you."

Aunt Lizbeth arose from her chair and filled a trencher for Charlotte. "Here, my dear. You must be starving."

"Thank you, Aunt Lizbeth." Char ate small bites, and it seemed as if she had difficulty swallowing each one. She stopped midway through her meal. "I'm not terribly hungry. Might I go for a walk, Uncle Silas?"

Uncle Silas and Uncle Samuel looked at each other. They both narrowed their eyes as they looked at Charlotte.

"May I go with you, Charlotte?" Abigail quickly finished her gruel, then stood up.

"Sure."

The two girls headed out the door into the sunshine.

"Silas, I'm concerned about Charlotte. Something troubles her." Aunt Lizbeth picked up the dirty dishes from the table.

"I know what's wrong." Elias grabbed one more bite of breakfast, set Gabriel onto the floor then stood up from his chair. "I was with her when she had to shoot that King's soldier. Char was quite upset."

"Oh my. No wonder the poor lass is troubled. I'll see if I can find her." Aunt Lizbeth turned to Elias. "Would you be able to watch little Gabriel for me?"

"Of course. Maybe I can take him to visit Alex while he recovers."

"I imagine he'd like that." Aunt Lizbeth strolled out the front door.

Elias held the toddler's hand while walking to Alex's room.

"I brought you a visitor, Alex."

A grin appeared on Alex's countenance. "And who is this little man?"

"My cousin Gabriel."

Gabriel toddled toward the bed, climbed on it, and promptly sat on Alex's lap.

"Let me know if you tire of holding him," Elias said. "He's pretty big for a two-year-old."

"I'm happy to have a distraction. He reminds me of my little brother, Willem."

"I didn't know you had a little brother, Alex."

"You wouldn't know. It's all right. He died a few years ago of a throat malaise."

"I'm sorry, Alex. That must have been hard."

"Aye." Alex stroked the baby's back when he lay against him. "How is your sister, Elias?"

"Not so well today. I think she's wrestling with some bad memories."

"You mean the killing of that redcoat?"

"Aye, she's not very hungry, and she went for a walk after breakfast with my cousin Abigail."

"When you see her next, please tell her I'd enjoy her company."

"I will. Thanks for thinking of her."

"The trouble is, I think about her a great deal. It will make it more difficult to return to the army when I'm well."

Elias frowned at him. "Do you have to go back? What if you can't shoot a musket anymore?"

"Well, if I can't shoot, then they won't want me back. But I'm pretty sure I'll be able to shoot just fine."

Elias wondered if it was wrong to pray that Alex would not be able to fire a musket. There had been so many losses for him and Char, could not God see they needed Alex here in Connecticut? Wrong or not, Elias determined that was what he would pray.

Eleven

Elias's prayers that Alex would stay weren't answered. At least, not in the way he'd hoped for. The Continental soldier gained strength each day, and he healed into the capable soldier he'd been when they met.

Alex spent as much time as he could with Charlotte. They went on lengthy walks, and one time when Elias was in the woods, he found them kissing.

All too soon, the day came when they had to say goodbye.

Before Alex left, he pulled Elias to the side. "Please watch out for Charlotte. I know that incident with the lobsterback left a pain in her heart. I fear her tender sensibilities could carry on with that grief. Please remind her that 'twas a necessary killing. It was him or all of us."

"I will." He sniffed sharply. "Are you sure you need to go?"

"If I could stay, I would. But like I told Charlotte, I will return here. Heading back to war holds no joy for me. 'Twas an adventure at first, with Thad signing on. But when my brother was killed, I lost hope of ever feeling the strength to fight again. I now have the strength, but I've grown so fond of your family, 'tis difficult to leave."

Elias squinted in the sunlight. "Thad was your brother?"

"Aye, I thought you knew."

Just then, Charlotte approached with tears in her eyes. She handed Alex a lock of her flaxen hair, tied with a ribbon.

"Please think of me when you see this."

"I'll think of you all the time." He held her close as she sobbed on his chest.

Elias felt terrible. For Charlotte. For Alex. For himself. He sauntered toward the barn, where he found Uncle Silas holding a wooden box.

"I thought you might like to keep busy with Alex going away. These tools have been in the Hawkins family for some time. They are the same ones your papa used to craft your lamb."

Fascinated by the intricate wooden handles with a variety of cutting edges, Elias picked each tool up with great care. Some were curved, some straight. "Papa used these?"

"Absolutely. He was the best whittler in the family. Although I'm not as good, I can teach you the skill. I have a feeling you'll become far better than me."

"You brought these from Taylorstown?"

"Aye. I want you to have them. Someday, you can give them to your own son." Uncle Silas grinned.

That seemed a strange thing to think about. Elias would have to ponder that one later. After he'd learned to whittle.

"Can you teach me now, Uncle Silas?"

"Aye, take a seat on a hay bale."

Uncle Silas sat next to him and showed him how to choose a piece of wood, hold on to the tools, and how to begin. It was not long before Elias had started a wooden image of Ranger, the dog. "I could give this to Abigail for her birthday."

"I believe she'd like that very much. See, you're already better at whittling than I am." Silas patted him on the back. "The more you do, the more realistic your sculptures will become."

"I like doing this. Thanks, Uncle Silas."

"You're welcome, lad." Silas stood, watched Elias for a moment, then sauntered out of the barn.

~

A FEW DAYS LATER, Silas announced he needed to return home. He worried about leaving Aunt Margaret for so long and would have to take a longer route to avoid New York City.

Char and Elias both grew quiet at his announcement.

The wagon was prepared, and bags were packed along with fodder for the horses.

"I wish you could stay longer, Uncle Silas." Char's eyes welled with moisture.

"I do as well, Charlotte. I will return for a visit as soon as I'm able."

Both children hugged him tightly, and he kissed the tops of their heads.

"Fare thee well, Silas. Do write and let us know when you arrive home." Samuel hugged his brother. "We shall pray for you. Please look sharp for any trouble."

"I shall. Take good care of these children. They are a treasure."

"Aye, they are."

Uncle Silas's mouth began to tremble, and he jumped aboard the wagon. Waving goodbye to all, Silas clicked his tongue to get the horses moving.

Charlotte stared at the ground, folded her arms, and walked slowly indoors. Abigail followed her, for she always seemed to sense when Charlotte had need of her company. Elias wished that Gabriel were old enough to share comfort and wisdom with him when he was downhearted.

At least he had the whittling tools. He took comfort in holding the same wooden handles his father had held and crafted wooden figures with, which brought joy to others. It was a skill that seemed so natural to Elias. It helped him feel even closer to Papa.

~

THE WARMTH of summer shifted to the cooler days of autumn. The golden hues of red and gold dappled the maple trees and soon immersed the entire forests with spectacular displays of fiery splendor.

Elias loved this season most of all, as it foretold of days of frost, then snow ... then Christmas.

Aunt Lizbeth seemed consumed in preparation for Thanksgiving. 'Twas always a huge event, but even more so in New England. Each state had its own date chosen, so families in other locales could celebrate more than once if invited to relatives' homes. At least, that's what cousin Abigail told him. She said last year they had three Thanksgiving dinners!

Elias wondered if traveling was as safe this year with the Declaration of Independence making England angrier than ever. No one at Uncle Samuel's house had mentioned going anywhere else for Thanksgiving. Besides, with the amount of food being prepared, Elias doubted he'd have enough room for any more Thanksgiving meals.

He wondered that no one had spoken of Christmas. By this time in Virginia, his mother and Aunt Margaret had turned their home into a delightful display of evergreens and ribbon. Elias decided to ask Abigail why no one spoke of his favorite holiday.

"Christmas?" Abigail turned pale and held her finger up to her lips. In a whisper, she declared to her cousin, "Christmas is unholy in our congregation. We never celebrate it."

It was Elias's turn to go pale. "Why not?" His lips trembled. Abigail placed her hand gently on his arm.

"I'm sorry, Elias. 'Tis just our minister preaches that 'tis a pagan holiday, and we must not participate."

"But we are Christians, and so were my parents. So is Uncle Silas. We are not pagans." By now tears rolled down his cheeks.

"I know you are a Christian, cousin. My father says many Christians celebrate Christmas, but some feel 'tis wrong. I know my father celebrated it when he lived in Virginia. I think honoring Christ on his birthday seems lovely. I don't really understand."

"Nor do I." Elias walked slowly outdoors and headed to the barn. He decided that he would still celebrate Christmas in his own way, no matter what.

He headed toward the wooden box and removed one of his whittling tools. Searching for just the right size of wood block, he began carving a small lamb, similar to the one his father had made for him. Every spare moment that he had, Elias carved numerous sheep, some in a reclining position, some eating, some standing. By Christmas Day, he had completed his plan.

Late at night, he brought a sheep to each member of his new family. Carefully he tucked a wooden sheep next to Gabriel, Abigail, and Charlotte as they slept. When he approached Uncle Samuel, his eyes opened, and Elias held his finger to his lips. Uncle Samuel grinned as Elias placed the gift next to him and then one next to Aunt Lizbeth.

"Merry Christmas," Elias whispered to his uncle.

"Merry Christmas, to you, Elias."

Elias grinned with satisfaction and returned to his bed. He could not imagine anyone objecting to the symbol of the Lamb of God being given on December 25.

Twelve

Three years later
New Haven, Connecticut, 4th day of July, 1779

Another Fourth of July celebration. Elias found it difficult to realize three years had come and gone since he arrived in Connecticut. Much had changed in that time, including the unexpected delight of Aunt Lizbeth carrying another baby Hawkins. She was so close to her confinement, Elias wondered if the child might be birthed on such an important day.

Charlotte and Abigail were, indeed, young ladies now. Charlotte still corresponded by letter with Alex, although recently the communications were few and far between. Elias watched with sympathy whenever Char hurried to greet a post rider, only to be told, "Nothing today for you, miss."

They all still missed Uncle Silas, and he wrote to them often. With the war ongoing, it did not appear a visit from him would happen anytime soon.

Elias, now thirteen years old, clung to Gabriel's hand outside of the meetinghouse. The rambunctious five-year-old held tightly to his cousin. Such a large crowd was unusual for New

Haven, but the celebration of America's birth was cause for excitement and a large gathering of celebrants. But Elias wondered if the American army would indeed win this conflict, or would all the colonists suffer at the hands of an angry king if his army carried the sword of triumph?

Sabbath service at the meetinghouse had just ended and the minister called for everyone to meet on the town green.

Suddenly, a horseman, riding at breakneck speed, arrived on the scene. "To arms! To arms," he cried.

The sheriff pushed his way through the throng and addressed the man. "What is the meaning of this interruption to the day's activities? Do you not know what the date is, sir?"

"And do ye not know that an entire fleet of the King's Navy is approaching our harbor?"

Gasps could be heard rippling through the crowd. The sheriff grew pale, and another man shouted, "Grab your muskets and pistols! Then head for the harbor!"

Elias froze in place until Gabriel tugged on his arm "What shall we do, Elias?"

"Head home. Quickly!" He hoped that Charlotte and Abigail had already sought refuge there and was relieved to see the backs of their gowns ahead of them. Aunt Lizbeth had stayed home, since she was close to confinement, and Uncle Samuel had stayed with her. Elias pulled Gabriel's arm to hurry him on, but the little one's legs couldn't keep up. Elias picked up his cousin, who by now sobbed loudly.

"It'll be all right, Gabriel." Elias prayed that would be true.

He'd not experienced such terror since that day in New York, when they were attacked in the woods by the King's soldiers. It was a nightmare he'd rather not revisit.

The two young ladies arrived home ahead of them, and as Elias and Gabriel neared the farm, Uncle Samuel raced out the front door looking for the boys. "Thank the good Lord you are safe." He reached for Gabriel and held him close.

Elias put his hands on his thighs and breathed hard. When

he caught his breath, he looked up at Uncle Samuel. "What do we do?"

"First, we gather our weapons, along with flints and powder and ball. Then we must gather other important items like food and canteens and hide in the woods." Samuel held his hand over his mouth, his lips pulled taut, then he met Elias's gaze. "Aunt Lizbeth will have the child soon, and I fear 'twill be impossible to find the midwife when she needs her."

"Do you wish for me to go find her right now?" Just then, musket fire could be heard not far from the direction of the meetinghouse.

"Nay, son, 'tis already too dangerous. We must hasten to the woods."

Gabriel sobbed again when they heard cannon fire. Whether the sounds were coming from the ships or the American militia, Elias could not tell. He ran inside, followed by his uncle, who still carried Gabriel.

Char's eyes were as wide as he'd ever seen them. Even Abigail, normally calm, appeared to be undone by the terror. Elias wanted to calm them both. "Lassies, be at ease. Gather some victuals and blankets. We'll be hiding in the woods, and we'll be safe."

No sooner had the words escaped him than a cry from Aunt Lizbeth's bedchamber startled them all. Abigail ran down the hallway to check on her mother. When she returned, her face had paled. "Mother is in terrible pain. What can we do?"

"I'm going to find the midwife. Please go stay with your mother." Elias raced out the open doorway.

Char started to object, but he ignored her.

He avoided Uncle Samuel, who was entering the barn. When he was out of sight, Elias rushed to town. Panicking residents of New Haven ran every which way. Confusion seemed to be everywhere as babies cried and their mothers carried them into the forests surrounding New Haven.

Men grabbed muskets and consulted with Continental

soldiers, then cried "Huzzah" and split up into two groups. The soldiers ran up a road, while the armed men hid behind bushes lining the road. Elias observed from a distance. When the soldiers ran up the road, the King's Army ran after them. Suddenly the townsmen stood and fired at the regulars, felling most of them. The Continental soldiers then turned and fired on the rest.

Elias nearly panicked, however, when he saw hundreds more of the king's soldiers debarking the ships that had just landed. He prayed that the Americans would not run out of gunpowder, as they seemed to be outnumbered.

The midwife! He'd become so engrossed in watching the fighting, he'd forgotten his purpose in coming. In all the confusion and smoke from the spent gunpowder, he had difficulty seeing clearly. When some of the smoke cleared, he saw a neighbor filling a wagon.

"I say, please tell me where I can find a midwife. My aunt needs one forthwith."

"Go try at the meetinghouse. Many are taking refuge there."

"Thanks."

Although well familiar with the meetinghouse, Elias had to rub his eyes a bit before he could focus on it in the distance. He dashed toward the tall building he'd just been at that morning, then scurried inside. He yelled to the crowd, "I say, is there a midwife here? My aunt has a great need of one if you can help her."

Not one lady raised her hand. Elias's shoulders sank. What would he do now?

He was approached by a young woman about his age. "Perhaps I can help you."

"You seem to be no older than I." Shaking his head, he started to thank her but was ready to decline her help.

She held up her hand to stop him from speaking further. "I know I'm young, just fourteen years old. But all the midwives are with other mothers, and my mother is one of them. She trained me since I was small, how to help with birthings. So you see, I've been doing this for a long time. I suppose I am better than no help at all."

Elias pondered the situation. Did he have a choice?

"Very well. I do applaud your bravery, and I thank you." He drew her toward the door. Seeing several British soldiers milling about with muskets and torches, he led her to the back door instead. As he walked, he cautioned those seeking refuge in the meetinghouse that they might need to leave. "Look sharp, everyone."

Several older men went to the front door, muskets at the ready.

Elias saw no one out back and ran alongside the young woman toward the woods. Reports from musket fire sped up their footsteps.

"Don't stop," he gasped.

They reached the edge of the woods and took refuge behind trees. He held his finger to his lips so she would stay quiet. It was difficult not making a sound, as their breathing seemed so sonorous in the quiet forest. Elias was not certain if the regulars were after the two of them, but he wasn't taking chances. He'd already seen what those troops could do. He had to protect the young lady by his side.

As their breathing slowed down and the main sound he heard was the birds of the forest, he carefully glanced around the tree's edge. "Looks like they're gone."

"Where is your aunt?"

"Hiding in the woods behind my uncle's cabin, I hope. By the way, my name is Elias. Elias Hawkins."

"I know who you and your sister are. The orphans from Virginia." She smiled at him. "My name is Molly Hale."

"Pleased to meet you, Molly." He could feel blood warming his face. That was a new experience for him. The only lassies he usually spoke to were his sister, his cousin, and his aunt. He'd never felt this way before.

"Come on Elias, let's hurry lest the soldiers come any closer." They pushed their way through the thick bushes, stirring up the mosquitoes hidden in the foliage. Their hair became entangled with leaves and burrs and an assortment of twigs. There was no time for stopping to bring relief from the itchy bug bites, so they ignored them and pressed onward.

Elias had never appreciated the cleared roads for travel before now. He also had a new appreciation for explorers who used crude tools to slash their way through virgin territory. They were unsung heroes in his mind.

"How much farther, Elias? I'm concerned for your aunt."

"I am as well. This is the safest way, although certainly not the fastest." He peeked through the forest when they were near the cabin. In horror, he observed three regulars setting fire to his uncle's cabin and barn. He pulled Molly downward so the soldiers would not see them. As he squatted on the ground next to her, he covered his face with his hands. "My tools."

Molly placed her hand on his arm. "Did you say your tools?"

"Aye. They belonged to my father, and Uncle Silas brought them to me. They were inside the barn." He might be able to replace them, but no other set would bear the imprint of his father's fingers. Nor the memories that the tools stirred.

Molly's eyes narrowed. "I'm so sorry, Elias."

The soldiers took their torches elsewhere, he assumed to burn more homes and barns. Anger rippled through his bloodstream, and he leaped upward to find the toolbox. Fire or no fire.

Molly screamed after him. "Elias! No!"

Running after him, she could not catch up with his longer stride. The fire exuded so much heat, Elias threw his hat and coat on the ground before racing into the barn. The smoke choked him, but he pressed onward. He thought he knew where the tools should be, but the smoke obscured his vision. He knew about where the worktable stood, and he stumbled toward it. The table was on fire, and he burned his hands, but he didn't stop until he felt the edges of the toolbox. He picked it up and ran toward the open door. The box singed his fingers, so he threw it on the dirt outside and fell onto the ground in pain.

Molly was at the water pump and filled a bucket as fast as she could. Bringing it over to Elias, she poured it over him, then returned to the pump. She filled it twice again. The third time, she plunged his hands into the cool water, and he screamed in pain. The water's coolness eventually helped, but the intense anguish in his hands was incessant.

Elias coughed like he never had before. Molly brought him a cup of water to drink, and she had to hold it to his lips because of the discomfort in his hands. When he stopped coughing, he closed his eyes and shook his head back and forth.

"Not certain if I feel heroic or like a complete dunderhead."

"I think it was misplaced bravery." She spoke to him in a soothing tone of voice. "But I understand the box of tools meant a great deal to you."

"It wasn't just the tools." His voice was gravelly. He opened the box and pulled out the wooden lamb his father had made for him. "This was inside as well."

He stared at the burning cabin that was their home, then looked downward. "Let's find my Aunt Lizbeth."

"But your hands." She wrinkled her brow. "They need tending."

"After we find Aunt Lizbeth."

"Don't touch the dirt with them. They must stay clean. I'll help you up." She grinned. "You are one stubborn young man."

"I've been told that before."

"I imagine you have."

Elias wondered if they'd ever find his uncle and aunt, but hurrying through the woods, relief filled him as he heard Aunt Lizbeth's birthing groans. Molly ran toward the sound.

"Thank the Lord." Uncle Samuel wiped the sweat from his forehead. He looked back at Molly, then spoke to Elias. "She seems rather young to be a midwife."

"'Tis a long story."

Then his uncle noticed Elias's hands. "What ... what happened to you?"

Elias inhaled deeply before coughing again. When he finished, he dreaded telling Uncle Samuel the news. "The cabin, the barn ... they're all gone." Tears rolled down his cheeks. "Those redcoat blaggarts burned most of the town."

Uncle Samuel's face paled, and his eyes widened. He stepped backward, nearly stumbled, and sat on a log.

"Uncle Samuel!"

His uncle remained silent then breathed in deeply before exhaling "Do not fret, son. We will build again. The whole town will. We are not alone in this calamity. If anything, this debacle will stir the anger of the American troops even more. Give them more reason to fight for our cause."

Just then, the cry of a newborn could be heard. Samuel hugged Elias. "Let's go see our new American baby, born on this fourth of July."

Thirteen

Uncle Samuel and Aunt Lizbeth named their new daughter Remember. Aunt Lizbeth proclaimed to all who would listen what a wonderful and capable midwife Molly Hale was. Although she seemed too young to have birthed a child herself, she was mature beyond her years, having developed the skills of an experienced nurse.

Since most of the buildings and homes in New Haven had been burned, the midwives set up a hospital of sorts in the meetinghouse. Molly tended to Elias's wounds on his hands every day. She declared it was a relief to see the burns had blistered but not turned black. Her mother prescribed a concoction of herbs to soothe and heal the skin on his hands. After it was applied, clean, dry linen that had been boiled in lye soap was wrapped around his hands.

While Molly worked on his hands, Elias smiled at the way she concentrated so intently on applying the bandages. Her fingers were gentle, and he became mesmerized by her touch.

A week following the attack, she declared she was finished. He looked at her with heavy eyelids and said, "Are you certain? I don't mind if you continue."

"I dare say, Mr. Hawkins, you are a flirty one. Now, I have work to do."

He sighed and winked his eye. "Very well, nurse Molly."

He began to leave the meetinghouse when he heard someone call his name. He searched until he found the source. "Alex! Are you well, man? How did you get here?"

His friend had a beard that was several days old, and dried blood stained several parts of his uniform.

"Where were you injured?" Elias sat near him on a chair and gripped his hand.

"I think my leg. I'm not certain what occurred." His weak voice emphasized the seriousness of his condition. "Perhaps you could ask the doctor?"

"Aye, I will. I'll return forthwith, my friend."

Elias searched for the physician, hoping to get some answers. He asked several women working there who carried basins of bloody water. None of them knew where the man was. Frustrated he walked out the back door of the building. He found him, lying on the ground, next to a half empty bottle of rum. The doctor reeked of the smell of alcohol. Elias attempted to smother his anger. He grabbed the doctor by his jacket and dragged him to a tree, where Elias propped him up.

"You are the doctor, are you not?"

The physician's eyes slowly opened and he appeared to be confused. "Who are you?"

Elias crouched down and gripped his hands tightly lest he punch the man. "I am Elias Hawkins and you are supposed to be tending these patients inside the meetinghouse."

"So what do you want from me?" The doctor's words slurred.

Elias gripped his own hands more tightly. "I want to know what is wrong with my friend, Alex Popkins. He is a wounded Continental soldier, SIR." At this point Elias grabbed the doctor's loose cravat and spoke close to his face.

"And you expect me to know who Alex is?"

"I *do* expect you to take better care of him than you are."

Appalled by the man's condition, Elias determined then and there to take his friend home. The renovation of the cabin had not been completed since the fire, but there were two usable rooms. Anything was better than this hospital and the care given by that man.

He approached Alex. "Is that doctor always drunk? His behavior is appalling. I'm taking you home as soon as I can contact my uncle. He and I can make a litter for you and bring you back to our cabin."

Alex touched Elias's arm. "Is Charlotte well? Has she married?" He swallowed with difficulty.

"Married? She's been waiting for you." Elias grinned. "I'll return forthwith."

WITH ELIAS'S hands still healing, a neighbor came and helped Uncle Samuel make a litter to drag behind a horse and carry the wounded soldier. When Elias informed Charlotte about Alex, she wanted to race to the makeshift hospital, but Elias cautioned her that Alex was weak. He was not certain what was wrong, but he determined to ask Molly and her mother to examine him to be certain there was nothing the doctor had missed. Given that man's state, any number of things might have gone unnoticed.

Charlotte accompanied Uncle Samuel and Elias to the hospital, along with the horse that could pull the transport litter. "I'm so nervous." Charlotte touched her hair frequently to be sure it was not coming undone. Elias grinned at her.

"He will be smitten once again with you, Char. He'll be amazed at how you've changed. You look different than you did when he left."

"It's been three years since we saw each other. Will he seem like a stranger?"

"I think you'll both be so happy to see one another again that the three years will melt away as if it was just three moments."

"I hope so."

When they arrived at the meetinghouse, Charlotte hesitated at the top of the stairs.

"Come on, brave lady." Elias held out a bent elbow so she could grab on to him.

The look of longing on Alex's face when he saw Charlotte almost brought tears to Elias's eyes. The soldier held out both arms to Char and could barely speak. "My precious Charlotte. I prayed every day I'd see you again."

Char ran to his bedside. "Oh my dear, Alex. I've missed you so much." Tears rolled down her cheeks as she kissed his pale face.

Elias and Uncle Samuel both turned away. Samuel smiled and whispered. "Let's give them a moment."

They walked away and saw Molly changing a bandage on a wounded man.

"Molly, do you know much about Alex's condition?"

"The corporal? I know he's having difficulty walking, but the doctor has not been very forthcoming about the reason."

That doctor is hardly in any condition to be helping patients. He needs help himself.

Elias looked back at Alex and Char and saw they were having what seemed to be a serious conversation. Turning back to Molly, he said, "Alex is my good friend. He's even better friends with my sister. Is there any other doctor we might get, to see what can be done for him?"

"Let me inquire for you. We've had many complaints against Dr. Sullivan."

Uncle Samuel elbowed Elias. "I think it's time to break up the reunion over there." They both strolled over to Alex and Char. "Hate to interrupt, but we need to get you to the Hawkins Hospital, well known for its fine victuals and very attentive nurses."

"I'm more than happy to go there." Alex held on to Char's hand, and they smiled at each other.

Elias displayed his bandaged hands to Alex. "Sorry I'll not be much help to ya."

Alex's eyes widened. "What happened?"

Before Elias could answer, Alex stood up from the cot and tried to bear weight on his left leg. The effort elicited a painful cry from the man.

"Let's sit you down a moment, Alex." Uncle Samuel's eyes blazed. "That pathetic man, the so-called physician, has not treated you for whatever the problem is."

"I feel sick." Alex turned a ghastly shade of white. Elias grabbed a bucket for his friend to vomit in.

"Let me carry his legs, held up by a blanket, and the rest of you carry his torso." Molly grabbed the blanket off Alex's cot.

Charlotte clenched her fists and moaned. "My poor Alex. I'd gladly take this pain for him, rather than see him go through this."

"Let's get him out to the litter." Samuel picked the patient up under his arms while Molly lifted his legs with the blanket.

"I'll back the litter up to the door." Elias scampered outside, happy to be able to help in some way.

As they placed Alex on the transport, Charlotte held his hand. "I'll walk with you, my love."

It seemed to Elias like a long pilgrimage back to Uncle Samuel's cabin. Although partially destroyed by the fire, the men had worked many hours to restore it. He and Molly walked on the other side of the litter from Charlotte all the way home.

Elias was grateful for Molly's friendship, as well as for her care for his family. He wondered why they'd not met before the invasion by the redcoats. He supposed it was not yet their time.

Fourteen

hanks to Molly's efforts as well as her mother's, a new physician from a nearby town was brought to New Haven to assist the wounded patients.

When he arrived at the Hawkins home, Dr. Walters asked for the assistance of Mrs. Hale, Molly's widowed mother, while he examined Alex.

Charlotte paced back and forth in front of the steps leading into the cabin.

Elias attempted to put a smile on her face and lighten the mood. "Why don't you do something constructive, like washing the floors in the back bedrooms with vinegar? The soot is so thick we could use it to smear on our faces like they did at Boston for the Tea Party."

"I suppose I could." Charlotte grabbed a bucket and went to the water pump to fill it. She hauled the container up the stairs and set it down on the porch. "Where did the vinegar get put? Everything has been moved around inside."

Aunt Lizbeth held the baby while sitting at their new table, set on the porch by Uncle Samuel. "'Tis over in the corner, Charlotte. Thank you, dear." The baby began to cry, and Aunt Lizbeth nursed her.

Elias looked at Molly. "Let's go to the orchard and gather apples. Come on, Gabriel. Come, Ranger." The dog wagged his tail and followed the group with enthusiasm.

Gabriel raced with them, gathering fruit that had fallen from the peach tree.

Molly called to Gabriel and grinned, noting the juicy mess that already covered his face. "Be sure to stay away from the worms in the fruit."

Appearing glum, Abigail sauntered out the front door.

"What's wrong, Abigail?" Molly walked toward her.

"Now that Charlotte has Alex, and Elias has you, I feel rather alone."

"I do understand. When my older sister got married, I felt like she had deserted me." Molly put her arm around Abigail's shoulder and walked with her. "But Elias and I are not yet ready to be wed. We're too young."

"I think we may be losing my sister, however, to Alex, as soon as he is well." Elias grinned.

"Let's pray he does recover." Molly looked up at the open doorway. "I think I hear the doctor. Let's go listen."

The three joined the attentive audience standing next to Dr. Walters in the kitchen. Uncle Samuel looked back at Elias. "'Twas as I thought. There's a break in his leg."

The Doctor turned to Uncle Samuel. "I'll need your help, Mr. Hawkins." He motioned for Uncle Samuel to follow him back to the room. The two men closed the door.

Charlotte went to the door and touched it. "Why cannot I go in?" She turned and swiped moisture off her cheeks. Suddenly a heartbreaking scream emanated from within.

"I believe that's why, Char." Elias gathered his sister in his embrace and held her.

Soon the doctor emerged. "I placed a temporary splint on his leg. Let me gather all the materials I need, and I shall return forthwith."

"Doctor, why did he scream?" Charlotte sobbed as she spoke.

"His bones have been out of alignment for a week. Much irritation has occurred. Once we get his leg wrapped to keep the bones together, he'll begin to heal." He started to leave then turned to look at her again. "One good thing, miss. He'll not be returnin' to the army. And he'll be able to walk, probably with a cane." He patted her arm then left.

Elias followed his sister into the room where Alex was lying. She sat next to his bed and laid her head on his chest. He wrapped his arms around her and stroked her back.

RECOVERY FOR ALEX was long and painful, but each day saw small steps of improvement. Eating was a challenge, as the bone break caused a great deal of nausea. After a few weeks, his appetite returned.

Either Elias or Charlotte spent every meal with him to encourage him to eat as much as possible. Aunt Lizbeth made his favorite meals, and even Gabriel showed up at mealtimes to make sure the victuals had "disappeared."

Dr. Walters came as often as he could to ensure all was progressing as it should. Privately, he expressed his anger about Alex's treatment at the hospital, as well as the care all the patients there had been given. He shared with Elias how grateful he was that Molly and her mother had contacted the medical society.

In the meantime, the leaves began changing to brilliant hues of red, orange, and gold. Elias was grateful for the cooler weather that made the reconstruction of the town from the attack more bearable.

The doctor checked Elias's hands whenever he came to examine Alex. "'Tis important to keep your fingers moving, lest you lose the function of them."

"I whittle on wood with my tools. Would that help?"

"Aye. It might hurt at first, but keep it up."

"I shall. I have a few projects I'd like to try."

"Well done." Dr. Walters started to walk away, but Alex called the doctor back from the bedchamber.

Elias followed the doctor inside.

Alex inhaled deeply. "Dr. Walters, I have a question for you."

"Ask away."

"It's rather obvious Charlotte and I are in love. When do you think we might get wed?"

"I'd say, as soon as you can stand up with a cane long enough to say, 'I do.'" Dr. Walters laughed. "Will I be invited as a guest?"

"You'll be at the top of the list." Alex grinned.

Dr. Walters tipped his hat and left, still laughing as he went.

THE WEDDING TOOK place in early October. A soft wind rustled through the trees, and the scent of burning piles of fallen leaves filled the air. Elias could not believe how grown up Charlotte appeared in her soft linen dress that Aunt Lizbeth had made.

As they prepared for the outdoor ceremony, Molly leaned toward Elias and whispered,

"Where is your Uncle Silas? I thought he might come."

Elias tried to smile, but he ached to see his uncle as well. "'Tis dangerous to make such a long journey. Char and I are disappointed, but we'd rather he stay safe than attempt to come."

Dressed in his military uniform, Alex stood as tall as he seemed able, while leaning on his cane for support. Despite his injury, his face beamed with joy. Every time Charlotte looked at him, she blushed red and grinned.

Gratitude filled Elias that, despite the ongoing war, joy could still be found in the love of Charlotte and Alex.

After the ceremony, Uncle Samuel handed Charlotte a letter. "It's from your Uncle Silas."

Tears filled her eyes as she read the note. His absence was the one distress on an otherwise perfect day. Elias had comforted his sister the night before as she wept over this last connection to her parents.

Uncle Silas must have understood that, for his gifts to the couple reflected that need. Several items that had belonged to their mother were sent: a pewter candelabra, the family Bible, and linens that she had adorned with her needlework. Charlotte cried when she saw them and hugged them close to her heart.

Aunt Lizbeth, Abigail, Molly, and her widowed mother all helped serve up a mountain of victuals to the guests.

The fiddlers came just in time to lead everyone in dancing.

"Elias, do you like to dance?" Molly's toes were already starting to tap a beat.

He scratched the back of his head. "Well, I don't know how. But I'd be happy to learn, Molly, if you'll teach me."

"I'd be happy to. You start with a bow. Bow, Elias."

"Oh." He finally bowed, and she laughed.

"Very good. Then I curtsy." She curtsied. "Then you take my hand and lead me to the dance floor."

"But there's no floor."

"Elias, the ground is acceptable. Especially on such a cool evening outdoors. Then follow me and the beat of the song."

She began to move so gracefully that Elias became mesmerized. Whether it was the wine, the music, or the festive spirit, Elias hoped that someday he and Molly would be able to marry. He prayed that when he was old enough, he would be a good husband.

Whether the years passed quickly or slowly, he prayed to the Lord that this war would finally end. After four long and dreadful years, there seemed to be no end in sight.

How many more Americans would die defending freedom? In three years, he'd be old enough to go a soldierin.'

Will I be another casualty of this war? Or will I be on the receiving end of liberty, bought with the blood of so many others?

Fifteen

Four years later
New Haven Connecticut, 1783

The letter in familiar handwriting arrived at Uncle Samuel's farm. 'Twas addressed to Charlotte and Elias, and the contents were shocking. Their Aunt Margaret had passed away suddenly from a terrible fever. Uncle Silas was grief-stricken and living by himself in that big home.

"Char, he's all alone. What do we do?" Elias re-read the letter before handing it to his sister.

"I know not. I do know I cannot go to him right now." Her pregnant belly explained that quite clearly, and her firstborn was barely two, the same age Gabriel had been when she and Elias moved there.

"We need to pray. Poor Uncle Silas."

They held hands, and Elias prayed.

"Dear Lord, please give me wisdom. Help me to know what I should do. Uncle Silas risked his life to bring us here, and now he needs me. You know I do not have fond memories of Aunt Margaret, but I love Uncle Silas, and I'd do anything to help him. Lord, help me to know what to do. Amen."

Uncle Samuel had heard the postrider and approached the two. "By the looks on your faces, you must have received difficult news." Samuel's forehead wrinkled when he realized Charlotte was crying.

"Aunt Margaret died, and Uncle Silas is all by himself. What should I do?

"Praise God the war is over so travel is not so difficult. What are you two thinking? Surely you're not going, Charlotte, with your confinement so near."

"Nay, I cannot. I feel so terrible for Uncle Silas."

"As do I. My poor brother." Samuel turned and gazed into the distance, a faraway look in his eyes.

"I'll go." Elias could not live with himself if he did not help his uncle in Virginia.

"What about Molly? I thought you'd spoken of marriage?" Uncle Samuel put his hand on Elias's shoulder.

"Aye. We have. But how can I ask her to leave her family? Her mother is widowed and all alone."

"I think perhaps you need to speak to her and leave the decision in her hands." Samuel squeezed Elias's shoulder and left him to his thoughts.

He watched Char waddle back to the cabin with Uncle Samuel. His sister had been visiting that day while Alex plowed a field. Although the doctor thought Alex would always use a cane, he somehow managed to drive a team of oxen pulling a plow. Elias was grateful for unexpected blessings.

He needed to speak with Molly as soon as possible. His mind wouldn't rest, wondering about his future. When he arrived at her home, he saw Dr. Walters entering the front door. Was someone ill? Molly?

Elias raced toward her cabin and ran inside without knocking. Dr. Walters, Mrs. Hale, and Molly all stared at him in surprise. "What is the matter, Elias?" Molly hurried to his side. "You seem most upset."

"I do? Oh yes, I—I actually feared you might be ill when I

saw Dr. Walters here. You look quite well. In fact, you look lovely, Molly."

She blushed. "And you look quite handsome."

He looked down at his clothing, dirty from working in the field, and his linen shirt covered in his sweat. Elias could only imagine how unkempt his hair must look.

"Dr. Walters, have you examined Molly's eyesight recently?" He could feel the heat rising in his face.

"I'm afraid there is no test I can do for eyes that view someone with love." Smiling, the kind physician placed his arm around Mrs. Hale's waist. "That's why I am here, Elias. Mrs. Hale has agreed to marry me. I am a most fortunate man."

Elias's mouth dropped open. "That's splendid, Doctor, and Mrs. Hale! I am so happy for you."

"I've never seen my mother look so happy." Molly grinned.

"Molly, there is something I must tell you. Would you walk with me?"

"Of course. You sound so very serious."

"Well, it is serious." The two left Molly's cabin and Elias was quiet for a few moments. "My Aunt Margaret in Virginia has died suddenly, leaving my Uncle Silas all alone."

"I'm so terribly sorry, Elias. Isn't Silas the uncle who brought you here?"

"Aye. He is a much-loved relative who helped raise us. When my parents died, their will designated Uncle Samuel should raise us, and Uncle Silas had to bring us here, right as war broke out. It was a dreadful time and a frightening trip. That's when we met Alex, and he and Char became friends."

"Amazing, is it not?" Molly placed her arm through his.

"What is amazing?"

"How God designed those events to bring Char and Alex together."

Elias stared at the ground for a moment then looked at Molly. "I never thought of God having anything to do with it. I just looked upon it as a difficult time."

"Does God not use difficult times to bring some good to us? To design His purposes for our lives?"

"I suppose He does." He stopped walking and turned, taking her hands in his. "Molly, you know how much I love you. I want to marry you. But I'll be leaving for Virginia soon to help my Uncle Silas. It's the least I can do to repay him in some way for all he's done for us."

"I agree you should."

"I should?" He kissed her tenderly on her cheek.

"Aye." She smiled and touched his face. "So, when do we leave?"

THEIR WEDDING WAS SIMPLE, with their closest friends and family attending. Molly wore her mother's wedding dress of dark blue satin, and Dr. Walters gave her away to her new husband.

Elias smiled so much his face hurt.

After the ceremony, the fiddlers played a lively tune that elicited much enthusiasm on the dance floor. The wedding was indoors, as a summer rainfall had baptized the happy group. No one minded the change of venue, as not even a summer storm could dampen their spirits.

The town had watched this young couple grow up, and to see their new lives beginning as husband and wife seemed to fill the entire community with bliss. It helped that the war was finally in the past. Everyone hoped for better days ahead.

Many tears were shed, especially by Charlotte and Molly's mother, when the couple prepared to leave for Virginia. Even Gabriel's lips trembled when they waved goodbye to everyone.

"Please come and see us. Anytime," Elias shouted to the group.

Molly clung to his arm, and she swiped some moisture off her own cheeks.

Elias leaned over and kissed her. "We're off on an adventure."

"And we're together." Molly kissed him back.

"Aye. Truly the best part." Elias called out, "Get up," to spur the horses on.

She laid her head on his shoulder as he managed the team.

"Molly?"

"Aye?"

"I forgot to write Uncle Silas that we were coming. I kept thinking about other things." Elias paused. "Like what comes after the wedding." His face turned red, and when he looked over at her, he laughed at the relief in her eyes.

Molly smiled shyly, laughing with him. "It's been on my mind as well."

Elias stopped the horses, set the wagon brake and embraced his wife.

Sixteen

Five days later, they arrived at Uncle Silas' home. He was expecting them, as they'd stopped along the way to mail a letter to him.

Elias was shocked at his uncle's appearance. The death of Margaret had truly left the mark of grief upon him. Seven years had also turned his hair gray and added wrinkles that aged him even more. Although he was just two years older than Samuel, the difference in their ages seemed to stretch further apart.

Uncle Silas hugged him so tightly, Elias thought he might break a rib. He held Elias away and said, "Look at you. All grown up and married? I never thought I'd have the joy of seeing you again!"

"When we received your letter, I couldn't stay away. Char would have come to visit, but she is near her confinement."

Uncle Silas's shoulders slumped, and he looked down. "So ye'll not be stayin'? Just here for a visit?"

"What? Nay, Uncle Silas. Molly and I plan on staying with you. If that be all right."

"So ye're stayin'?"

Elias grabbed his arms with affection. "Aye, Uncle Silas. We came to stay with you so you wouldn't be alone."

Silas covered his mouth with a palm pressed against his lips. "I prayed ye'd come."

Molly put her arm around his shoulder. "We're here for you, Uncle Silas. Let's come inside, and I'll fix ye some victuals."

"Go with Molly, Uncle Silas. I'll tend the horses and be right there."

Elias watched his uncle walking next to his wife. *There goes a broken man.*

He prayed as he worked. *Dear Lord, thank You for bringing us here. Thank You for bringing Molly to my heart, and for her love. Please bless this home and bring joy to my uncle. Amen.*

As Elias and Molly lay on clean sheets for the first time in days, Elias mused on simple things. "Molly, I've never appreciated the joy of a bath and clean sheets as much as today. "'Tis a gift. One of life's simple gifts, yet it means so much."

Molly lifted one eye open and smiled. "Aye."

"Like that wooden lamb my Papa made for me. So simple and small. Yet it has brought me comfort so many times and been such a blessing."

"Aye." This time her eyes remained closed.

"And my box of whittling tools. It's small yet brings me such joy and then brings joy to others when I make something for them."

This time Molly was silent. *Sound asleep.* He leaned over and kissed her, whispering, "Good night my love."

He leaned over and blew out his candle.

THE WEEKS ahead were filled with repairs needed on Uncle Silas's home. He must have been too busy to fix the roof and windows. Or perhaps he was too lonely, and it sapped his energy. Even before Aunt Margaret died, it appeared that melancholy had set in. Elias hoped that he and Molly could lift his spirits.

"Elias, didn't you say Uncle Silas used to whittle some?"

"Aye. He did." He ran to find the small box of tools he'd brought with him. When he showed it to Silas, his uncle beamed.

"The whittling tools! Did ye make a few things?"

"Aye, several. As soon as I made them, I gave them away as gifts."

"But you still have the lamb your father made?"

"Of course." Elias grinned from ear to ear. "It's been my constant companion."

Grateful to see the joy on his uncle's face, Elias handed the box to him.

"Why do ya not make a few things? For old time's sake?"

Uncle Silas took the box and met Elias's gaze. "I do believe I will."

Seventeen

They'd been there almost three months when Molly took to her bed, "Elias, I'm quite tired today. I can barely keep my eyes open."

"Perhaps you've been working too much. Please rest, my love."

The fatigue persisted for several days, and Elias went to find a doctor. When he arrived, Dr. Gregory asked to see her. Elias followed him into their bedroom and found her asleep.

"Mrs. Hawkins, might I ask you a few questions before I examine you?"

Molly awoke and rubbed her eyes, then narrowed them when she looked at the doctor. "Who are you?"

"I'm Dr. Gregory. Your husband asked if I'd come."

"Because I'm sleeping so much." Molly finished his sentence. She sat up, then grew dizzy, which sent her head back to the pillow, eyes closed. Molly pushed herself up, slowly this time. "I believe I know what's 'wrong' with me. I've been a midwife for a few years now, and I know these symptoms." She looked up at her husband, a small smile on her face. "Elias, I do believe you're going to be a papa."

"He plopped down on the edge of the bed., "A papa?"

Dr. Gregory laughed. "Maybe *you* need to lie down, son."

"I just might have to."

Molly looked up at the doctor, a worried look on her face. "Dr. Gregory, are there midwives near here?"

The doctor grinned. "Quite a few, I believe. With the war now over, we have much need for midwives. Perhaps, after your little one is born, you might be able to help ..."

She yawned. "Perhaps."

"I'll let you two rest now." He stood, chuckling, and closed the door when he left.

Molly put her head back on the pillow with a relieved sigh. Elias followed her lead.

He rolled onto his side facing Molly, caressing her face. "A papa. I can hardly believe it. Thank you for having our baby." He reached over and kissed her tenderly.

"Good night, my love." Molly smiled at him and went back to sleep.

~

When Uncle Silas heard the news of the coming baby, he whooped out loud. "A baby! My nephew's havin' a baby!"

He hugged Elias in a big bear grip and gave Molly a gentler embrace. "Let's see, you can have the room adjoining your bedroom for the little one. And I'll go lookin' in the barn for a few pieces of furniture that might come in handy."

"We don't need to figure everything out right away, Uncle Silas. The baby won't arrive tomorrow." Molly chuckled at his enthusiasm. "I'm so pleased you're excited for us, though. I hope this won't upend your life too much."

"My life could use a little upending right now. It's been lonely and quiet for far too long."

Right after the noon meal, Uncle Silas disappeared to the outdoors. He said he was on a mission of sorts and would not reveal what it was.

In a few days, his secret mission revealed itself: he'd discovered Elias's baby cradle in the barn and cleaned and fixed it.

"Uncle Silas! What a wonderful gift. Thank you so much." Molly hugged him and kissed him on the cheek.

Elias and Uncle Silas carried the cradle upstairs. "Right here, next to where Molly sleeps."

"This means so much to us both." Tears welled in Molly's eyes.

"You've no idea, Miss Molly, how much your coming to stay with me means," Silas said. "I know you left your mama behind in Connecticut, and that wasn't easy. But it brings such joy to this old man. Thank you."

"Like Molly always reminds me, God uses difficult times to bring about blessings and goodness. To design His purposes for our lives."

"That sounds about right." Uncle Silas grinned. "Let's get some victuals. I'm gettin' hungry."

THE END

Discussion Questions

1. Did you ever have to move as a child? Describe the experience.
2. Think of a situation where you might have experienced fear of losing your life. Were you able to trust the Lord to give you strength? What verses from the Bible helped you?

Acknowledgments

I want to thank my co-authors, Cynthia, Candace, and Kelly. It has been such a blessing working with you. And thank you to Linda Fulkerson of Scrivenings Press for this opportunity to do a novella collection.

About the Author

Elaine Marie Cooper has penned nine books and several have won awards. Her most recent accolades were received for *Scarred Vessels*, which won the Selah Award for best historical romance.

Cooper grew up in Massachusetts and Connecticut and has many fond memories of her formative years there. As a child, she was devastated to find out her ancestor was a Redcoat soldier fighting for England during the American Revolution. As she grew however and studied about him, she imagined a sweet love story that piqued the romantic part of her. Her musings became her first book, *Road to Deer Run*.

She is a registered nurse and currently works as a caregiver for the elderly. She is married, has two sons and 5 grandchildren. Her only daughter died of brain cancer in 2003. Her memoir entitled *"Bethany's Calendar"* was written to help others who care for the ill and dying.

A Lasting Legacy

Cynthia Roemer

To my kindred spirit, Cindy Snyder, who showed me the blessings of true friendship and courage. Until we meet again in God's kingdom. You are loved and missed.

"Therefore, I take pleasure in infirmities, in reproaches, in necessities, in persecutions, in distresses for Christ's sake: for when I am weak, then am I strong."
(2 Corinthians 12:10)

One

Wednesday, August 24, 1814
Bladensburg, Maryland

"Something's not right. I can feel it."

"Hush, Noah. You'll have the entire militia on edge," Private Daniel Hawkins cautioned his friend. And yet, he sensed there was something to what his companion surmised. He peered out at the landscape, squinting against the noontime sun. From their heightened vantage point on Lowndes Hill, they had a clear view of the narrow, wooden bridge across the Anacostia River—the only access to Washington that hadn't been destroyed.

His nervous cohort shifted his feet, wiping sweat from his brow. "But surely you realize the threat. You heard as well as I the redcoats are not far from Bladensburg. Washington is but a few miles away. If they overpower us and seize the capital, all is lost."

Daniel widened his stance and tipped his chin higher. "Nearly six thousand strong, we should have little trouble repelling the British should they launch an attack."

It was rumored that President Madison himself had joined the ranks somewhere between here and the capital.

"I see them!"

The sharp tenor voice of a sentry farther up the rise brought every soldier to his feet, musket at the ready. Daniel scoured the east side of the river, finally spotting the long line of red-coated soldiers in the distance as they marched along the road to Bladensburg. Whether from the blistering heat or his own raw nerves, sweat droplets slithered down his temples onto his cheeks. He swiped them away with the sleeve of his dark-blue uniform jacket.

He'd faced redcoats before. Why should this time be any different?

His thoughts flickered home, and one corner of his mouth lifted. Mayhap it was that Maggie had given him more reason to stay alive.

He reeled in his thoughts. If he were to prevail, he must stay focused. These soldiers were well trained, formidable opponents. Far better equipped than he and the rest of the American militia. The prattle of drums thrummed in the distance, announcing their enemy's approach. As they neared the river, the soldiers fanned out in all directions. Some headed toward the bridge; others dispersed themselves among the buildings in the settlement on the east side of the river.

Daniel squinted at the spindly contraptions the soldiers were setting up along the river's edge. The odd devices resembled firecrackers fastened to long poles.

"What do you suppose those are? Some sort of weaponry?" Noah's nerve-shattered voice carried across the stillness.

Daniel arched a brow. "Possibly. They don't appear too intimidating, but by the way the redcoats are flittering about them, it appears we'll soon find out."

The command from General Winder to open fire set off a barrage of musket rounds. Several British soldiers fell instantly to the ground, while others knelt to return fire. Daniel set his sights on the column of soldiers attempting to cross the bridge. Singling out the one on the far left, he steadied his aim, pulled the trigger, then watched his target drop to the wooden planks. Another American bullet found its mark, and a second soldier collapsed to the bridge floor. Others in the squad fell back, retreating into the small settlement nestled across the river.

As Daniel reloaded his Springfield 1795, a loud whistle split the air. He flinched and glanced up to see a flaming projectile soar through the sky, arching high overhead as it spiraled toward them. On its descent, the shaft exploded in midair, sending a spray of shrapnel in all directions. Though dozens of yards from the blast, Daniel flattened himself on the ground, heart pounding.

A man's shrill cry pierced the air.

Daniel ventured a glance in the direction of the sound. Several yards in the distance, a man writhed on the ground, while another ran to offer assistance. The rest of the soldiers in the vicinity scattered.

Still half stunned, Daniel stood and brushed off his soiled uniform. "Indeed, they *are* weapons."

Coming up beside him, Noah cut a glance at the far side of the river. "How will we defend ourselves against such weaponry?"

"The best we know how—with much faith and courage." Gripping his musket, Daniel pointed it at the nearest redcoat and fired. His aim rang true, finding its mark in the chest of the British soldier.

More rockets flared overhead.

Noah stumbled backward, face blanched. "Heaven preserve us. Come. We must flee!"

Daniel hesitated, his gaze vacillating between the rockets and his fellow militiamen. Many had fallen back, blasting a final shot before seeking refuge or fleeing. Would they be routed so easily?

He heard their sergeant call to them. "Courage, men! Stand firm and fight!"

A few soldiers paused and turned, but as the missiles

continued to explode around them, they took flight once more. Daniel fell back a few paces and fired off another shot, conscious of the constant barrage of rocket blasts peppering the landscape. Not one to shy away from battle, he balked at the thought of fleeing. And yet, the intruders would have to face two more waves of soldiers guarding the capital. Mayhap it would be best to regroup with his comrades and combine their efforts.

Noah paused his running and pointed frantically to the sky. "Daniel, above you!"

Daniel caught a glimpse of the projectile bearing down at him. Drawing a hurried breath, he sprinted forward, his heart drumming in his ears. He prodded his muscles harder, faster up the incline, dodging obstacles in his path.

Thoughts of Maggie and the babe in her womb spurred him on. They had their whole life ahead of them. He must live.

He must.

With every stride, he breathed a prayer. *Preserve me, Lord. For Maggie's sake.*

For our child's.

A deafening "pop" sounded, and sharp pain pierced the back of his left leg. Another, his side. He tumbled to the ground, lurching to a stop face down in the grassy field.

Muffled voices called from every direction. Most, unfamiliar ones.

British voices.

Shots zinged overhead.

Daniel's mind whirled. His musket had flown from his hands in the fall. With no means to defend himself, he had no choice but to lie still and pray he would be presumed dead. He ground his teeth against the excruciating pain in his upper thigh. He could feel the steady trickle of blood seeping from the wound. The shrapnel must have cut him deeply. As soon as able, he needed to rig up a tourniquet to stem the flow.

But for now, he must remain still and wait.

When the battle ended, someone would come for him. Noah, most certainly.

Some time passed before the blare of rockets and gunfire faded. When all went quiet, Daniel lifted his head. Sweat streamed down his face, the pain in his leg almost more than he could bear. He blinked, weak and struggling to focus. The bodies of soldiers—more American than British—lay strewn about the battlefield. The rest, it seemed, had been routed toward the capital. He could only pray the British attack had been stymied somewhere along the way.

His gaze fastened on one fallen soldier farther up the rise, and his breathing shallowed. Though the body lay twisted and bloodied, there was no mistaking the dark mop of hair and familiar lean frame of his friend. "Noah," he murmured, loud enough for only himself to hear.

Daniel tried to rise, but his leg gave way, the pain intensifying. With a groan, he propped himself onto his forearms and pushed himself along with his good leg. After several yards, he collapsed to the ground, breathless, his strength sapped. His injuries and blood loss were significant. And yet, if not for Noah's warning, Daniel would likely have suffered much worse.

Through blurred vision, he studied his friend from a distance. The dark stain on his uniform gave clue that Noah had taken a musket ball to the chest. His limp, unnatural position assured he hadn't survived.

Moisture pooled in Daniel's eyes. Since their youth, he and Noah had been inseparable. When Daniel determined to enlist in the militia, Noah had reluctantly followed, hopeful their efforts would bring a quick end to the unwanted threat to their freedom.

They'd boasted such plans for the future. When their thirteen months of service were up, they would claim the one hundred sixty acres promised them and settle on adjacent plots and share the work and produce of their land.

Daniel's throat caught. Now his friend was gone, and their dream had died with him.

He tensed at the shuffle of boots in the grass. Fighting fatigue, he slowly shifted to his side, cringing at the sight of approaching British soldiers. Whether from the sweltering heat or loss of blood, his limbs felt drained, heavy. The soldiers faded in and out as his vision blurred. He closed his eyes, powerless to fight them.

His thoughts returned to his sweet Maggie and the wee one she now carried. What would become of them if he were imprisoned or killed? He tried to rally but dropped back down from his elbows with a groan.

He dug his fingernails in the grass. Earlier, he'd spoken with such courage and fortitude. Now, he hadn't the strength to even put up a struggle. *Have mercy, Lord.*

Yielding to his weariness, Daniel laid his head down in defeat, wondering if Noah had suffered the lesser fate.

Two

Thursday, August 25, 1814
Loudoun County, Virginia

Maggie spread the freshly laundered dress on the boulder to dry, then pressed a hand to her swollen abdomen, a grin pulling at her lips. "He's moving again."

Her sister, Emma, finished wringing out the garment she held and tossed it in the basket. With a shake of her head, she peered over at Maggie. "Always, you refer to the baby as *he*, as if you know for certain the child is a boy. You do realize there's an equal chance the baby is a girl?"

Maggie's smile deepened. For better than a week now, she'd relished the feel of the babe's quickening within her. Daniel's letter sharing his excitement over the news had only accentuated her joy. "Somehow, I just know."

Emma rested her hands on her hips and scoffed. "The way my Jonathan was certain we were to have a lad each time, and yet the Lord has given us three lasses?"

With a chuckle, Maggie glanced at the three young girls

playing beneath the sycamore tree, their strawberry-blonde hair catching flecks of sunlight betwixt the shade of the tree's broad leaves. "Mayhap his intuition was misguided. But something deep within assures me *this* baby is a boy."

"And, pray tell, what leads you to that assumption, sister?"

"Just a notion." Maggie tossed her older sister a curious glance, certain of the answer before she mouthed the question. "Did you never have such impressions?"

With a shake of her head, Emma doused another piece of clothing in the stream. "I left that knowledge in the Lord's hands. As well should you, dear one."

Maggie released a long breath and pressed a hand to her womb. She didn't expect her serious-minded sister to understand.

But Daniel would. And if he was agreeable, she also knew the name she wished to bestow on the child.

"I did say I would *help* with your chores, not do them entirely."

At her sister's gentle scolding, Maggie pushed her thoughts aside and reached into the basket for another piece of clothing. "Forgive me. 'Tis difficult to concentrate when my mind is so full."

Emma's expression softened, a faraway look in her eyes. "Married these seven years, I'd nearly forgotten what it is to be so smitten. You and Daniel had so little time together after you married and, this being your first child, I reason a bit of grace is in order." With a telling grin, she returned to scrubbing. "Have you received word from Daniel of late?"

Shaking the wrinkles from the wet garment, Maggie gave a soft sigh, the humid air weighing heavy on her chest. "None these past couple weeks. But I'm certain I'll hear from him soon. He rarely goes more than a fortnight without writing." She flattened the undergarment on the far side of the boulder. "And what do you hear of Jonathan?"

Emma peered over her shoulder, swiping a strand of her

wheat-blonde hair from her sweaty brow. "His term with the militia is up the end of next month. What a blessing it will be to have him here in time to help prepare for the sparse winter months. Not to mention your wee one's arrival with Daniel away."

"Indeed." A flurry of hopefulness swept through Maggie. "Do you suppose they will allow Daniel at least a short leave when our baby is born? Surely the fighting will slacken come winter."

As if guessing Maggie's need for reassurance, Emma offered a slight grin. "Mayhap. 'Tis more than likely, I would venture."

And yet, the pitch in her sister's voice sounded forced, unconvincing.

A nervous twinge kneaded through Maggie. The thought of Daniel being away when their baby came was heartbreaking. Eight long months remained of his term of service in the militia. The harsh winters here were difficult enough to withstand when she was not carrying a child. How would she manage without Daniel?

She placed a hand on her belly as the babe fluttered once more. Each day she prayed for Daniel's safe return and that, by some miracle, he would be here when their son was born. In some ways, January seemed as though it would never come. Yet, when she considered all the necessary preparations, it seemed but a breath away.

~

Evening, August 25, 1814
Bladensburg, Maryland

DANIEL STARTLED awake to the sound of pelting rain, his forehead damp with sweat. Lantern light flickered on the ceiling of the unfamiliar cabin. Fatigue coursed through his limbs, the throbbing in his leg bringing to mind his injury.

Along with the loss of his friend.

The fierce-sounding wind pulled his eyes to the nearby window. Gray clouds blanketed the sky, making it difficult to distinguish night from day. He drew a heavy breath. The air in the room was stifling. How had he come to be here? Last he recalled, the British were all but upon him. Had he lost consciousness?

A lean man approached, shoulders slumped and silvery eyes bloodshot. His white shirt and fitted breeches were not those of a soldier, but neither did they resemble typical American clothing. Thunder rumbled in the distance as he squatted beside Daniel.

"So, the storm has finally awakened you."

The man's British accent confirmed Daniel's fears. He swallowed, the dryness in his throat nearly stealing his voice. "Where am I?"

"I believe the village is called Bladensburg. We found it abandoned and converted this building into a hospital for the wounded."

Daniel glanced about the dim room filled with maimed soldiers, noting most wore the trappings of redcoats. "You're a British physician, then?"

"Aye. A surgeon."

"And you intend to treat me, your enemy?"

"Indeed. All of the wounded were brought here—American and British."

A surge of bitterness washed through Daniel, edging out the weakness in his limbs. "That's quite liberal of you. I don't know that I would be as generous with those who killed my dearest friend."

"I'm sorry." The doctor's long, thin nose flared. "War is fraught with tragedy, to be sure."

Pain shot through Daniel's thigh, and he cringed. "If you intend to be so benevolent, then mayhap you'd care to remove the shrapnel in my thigh and side. Or at least offer something to stifle the pain."

The doctor's eyes flicked from Daniel's face to his leg and back again. "I can get you some morphine for the pain. But ..."

Daniel's brows pinched. "But what?"

The man's tone deepened. "The shrapnel has already been removed and your wounds ... tended."

"I recall no such treatment or doctoring."

"You were unconscious when the soldiers brought you and have remained so more than a day. I performed surgery on you soon after your arrival."

Daniel felt his bandaged side, then reached to touch his leg. His heart hammered. Instead of his dressed limb, his hand raked over a rounded stub. Panic rose in his throat as he struggled to lift his head for a look. Every fiber in him revolted at the sight of the sunken sheet where his leg should have been. "Lord, have mercy. What have you done?"

Something akin to compassion streamed from the doctor's eyes. "The shrapnel was embedded deep in your thigh and shattered your bone. The damage to your leg was beyond repair, and you'd lost a great deal of blood. There was no other option but to take the leg."

"No!" Daniel squeezed his eyes shut, willing himself to drown out the surgeon's words.

His thoughts turned to Maggie. They'd had a mere three months together after their wedding. He'd barely seen them through the winter before joining the militia. Since learning he was to be a father, he'd prayed fervently for the war to end so that he could be home when the child came.

His stomach clenched. Was he to return to her half a man?

The sound of the wind and rain slackened as he opened his eyes and glared up at the surgeon. "You've ruined me. How am I to provide for my wife and child with only one leg?"

The doctor arched a brow, his mouth taut. "'Twas your leg ... or your life."

The sobering words pierced Daniel to his core. Twenty-three

years of age was too young to be robbed of life *or* limb. He and Maggie had such plans and dreams for the future.

Not once had he given thought to an injury shattering those dreams.

Three

Loudoun County, Virginia
September 28, 1814

The wagon jostled along the worn path, keeping Daniel from any semblance of rest. He folded his arms, weary of the sound of cackling chickens eager to be freed of their crate prisons. A feather flittered past his face, and he blew out a puff of air, watching the downy plume dive and swirl over the side of the wagon.

Daniel sighed. Hitching a ride in the bed of Judd Cravens's rickety cart wouldn't have been his first choice of travel, but upon witnessing Daniel's plight, the aged neighbor insisted on offering a ride home.

Sitting up straighter, Daniel craned his neck for a look around. Not much had changed since he'd left in the spring. Mr. Newman's split-rail fence was still in dire need of repair. The rolling landscape still held its charm. Mr. Benson's cattle— plumper after months of grazing the lush, green pastureland— continued to roam the meadow to the west.

There were changes, however. The September day held more warmth than the raw April morning he'd departed. The once bare trees now boasted thick foliage which would soon burst with autumn color—a change Daniel always relished but for the cold, harsh winter certain to follow.

Maggie, most certainly, would have changed too, her slender frame blossoming with the child in her womb. Warmth surged in his chest. So much love had passed between them in the few short months after they'd wed. Dear, sweet Maggie. Her letter bearing the news she was with child had oozed with joy and excitement.

Enthusiasm Daniel had shared.

His throat clenched. But now ... could he even manage being a father?

A glance at his stubbed leg shot a wave of trepidation through him. How would Maggie react to seeing him in such a state? Would she look on him with disgust? Pity?

Daniel couldn't bear the thought of either.

His gaze returned to the roadside, the landscape growing more familiar with each turn of the wheels. He could almost envision Maggie bursting through the cabin doorway, face aglow, only to slow her pace, her countenance falling like that of a child deprived of a favorite toy at sight of his infirmity. The agonizing image pricked his very soul.

He scrubbed a hand over his face. What good was he to her now? Unable to protect or provide for her or their child, he was but an encumbrance.

A burden.

Daniel gripped the bundle at his side, the wound of his friend's passing still raw. Returning Noah's things to his family and facing his friend's intended were not tasks he relished. But at least Elizabeth would not be burdened by Noah as Maggie would with him.

"Does your missus know you're coming?"

The question stirred Daniel from his thoughts. "I sent word, though she knows not when to expect me."

Judd spoke over his shoulder. "Does she ... uh ... know of your ... injury?"

Heat burned Daniel's cheeks. The intrusive query was not one he was inclined to respond to. Maggie knew his reason for returning home months earlier than anticipated. He'd simply neglected to offer specifics.

He hadn't the heart to.

A twinge of pain throbbed in his still tender nub as he blew out a breath and reluctantly gave answer. "She knows."

The neighbor's head bobbed, his straw hat concealing his features. With a tap of the reins, he returned his attention to the road ahead.

Daniel shifted, his hands growing clammy as his cabin appeared in the distance. Soon there would be no more hiding behind half-truths. Maggie would view for herself that the man she'd married with such eager anticipation was but an invalid.

MAGGIE STILLED her dishwashing at sight of Mr. Cravens's wagon veering toward the cabin. She dried her water-soaked hands on her apron, not bothering to tidy herself before stepping outside. With a shake of her head, she noted the pile of crates in the wagon bed. If he'd come in hopes of selling her more chickens, he was sorely mistaken. At this point, she hadn't the stomach or will to butcher the poor creatures. When Daniel returned, mayhap he would take up the task.

Poor Daniel. He'd been so vague in his letter alerting her of his injury. And yet, his distraught tone had been telling. Whatever the wound, she would simply be thankful to have him home. 'Twould be an answer to her prayers for him to be here when the baby came. Though him returning injured was not what she'd had in mind.

As the wagon neared, she noted more than chicken crates in the rickety bed. Shielding her eyes against the evening sun, she caught a glimpse of a man's head of chestnut hair. He turned his head enough to allow her a glimpse of his profile, and her breath caught. She clapped a hand to her mouth, moisture pooling in her eyes. "Daniel."

Hiking her skirt, she trekked toward the wagon as swiftly as the growing baby in her womb would allow. As Daniel pivoted toward her, his eyes flashed recognition, and he sat taller, a gentle smile spilling across his face. She waved to him, tempering her emotions, uncertain whether to laugh or cry.

Mr. Cravens tugged on the reins, bringing his aged mare to a halt before her. So fixated on her husband, Maggie barely noticed the older man's tip of his hat or his spry, "Good day to you, ma'am."

With her gaze still trained on Daniel, she returned a slight nod. "'Tis a good day for certain that you've brought my Daniel home." She stretched out her hand, and Daniel clasped her palm in his, the warmth of his touch spreading through her like sunshine on a spring morning.

For a blessed moment, they took each other in, the depth of expression in Daniel's olive eyes challenging to read. One moment his gaze radiated love and longing. The next, a curious sort of hollowness seeped in. Did he find her expanding waistline unappealing?

No. Daniel would never be so petty. He'd been as excited as her at the news of their coming child. Mayhap his injury was what troubled him. She let her gaze drift to his shoulders and chest. How handsome a soldier he made. Though his uniform showed smudges and wear, there were no visible signs of a wound. And yet some harm must have befallen him to cause his early discharge.

She squeezed his fingers, giving his hand a gentle tug. "Come. I'll get supper on the table whilst you tell me all that has happened."

His smile faded as he pulled his hand away. "'Tis best Judd drives closer to the cabin."

Maggie knit her brows. "Why? What is it?"

"You'll know soon enough. Let's go Judd."

The elderly neighbor flashed her a sympathetic glance then slapped the reins across the horse's back.

Maggie strode alongside, pricked by the coolness in Daniel's tone. Her mind whirled. Was that it? Had his injury rendered him lame?

She tipped her chin higher. Well, no matter. She and the Lord would have him back on his feet within a matter of weeks.

As Mr. Cravens brought the wagon to a halt outside the cabin, Daniel reached for something at his side. Maggie craned to see past a crate of chickens, and her heart plunged when the object proved a wooden crutch.

"Let me give you a hand." Lighting from his driver's seat, Mr. Cravens moved to the back of the wagon and unfastened the end gate.

Maggie inched closer, gnawing her lip as she watched Daniel slide his way toward the opening, the sideboards and crates concealing much of him from view. She pressed a hand to her abdomen, the quickening in her womb rekindling a smile. No matter their hardships, she and Daniel had the joy of this child to share. A testament of their deep love and of the Lord's tender blessings.

Ignoring Mr. Cravens's attempt to help, Daniel lowered his crutch to the ground. "I can manage."

The shortness in Daniel's tone sounded so uncharacteristic of his usual jovial voice that it hardly seemed his at all. As he scooted to the edge of the wagon into Maggie's view, she sucked in a breath and stifled a cry. Oh, her dear, sweet Daniel. His leg was nothing but a stub.

No wonder he seemed so on edge.

He sat with head bowed, not venturing a glance her way, as if afraid what he might glean in her expression.

Moisture pooled in her eyes, and she blinked it away, surrendering her own emotions for his sake. She refused to cry even a single tear in his sight. Though mayhap she would shed a bushelful when left to herself.

A thousand misgivings pummeled her as she watched him painstakingly lower himself from the wagon. How would they manage these coming months—her laden with child and Daniel barely able to maneuver and reluctant to accept help?

Lord, render strength to us both.

With a tip of his hat, Mr. Cravens moved to replace his end gate. "Be there anything me or the missus can do to lend a hand, jus' say the word."

"We'll be fine." The firm set in Daniel's jaw spoke of manly pride rather than conviction.

Maggie forced a smile at the elderly neighbor. "Thank you, Mr. Cravens. That's most generous."

He pursed his lips and nodded, understanding in his pale blue eyes. "Well, I'll be on my way then and leave you two to get reacquainted." The creases in the corners of his eyes deepened as he flashed a quick wink at Maggie.

She returned a weak grin and then shifted her gaze to Daniel who continued to stare somberly at the ground.

As Mr. Cravens's wagon pulled away and the cackle of poultry faded, Maggie drew a cleansing breath. "Well. Shall we go inside? We have much to talk over."

Without a word, Daniel started forward. He swayed, leaning heavily on his crutch. Maggie resisted the urge to grasp his arm, refusing to further wound his pride.

As he steadied himself, his eyes lifted. "I'm sorry, Maggie."

She forced a grin, doing her best to conceal the ache gnawing at her insides. She'd expected a limp or gash in his side, one that would heal in time.

Not this.

Not a loss he could never regain.

Swallowing her hurt, she stepped toward him, never allowing her eyes to stray from his. "There's nothing to be sorry for."

"But I'm no good to you now, love." His gaze drifted to their cabin, then to the small field in the clearing and to the abundance of trees dotting the landscape. "All our hopes and dreams of this place and of our lives together are shattered. I'm more worthless than a man thrice my age."

She clutched his arm. "You mustn't speak so, Daniel."

He glared at her. "It's true. I can no more provide for you and our child than ... poor Noah can Elizabeth."

The catch in his voice sent a shiver through Maggie. "What of Noah? Has he been injured as well?"

Daniel's eyes glazed over, his tanned complexion paling as he turned away. "Not injured." He swallowed, seeming to struggle for words. "Fallen, without a chance to voice a goodbye."

Maggie gasped, unable to stem the flow of tears. "Poor Noah. And Elizabeth. She will be heartsore at the news."

Daniel hung his head. "Her burden will be great, to be certain, but she is young and fetching. No doubt, in time, she will love again." His voice softened. "It's you who carries the bleaker lot, chained to a husband who'll be nothing but a hindrance."

Pricked at his words, she again clutched his arm. "I could never think of you as a burden."

He shifted his head toward her, lips taut. "Oh, no? Then tell me. How will we manage the coming winter when I can barely stay afoot? How will you bear the burden of tending me when you have a newborn to nurture?"

Before Maggie could form a response, he tugged his arm away and shuffled forward, his voice so soft and gritty she struggled to hear. "'Twould have been better had I suffered the same fate as Noah."

She squeezed her eyes shut, too aggrieved to reply. As though in response to the effects of the painful declaration on Maggie's heart, the babe twisted in her womb. She stifled a sob. The homecoming she'd longed to rejoice in had instead left her hollower than Daniel's absence ever could.

Four

Sunday, October 2, 1814

"Can I get you anything before I go?"

Maggie's tender voice butted against the thick hedge around Daniel's heart but could not penetrate it. He shook his head. "No. Nothing."

"You're sure? I'll stay if you wish."

"Go." The word came out harsher than intended, and the wounded expression on Maggie's face tore at Daniel, causing him to look away.

Soft footsteps sounded, followed by a thud of the door.

He jerked his head to where she'd stood, the emptiness shrouding him like a cloak of darkness. In the three days since his return, he'd done nothing but cause her grief. And yet, she'd remained pleasant, forbearing. Not at all what he deserved.

While some might consider Maggie plain, he thought her fetching. Beautiful, in fact. Even more so with the glow of motherhood shining in her eyes. Being with child suited her. Everything in him longed to take her in his arms and caress her as he'd envisioned himself doing countless times over the months away. But, ashamed of his failings, he could not bring himself to show his affection. Instead, he chose to remain aloof, feelings of inadequacy and longing at war within.

Oh, the anguish of loving someone so deeply and yet keeping such emotions bottled inside. Like a simmering pot threatening to overspill, his heart nearly burst each time he glanced her way.

Daniel raked a hand over his face, the lonesomeness of the dim cabin taunting him. He should have gone to church service with her. Together they might have managed it. Instead, he'd played the part of a coward, choosing to let his dear Maggie walk the near mile trek alone while he stayed to lick his wounds.

He didn't blame the Lord for his predicament. After sharing news of Noah's fate with his family and young Elizabeth, he'd simply lost all will to face anyone. The encounter had proven every bit as heart-wrenching as he'd imagined. Mayhap even more so. The dense log cabin seemed a fitting place to hide away and attempt to forget what had transpired.

A twinge of pain shot through him, and he peered at the blanket draped over his lap. All but his leg. *That* inadequacy he could never forget.

It would plague him to his dying day.

"AUNT MAGGIE!"

Her three nieces dashed over, faces aglow, dressed in their Sunday finest. Maggie pasted on a smile, relieved to find them still at home. She gave them each a touch on the cheek. "Good morning."

Nina pressed a hand to Maggie's rounded middle. "When will the baby come?"

"Not for a while yet. After the new year." Maggie turned to Liddy. "Is your mother inside?"

Liddy nodded. "She sent us out here so she could finish readying for service. You can go in, if you like."

"Thank you." Maggie mustered a weak grin, then skimmed past. Lifting her hand, she rapped her knuckles on the pine door.

Hurried footsteps approached, and the door swung open. Emma's eyes widened. "Why, Maggie. I thought you would go to service with Daniel." Her gaze drifted past Maggie, her smile fading. "He's not with you?"

Maggie shook her head, chin quivering. Moisture pooled in her eyes. She'd held in her emotions before Daniel and the children, but with her sister, could no longer stem the flow.

Taking her by the arm, Emma tugged her inside. "Come, dear. Tell me what's troubling you."

Before Maggie crossed the threshold, the tears streamed down her cheeks. She swiped them away, annoyed with herself for giving vent to her feelings. "I'm sorry. I don't wish to burden you."

With a shake of her head, Emma clasped Maggie's hands in hers. "Nonsense. What good are sisters if not to share one another's struggles?" She ushered Maggie to a chair, then took a seat across from her. "Now. Is it Daniel's plight that's troubling you or something more?"

Drawing a breath, Maggie fought to steady her voice. "I could handle his limitations. It's his indifference that troubles me. He's not the same man I married just a short time ago."

Emma breathed a soft sigh. "I don't suppose any man returns from war quite as he left. I'm certain my Jonathan will have some challenges of his own to work through. Injured or whole, war penetrates the heart of a man."

"But it's more than that with Daniel. His spirit is depleted." A tinge of heat stung her cheeks. "He ... has no wish to ... be near me." She hung her head. "He's ... not my Daniel."

Gentle fingers cupped Maggie's chin, drawing her eyes back to her sister. Leaning closer, Emma flashed a reassuring grin. "Give him time, dear one. His manhood has suffered a harsh blow. Lord willing, in time he will find himself once more. Love him with the same vibrancy you always have. His spirit will revive."

Unconvinced, Maggie sniffled. "And if it doesn't?"

Emma arched a brow. "Jonathan will be home in a few days. He will light a fire under your Daniel."

With a sigh, Maggie bowed her head. "Jonathan may hold influence over Daniel's zeal for work, but no one can rekindle his spirit but the Lord and Daniel himself."

"Then, we will pray. Even Daniel's stubborn will is no match for the Lord's promptings." She handed Maggie a kerchief. "Now dry your eyes, and let's be off or we'll be late to service.

Taking the kerchief, Maggie dabbed her eyes, a spark of hope flickering within her. She would do just as her sister suggested— love Daniel with all the affection she'd held pent up inside these many months apart.

And leave the rest to the Lord.

Five

Thursday, October 13, 1814

Daniel breathed a soft sigh as Maggie stooped to gather another log for the fire. She was indeed fetching. Truly a rare woman. In the weeks since his homecoming, she had worked tirelessly without complaint while he'd barely managed to maneuver his way about the cabin. Shamed, he pulled himself up with his crutch. "Let me do that. You sit a while."

She turned to face him, a weak smile edging out the tiredness in her eyes. "Thank you."

Hobbling over, he took the log from her, his fingers brushing the back of her hands. Their eyes locked, and the flush in Maggie's cheeks took him back to when their love was new. When they'd strolled together along the banks of Willow Creek, and he'd held her soft hand in his for the first time. In that moment, he'd known he and Maggie were meant to be together.

Enthralled in the memory, he barely heard the spry call from outside the cabin.

With a shy smile, Maggie slid her hands away and moved to the door.

Daniel leaned to toss the log on the fire, forcing himself back into the present.

Peering outside, Maggie clasped her hands together. "It's Emma ... and Jonathan's with her!" With hurried steps, she rushed outside to greet them.

Edging his way to the window, Daniel pulled aside the thick muslin curtain and peered through the dusty pane. With sure steps, his brother-in-law strode forward to give Maggie a gentle embrace. Though the crackling fire and closed window muffled the conversation, plainly Jonathan was exchanging pleasantries and complimenting Maggie on her appearance.

A wave of envy coursed through Daniel as he took in Jonathan's tall, lean physique. It didn't seem fair that Jonathan had returned home in such good measure and he had not. Daniel shoved the curtain back into place. *Envy rotteth the bones*, scripture said. But how could he not be jealous of his brother-in-law's wholeness as opposed to his privation?

As their voices grew louder, Daniel moved away from the window. Leaning his crutch against the wall, he braced himself on the back of a chair. He tensed, drawing himself taller as the three entered the cabin. 'Twas prideful, he knew, but he could not stomach the thought of baring his weaknesses before Jonathan at first glance.

Their expressions sobered as all eyes veered in his direction. After a slight hesitation, Jonathan stepped toward him, hand outstretched. "How are you, Daniel? It's good to see you."

With a crisp nod, Daniel clasped his brother-in-law's hand. "As well as can be expected given my limitations."

Jonathan's dark eyes crimped slightly but remained fixed on Daniel's. "Yes. Well, now that I'm home, I'll be happy to assist you in any way."

Daniel's cheek flinched. Until now, he'd been content to sit idle and mourn his restraints. But the thought of his brother-in-law shouldering Daniel's responsibilities to tend to his property and see to Maggie's needs didn't sit right. Jonathan meant well, he knew, but Daniel's pride balked at the notion of another man managing his household. And yet, given his and Maggie's circumstances, there seemed no way around it. With the baby coming, it wasn't fair to ask Maggie to pull his share as well as her own. Unwilling to voice his thanks, he merely nodded.

Maggie slid one of the chairs from the table. "Have a seat, won't you?"

With a shake of her head, Emma cut a glance at Jonathan. "We left the girls in the care of Jonathan's mother and promised not to be away long. We only wished to let you know he'd returned and is willing to help out where needed."

Jonathan's gaze drifted to the near-empty kindling box. "Like replenishing your wood supply." He edged toward the door, casting Daniel a sideways glance. "Shall I tote a few armloads before we go?"

Daniel's shoulders stiffened. For Maggie's sake, he knew he should accept, and yet he couldn't bring himself to do so. "No need to bother. We can manage it."

"'Tis no bother. I'm pleased to help." Jonathan paused, fixing his gaze firmly on Daniel. "Or, mayhap the two of us could work at it together."

Daniel wavered, torn between accepting the challenge or suffering the embarrassment of displaying his inabilities. He eyed his crutch, tempted to reach for it. Instead, he turned to Jonathan, chin dipped low. "I suppose a few armloads wouldn't hurt."

With a hesitant nod, Jonathan took his leave.

Tension hung in his absence. Certain Maggie and Emma's expressions would convey either pity or disappointment, Daniel kept his gaze fastened on the puncheon floorboards. Eventually, the two women broke into quiet chatter, easing the strain.

Tired of standing, Daniel clung tighter to the back of the chair, eager to regain his solitude. His leg began to quiver and then shake, yet he forced himself to remain standing until

Jonathan had deposited his last load and he and Emma had spoken their goodbyes.

As Maggie closed the door behind them, Daniel snatched his crutch and sank down onto the chair, grateful for the briefness of their visit. He draped a knitted blanket over his lap, reluctant to allow even Maggie to look upon his stub. How long would he let his injured pride have the better of him?

Maggie's eyes were moist as she pivoted toward him. Though she spoke not a word, her grieved expression conveyed her disappointment. As if to say, 'Twould be a terribly long, lonesome life if he continued to shut out all those around him.

Cut to the quick that he'd caused her grief, Daniel knew his attitude must change.

He just wasn't sure how. *Lord, help me.*

MAGGIE SNUGGED her shawl tighter around her and breathed in the cool October air. She'd had to get out of that dungeon of a cabin. Out here in nature the Lord seemed so near, His signature painted across the sunlit hills and misty valleys. Yet, even here she could not escape the pang of loss. Her once cherished bond with Daniel had disintegrated to little more than strained silence.

She fingered her thin wedding band, tears dampening her cheeks. For one fleeting moment, when their hands had touched, she'd caught a glimpse of the true Daniel. The one she'd come to admire and love. But the instant the tap on the door sounded, the hint of closeness had vanished like morning dew.

With a deep sigh, she pressed a hand to her abdomen. She'd longed to share this special time with Daniel. Together experiencing the baby's growth and movement, seeing him take his first breath, and hearing his first cry. But despite her many attempts, Daniel had shown little interest in her or the baby. Deep down, she knew he must be pleased at the thought of being a father. His joy was merely buried beneath layers of self-doubt and bereavement over his lost limb.

Nothing she said or did seemed to penetrate his defenses. Emma said to give him time, but with each failed attempt, Maggie's hopes plummeted. Every day she sensed Daniel retreating further into his shell ... and her own heart growing colder.

Lifting her eyes heavenward, she folded her hands together at her chest. "Father, I've tried to be patient, tried to love Daniel despite his lack of affection. How I miss him, Lord. Now more than ever. While apart, I could dream of his return. But now, there is nothing left to hope for. Please, Lord, may he realize how much this baby and I need him."

A scuffing noise from behind stilled her wispy voice. She turned to see Daniel several yards away, a pained expression in his eyes. Leaning on his crutch, he hobbled closer, his eyes never straying from hers. When he was but an arm's length away, he raked a hand through his flaxen hair.

"Forgive me, Maggie. My homecoming has been a disappointment."

Maggie worked to still her quivering chin. "Your homecoming could not have brought me more joy, Daniel. It's just ..."

His head lowered. "You wish for a whole husband. Like Jonathan. One who will care for you as you deserve."

"No, Daniel. That's not it at all." She stepped toward him, the tightness in her throat straining her voice. "I can accept the loss of your leg. But I cannot bear losing *you*."

His head lifted, and a strange sort of quandary filled his face. He leaned harder on his crutch, brow furrowed. "Is that how you feel? That you've lost me?"

"How could I not?" Before she could still them, the anguished words poured from her lips. She stifled a sob, letting her gaze drift to the ground beneath. "You ... you've hardly given me notice since you've been home."

He reached out and clasped her hand, the warmth of his long-awaited touch sending a tremor through her. "I'm sorry, Maggie. I don't wish to hurt you. I merely hate for you to see me like this. Half a man."

Tension tore at her brow. "Is your opinion of me so small that you reason losing a leg would make me think any less of you? 'Tis *you* I love, Daniel. Not your leg or your arm or ... anything else. *You*."

He stared at her, eyes wide, as though her words rent away blinders to a clearer view. "But we had such dreams for our future. Surely having them snatched away must disappoint you."

She squeezed his hand, gazing up into his olive eyes. "My only disappointment is that you've pushed me away."

He perused her face, his gaze settling on her lips. He closed the gap between them until her rounded belly pressed against him. "Do you know how torturous it has been to be so near you these past weeks and not hold you in my arms?"

Maggie's heart beat faster, and the baby in her womb leaped as though responding to the stir of emotions swirling inside her. She arched a brow, a grin edging onto the corners of her lips. "Much like the torturous feeling of not having your arms around me, I would venture."

His gaze snapped back to hers and his expression softened. "I'm sorry, love. This is not what I anticipated our life together to be. The Lord has dealt us a difficult lot."

Maggie raised her head higher. "War has dealt us the blow, not God. And we must make the best of things."

"But there's so much I can't do. I don't know how to be anything but a farmer."

"Then you must find what the Lord has in store for you instead. He will not leave you to flounder. You must have faith and not give up."

As if unconvinced, he offered a tentative nod.

"Promise you'll try, Daniel."

Wrapping his free arm around her, he gave her shoulders a gentle squeeze. "I will try."

As he leaned closer and pressed his lips to hers, Maggie melted into his embrace, praying the words were heartfelt ones and that the Lord would allow them a fresh beginning.

Six

Friday, December 2, 1814

Maggie rubbed a hand over her rounded belly. "That was such a good meal. Thank you for bringing it to share with us."

Emma's chin dipped. "For a good meal, you didn't eat much."

"I fill up rather quickly these days. The baby seems to take up most of my eating room."

Casting Maggie a sideways glance, Emma stood and hefted the half-empty pot of stew. "That will only worsen as the baby grows. Small, frequent meals are best."

"May we play, Mama?" asked Nina.

All three tow-headed girls perched on the edge of their shared bench and peered with hopeful faces at their mother.

With a tip of her head, Emma nodded. "Go on."

The three youngsters giggled as they skirted past their father, dodging his teasing attempts to slow them.

Maggie warmed at the sight, imagining the small cabin filled with the elated voices of her and Daniel's own children. She glanced his way, noting his somber expression. Would he relish seeing children at play as Jonathan seemed to?

The old Daniel would have.

But *this* Daniel, the straight-faced one who sat before her, would likely be put off by the lively activity.

Since their tender exchange outside the cabin more than a month ago, Daniel's emotions had ebbed and flowed. One moment he seemed to truly attempt to start anew. The next he retreated back into his sullen shell, impossible to reach. The few moments of affection they'd shared made her hunger all the more for what they'd once had.

She stifled a sigh, her attention pulling to Jonathan as he rose to his feet and stared down at Daniel. "I've some business in town. Would you like to come along?"

Maggie's breath caught as Daniel's expression wavered. Was he considering the possibility? Though Jonathan's frequent attempts to draw her husband out often fell short, she appreciated each effort.

At last, Daniel shook his head, locking his fingers together on the table. "Mayhap another time."

Disappointment gnawed at Maggie as she gathered some of the dishes and carried them to the dishpan. Another failed attempt. Daniel needed something to hold his interest. Some worthwhile endeavor to stir his mind and body. He seemed to prefer idly gazing out the window, his ambition all but sapped.

Choosing not to press, Jonathan merely bobbed his head and peered over at Emma. "Shall I pick you and the girls up when I'm through?"

With a shake of her head, Emma poured a pot of hot water into the dishpan. "I'll just help Maggie tidy up the dishes, and we'll be on our way." Softening her voice, she cupped a hand to the side of her mouth. "The walk home will ensure the girls are set for their naps."

He returned an understanding nod and strode toward the door, his large frame making the cabin appear smaller. "See you at home then."

As the door closed behind him, an uneasy quiet settled over

the household. While the girls played with corn husk dolls, Maggie and Emma set silently to work on the dishes.

At the creak of a chair, Maggie paused her dish drying and pivoted, surprised to see Daniel pulling himself up with his crutch. He cleared his throat. "Think I'll ride along with Jonathan. Is there anything you need from town?"

She flashed him a warm smile, a glimmer of hope threading through her. "We're rather low on salt and flour."

With a nod, he hobbled across the room. Donning his coat and hat, he turned to Emma. "You'll look after her while I'm away?"

Emma's hands stilled in the soapy water, and her chin angled higher. "You needn't ask. 'Course, I will."

Maggie caught Daniel's quick wink, and her heart soared at the glimpse of his old self. He always had enjoyed rousing her sister's defenses. Recalling his offer to purchase supplies, she touched a hand to his sleeve as he started to go. "Just a moment. I've some eggs for trade."

Retrieving the basket, Maggie held it out to Daniel. A tinge of redness lined his cheeks as he tentatively took the eggs from her. She knew at once what troubled him. He wished for something more substantial than eggs to trade, as in times past. Mayhap the awkwardness would spur him to try harder? At least that was her prayer.

As the door closed behind him, Emma gave Maggie's arm a gentle nudge. "That's heartening, is it not?"

"Indeed." Maggie inched her way to the window and watched him shuffle toward Jonathan's wagon. Since his return, Daniel had rarely left home except to meet with Noah's family to share the unwelcome news of his death. To have him willingly make the trip into Taylorstown, be it ever so reluctantly, conveyed true progress. She breathed a quiet sigh. "It's heartbreaking to watch him struggle, but every now and then I get a glimpse of the man he once was."

"When the baby is born, he'll come around. You'll see."

Emma nodded toward her daughters playing before the fireplace. "Nothing softens a man's heart quicker than young ones."

Maggie glanced at her three nieces and cradled her rounded abdomen, lips lifting in a cautious grin. "I truly hope so. I can think of no greater joy."

With a nod, Emma handed her a washed plate. "Joy, certainly, but children bring challenges as well. 'Twill not be easy for the two of you, given Daniel's limitations." Ever the realist, Emma minced no words. She pivoted toward Maggie, a look of resolve in her eyes. "The time is quickly approaching when you'll need more than an occasional meal to manage. You'll need someone near at hand."

Dismissing the concern, Maggie finished drying the plate and set it in the cupboard. "There's plenty of time to consider that. The baby isn't due for six weeks yet."

"Even so, I think it best I make arrangements to stay with you when your time nears."

Maggie released a long breath, doing her best to tamp down the urgency in her sister's words with firmness of her own. "Mayhap. But that time has not yet come. We'll speak of it after the new year." When her sister offered no argument, Maggie traced her fingertip along the rim of the plate, her voice softening. "This will be Daniel's and my first Christmas together, and I want it to be special."

"'Tis true. I'd forgotten." Understanding streamed from Emma's eyes as she cupped a hand under Maggie's chin. "You're right. This one deserves to be special. Yours and Daniel's alone."

Warmth blanketed Maggie's cheeks. "Thank you."

The firmness in Emma's jaw returned as she slid her hand away and wagged a finger at Maggie. "But I will keep close watch on you and, by the new year, will not let you out of my sight. Babies come when they are ready, not on our time schedule, you know."

With a humored nod, Maggie reached for another plate. "Agreed."

Despite the optimism she showed her sister, Maggie's thoughts churned. 'Twas a comfort to know her sister would be around to help. But for how long? Emma had her own family to tend and would not stay indefinitely. Nor would Maggie wish her to.

A sliver of unease coiled through her. How would she and Daniel fare in dead of winter, when it would be difficult for Jonathan and Emma to make the half-mile trek to check on them? Would they have the provisions to see them through? Though Jonathan had split and stacked a fair supply of wood, it likely wouldn't last until spring.

Truth be told, Maggie wasn't sure how she and Daniel would even manage the means to live on.

But the Lord knew. And that was what mattered.

DANIEL LOOSENED his grip on the wagon bench, grateful when Jonathan pulled the team to a stop outside Taylorstown's general store. A bit tousled by the rough two-mile ride into town, Daniel pushed himself more solidly onto the seat with his good leg and readjusted the basket of eggs in his lap. Though the sharp December air nipped at his exposed skin, it felt good to be out in the elements. Every day he remained holed up in the cabin, his body and spirit seemed to waste away more.

A pair of ladies walking nearby glanced his way, their gazes settling on his stubbed leg. The lankier woman cupped a hand to her mouth and leaned toward her weightier companion, whose expression took on a sorrowful air.

Heat burned Daniel's cheeks as he looked away. He'd sacrificed his leg in defense of his country. Was he to feel disgrace for that? Mayhap he'd made a mistake in coming. It seemed safer to remain at home, where he didn't have to face the piteous stares of onlookers. Leastways, with his sweet Maggie he had no need for pretense or shame.

Hopping from the wagon, Jonathan peered up at Daniel. "My business won't take long. Were you coming?"

Daniel clutched tighter to the basket, his first inclination to remain. Bartering eggs was woman's work. Yet he'd promised Maggie. His gaze returned to the pair of women who had ceased their gawking and continued on. Plainly his injury would garner attention whether he stayed or went. With a tentative sigh, he reached under the seat for his crutch. "I'll come."

As Jonathan tethered the horses' reins to the post, the store proprietor, Oliver Sullivan, appeared at the storefront, broom in hand. The bright sunlight gave his thick head of hair a reddish cast as he stepped out into the open, his thin face lifting in a ready smile. "Well, hello, Jonathan. In need of goods again so soon? Those youngsters of yours must be difficult to fill."

With an emphatic nod, Jonathan swiped his hands together. "That they are. I believe they can out-eat boys twice their size."

The storeowner gave a loud chuckle then leaned on his broom handle, squinting up at Daniel. "Good to see you, Daniel. I heard you were back some time ago. I've been eager to welcome you home, but until now haven't had the pleasure."

"Thank you, Oliver." A twinge of regret ripped through Daniel as he unwittingly stared down at his stubbed leg. "With my injury, I've not strayed far from the cabin."

In the brief pause that followed, he expected Oliver to either sympathize with his loss or gloss over it. Instead, he addressed the matter straightaway. "Your lost leg is a hindrance, to be sure, but your sacrifice for our country is not a matter of embarrassment to hide away, but one of honor."

Daniel's head lifted, his chest expanding in the first unhindered breath since entering town. He met Oliver's steady gaze, reading a sincerity in his eyes that all but erased the harm done by the chatty women passing by.

The storeowner reached out his arm. "Now, if Maggie has sent those eggs for bartering, what say we head inside and find what you need?"

With a determined nod, Daniel handed him the basket. Slowly, he lowered himself from the wagon seat, a tad less self-conscious than he'd been moments earlier. Jonathan edged closer as though to catch him if he fell. The protective measure further bolstered Daniel's determination to accomplish the task on his own.

A slip of his foot threw him off balance, causing him to drop faster than anticipated. Pain surged through him as his stub raked the side of the wagon on the way down. When his boot met the ground, he wobbled, and Jonathan reached a hand out to steady him. Tugging free of his grasp, Daniel leaned against the wagon wheel. "I'm fine."

His well-meaning friend took a step back, a flash of hurt in his eyes.

Eager to remedy the situation, Daniel forced a grin. "It's time I stand on my own feet ... er ... foot."

Jonathan's lips hinged upward. "That it is."

With a satisfied breath, Daniel reached for his crutch then pivoted toward his companions. "I think Maggie was pleased to have me out of the house a spell."

Oliver clapped him on the shoulder. "How is your wife? Not ailing, I hope."

"No. She is well." *Though a bit grieved by my dispirited nature since my return*, he neglected to add.

That must change.

"More eager by the day for the little one to come, I'll wager."

The man's friendly demeanor had Daniel almost wishing he'd ventured out sooner. If only everyone held to Oliver's way of thinking. Daniel started forward, his own enthusiasm beginning to rise. "Indeed. Only a few weeks to go."

Oliver and Jonathan fell into step beside him, matching his measured gait. The proud storeowner pointed toward the cluttered storefront, its narrow windows decorated with pine boughs laced with red and gold ribbons. "Ah. Then you'll for certain want to look over my wares." Ushering him through the narrow doorway, Oliver gestured toward the display of goods crowding the store. "A new babe requires a number of necessities you aren't accustomed to."

Daniel skimmed the display of items. So enthralled with his predicament, he'd given little thought to how he and Maggie's new son or daughter would alter their lives ... as well as their expenses. He swallowed. If they were to manage, he must find some means of income. A trade that required use of his hands. One not hindered by his missing limb.

His chest tightened. Maggie deserved more than he could give her. How he wished he could fill their cabin with the fine tableware, shiny lanterns, sleek rocking chairs, and stylish dress material. As things were, they could afford none of it. He would return home empty-handed, but for the requested items. He held back a sigh, his gaze stalling on an object tucked in among the furnishings. A wooden cradle, so trim and low to the floor he'd nearly overlooked it. Stooping over, he ran his fingers along the smooth pine hood shading its top.

"Say now, that's something you're sure to need." Oliver's voice carried from where he stood behind the counter. He paused from transferring eggs from the basket to his own container. "A cradle to rock your little one to sleep."

Daniel gave it a light tug then let it go, watching it sway easily to and fro. "It's a fine-looking one."

Abandoning the egg count, Oliver joined Daniel, arms crossed over his chest like a proud father. "A fine-crafted one too, all the way from Leesburg."

Daniel straightened and clenched his jaw, certain it carried a fine price as well. He grudgingly pushed the notion of surprising Maggie with it aside. Something plainer would have to suffice. He wet his lips. "Just some salt and flour today, however much the eggs are worth."

Understanding brimmed in the storeowner's eyes, and he gave a slight nod. "All right, Daniel." The hint of regret in his voice lingered in the quiet. With practiced ease, he gathered the items, then turned to Jonathan. "And what can I get for you?"

Shuffling aside to allow Jonathan the opportunity to conduct his business, Daniel ventured another glance at the cradle. The fine piece would make a fitting Christmas gift for Maggie. Yet coming up with the funds in such a short time seemed an impossibility. The Lord Himself would have to provide the means. *Please, Lord. Show me a way.*

Daniel mulled the thought as Jonathan loaded their supplies for the trip home. If he couldn't afford to barter or purchase what he and Maggie needed, he must find other means. He'd succumbed to feelings of uselessness far too long. Maggie had tried to make him see that.

He should have listened.

His mind snagged on a remembrance, sending his heart pounding. The adze and saw his father had bought him still hung in the barn. His grandfather's set of chisels remained tucked away inside their trunk. Though Daniel had rarely put the heirloom tools to use, he recalled watching his father skillfully carve an item or two on occasion. Mayhap Daniel would share his gift for carving.

Daniel clutched his hands into fists. He might be minus a leg, but he still had two strong arms with which to work. Why could he not fashion his own cradle? Having put the form of it to memory, he could at least make an attempt. It might not turn out as refined as the store-bought one, but it would mean more to Maggie fashioned by his own hands. If Jonathan would be willing to provide the wood, he could surely manage the smoothing and carving.

Tying up the end gate, Jonathan nodded to Daniel. "All set?"

"Yep." With a wave to Oliver, Danial slid his crutch under the wagon seat. Hoisting himself up with his good leg, he clambered higher using his knee and arm strength to inch his way along. Winded from the effort, he collapsed onto the wooden bench.

If his limitations had taught him one thing, it was that it would take effort and determination to accomplish anything of significance—along with a lot of faith and prayer.

Virtues he'd regretfully allowed to slip away.

Seven

Saturday, December 3, 1814

"You're a fine cook, Maggie."

Taken aback, Maggie stilled. Until now, the noontime conversation had proven rather sparse. Daniel's unforeseen compliment brought an airiness to her voice. "Thank you."

He pushed his plate aside and gazed across the table at her, a curious gleam in his eyes.

Setting her cup of tea on its saucer, she grinned and tipped her head to one side. "What is it?"

He reached a hand out to clasp hers, sending a wave of warmth rippling through her. "I've asked Jonathan to come take us both to church service tomorrow."

Maggie's smile deepened, and she gave his hand a gentle squeeze. She'd grown accustomed to his absence next to her in the church pew while he was away at war, but since his return, the vacant space seemed twice as unbearable. "Truly, Daniel? I'm so pleased." She stopped short of asking what had inspired him to make the unexpected decision. Instead, she drank in the blessedness of the moment as though it might vanish like a late-night dream.

The rumble of a wagon broke through her concentration. "Who could that be?" Reluctantly, Maggie slid her hand from Daniel's and slowly rose to her feet, the cumbersome baby in her womb limiting her movements. Striding over to the window, she pulled the curtain aside for a better look. Unable to conceal her surprise, she pivoted toward Daniel. "It's Jonathan. Odd him stopping by again so soon. I hope all is well."

Daniel cleared his throat, his face flushing red as he reached for his crutch. "I, uh, asked him to bring something by. I'll go meet him."

Now Maggie knew something noteworthy had taken place. Since returning home, Daniel had never so much as attempted to greet Jonathan at the door, let alone make the trek outside to meet him. "Will he not simply come to the house?"

With a shake of his head, Daniel pulled himself up. "What he's bringing must go to the barn."

"Oh. Then I'll get my cloak and go with you."

"Uh-uh." A hint of a grin lined his lips as he motioned her away from the window. "You're to stay in here ... with curtains drawn. Jonathan and I can handle things."

"I see." Maggie bit back a smile, trying to convince herself this was the same Daniel who days ago would hardly move from his chair. Though he'd relayed little about yesterday's trip into town other than his agreeable encounter with Oliver Sullivan, something had changed within Daniel. His spirit seemed ... lighter.

As he hobbled his way to the door, she cleared away their dinner dishes, observing him out of the corner of her eye. Whatever had transpired, she prayed its effect would be long-lasting.

⁓

Daniel ran his fingers over the slab of pine wood, its strong scent wafting up at him. "This will do nicely. Thank you, Jonathan."

Standing taller, Jonathan thumbed his suspenders. "There should be plenty—several larger pieces for the sides and bottom, and smaller ones for the hood and rockers. If you need more, just give the word."

"This should do, so long as I don't ruin some in the process." He glanced to the mallet, adze, and saw hanging on pegs along the north wall. "It's been a long while since I've tried my hand at woodworking."

Jonathan followed Daniel's gaze to the display of tools. He lifted the adze from its place and touched a finger to its sharp edge. "Nice set of tools. Were they your father's?"

Trundling over, Daniel took the mallet in hand, brushing aside the thick coat of dust and cobwebs. "Only the mallet, passed down from his Uncle Silas. The others he bought for me, hoping to stir my interest in the hobby." He clutched the smooth handle, the memory of watching his father skillfully strike a chisel into a block of wood flooding back. "He could carve or build just about anything he set his mind to."

Jonathan swiped a layer of dirt from the adze handle. "I take it you've not put them to much use."

With a tentative shake of his head, Daniel replaced the mallet to its spot. "My father longed to teach me, but I was young and hadn't the patience to try my hand at carving. I had other ambitions to chase."

His thoughts careened back to his youth when he and Noah had spent long days plotting their futures. His throat thickened. Their plan to farm adjacent plots of land and share its bounty had not fared well for either of them.

A chuckle sounded from his companion. "Ambitions such as Maggie?"

A sliver of pleasure broke through Daniel's fog at the remembrance of the first moment Maggie had caught his eye.

Once they started courting, he'd had even less use for pursuits such as wood carving. His lips lifted. "Mayhap."

"You may wish you'd paid closer attention to your father's instruction. Do you even recall how to use the tools?"

Taking the adze from him, Daniel gave a brisk nod. "I watched enough to get the idea." He limped over to the stack of pine wood and stared at the tool in his hands, longing to see his father wield it once more. A wistful grin tugged at his lips as he recalled the numerous times he'd abandoned his father's gentle instruction for other pursuits. "It was endurance and motivation I lacked."

A twinge of remorse trickled through him. In the three years since his father's passing, Daniel had often regretted not taking more interest in the pastime. Bracing himself against the stall post, he swung the adze at the hunk of pine. A thin layer of wood dropped to the strawed floor. Again and again, he chipped away at the slab until he'd achieved the desired width for the side of the cradle.

Bending down, Jonathan lifted the piece of wood and ran a hand over the flat surface. He jutted out his lower lip and bobbed his head side to side. "Not bad."

Daniel drew a satisfied breath and shrugged. "It's a start." Sliding another slab from the pile, he lifted the adze, a sense of eagerness engulfing him. Hopefully he'd matured in his focus and abilities enough to satisfy Maggie ... and himself with the job.

With Jonathan supplying the wood, Daniel's cradle would not be a costly gift, but rather one fashioned from the heart.

Something Maggie was certain to count of greater value.

THE LAST RAYS of sunlight fringed the western sky as Maggie trekked from the cabin to the barn. Jonathan's wagon had pulled away more than an hour ago. What could Daniel be doing in there?

The gentle December breeze held a chill, and she snugged the front of her cloak tighter, her enlarged middle no longer allowing it to fasten. She stopped beside the chicken coop, listening. Contented squawks ensured all was well within as she latched the door shut for the night.

Maggie edged toward the barn, recalling her promise not to intrude on Daniel's obviously private task. She paused outside the barn door, wondering how he was able to see inside the dim interior. "Daniel? Is all well?"

"Yes. Don't come in!" came the fervent reply.

She shivered, eager to return to the warmth of the cabin. "Supper is all but ready. Will you be much longer?"

"No. Only a few minutes more."

Willing herself not to question him further, she rounded the corner of the barn to shield herself from the wind. Shuffling noises sounded from within the log structure. With effort, she resisted the urge to sneak a glance through the unchinked walls. "You must be chilled to the core by now."

"I'm fine. Go inside and get warm. I'll be in soon." After a short pause, he added, "But could you bring a blanket, one you don't care about being returned for a time?"

Maggie knit her brows. She could understand him wanting the blanket to temper the cold. But why would he wish one to be kept out here indefinitely? Daniel's odd behavior had her not only puzzled, but a bit unsettled.

With a shake of her head, she traipsed toward the cabin. Whatever had captured Daniel's attention beat watching him waste away sulking in a chair. She only hoped, in time, he'd be less guarded about what he was up to.

Eight

Monday, December 5, 1814

Daniel drummed his fingers on the table until Maggie's look of displeasure stilled them. He couldn't contain his eagerness. With Jonathan's help, he'd fashioned a rough framework of the cradle pieces. Not until he searched through the trunk for his father's set of carving knives and chisels could he continue work on the project. And he couldn't very well dig through the chest with Maggie nearby. Not without spoiling his gift to her.

"You seem quite anxious this morning," she commented, tying on her bonnet. "Mayhap you should gather eggs in my stead today."

Though her words held an element of jest, his shoulders tensed. With the more frigid weather and the fatigue of carrying their child, much of Maggie's time was spent indoors. If he didn't watch himself, he would miss his opportunity to seek the box of tools. He shrugged, feigning indifference. "If that's what you wish." He reached for his crutch, praying her threat had been a hollow one.

She shook her head, motioning for him to sit still. "Don't

bother. Emma tells me I must 'stay fit and strong for when the baby comes.'"

A wave of relief coursed through Daniel, and he grinned at the singsong tone Maggie used when recalling her sister's words. In this instance, he was grateful for the unwarranted advice. He only hoped the scanty amount of time in Maggie's absence would be sufficient to locate the tools and reposition the items in the trunk as he'd found them. If caught rummaging through the chest of treasured keepsakes, he would have difficulty explaining his purpose.

With a yawn, Maggie donned her frock coat, the shadows beneath her eyes evident. Sleep often evaded her of late, the discomfort of the growing babe in her womb causing her to toss and turn most nights.

Daniel wagged a finger at her. "All right. But when you return, you must sit and rest. You lost too much sleep last night, I fear."

At his concern, a warm glow enveloped her rounded face and cornflower blue eyes. "I shall be pleased to take you up on that, dear husband."

He returned a smile, finding her more attractive in that moment than the day they'd wed. Despite their hardships, he had much to be thankful for.

"I won't be long." Turning, she lifted the latch and tugged the door open.

He gnawed at his lip, resisting the urge to instruct her not to hurry.

The instant the door clicked shut behind her, Daniel slid his crutch under his arm and rose from the chair. Three hasty strides took him to the flat-topped trunk at the foot of the bed. With effort, he worked his way down onto his knee and set the crutch aside. He slid the folded hand-stitched quilt from atop the trunk, revealing the lid of polished oak.

Casting a hurried glance over his shoulder to ensure she hadn't returned for some unknown reason, he reached to lift the lid. Maggie had placed his father's smaller tools inside the trunk alongside her own valued keepsakes. Gently, he lifted the layers of table linens, bed sheets, and Maggie's wedding gown and laid them on the bed. A quick glimpse at the remaining trunk contents revealed nothing more than an infant gown, an ornate candle holder, and several tins filled with unknown treasures.

At last, his eyes locked on his father's toolbox, and his heartbeat quickened. He lifted the neglected treasure, eager to open it and look over the various pieces. Instead, he set it beside him. Viewing the tools would have to wait. Little time remained to put things aright before Maggie's return.

With another leery glance over his shoulder, he began replacing the keepsakes. His knee popped, groaning under the strain of weigh thrust upon it. His leg half numb, he reached for his crutch and pulled himself up. As he worked to return the dress and linens to the trunk, faint humming sounded outside the cabin. His heart drummed as he quickened his pace, no longer caring in what order he returned the items. Maggie rarely delved into the chest. He would straighten the mementos another day, before she had opportunity to see their disorderly appearance.

As he rushed to fit them into the trunk, something hard dropped onto the floor. In that moment, the door creaked open. Daniel lowered the lid, almost toppling in his haste. He slipped the object in his pocket without noting what it was and snatched up the box of tools.

Maggie entered just as he placed the quilt atop the trunk. She flashed him a questioning look. "What have you been up to?"

"Nothing." Face flushed, he concealed the box behind him. "But I ... uh ... think I'll head out to the barn a while so as not to disturb you while you rest."

"How considerate of you." Suspicion streamed from her eyes.

He flashed a sheepish grin. As perceptive as Maggie was, she'd likely unravel his plans within a week, well before

Christmas. Already, he'd aroused her curiosity by banishing her from the barn.

Waiting until her back was turned, he slipped the box under his free arm and ambled toward the door. Awkwardly donning his coat, he glanced over at the trunk and cringed at the bit of linen protruding from beneath the lid. He could do nothing to resolve it now—other than pray Maggie was too weary and distracted to notice.

❧

MAGGIE SWIPED a loose strand of hair from her forehead, staring at Daniel's back as he closed the door behind him. How could she rest? His odd behavior was enough to set anyone on edge. What was he up to? Did he think she hadn't noticed him trying to conceal something behind his back or the mussed quilt?

She peered over at the trunk. Was that a fragment of linen dangling from its side?

Stepping toward it, she puzzled over what cause Daniel would have to rummage through the chest of keepsakes. Since returning with Jonathan from town Saturday, he'd seemed full of mystery. First his secretiveness in the barn, then his willingness to attend church service, and now his unexplained behavior in the cabin.

One glimpse inside the trunk confirmed her suspicions. She pursed her lips. Daniel had indeed rifled through the linens and her wedding dress, leaving them in disarray. She sorted through them, tempering her annoyance. Did this have anything to do with his strange behavior? If only he'd told her what he was after, she'd gladly have fetched it for him. What could he possibly have ...

Her breath caught. Setting the linens aside, she dug deeper in the trunk. After a thorough search, a smile edged out her frustration. His father's tools were missing. Every ounce of irritation fled from her spirit. Lifting her eyes to the ceiling, she released a long breath. "Thank You, Lord, for stirring renewed hope and purpose within Daniel. May You grant him success in whatever it is he plans to do."

~

DANIEL RAN his fingertips over the smooth wooden handles of the carving knives and chisels, the stain of use rendering them all the more endearing. His father's deep voice echoed through Daniel's head as clearly as if he stood beside him. *I hope someday you'll find use for these, son. Passed down from my own father through your Great Uncle Silas, they've served me well many a year. One day, I pray you'll have an heir to pass them on to as well.*

Remembrance of his father's words stirred a slew of emotions within Daniel. He'd stored the treasured tools away with little intention of ever putting them to use. Had it taken the loss of his leg to perceive their value?

Reaching in the box, he took up the gouge chisel and clasped it tightly in his palm. It felt good. Right. As if it had found where it belonged. Daniel replaced it in the box and picked up each knife and chisel in turn, attempting to recall its specific use. He sighed, regretting not having given his father's instruction more attention. Could he do the tools justice?

For Maggie and the baby's sake, he was willing to try.

As he peeled back the blanket covering the pine pieces, something pressed into his thigh. He fingered the bulge in his breeches pocket, recalling the object that had spilled from the linens onto the floor.

Curious, he reached in and drew the item out. Fond recollection seeped through him as he turned it over in his palm. 'Twas the sheep his grandfather had carved as a boy—the very carving that had spawned his love for creating. Daniel examined the sheep's chiseled wool and smooth legs, amazed at the rich detail. Though flaws marred the sheep's tiny face and hooves, the piece was truly a work of art at the hands of a young boy. Pride told in his father's voice during each retelling of how Grandfather had fashioned the sheep.

Daniel tenderly set the sheep on the stall rail beside him. The carving would be his inspiration as he fashioned the cradle. With a cleansing breath, he took up one of the pieces of pine. Lord willing, he could do the Hawkins family tools and legacy justice.

Nine

Friday, December 9, 1814

A rap at the door stirred Maggie from her afternoon nap. Slowly coming to her senses, she pushed herself up from the rocking chair. As she eased the door open, Emma peered in at her, young Ada propped on her hip. A gust of cold air burst in as Maggie widened the door.

"Well, good afternoon." Liddy and Nina peeked at her from behind their mother's skirt, their noses red from the chill. Maggie motioned them in. "Come in and warm yourselves."

Without further invitation, the girls trotted inside and plopped down before the fireplace, holding their hands out to absorb the fire's warmth. Emma stepped in and set a wriggling Ada down to join them. "I hope you don't mind us stopping by. Jonathan was headed this way, so we decided to tag along and pay you a visit."

"Not at all. It's good to see you."

Emma touched an icy hand to Maggie's cheek. "Are you well? You look a mite peaked."

"I've been resting. I just need to move about and stir my blood a bit."

Removing her bonnet, Emma offered an affirming nod. "Well, all right then. 'Tis good to hear you're behaving yourself."

Maggie shook her head at Emma's mothering words. Admittedly, she tired more easily these days, the added weight of carrying the child pulling at her back and making her breaths shallower. But she could do without her older sister's constant coddling.

Eyes wide, Emma slipped off her frock coat and hung it over the back of a chair. "What a pleasant surprise to have Daniel join us for services last Sunday. How did you ever convince him?"

Memory of her husband seated beside her on the church bench brought a smile to Maggie's face. "I didn't. 'Twas entirely his idea."

"Well, now. That *is* progress. Jonathan said the ride into town Saturday appeared to have done Daniel some good."

"I believe it did. He seems in better spirits and has spent more time in the barn than here ever since."

"Ah, yes. Jonathan was eager to see how Daniel is coming with his project."

"Daniel's ... project?" Curiosity nipped at Maggie like a cold wind. "Do you know what it is?"

"Not a clue."

"Does Jonathan?"

Emma threw out her palm. "All I know is, Jonathan said I was not to ask questions."

"And *I've* been instructed not to go near the barn." Maggie moved to the window, rubbing a hand over her belly. "What do you suppose they're up to?"

"Hmm. Sounds like some sort of Christmas present conspiracy to me."

Maggie snapped her head toward her sister. "Do you truly think so?"

"I would venture to guess nothing but." Emma pulled up a chair and joined her daughters by the fire.

The thought seemed so out of step with Daniel's recent

behavior. And yet, something had changed within him. Maggie tapped a finger to her cheek. "I did notice his tool set missing from our trunk."

"Aah! And I saw Jonathan loading wood into our wagon earlier this week."

Maggie's mind churned. Was Daniel attempting to build something for her?

Her lips tipped upward in a slight grin. "Then I'd best get to work. I intended to knit him a scarf, but he's been in the cabin so much, I've not had opportunity."

Emma motioned her to the rocker. "Don't let our presence stop you. We can visit quite well while you work."

"All right." Warmth enveloped Maggie as she collected her yarn and needles. She'd given little thought to her and Daniel exchanging gifts at Christmas. With the baby coming and Daniel's inability to supply an income, gift giving seemed an extravagance they couldn't afford. But surely she had enough yarn to knit the baby a blanket and stockings as well as a scarf for Daniel.

As to the rest of their needs, she would entrust them to the Lord. He had been faithful to provide in the past. He would do so in the future as well. Already He was answering her prayers for Daniel. Whatever the Lord had placed on his heart to build, no matter how rickety or imperfect, she would cherish it always.

"SAY, YOU'RE MAKING PROGRESS."

Daniel tapped the chisel with the wooden mallet, cutting a small diagonal wedge at the base of the slab of pine. He blew off the shaving, then stretched his back and nodded to Jonathan. "Now I know why my father was such a patient man. Woodworking is indeed tedious work."

"And it appears you have a knack for it. If you keep on as you are, I wager you'll have a cradle every bit as fine as Oliver's store-bought one."

Daniel sat taller on his three-legged stool. "I doubt that, but at least one I hope will please Maggie and serve our child well. A less expensive one to be sure."

"Agreed." Jonathan lifted the carved sheep from its spot. "And what's this? Another project of yours?"

With a shake of his head, Daniel repositioned the chisel for another strike. "I keep it there for inspiration. My grandfather carved it. He had a gift, did he not?"

Holding the sheep in his palm, Jonathan examined it closer. "Indeed he did." His gaze shifted to Daniel. "And by the looks of things, he may have passed it on to his grandson."

Daniel paused, his eyes drifting to the carved sheep. "I could never fashion something so small and detailed. Though it might be fun to try."

"And try you should. A sheep needs other sheep and a shepherd, don't you think?"

A grin tugged at Daniel's lips. "Maybe so, but I'll be fortunate to have the resolve to finish this cradle."

Jonathan returned the sheep to its spot and rubbed his hands together. "Then tell me what needs done."

Ten

Wednesday evening, December 14, 1814

Daniel held his breath as he joined the two slotted ends of pine together. The dovetail joints snapped into place, and he released the mouthful of air. A near-perfect fit. Reaching for the other side piece, he repeated the action, his anticipation growing as the cradle began to take form. He popped the second end piece in position, then tamped each joint with his mallet to snug it tighter in place.

A wave of satisfaction surged through him as he ran his fingers over the rectangular box. Two long weeks of work had paid off. All that was left was to slide in the bottom and fasten on the hood.

He stretched, knowing he should quit for the night. Christmas was still a full ten days away. But he was so close to finishing and longed to see the cradle to completion. He hoped Maggie would forgive him for keeping such late hours. She seemed genuinely happy to have him occupied with something besides moping around feeling sorry for himself.

As was he.

A glance down at his stub resurrected his loss, but somehow

thought of it didn't sting as harshly as it had at first. The woodworking project had rekindled his sense of pride and manhood. With it finished, would he fall back into his old piteous ways?

His eyes lifted to the sheep resting on the stall ledge. He snickered at the memory of Jonathan's challenge to carve a companion sheep and shepherd. Taking the sheep in hand, he rubbed his thumb along the chiseled lines. Could he follow his grandfather's design to craft another like it?

Several scraps of wood lay on the strawed floor beside him. Reaching for one of the larger blocks, he twisted it in his hand. Just about the size needed to carve a small lamb. He shrugged. At least he could make an attempt. His son or daughter might one day cherish the carvings as he did his grandfather's.

He rubbed a hand over his stubbled jaw. Ten days remained until Christmas. Surely enough time to carve a sheep and shepherd. Maggie had always wanted a nativity. If all went well, mayhap he could fashion a simple one good enough to suit her.

Daniel set the block next to the sheep on the ledge and blew out a breath. For now, he had a cradle to complete. The air grew chillier as evening shadows settled in to replace the last glimmers of twilight. With a shiver, he reached to brighten the lantern flame. No matter how cold or dark the night, he was determined to stay until the cradle was finished.

Maggie peered out the frosty windowpane, rubbing a hand along her arm. Lantern light pulsed from within the unchinked cracks of the log barn walls. What could Daniel be doing all this time? She quivered to think of him being out there in that drafty barn so long.

With a sigh, she let the curtain fall back into place. He could at least quit when the sun set so she wasn't forced to spend so much time alone. Her stomach rumbled. *And so we could have our supper at a decent hour.*

Easing down in the rocker, she scolded herself. *No.* The Lord had answered her prayers for Daniel to find something worthwhile to occupy him, and she refused to complain. Although, it was difficult to determine how worthwhile his activity was without knowing exactly what it entailed. His secrecy niggled her, and yet, she thrilled at the thought of a gift fashioned by his hand.

Taking up her knitting needles, she began the practiced knit and purl movements. Already she'd finished Daniel's scarf and stashed it under the mattress for safekeeping. Now the baby's stockings were well underway—the first one completed and the other newly begun. She smiled, holding the finished one out in front of her. So very small. It was hard to imagine such a tiny foot to fit inside. With a full month yet before the babe was to be born, she should have time to knit the small blanket as well.

Nearly another half hour passed before Daniel's familiar lopsided gait approached the cabin. Relieved, she set her knitting aside and rose to her feet. Giving the stew a quick stir, she did her best to temper her annoyance at it having stuck to the sides of the kettle. The door opened, and she turned to greet Daniel, her frustration waning slightly at the pleasant smile on his lips. Though he looked eager to burst with news of something noteworthy, he held back like a dog unwilling to forfeit its favorite bone.

Removing his hat, he raked a hand through his flaxen hair, his eyes searching hers. Something in her expression must have hinted of discontent, for his grin faded. "Forgive me, love. I didn't mean to be so long in coming."

The apology, though sincere, only half diminished her pent-up ire. Contentment seemed to escape her. Either she was eager for Daniel to have something to occupy him or longing for his company. Her gaze drifted to the table, and she reached for the soup bowl. "You must be chilled and famished."

As she reached for the ladle to dip the soup, a gentle hand clasped her shoulder. Straightening, she pivoted toward Daniel. The tenderness in his gaze made it easy to lean into his one-armed embrace. "From now on, I promise I'll limit my work to daylight hours."

The gentle words whispered in her ear were like sweet balm for her spirit. Daniel hadn't lost his ability to discern her thoughts. She lifted her eyes, her face only inches from his. The irrepressible urge to press her lips to his overwhelmed her. Daniel bent lower, his warm breath mingling with hers. As their lips met, the ladle slipped from her grasp. Maggie slid her arms around his neck, her hunger—and discontent—forgotten.

Eleven

December 24, 1814

A cold east wind funneled through the barn, sending a chill through Daniel. He rubbed stiff hands together, his breath steamy. He'd endured the cold long enough. Time to move indoors. He shaved a final bit of wood from the corner of the manger that held the carved baby Jesus and dusted it off, a sense of satisfaction spilling over him. Over the ten days since he'd started the nativity set, he'd managed to fashion not only a lamb and shepherd, but Mary and baby Jesus as well, along with a crude stable.

Shaping the small figurines had proven a challenge, but each one became easier and more satisfying to create. He was beginning to understand his father's passion for carving. So long as Jonathan stocked him with wood, Daniel hoped to continue the new pastime.

A blast of cold air whipped in at him, and he peered through a crack in the log wall. Heavy gray clouds held the promise of snow, shadowing the light of midday. Daniel clutched the block of wood that he'd begun to form into the likeness of Joseph. The rest of the nativity would have to wait.

He perused the row of figures, his mouth twisting. It seemed a shame not to let Maggie in on his surprise. If a heavy snow came, it would be near impossible to make it to the barn to retrieve the cradle and partially finished nativity. This being Christmas Eve, it would not be too early to give Maggie the gifts. Mayhap he could finish the nativity before the baby came.

Gathering the carvings, Daniel bundled what he could of them in a handkerchief and stuffed the rest loose in his pockets. He covered the cradle with the blanket and tucked it under one arm and took up his crutch with the other.

Large flakes pummeled him as he hobbled toward the cabin. Already a thin coating of snow blanketed the ground, making it slick to walk on. He slowed his pace, fearful of falling. Maggie met him at the door, her head tilted to one side. "What's all this?"

"The reason I've spent so much time in the barn of late. With the snow, I thought it best to bring your Christmas presents in early."

A smile transformed her face. "Well then, by all means, bring them in." Ushering him inside, she brushed snowflakes from his coat.

As Maggie closed the door behind him, Daniel set the bundle on the bench inside.

Maggie reached to help him out of his coat. "Why, your pockets are bulging. What sort of surprises are you toting?"

"Reach in and see for yourself."

Like a child seeking treasure, Maggie dug in his pockets and pulled out first the shepherd then his grandfather's sheep. Her brows pulled together. "Isn't this the sheep your grandfather carved?"

Daniel nodded. "I ... uh ... found it in the trunk while looking for his woodcarving tools."

A curious grin crossed her lips. "I noticed." She stared at the carving in her hand then blinked up at him. "Did your grandfather carve the shepherd as well? I don't recall seeing it."

With a hesitant shake of his head, he answered, "I did."

Her eyes flashed wide as she traced a finger along the carved edges. "I didn't know you could carve like this."

"Neither did I." Daniel jiggled the coat in her hands. "There's more."

Slipping an eager hand in his other pocket, she pulled out the lumpy kerchief. She unfolded the ends and stared at the carved figures. "Oh Daniel, they're lovely." Her eyes lifted to his. "You have a gift."

Daniel's face warmed under her praise. "You've wanted a nativity, so I thought I'd give it a try. Never dreamed I could actually carve anything so intricate."

"Well, you've definitely succeeded." One by one, she set the pieces atop the mantel and smiled. "No Joseph?"

"Not yet. I ran out of time. I've built a stable as well but didn't have an arm to carry it. I hope to finish the rest before the baby comes."

Maggie's eyes danced as she gazed at the figurines. "I can't think of a finer Christmas present."

Daniel nudged her elbow. "You haven't yet seen what's in the blanket."

She swiveled toward him, her expression childlike. "True." Her eyes shifted to the bundle on the bench. A corner of the blanket had slipped down, revealing the hood of the cradle. Her sudden intake of breath left no doubt she'd deciphered what it was.

Gratified by her response, Daniel gestured toward the gift. "You may as well have a look."

Touching her hands prayerlike to her lips, she ventured toward it. Carefully, she peeled back the blanket, and her eyes widened. "Oh, Daniel. It's beautiful. You made this?"

He shrugged a shoulder as he came up beside her. "I saw one like it at Oliver's store. I used its design to fashion one myself. Jonathan was kind enough to supply the pine."

She ran her fingers over the smooth sides and along the

dovetail joints. "I never dreamed of something so lovely." Turning moist eyes on Daniel, she pressed a kiss to his cheek. "What a precious gift for our baby. Thank you."

Uncertain how to respond to the tender display, he cleared his throat and nodded toward the cradle. "Once we've settled on names and know if the baby's a boy or girl, I figure on carving his or her initials in the side."

"NH." Maggie's eyes sparkled as she ran a hand over her belly.

"NH?"

A grin inched across her face. "For Nathaniel Hawkins. If the name suits you."

With an amused chuckle, Daniel eased into a chair. "You speak as if you know for certain the baby is a boy."

"I *am* certain." The lilt in her voice almost made the declaration plausible. "I have such a strong sense the baby is a boy. Nathaniel means gift of God, and our baby is surely that."

Daniel crossed his arms over his chest with a grin. "Nathaniel is a fine name, and I'll not dispute it. But don't you feel we should choose a girl's name as well, in case you're mistaken?"

She rocked the cradle back and forth, its movement smooth and even. "Choose one if you wish, but I'm confident Nathaniel is the only name we need."

Humored, Daniel couldn't resist offering a challenge. "All right then. I'll give thought to a proper girl's name, and in a couple of weeks, we'll see what initials are fit to carve in the cradle's side."

"Agreed." With a mischievous grin, Maggie glanced out the window at the darkening landscape. Her face sobered. "The snow is beginning to mount."

Daniel shifted his gaze to the half-filled kindling box. "I should bring in more wood before it's buried beneath the snow."

Maggie held up a finger. "Then you'll need your Christmas gift now as well." Striding over to the bed, she slid something from beneath the mattress. She concealed it behind her back until she neared, meekness shadowing her expression. "Though not nearly so impressive as your gifts, 'tis something useful and made with love."

She unfolded an ivory scarf, knitted by her own hands. Daniel felt of its softness. The hours she must have spent working at it. Though lacking in length, the scarf was finely stitched and would keep his neck warm. His chest squeezed, certain the scarf's shortness was due to Maggie's attempt to be frugal with their store of yarn. "'Tis lovely. Thank you."

With a shy grin, Maggie wrapped the scarf around his neck, leaving her arms looped around him as well. Love glistened in her azure eyes as she pressed her forehead against his. "Looks like we'll be snowed in."

Daniel cupped a hand to her cheek, his pulse beating faster. "Good. Then mayhap we can have Christmas all to ourselves."

"Our first Christmas together." She stretched to give him a kiss, then smiled, her voice soft and wispy. "I can't think of anyone I'd rather spend it with."

He leaned for another kiss, feeling more alive than he had in months. Since the day of his arrival, not once had Maggie treated him as less of a man. Did she truly see past his defects to the man he was inside?

Daniel teetered on his crutch, old feelings of inadequacy attempting to rob him of the moment's joy. If only he knew how to better provide for her and the baby. How could he hold their respect if he continually depended on Jonathan and Emma for aid? There must be something he could do to earn income for his family. His dear wife deserved better than scraping by to have what she needed.

When I am weak, then am I strong.

The words of scripture wove through him. Most assuredly, he'd felt weak since his leg had been rent from him. But how could his weakness become his strength? It seemed an impossibility.

Shaking off his insecurities, he determined to leave his

doubts and fears with the Lord and make this Christmas a special one.

∼

Maggie turned on the bed, tightness squeezing her abdomen. She'd lain awake for what must have been an hour, listening to Daniel's steady breaths beside her. But the pressure in her abdomen was growing more and more difficult to ignore. A twinge of pain forced a soft moan from her throat.

Daniel stirred in his sleep.

Determined not to let her restlessness disturb him, she eased from the mattress. A chilling wind whistled outside the cabin. If snow was still falling, she and Daniel would likely be snowed in for a number of days. A twinge of nervousness washed through her as once again her abdomen gripped. She stilled, holding her taut belly. Was she having labor pangs?

She swallowed. The baby wasn't due for at least a couple of weeks. What if he came early? Before Emma could get there? *Oh, Lord. Please don't let the baby come too soon.*

When the tightness eased, she inched her way toward the window, the whiteness of the snow reflecting dim light into the cabin. She drew back the curtain but was unable to see past the frosty, snow-covered pane. Was it still snowing? 'Twas difficult to tell. If the howling wind was any indication, they were certain to be drifted in.

And if need be, they would not be able to retrieve Emma. Maggie gnawed at her lip. Suddenly, their perfect Christmas appeared a bit shaky. Mayhap she should not have been so quick to discourage her sister from staying with them. Maggie drew a deep breath and forced herself to calm. She mustn't fret. Come what may, the Lord would look after them.

Rubbing her arms against the chill, she glanced at the fireplace, where last night's warm fire had dwindled to glowing embers. A shiver kneaded through her. Thank goodness Daniel

165

had thought to stock them with sufficient dry wood. With careful steps, she weaved her way past the table and chairs to the hearth. Daniel's steady breathing droned at her back. What she wouldn't give to sleep so soundly.

She lifted the poker from its spot and squinted at the clock on the mantel. Half-past three. Still hours till daylight. Smothering a yawn, she gave the hot embers a stir. A small flame fanned to life. If the wee morning hours were to be restless ones, she at least wished to be warm. She reached for a handful of kindling and leaned to place it on the fire. As she did, another pain stole over her, robbing her of breath. Wrapping her hands around her firm middle, she stifled a groan.

A burning sensation stung at her, and wetness drizzled down her legs. Her hands grew clammy as panic seized her. No doubt about it. This baby was coming.

And, Lord help them, she and Daniel would face it on their own.

<h1 style="text-align:center">Twelve</h1>

"Daniel, wake up." The soft-spoken yet urgent words sliced through Daniel's deep slumber. The tug on his arm further startled him awake. Even in the dim light, he could see the distress in Maggie's eyes as she hovered over him. "What is it?"

"The baby. He's ... com-ing." Her words spilled out through jagged breaths. She eased onto the mattress, rocking forward as she hugged her abdomen.

"But it's not time." Sitting up, Daniel slid an arm around her shoulders. There was no need asking if she was certain. Her rapid breaths and anguished state were telling enough. The question was what to do about it. Jonathan and Emma lived a half mile away. Quite a jaunt for him to manage with one leg in dark of night. He didn't wish to leave Maggie alone, but what choice did he have? Many a woman and infant died during childbirth. If something went wrong, he couldn't bear it. "I'd better fetch Emma."

Maggie shook her head. "You'd never ... make it. Too much ... snow and ... wind."

Daniel tensed and cast a leery glance at the window. He'd forgotten about the snow. And by the sound of the wind, he'd not make it ten feet from the door without losing his way. At a loss, he tugged at her shoulders and shifted to make room on the bed. "Lie back. Mayhap the labor pangs will cease."

Though she gave in to his pull, her tortured expression told otherwise. "My water has broken. The baby … is coming."

Daniel raked a hand through his hair. "I know nothing of birthing a baby. What if something were to go wrong?"

"It won't." She reached to clasp his arm. "The Lord will … guide us."

He met her gaze, gaining strength from her faith-filled eyes. With a halfhearted nod, he eased her down, propping a pillow beneath her. "Are you comfortable?"

She gave a nervous chuckle. "That is not a question … one should ask a woman … in my condition."

"Forgive me." He returned a feeble grin and brushed hair from her cheek, unable to fully distinguish her features in the darkness of the cabin. "You see how inept I am at this? I'm at a loss at what to say or do."

"No more than I. If you'll recall … this is my first birthing as well."

At the sound of her quivering voice, Daniel chastened himself for adding to her distress. No matter how brave her exterior, Maggie's worries mirrored his own. He leaned to kiss her. "We'll walk this together and trust the Lord to see us through."

"Yes." Her breathing calmed as she gazed up at him with moist eyes.

Daniel straightened and gave her a reassuring pat on the arm, feigning a confidence he didn't feel. "The first thing we need is some light to see by." Swinging his leg over the side of the bed, he reached for his crutch. With a quiet sigh, he paused and bowed his head, struggling to still his uneasiness. *Lord, I'm unprepared for this. Lend me Your strength. Clear my thoughts and grant discernment on what to do. And please, see to Maggie and the baby, that they are kept safe and well.*

DROPLETS OF SWEAT trickled down Maggie's temples as she lay back on the pillow, breathless. Slowly, she shook her head side to side. "I can't. My strength is sapped."

Daniel leaned forward on his crutch, his olive eyes pleading. "You can, Maggie. You must keep trying."

Exhausted, she wetted her lips. Morning light shone through the windowpane. For hours, she'd endured endless pains, each stronger than the previous. With each one, she sensed her vitality draining. Though Daniel did his best to spur her on, the beads of perspiration lining his furrowed brow hinted of weariness and concern.

You'll need stay fit and strong for when the baby comes, Emma's insightful words taunted Maggie. Her sister had known best after all. She and Daniel lacked experience at birthing a child.

Bolstering her resolve, Maggie drew a deep breath and readied herself for another attempt. When the effort proved futile, she lay back, fighting tears. How much more could she endure?

Seeming to sense her discouragement, Daniel abandoned his position at the foot of the bed and hobbled closer. He brushed damp hair from her forehead, his lack of words and forlorn expression hinting of concern.

Tears slid down her temples to her ears as she stared up at him. "What are we to do, Daniel? I have nothing left to give."

He clasped her hand in his, the warmth of his touch offering a flicker of comfort. "We pray."

Maggie closed her eyes as Daniel bowed his head. Moments of silence passed before he found his voice. With quivering words, he spoke his heart.

"Lord, You know our needs before we even ask. You know our limitations and the very time and circumstances surrounding the birth of this child. As Mary and Joseph were in a crude stable on the night of the Christ child's birth, so we are without guidance or provisions. I ask You to give Maggie and the baby strength to endure this labor. May You enable me to remain ready and able to receive this baby when he comes. We love You, dear Father. Come what may, we commit ourselves and our offspring into Your care. In our weakness, be our strength."

No sooner had Daniel's heartfelt words left his mouth than Maggie's muscles tightened, and she had the overwhelming urge to push. She gripped the edge of the mattress, her breaths hurried and shallow. "Something's ... happening."

With the quickness of a two-legged man, Daniel whisked back to the foot of the bed.

Closing her eyes, Maggie gritted her teeth and arched forward, giving another vigorous push.

"Keep pushing, love. I can see the head. Our Nathaniel is almost here."

With a winded giggle, she gave another resolute exertion. Something gave inside her., The pressure eased and the urge to push subsided. Exhausted, she lay back, listening for a baby's cry.

When none came, she strained for a look. Daniel turned his back to her, blocking her view. Why? A moment of panic robbed her of peace. Fear coiled a stranglehold around her throat, choking off her ability to speak. Had the difficult birth taken their baby?

Then it came.

A loud *smack* followed by a vibrant cry.

Her whole body fell limp, tears of joy and relief welling within her. *Thank You, Lord.*

At last, she found her voice. "Is the child well?"

"Yes, indeed. A fine, healthy baby."

Daniel neglected to mention whether they had a son or a daughter, and yet his reference to their baby as Nathaniel even before the birthing had not escaped her. "A boy?"

Daniel mumbled something indistinguishable, casting a seed of doubt within Maggie. She'd been so certain, and yet, it mattered not if she'd been wrong or right. Either son or daughter was a gift from the Lord. She only hoped Daniel had chosen a fitting name for a girl.

The newborn's cries died away as Daniel worked to clean and swaddle the infant. At last, he shuffled over, the baby nestled in the nook of his arm. His eyes sparkled as he leaned to lay the child next to Maggie. "Meet Nathaniel."

A wide smile spilled across Maggie's lips as she cuddled her son in her arms. She'd been right all along. This dear child born to them was indeed a precious gift of God.

As though worn out from all he'd been through, Nathaniel's eyelids remained closed, short lashes resting on his pink cheeks. Maggie brushed a finger over his thin hair, the color of wheat at harvest. She smiled at Daniel as he eased onto the mattress beside her. "He's beautiful, is he not?"

Though dark circles lined Daniel's eyes, they shimmered with merriment. "Indeed. Like his mother." He leaned toward her, cupping a hand to her cheek. "What a Christmas present the Lord has given us."

Maggie stretched for his kiss, the pain and uncertainties of the birthing forgotten. Though she knew not what their future held, she was certain the Lord would faithfully guide their way.

Thirteen

Tuesday Morning, December 27, 1814

The pounding on the door startled Daniel from sleep. Maggie stirred beside him, but the baby's sleep went undisturbed. Awake off and on throughout the night from Nathaniel's cries for nourishment and attention, they'd overslept. By the amount of daylight streaming through the window, half the morning must have lapsed.

Daniel yawned as he sat up and reached for his crutch. He cringed as another thump sounded on the door. "Daniel? Maggie?"

"Coming." He shot another glance at Nathaniel. Still sleeping soundly.

"Who is it?" Maggie's whisper sounded beside him.

"Jonathan, no doubt." With all the snow, Daniel hadn't imagined even his brother-in-law would venture out so soon. "Emma must have sent him."

Slowly, Daniel made his way to the door and lifted the latch. As he eased the door open, Jonathan stared in at him. "You folks all right? Emma's been worried sick about you since the snow came. When I didn't see any tracks around the place, I began to fret some myself."

"We're fine." Daniel stood aside to let him in, keeping his voice low. "I brought some extra wood in ahead of the storm and have been melting snow for water."

Jonathan stomped the snow from his boots, then sauntered inside. He gestured over his shoulder. "Your chickens were squawking for their breakfast. I'll see to them and gather your eggs before I head back."

"We're obliged to you. It's difficult for me to trudge through snow. And we've been ... preoccupied the past couple of days." Daniel couldn't hold back a grin as Maggie walked toward them, Nathaniel cradled in her arms.

"I can see that, you being still in your night clothes." Edging closer to the fire, Jonathan snickered and rubbed chapped hands together, still unmindful of Maggie's approach. "Emma said you two were set on spending Christmas alone, but this snow and cold had her spooked the baby might come before she could get here."

With a soft chuckle, Maggie eased up beside him. "She was right."

Intent on warming himself, Jonathan cast only a casual glance her way. "How's that?"

"I said, she was right about the baby coming early."

Jonathan's face snapped toward her, eyes wide. "What? You've a baby!"

Ambling over, Daniel slid an arm around Maggie's shoulders. "Jonathan, meet Nathaniel Hawkins."

Jonathan scratched at his chin. "Well, I'll be. A fine boy. Won't Emma be tied in knots to learn she missed out?" His gaze flicked between Daniel and Maggie. "You two manage it on your own?"

"With a lot of help from the Lord." Daniel met Maggie's loving glance with a wink.

Jonathan hiked a brow. "You're a brave man, Daniel. My

wife's been through three birthings, and I did good to stand outside the door without my knees buckling."

"Didn't have much choice in the matter. Our son had his mind set to come when we were snowed in." Daniel pulled the blanket away from Nathaniel's face and leaned to kiss his cheek. The infant's mouth made a sucking motion, his blond lashes brushing rosy cheeks as he slept. Daniel grinned. "But I wouldn't have had it any other way."

A sense of contentment washed over him as he gazed at the tiny bundle in his wife's arms. Though he had no inkling how the three of them would manage, in that moment, his heart told him the Lord would provide, just as He had guided them through the birth of their son.

"Say, now. That cradle of yours turned out right well." Jonathan strode over and bent down beside it, rocking it back and forth. "Why, this is as fine as the one in Oliver's store."

Daniel slid his arm from around Maggie and stood a bit taller. "Considering a first attempt, I'm rather pleased."

"Rather pleased? My dear husband, you have a rare talent." Maggie moved to the cradle's far side and laid Nathaniel on a cushion of blankets. She nodded to the figurines on the fireplace mantel. "Take a look at those carvings, Jonathan, if you don't believe me."

Straightening, Jonathan followed her gaze to the nativity figures. "Daniel carved those?"

Maggie stood and gave a brisk nod. "He did. Aren't they fine?"

"Sure are." Lifting first one and then another, Jonathan shook his head. "Why, I declare, Daniel. You may have found your calling."

Cheeks burning under the praise, Daniel dropped his gaze to the puncheon floorboards. "Carving figures may make a fine hobby, but it won't provide for a family."

"What about that cradle over there?"

With a shrug, Daniel peered over at Jonathan. "What about it?"

"If you made more like it, you could sell them. Oliver might even be willing to put them in his store for commission."

Daniel's heart pounded harder. The idea had never crossed his mind. Woodworking and carving had never been an ambition he'd considered undertaking. And yet, he'd enjoyed crafting the cradle and nativity figures. Could he make any sort of living at it? At last, he shook his head. "Nay. I may have a bit of natural ability, but I could never take it up as a profession. Besides, Oliver has more than enough goods cluttering his store without my feeble attempts at furnishings."

The comments brought Jonathan a step closer. "Oliver said himself he must travel clear to Leesburg to find such quality. Your work is every bit as good. Do you not think he would rather do business with someone close to home?"

Though the possibility excited Daniel, it seemed but a fanciful notion. "I could never manage it."

Maggie propped her hands on her hips, blue eyes crimped. "You think too little of yourself, Daniel Hawkins. With the Lord's help, you can do anything you set your mind to."

'Twas true. Since he'd lost his leg, he'd lost faith in himself. But mayhap it was time to start putting faith in the One who truly held life's answers.

Fourteen

Thursday, December 29, 1814

Emma held out a finger for Nathaniel's tiny hand to latch onto. "I still can't believe I missed this little one's birthing. It's been torture waiting four whole days to meet my sweet nephew."

Maggie glanced over her sister's shoulder, still in awe of the tiny infant born to her. "And in that time, he's changed our lives."

Three mesmerized pairs of eyes peered at the babe on their mother's lap. "Why is he so wrinkly?" Nina's high-pitched voice cut through the moment of quiet.

"All babies are wrinkly at birth." Emma gave his fingers a kiss. "He'll grow into his skin once he fills out."

Liddy's nose scrunched. "Is all he does is sleep?"

"Much of the time." Maggie smothered a yawn. "He seems to get night and day confused."

Coming up beside her, Daniel slid an arm around her waist and leaned toward the girls. "You'll know when he gets hungry or needs a change."

"He announces that rather boldly," explained Maggie.

Emma leaned her head toward them, speaking in a whisper. "You having a boy has put Jonathan in the mindset of trying for one ourselves. But if you ask me, we'll only gain another lass."

Maggie chuckled. "I didn't think you liked to venture a guess as to what a child will be."

Nodding to her tow-headed daughters, Emma raised a brow. "'Tis not much of a guess when the record is so clear."

Daniel and Maggie shared a grin, then turned toward the window at the rattle of a wagon outside the cabin. "Sounds as though Jonathan has returned," Daniel said.

Maggie stepped to open the door, surprised when not only Jonathan but Oliver Sullivan greeted her. "Mr. Sullivan. Come in, please."

The small cabin seemed to shrink as the two men stepped inside. With sorrowful eyes, Jonathan paused in front of Daniel and held something out. "Forgive me. I confess I borrowed your shepherd."

With furrowed brow, Daniel took the figurine and peered at the mantel. "We've been so occupied, I hadn't noticed it missing."

Maggie shared an inquisitive look with Daniel, both obviously wondering the same thing—what was their brother-in-law up to?

Jonathan cleared his throat. "I took it upon myself to show the carving to Oliver and asked him to have a look at your cradle. I hope you don't mind."

Maggie gnawed at her lip, praying Daniel would not take offense at the action. To her relief, his expression held a degree of disbelief but not anger.

Squatting beside the cradle, Mr. Sullivan slid a hand along its smooth side. "Jonathan didn't exaggerate. This is fine workmanship, Daniel. I'm impressed."

"Thank you." Daniel's unsteady tone hinted of uneasiness.

Mr. Sullivan stood erect, gripping his hat in his hands. "Do you think you can retain this same quality of work with other wood furnishings?"

Daniel cut a glance at Maggie, and she gave him a reassuring nod. This could be a new start for him, an answer to their prayers. Hopeful, she clutched her hands to her chest. *Oh, please Lord, give him confidence to try.*

He moistened his lips. "If I had a pattern to go off of, I might."

With a brisk nod, Mr. Sullivan offered a faint smile. "That's not a problem. From what I see here, I won't be making many trips to Leesburg for quality workmanship from now on. Not with a local talent such as yours." He held out a hand to Daniel. "If you're willing, I'd be pleased to buy up any items you're able to supply."

Daniel's face blanched as he left Mr. Sullivan's hand suspended in midair.

Maggie bit her tongue to keep from nudging him to seal the deal. This need be Daniel's decision. No one else's. He had to want this enough to choose it.

When Daniel remained silent, Jonathan gripped his shoulder. "What do you say, friend? We've plenty of pine trees to supply you with wood."

Slow and steady as a sunrise, Daniel's face regained its ruddiness, and his lips lifted as he clasped Mr. Sullivan's hand. "That sounds good, Oliver. I'm obliged to you."

"Don't thank me. I'm thrilled to have a gifted craftsman so close at hand. When you have a few items ready, bring them by and we'll talk price."

Moisture stung Maggie's eyes as she witnessed the pride on her husband's face. He'd returned home a broken man. Now, months later, the Lord had renewed his hope and sense of purpose.

Her Daniel was finally home.

~

Daniel gently laid the figures of Mary, Jesus, the shepherd, and sheep inside the crude stable and set them at the bottom of the trunk where his box of keepsake carving tools once rested. Now that the chisels were in use, the spot was the perfect place to store the unfinished nativity. Someday he hoped to complete it. But for now, it would remain safely tucked away, a vivid reminder of not only Christ's coming, but of the awakening within him to the faithfulness of God's leading in his life.

Never would he have chosen to lose his leg, his friend Noah, or his dream of farming. The direction of his life had forever changed that fateful day when war stripped him of so much. There'd been days he wished he'd not survived, longed to join Noah as a casualty. But now, as he listened to Maggie's soft humming as she rocked young Nathaniel to sleep, Daniel counted himself most blessed.

He'd never envisioned one day making woodworking his profession or finding renewed purpose in something he'd once avoided. And yet, the Lord had planned it all along. If not for his weakness, Daniel would never have gained his truest strength and calling.

He smiled over at Maggie as he pulled himself up. "I'll let you put the rest in. I need to get to work."

Nodding, she returned a wide grin. "Your father would be so proud of you."

"'Tis a shame he'll never know his wish for me finally come to fruition. That I've gained his love for working with wood."

"He'd have been pleased indeed." Maggie peered down at Nathaniel. "Mayhap someday this little fellow will share your family's gift of woodcarving."

Daniel tipped his chin higher. "Possibly. But our son must choose his own path. I can only demonstrate the same love and guidance my father showed me and pray Nathaniel chooses well how to spend his days."

Hobbling over, Daniel gave Maggie a soft kiss then gazed

down at his son, his heart swelling with humble gratitude. Greater than the wish to have Nathaniel follow in his family's tradition was Daniel's desire to provide him a lasting legacy of faith to guide his way.

Epilogue

Five Years Later
November, 1819

"Did you always wish to be a woodcarver, Papa?"

Nathaniel's soprano voice cut into Daniel's concentration. His hands stilled, his young son's inquiry taking him back to his own youth, when he'd watched his father wield the very tools he now used. "No, Nathaniel. I wished to be a farmer."

Daniel warmed at the touch of Nathaniel's small hand on his shoulder. "Then why didn't you? Because of your leg?"

Relaxing his hold on the chisel and mallet, Daniel eased back on the three-legged stool. Years ago, the question would have stirred unwanted emotions, but now, he was at peace with his lost limb and even grateful for the path the injury had taken him down. He met Nathaniel's inquisitive stare, the boy's blue eyes a similar hue to his mother's. "Yes, son. It seems the Lord had different plans for me."

The boy's eyes widened. "To be a woodcarver, you mean."

Daniel tossed him a wink and again took up his tools. "Indeed."

The boy leaned in closer as Daniel shaved rough edges from the figure he was fashioning. "Is that going to be *our* Joseph?"

Daniel paused, regretting that, with the numerous nativities he'd carved to sell, he'd never taken time to complete their own. "Do you wish it to be our Joseph?"

A moment passed before Nathaniel spoke again. He puffed out his chest. "No. I think I should like to carve our Joseph someday. 'Cause I want to be a woodcarver like you when I grow up."

"Is that so?" Daniel held back a grin at Nathaniel's affirming "uh-huh." He knew from experience the boy's interest would likely ebb and change as he matured. And yet, it thrilled him to think, at this tender age at least, his son wished to follow in his footsteps. "All right, then. 'Twill be your duty to carve our Joseph."

The approach of a wagon drew their attention to the open barn doorway. "Sounds like your Uncle Jonathan has come for the load of goods."

Rushing over for a look, Nathaniel bobbed up and down. "It's him." He spun toward Daniel. "May I go with you into town this time, Papa?"

Daniel's mouth twisted. Maggie would likely balk at the idea, but if he approached her in the right manner, he might succeed in convincing her. "We'll see."

Setting his work aside, Daniel brushed shavings from his trousers and reached for his crutch.

"We-ell. Good day to you, young man." Jonathan's chipper greeting burst in at them. He lifted Nathaniel in one quick swoop and gave his belly a rub with his knuckles. "Are you helping your father today?"

"Uh-huh. And I'm gonna go into town with ya too."

Daniel cleared his throat, and the grin fled from his son's face. "I'm hopin', anyhow."

"Well, now. I don't blame you one bit. Those twin sisters of yours can be quite an earful. But then, so can my four girls." He lowered his voice as if sharing a secret. "That's why I volunteer to make so many trips to town. We menfolk have to stick together, outnumbered like we are." With a chuckle, Jonathan set Nathaniel on his feet and glanced over the stack of wares. "You've some fine pieces here, Daniel. They should bring a good price from Oliver."

Making his way over, Daniel gave an affirming nod. "He's been more than fair these past few years." Indeed, their arrangement had proven quite a blessing, with most of his goods selling within a matter of days or weeks of delivery. The Lord had blessed them immensely, providing for their needs in ways Daniel never could have imagined.

He tousled Nathaniel's blond hair. "Why don't we let Uncle Jonathan load these while we go speak to your mother?"

With a firm nod, Nathaniel grinned and reached to clasp Daniel's hand.

Small fingers latched on to his, and Daniel tightened his hold, watching his son willingly match his hobbled gait. In the nearly five years that had passed since the boy's birth, never once had the Lord ceased to provide for them. He and Maggie had been so frightened that Christmas Eve. But when things looked bleakest, the Lord had graciously turned their fear into joy.

That Christmas would forever hold a special place in Daniel's heart, for it was then he'd learned to trust God's plan for him. What Daniel had viewed as weakness, the Lord had revealed as strength. He'd given Daniel the gift of faith and purpose—a legacy he resolved, with God's help, to impart to his children and grandchildren.

THE END

Discussion Questions

1. When Daniel Hawkins loses his leg as well as his friend, Noah, he also loses his will to live. His plans for his life were shattered. What causes you to lose heart and want to give up? How does your faith help you through life's trials and discouragements?
2. Maggie is thrilled by Daniel's return, but is soon devastated by his depleted attitude and unwillingness to try. What attempts does she make to encourage him? How can you encourage someone who is downcast and without hope? How can prayer play a part in changing someone's heart or attitude?
3. Daniel mistakenly believes his impediment is the cause of Maggie's disappointment. How does her openness and honesty help him better understand the root of her feelings? Have you ever had to share hard truths with a family member or close friend? If so, was it difficult? Did it help alleviate the misunderstanding?
4. When Daniel finally realizes the Lord has a plan for his life, he finds renewed fulfillment and purpose. Have you ever had plans that don't pan out and

instead you sense the Lord leading you down a different path? How did you feel? Were you discouraged, frustrated, or angry? In the end, did you find peace and see the wisdom in God's plan?

Acknowledgments

When I consider all that the Lord has done and the beautiful people He's placed in my path these past several years, I am overwhelmed with gratitude. My dream of becoming a published author stems back to my high school days, and I am indebted to so many for helping make this novel-writing dream a reality. First and foremost, the Lord. Without His abundant love and guiding hand, none of this would have been possible. May His name be praised, and may each word I write bring glory to Him.

I'm so grateful to the staff of Scrivenings Press for believing in my stories. Thanks to Publisher, Linda Fulkerson, for her tireless efforts to aid, encourage, guide, and promote my work as well as the numerous other authors she's taken under her wing.

Thanks to co-authors Elaine Cooper, Kelly Goshorn, and Candace West for their collaboration efforts on this project. It has been a joy to work with you. May the Lord continue to bless your writing journeys.

About the Author

Cynthia Roemer is an inspirational, award-winning author who enjoys planting seeds of hope into the hearts of readers. Raised in the cornfields of rural Illinois, Cynthia enjoys spinning tales set in the backdrop of the mid-1800's prairie and Civil War era. .

Cynthia feels blessed the Lord has fulfilled her life-long dream of being a published novelist. It's her prayer that her stories will both entertain and encourage readers in their faith. Her Prairie Sky Series consists of Amazon bestseller, *Under This Same Sky, Under Prairie Skies*, and 2020 Selah Award winner, *Under Moonlit Skies*. Her fourth novel, *Beyond These War-Torn Lands*, is set during the final year of the Civil War and is Book One in her Wounded Heart Series. *Beyond Wounded Hearts* is the second book in the series.

She writes from her family farm in central Illinois where she resides with her husband of twenty-nine years. She is a member of American Christian Fiction Writers. Visit Cynthia online at: www.cynthiaroemer.com

Healing WITHIN THE Pieces

Candace West

For Grandma West who shared her love for family treasures with me.

*But he knoweth the way that I take: when he hath tried me, I shall come
forth as gold.*
-Job 23:10

One

Loudoun County, Virginia
December 1836

Freedom blustered in the winter breeze, sifting through Nathaniel Hawkins's cotton shirt and chilling his skin to the bone. Yet the prison chains still weighed his steps.

Until he remembered he wasn't bound any longer.

Casting a furtive glance at the travelers disembarking the train, Nathaniel turned up the collar of his shirt to block the wind's bite against his cheek. The musty odor of the fabric collided with his nose. When he arrived home, he'd scrub away that smell for good.

If home still existed.

Nathaniel crammed his hat farther down on his head and shuffled toward the end of the platform. Again, he remembered he wasn't wearing chains.

Quickening his pace, he jogged down the steps of the platform, turning in the direction of his farm. An eight-mile stretch of the legs. The smell of snow tinged the air. He scanned the cloudy horizon. Surely, he could arrive before it started covering the hilly landscape. Would it even matter if he didn't return?

"Hey, young feller, do you need a ride?"

Nathaniel's chest tightened. Slowly, he pivoted to find someone he hoped was unacquainted with the crime that had made him a stranger. "Are you headed for Taylorstown?"

"I am. It's a long walk in this weather." The man shoved a crate farther into the wagon and jumped down. After dusting off his hands, he held one out. "My name's Ben Greer. You're welcome to come along."

"Thank you. I'm Nathaniel Hawkins." He accepted the handshake, forcing himself to meet the man's direct gaze.

With a slight shake of his head, Mr. Greer skimmed Nathaniel's stained hat, unkempt beard, and threadbare clothes. "Never heard of you, but I've just lived here a year. Looks like you forgot to bring a coat."

"I brought what I could." Nathaniel pulled a taut smile over the bitter clip of his words, failing to dull the edge of his tone.

Mr. Greer didn't seem to notice while he rounded the wagon, gesturing for Nathaniel to climb aboard. "The wind is picking up. We'd better not waste time."

The seat jiggled and creaked under their weight. After a flick of the reins, the horses hurried forward as though eager to reach the safety of their barn.

Tucking his chin, Nathaniel crossed his arms to stave off the chill. He glanced at the sky, tempted to whisper a prayer of thanksgiving for the ride. The words jammed his throat instead. For two years, he hadn't been on speaking terms with God.

Truly, though, Nathaniel wouldn't have listened if the Lord had spoken.

"You got kindred waiting on you?"

Family. The word stiffened Nathaniel's shoulders while he shook his head. "No, sir." He fished for something else to say, but conversing no longer came easily. Too many quiet hours in a cell had rusted his manners.

"A shame, that." Mr. Greer's bushy, russet eyebrows dipped closer together. "There's just me and the missus, but it's better than nothing."

"You're a fortunate man."

"Less than some but more than most."

Memories of Mother's sweet singing coupled with Father's hearty laugh eclipsed the noise of the horses' plodding hooves on the country road. How were they faring? Were they still among the living?

Nathaniel slammed his eyes shut against a jab of guilt. He'd not written, deciding that silence would lessen their pain. Especially his, most of all. Perhaps a bit selfish. Prison had brought out the worst in him. To survive, he had to forget his folks. Forget everything.

All the while, their faces had trailed him like the hounds that had caught up with him that fateful night.

Mr. Greer talked through the next several miles for both of them, while Nathaniel answered when required. At least he needn't worry about keeping the conversation alive. The older man's stories whizzed along with the breeze.

At a crossroads, a horse and its rider waited. Mr. Greer raised a hand. "Hullo!" He reined in the horses.

"On your way home, Greer?"

Nathaniel's eyes snapped in the rider's direction. His pulse leaped against the skin on his neck. Would the man recognize him beneath two years of scruff and dingy clothing?

A broad smile spread across Greer's face. "Mr. Kimball, sir. What brings you out on a day like this?"

"An overdue visit at my daughter's. The clouds came up rather suddenly." Kimball's glance snagged on Nathaniel while Mr. Greer inquired about the family.

"How's Missus Carrie and the little one?"

Thank goodness his beard hid most of his expression at Carrie's name. Nathaniel's pulse ticked harder.

"They're both doing fine. The babe is the perfect image of her mama. It takes me back to my first days being a new papa."

Mr. Greer chuckled. "No doubt you'll be spoiling her."

Kimball's stare sharpened, but Nathaniel resisted the urge to dip his head. He held his breath.

Recognition dawned as the man's watchful eyes hardened like cold flint. He straightened in the saddle. "Nathaniel Hawkins."

Clenching his jaw, he sat frozen in the seat, his demeanor betraying none of the turmoil inside. He had nothing to say to Kimball.

Mr. Greer shifted sideways, surprise lifting his brows. "You know him?"

"I regret to say I do." A bit of sneer tweaked the corner of Kimball's mouth. "Perhaps I should say I *once* knew him. Prison hasn't agreed with you, my boy, but I trust it has tempered any remaining vices."

Fire raced along Nathaniel's veins. He wouldn't give him the satisfaction of answering or showing his anger.

Mr. Greer sputtered a cough. "Prison?"

"He didn't tell you?" Kimball's crafty smile displayed a perfect row of teeth.

"Not a word."

"He's well known for his ability to conceal things."

A frown turned down Mr. Greer's rotund mouth while he appraised Nathaniel through fresh, wary eyes. "I'll not take you an inch farther. Get off."

The sharp words cut deeper than the cold gusts buffeting him. Nathaniel rose. "I thank you for taking me this far." Without a glance at Kimball, he jumped down.

After a parting wave at his friend, Mr. Greer started the horses toward town, leaving the men to face each other.

The older gentleman adjusted the dark blue scarf around his neck, tucking the ends securely within his coat. "Stay away from Carrie. She's married, with a family of her own. She has no interest in the likes of you."

"I have no interest in the likes of her."

Kimball ignored the remark. "You'd better hurry before the storm catches you. If I recall correctly, you're not so adept at outrunning things."

Turning his head, he nudged his horse into a trot and followed in Mr. Greer's wake.

A tremor raced along Nathaniel's shoulders, but it had nothing to do with the coming blizzard. Cramming stiff hands into his pockets, he strode into a nearby field. Good thing he could walk this country blindfolded if need be. He'd cut the remaining four miles to two in this direction.

The longest part of his journey, however, promised no shortcuts.

Two

"Oh, not now," moaned Delia, gripping her rounded middle and slumping into the chair. Though the time neared for her unborn child's delivery, the sickness of those early months persisted.

The sweet smell of dried peaches assaulted her nose. Stifling a gag, she shoved the gunny sack of fruit across the table and tried to steady her breathing. Sweat prickled her forehead. For a few moments, the chill of the parlor numbed the waves of nausea.

Delia brushed trembling fingers across her brow while watching the small flames lick the wood in the fireplace. Soon the blaze would cast heat through the sparse room. She hadn't dared start the fire until after sunset. Rising smoke from the chimney of an abandoned house would attract folks like bears to fresh honey.

The thought of the sweet chunks of fruit made Delia choke down another gag. "If I lived a hundred years, it would be too soon to eat them." Shivering, she covered her lips with the palm of her clammy hand.

Her provisions were running low. The peaches, her least favorite fruit, were the last of the bunch. Only this bag remained.

A blast of wind pounded the shuttered windows of the farmhouse, a fierce yet lonely sound. Delia rubbed her forearms as the sickness receded, thankful she hadn't cast up her accounts. She hadn't the nourishment to spare.

No one but the Lord above knew her whereabouts. She had turned her back on home. Delia ground her teeth. *Home.* A veritable prison, but she had broken free.

Nothing would force her to return.

She'd die first.

In her condition, death loomed a possibility. Alone with no family, no doctor or midwife, she had no recourse. Neither did the unborn child kicking within her womb.

Pain tensed the muscles of her forearms. Glancing down, Delia realized she'd been squeezing them too hard. She stood, retrieved a quilt from the back of the chair, and draped it across her shoulders. She'd found quite a few in a dusty trunk upstairs.

Delia moved toward the window while the firelight cast distorted shadows throughout the room. The wind howled like a wild animal through the trees.

If I say, Surely the darkness shall cover me; even the night shall be light about me. Yea, the darkness hideth not from thee; but the night shineth as the day: the darkness and the light are both alike to thee.

The Bible verses brought strange comfort into the stark loneliness of her circumstances. The words wrapped around her like the quilt draping her frame.

Delia peered through a crack in the shutters, hoping they concealed the firelight from view. Snow pelted the landscape and highlighted everything it touched.

In the distance, something caught her gaze. She narrowed her eyes. A shadowy figure trudged toward the cabin, leaning into the rising wind.

Terror bubbled up Delia's throat. Could it be him, the man she'd fled? How would he have found her?

She stumbled backward. Frantically, she glanced around the

room, her mind scrambling for a way to escape. She could hide somewhere upstairs, perhaps in the attic.

Delia skittered toward the stairs, but the crackling fire halted her steps. Abandoned houses never had a burning hearth. He would realize her presence, no matter where she hid.

Better to face it now. But she would never go back willingly. She would never go back at all.

She yanked a long dagger from its place on the mantel. Likely an heirloom belonging to the previous owner, it fit perfectly in her hand.

He would overpower her at a price.

Footfalls padded onto the porch. Licking her dry lips, Delia pivoted to meet whatever fate brought through the front door.

The door jiggled, but the latch stopped the intruder's advance. The door shook once. Twice then harder.

Delia's fingers tightened around the weapon.

Without warning, the door burst open and crashed against the wall. A gasp escaped Delia's lips as she brandished the dagger.

The man lowered his boot, stepping across the threshold. The firelight struck his face.

"Who are you?" he demanded.

Delia's knees trembled beneath her skirts, relief edging around her. At least, it wasn't *him*. Raising her chin, she raked her stare over a half-starved scarecrow. A sodden hat covered his bushy mane badly in need of a haircut. His scraggly beard failed to conceal a scowl. Threadbare clothes covered his broad shoulders and narrow hips.

Delia forced ire into her question. "Who are *you*?"

The man's eyes glinted at her weapon, but he made no move toward her. "I'm Nathaniel Hawkins. This is my place."

"This farm was abandoned. I live here now." Delia's heart thundered against her ribcage.

"I'd say barely." Hawkins's wary gaze roved the room. "How long have you been here?"

"Long enough."

A frown pinched the skin around his eyes. With a sound akin to a growl, he shut the door. His fingers lifted the broken latch before dropping it back against the doorframe.

Stiffening her shoulders, Delia stretched to her full height. "What are you doing?"

"Like I said, this is my place. I'm not about to stay out in the storm." His intent stare skimmed over her. "You can put away my dagger. I'm not about to turn you out or harm you. I'd appreciate the same."

A pent-up breath slid over Delia's lips. Stepping cautiously away from the hearth, she relaxed her grip. Usually, she recognized the truth when she heard it. Candor glinted in the man's eyes.

"All right." She hated the traitorous tremble in her voice.

"Now, what's your name?" Hawkins neared the fire and flexed his fingers into the rising heat.

Delia swallowed a bitter lump, aware she owed the stranger an explanation. She ignored the memories lurking within the shadows. Her glance dropped to the blade in her hand.

"I'm Cordelia Evans. Most folks call me Delia.'"

Three

Nathaniel could see through the young woman's bravado. Fear shimmered behind her defiant brown eyes. Relaxing his shoulders, he gentled his tone. "You have no family?"

"Not now."

"How old are you?"

"Twenty."

For the first time, he noticed her round, protruding stomach. His breath stilled. "Where is your husband?"

Flinching, Delia took a step back. A crimson flush crept into her cheeks as she set her lips in a straight, hard line.

"Do you have a husband?"

Delia worked her jaw, but no explanation followed.

Nathaniel shook his head, ignoring the burning in his chest. Far be it from him to judge her, yet the assumption hammered into his thoughts. Here he stood, fresh from prison with possibly a loose woman on his doorstep. In his very home. What a way to start fresh.

Sighing, he gestured to the chair. "Please sit, ma'am. Looks like we have some things to sort out." He crossed to the table and lifted another chair to bring near the fireplace.

"I've nothing to say." She remained motionless, clutching the weapon.

"Not from the looks of it." Nathaniel set his chair near the hearthside. "But first, let me have the dagger."

She ignored his outstretched hand. "I'll do no such thing."

Nathaniel tamped down impatience, the first pangs of hunger gnawing at his gut. How long had it been since his last meal? Since yesterday's supper. He rubbed callused fingers over his eyelids. "Will you at least have a seat?"

Delia blinked, considering. Warily, she lowered herself onto the chair and rested the dagger across her lap. "I've a few questions myself. If this is your home, then why did I find it abandoned? It looks like it's been empty for years."

"Two, to be exact."

Her guarded perusal narrowed. "Why?"

"I've been in prison." Leaning forward a little, Nathaniel hardened his stare to test her reaction.

The color blanched from Delia's face. She drew in a breath but met his gaze without wavering. "For what crime?"

"You tell me why you're here, and I'll tell you my crime."

She swept trembling fingers over her mouth before balling them into a fist. "I can't," she said through clenched teeth.

Compassion whispered around the edges of Nathaniel's conscience, an emotion he thought he'd stamped out long ago. "Can't or won't?"

"Both." Delia's shoulders sagged. "I suppose I'm at your mercy."

Mercy. Another ideal he'd tried to forget. Sweeping his hands over his stained trousers, Nathaniel stood and turned toward the table.

"I said I wouldn't turn you out. We'll have to figure out our way forward. Until then, I'll have some of those peaches."

～

DELIA BIT down another wave of nausea while Nathaniel devoured the peaches like a starved creature. She raised a hand to press against her throat.

Nathaniel raised his eyes, catching her grimace. A glimmer of understanding touched his features. "Sorry," he mumbled, swiping a dirty sleeve across his mouth.

Delia darted her glance to the fire. She hadn't planned on being trapped in a snowstorm with a criminal. Despite his dour behavior, he didn't seem intent on harming her. If anything, his offended glare at her stomach hinted otherwise. Had prison sharpened his sensibilities?

The sarcastic thought heightened her shame. How could she blame him if she refused to answer his questions?

Unwanted memories blurred the corners of Delia's vision, threatening to erase the sounds of the rumbling wind along with the stranger in the room. The rancid smell of whiskey on Clive's breath snaked under her nose. Her breath thinned against a thudding pulse. Unseen hands closed around her throat until she realized her fingers squeezed the tender flesh.

"Ma'am, are you all right?"

Delia dropped her hand, shoving away the scenes. "I'm a bit shaken, as you can rightly imagine."

"You're safe here ... even with me. I'll need to sort things out around here tomorrow. We'll need food and supplies. Until then, I'll bed down here by the fireplace."

His gruff but calm words somehow soothed her spirit. Whatever his past, he looked like he'd suffered greatly.

Delia nodded, rising from the chair. "There's a trunk upstairs with quilts. I'll bring you several."

"No need." Nathaniel held up a hand. "I'd spoil them with my filth. I'll clean up tomorrow."

"In that case, I'll say goodnight." Delia returned the weapon to its place above the mantel and faced him. Her next words scraped the back of her throat. "Thank you for letting me stay."

Nathaniel dipped his head. "Wait a moment." He rushed from the room into the dark kitchen.

Confused, Delia listened to his rummaging through the pantry. Moments later, he returned with a kerosene lamp and a knife.

"There's still plenty of oil left inside," he said more to himself than to her. Once he had trimmed the wick and lit the lamp, he slid the glass dome into place. "Here. Take this with you." He held it out.

A tremor shook Delia's fingers when she took it. Without waiting for a reply, Nathaniel turned quickly away.

He didn't stop at the chair or the table. Instead, he strode to the front door and yanked it open. Frigid air whirled past him into the house, seeping under her skirts. After stepping outside, he thumped the door shut.

The sound jolted Delia from her shock. Stifling a shiver, she scurried up the stairs to a bedroom. What manner of man abode under the same roof with her?

After entering the room, she set the lamp on a cobwebbed dresser. One by one, she dug several quilts from the trunk. While she layered them on the bed, she mused over his behavior.

Never had a man been kind to her.

Getting the lamp had been unnecessary. She would've fumbled her way up the stairs without it. Making do taught her to survive without help.

However, she wasn't accustomed to kindness. From the look of it, neither was he.

In fact, he acted downright terrified of it.

Four

T he bottom step of the stairs squeaked under Delia's careful tread. Wincing, she glanced up to find Nathaniel stirring a pot over the fire.

"Rabbit stew," he said without glancing in her direction. "My gun and ammunition were still in the closet, so I set out early this morning."

The savory scent agreed with Delia's stomach. "It smells good."

"It's not much stew to speak of. There's no vegetables, just meat, and the broth."

"Anything is better than peaches."

Nathaniel cut a glance at her then, a wry smile cracking his somber expression. The next instant, it faded like a cloud shrouding sunlight.

"I'll get the bowls from the cupboard." Delia whisked into the kitchen, away from the piercing blue of those eyes.

"Lord," she whispered, "grant me wisdom. I don't know what kind of temperament this man has. Does he get riled easy? Please help me sense when to speak or be quiet."

When she had gathered the bowls and spoons along with her courage, Delia went into the parlor. She set their places at the table. After a cold night, she welcomed the warmth radiating from the fireplace.

"The food's ready." Approaching the table, Nathaniel picked up her bowl. "I'll dish up."

If that didn't beat all. A man serving her? Fumbling with the edge of her sleeve, Delia watched while he ladled the stew into the bowl. Upon returning, he laid it at her place.

"Thank you." Delia's dry throat cracked.

Without answering, Nathaniel grabbed his bowl and shuffled to the fireplace, walking as though still chained. A hint of pity touched Delia.

Only then did she notice a change in his clothes. Sliding into the chair, she cleared her throat. "I see you found some clothes."

"After I killed the rabbit, I brought in the washtub, melted some snow, and bathed. The clothes were packed away in my room. I have a cedar chest my father made. It kept them from the moths."

"You have family?"

Nathaniel's lips tightened. He lowered himself into the chair across from her.

Keeping the tremor from her voice, Delia held up a hand. "I'm sorry. I didn't mean to pry." She folded her hands together. "May we say the blessing?"

Shock furrowed Nathaniel's brow. "I suppose so."

Though he made no move to fold his hands or bow his head, Delia managed a hurried prayer. Venturing a peek, she found him staring at the stew, waiting.

Willing her fingers not to tremble, Delia slid the spoon into the broth and brought it to her lips. The warm, flavorful liquid ignited a hunger she'd been striving to ignore. "This is good, Mr. Hawkins. The best food I've had in weeks."

Nathaniel sampled his stew. "Same here, but I daresay it's because we're half-starved." A frown turned down his lips. "Last night, I wasn't thinking when I said I'd stay downstairs. I meant it for your privacy, but I sent you to the colder part of the house."

Unsure of what to say, Delia took another bite of stew, remembering how she spent most of the night shivering under the blankets. Before he'd come, she'd spent her nights lying near the fireside.

Nathaniel shifted in his seat, looking uncomfortable. "I'll clean out the fireplace up there for this evening. There's also a bed warmer in the pantry. I'll be sure to prepare it."

Swallowing, Delia stumbled over her response. "There's ... no need to trouble yourself. I can manage."

"I'm sure you can, but it's no trouble." Again, a hint of a smile softened the brusqueness of his words. He turned his attention back to the bowl and lifted another bite to his mouth.

NATHANIEL RUBBED the sore muscles of his forearms. Across from him, the young woman dozed in the chair, a quilt wrapped around her. The threadbare ribbon tying back her long tresses had loosened. Several wisps of dark auburn hair, the color of burnished copper, brushed her pale cheeks. A faint ridge of freckles bridged her nose. Sighing, Delia shuddered though she sat only a few feet from the fireplace.

He couldn't fault her work ethic. While he had scoured the upstairs fireplace, she had busied herself sweeping up the filth, emptying the dustpan, and doing whatever else she could to help. She'd refused to rest until he finished his tasks.

What had driven her into hiding? The purple shadows under her eyes emphasized sleepless, distressed nights. Beneath the quilt, the swell of Delia's stomach rose then fell with her breaths.

Nathaniel's chest clenched. Soon, the babe would come. How could he provide for them? Even more, why should he? They weren't his responsibility.

He dragged a hand over his face, stifling a groan. His life lay in shambles, without direction or purpose. To help someone else gather their shattered pieces stretched beyond his means and ability. The burden almost weighed him down more than the physical chains he had left behind in prison.

Outside, a sudden shuffling, jangling sound drove Nathaniel from his seat. He dashed across the parlor. Stooping low, he peered through the crack in the shutters.

Behind him, Delia stirred, her tone thick with sleep. "What is it?"

A horse-drawn piano box sleigh carrying two passengers stopped in front of the house. Frosty vapors streamed from the horse's nostrils as the driver laid aside the reins.

Panic crawled up Nathaniel's throat. Straightening, he scraped his fingers through his hair. They shouldn't be here. Not now.

The quilt puddled to the floor as Delia scrambled to stand. "What's happening?"

"It's my folks, paying a visit." His voice cracked beneath the pressure building in his ribcage.

"Mercy, no," she hissed, her eyes wild. "They mustn't find me."

Footsteps thudded onto the porch. Without delay, Delia whisked up the quilt and dashed upstairs to her bedroom, leaving no trace of her presence.

Nathaniel tugged his beard, dreading his parents' reaction to his bedraggled appearance. No doubt they would worry over him.

The door rattled with a firm knock. "Nathaniel? Are you there?"

Father's firm, steady tone swept Nathaniel back to happier times, a veil so thin it seemed he could walk through and abandon his past forever. Shaking himself, he unlatched the door and pulled open the door.

There they stood—Father and Mother, their hair a little grayer, the lines on their faces more pronounced. Holding a crutch under one arm, Father straightened and shifted his weight on his right leg. Even though he'd lost his left leg years ago, his strength and agility still awed Nathaniel.

Their eyes widened while they gazed at him as though he were a long-lost phantom.

"Son?" Mother reached out a trembling hand.

Any words Nathaniel might have said grew brittle and crumbled on his tongue. His mouth ran dry. Mother wrapped her work-worn fingers around his limp ones and lifted the back of his hand to her cheek. "Thank God you're home."

His feet moved of their own accord toward her, and she gathered him into an embrace. Her back quivered with shuddering breaths.

Father clasped Nathaniel's shoulder. "Amen and amen." A mist glistened in his gaze, spilling onto his cheeks when he tightened his grip.

Tears burned in Nathaniel's eyes, and he squeezed his eyelids together to contain them. Choked them down instead. "It's good to see you," he finally managed. "How did you know?"

"Word travels, even in a snowstorm." Father dabbed a sleeve over his eyes. "A neighbor told us Mr. Greer picked up a man who'd been released from prison. When Greer found out, he ordered him off the wagon and spread the story along his way home. We knew it had to be you."

"Unfeeling man." Wiping her cheeks, Mother stepped back to look up at Nathaniel. "He has no Christian charity."

"I can't blame him." Nathaniel shrugged.

"I can."

A fringe of a smile quelled the tension roiling inside him. Though his world had irrevocably changed, their love for him hadn't.

Father motioned toward the sleigh. "We brought food and supplies, enough to stock the pantry for a while. Come and help me get them."

"We've also brought one of your father's old coats. It's on top of the box. Put it on, first thing." Mother rubbed her mittened hands together.

"Yes, ma'am." Nathaniel braced himself against the sharp, icy breeze and followed Father. He sank knee-deep into the snow and plodded forward. "Did you happen to bring boots?"

"We did. I don't think your mother left out any detail." Reaching into the sleigh, Father tugged a heavy coat from the top of a box and handed it to Nathaniel.

He shrugged into it, thankful for the sudden warmth. Several crates sat on the floorboard, filled with dried provisions from Mother's garden and orchard, flour, and an assortment of other supplies. Nathaniel hauled them one by one into the kitchen while Mother unloaded the contents and arranged them in the pantry. The immediate pressure to provide for Delia and the babe eased a little.

"There's one more thing, son." Father lifted the hatch of the compartment in the back of the sleigh.

Nathaniel's pace slowed when he saw the heirloom trunk. "Why did you bring this?"

Father brushed his hand over the lid. "I figure it's high time I passed it down to you. I've made good use of it, but now it's your turn."

"I—" A flood of childhood memories crashed into Nathaniel —sitting beside Father and watching him carve, memorizing the movement of his hands, listening to the story of his family, and learning the skill himself. How he had loved it. Then.

But faith intertwined the pieces.

Father pushed the chest toward him. "You remember our nativity?"

Stifling a sigh, Nathaniel nodded. How could he forget? "I didn't think you'd want to part with it so soon."

"Soon?" Father chuckled. "I've waited a long time to pass it on to you. It's your turn to contribute to its history."

All his life, Nathaniel had waited to add a few pieces to be passed along to the next generation of Hawkins sons or daughters. He had dreamed of sharing the stories and teaching the skill to a wide-eyed little one.

His jaw tightened. Those aspirations had died in prison, where he'd learned to live day to day while the future mocked him. What kind of prospects did he have now?

Father's stare probed into places Nathaniel had buried. "Poverty and uncertainty were uninvited guests at the nativity. But redemption showed up, brightening mankind's hopeless future." Again, he gripped Nathaniel's shoulder. "You're free to pursue your prospects, but first, reacquaint yourself with these things. You'll find healing there."

Wrenching his gaze away, Nathaniel gathered the trunk into his arms. From the porch, Mother's shout pierced the stillness.

"Come quick! Something's happened."

Five

Nathaniel jogged the distance to the house and then deposited the trunk onto the parlor's table. Pointing at the ceiling, Mother hissed, "Something crashed upstairs. Where's your gun?"

"There's no need for it." Nathaniel pinched his lips together and strode to the stairs. Taking them two at a time, he tamped down his rising ire. What could have happened? Behind him, his parents' footsteps mounted.

When Nathaniel swept open the bedroom door, a pungent odor assaulted his nose. He froze. Crumpled on the floor lay Delia, unconscious, with shattered pieces of a basin scattered across the floor.

He dashed to her side and pressed his fingers against her neck. The smell of vomit twisted his insides.

"What on earth?" Mother gaped, pressing her hand against her chest.

"She's fainted. Looks like from vomiting." Nathaniel slid his hand under Delia's head, elevating it. "You didn't happen to bring smelling salts with the supplies, did you?"

Mother blinked away the bewilderment from her eyes. "No,

but a few handfuls of snow should bring her around. I'll get some." Pivoting on her heel, she rushed from the room.

Awkwardly, Nathaniel patted Delia's cheek. "Miss Evans. Miss Evans, can you hear me?"

Maneuvering farther into the room with his crutch, Father frowned. "What is going on here?"

"I'll explain when Mother returns." Nathaniel patted Delia's cheek a bit harder, but to no avail.

Moments later, Mother brought a snowball cupped in her mittened hands. Kneeling beside Nathaniel, she rubbed it across Delia's forehead before touching it to her neck.

The young woman's eyelids fluttered, followed by her gasp.

"There now," Mother soothed. "You'll be all right."

Horror rippled across Delia's face. "No. No." Her gaze bounced around the room until she found Nathaniel next to her still cradling her head. "Please help."

"It'll be all right, Miss Evans. You're with friends. These are my parents, Daniel and Maggie Hawkins. Mother heard you fall. You must've fainted."

Lifting trembling fingers to her lips, Delia winced. "The sickness hit me harder than usual. I tried to keep quiet but ..." She allowed Nathaniel to lift her onto her feet and ease her into a sitting position on the bedside. "My legs are weak."

"I should say so." Raising the window, Mother dropped the remnants of the snowball outside. After lowering the window sash, she tugged off her mittens and stuffed them in her skirt's pocket.

"I'm sorry for the mess," Delia murmured.

"Don't trouble your head another minute." Mother scanned her from head to toe. "At least, you're not seriously hurt."

Nathaniel racked his brain for an explanation of their situation. He crossed his arms. "I need to ask you both not to tell anyone about Miss Evans. She is in hiding. I found her already here when I arrived last evening."

"I thought the place was abandoned." Delia twisted her fingers together, her pale face draining of any remaining color.

"I'd say no harm has been done. We won't tell anyone of your whereabouts. Are you in danger?" Father used the gentle tone he always reserved for a spooked horse. In truth, Delia's panicked expression bespoke her desire to bolt.

"If I'm found, yes."

"Have you committed a crime?"

"No, sir. I've only run away."

Mother settled on the mattress next to Delia. "You're welcome to stay at our place. You would be safe. There'd be no risk to your reputation."

Delia braved a weak smile, her voice threaded with sudden tears. "Thank you, but I have no reputation to speak of." She placed a hand on her stomach. "It's best I stay here. The more I move around, the more I risk being found."

Sympathy entered Mother's eyes. "But you can't hide forever."

"That's true, but I'll be moving on when I'm able."

No one mentioned the unborn babe, but the unspoken thought loomed heavily in the room. Father straightened and moved toward the doorway. "No need to plan too far ahead for now. Take the days one at a time. We'll do all we can to help."

Patting Delia's shoulder, Mother rose. "We certainly will. Nathaniel, help Miss Evans downstairs. She needs the warmth of the fire. I'll be down after I finish cleaning."

An hour later, Nathaniel stood on the porch with his folks while Delia remained inside. The breeze whistled around the eaves of the house, a somber sound to match their mood.

"She has told you nothing about herself?" Mother squinted against the sunlight bouncing off the snow.

"No more than what she shared with you, but I haven't told her much about myself either." Nathaniel rubbed his scrubby beard. "She might think me a murderer."

Father frowned, unamused. "A released murderer? Hardly. You need to find out why she's hiding."

"It might help if you were forthcoming with her." Mother touched Nathaniel's arm.

A chill unrelated to the wind snaked down his spine. Revisiting the past tortured him. Mercy, he could hardly face the present, and thoughts of the future petrified him.

"I'll do what I can."

His folks shared a look full of concern before descending the steps. When they reached the bottom, Father tightened a scarf around his face, his next words muffled. "We'll be praying, son. The Lord will make a way."

Waving, Nathaniel watched them until they were out of sight, the familiar loneliness nipping at him like baying bloodhounds.

He reeled from the explosive memories. His pulse hammered his temples while the sounds deluged his mind. In one shoulder, an old, scarred gunshot wound burned. His fingers grasped the spot.

Would there ever come a day when danger wouldn't trail him?

DELIA EXHALED a long breath as the last of the nausea faded. Without warning, the babe kicked, and Delia pressed the spot with her hand. Soon the little one would run out of room, nearing the journey into the world.

Neither of them was ready.

Nathaniel returned inside, the creaking door hinges interrupting her worries. Snow swirled around the soles of his boots. After unbuttoning his coat and removing his tattered hat, he hung them on a peg near the door.

"Are you feeling better?" He barely glanced in her direction.

"Yes, thank you." She still didn't know whether to be relieved or wary when in his presence. Her limited experience with men hadn't prepared her for someone like him. After she had fainted, Nathaniel had been attentive, even concerned. Now, however, he had locked any tender emotions beneath a taut mask.

He eyed the trunk on the table, slowly approaching it. He tunneled a hand through the sandy mane almost reaching his shoulders.

What must he look like under such a mass of hair? Mostly, it cloaked his expressions, making it hard for Delia to gauge him.

Nathaniel touched the trunk's lid, his fingers absently tracing the woodgrain. Shadows of unspoken thoughts clouded his eyes.

The awkward silence squeezed Delia's ribcage. Better to break the tense quiet than endure it. She moistened her lips with the tip of her tongue.

"Your folks seem like good people."

Not a flicker of emotion passed over his face. "They are."

While she grasped for something else to say, Nathaniel lifted the lid and peered inside. For a moment, he hesitated before pulling out a thick book. The shadows in his eyes burned into a glower. He chucked the book to the side as though it scorched his fingers.

Before she could stop herself, Delia leaped from the chair. "A Bible? Oh, may I?"

Nathaniel jerked his head up in surprise. "You want to read it?"

"Yes, please."

Pulling his gaze away from hers, he nodded, staring into the trunk once more. Curious, Delia ventured a look. Another smaller box, carved with the initial *H*, lay inside.

Nathaniel lifted it out and set it beside the trunk. "These are my family's woodcarving tools."

"I can't think of anything more fitting than putting a Bible with tools," she mused.

"What do you mean?"

"Without God's Word, it's mighty hard to carve out a life. These belong to your father?"

"They've belonged to the Hawkins family for a long time, passed down through the generations. Father used them all my life. He taught me everything about woodwork. Now, he's given them to me." He clamped his eyes shut.

"You don't sound very pleased."

"At one time, I would've been."

"What about now?"

His chest expanded then fell. "I'm at a loss."

Delia blinked. What could she say? She focused instead on the trunk. "What else is in here? It doesn't look like a place to hold provisions."

"It's not." Nathaniel drew aside a quilted cloth protecting the second layer beneath.

Rounding the table, Delia drew closer. Straw lined the bottom and sides of the trunk, cradling a crude-looking stable. Individual items, wrapped in cloth, lay inside it.

Confused, she tilted her head to one side. "What is this?"

Without answering, Nathaniel picked up one of the pieces and unwound the yellowed fabric to reveal a carved sheep. He set it aside on the table. Plucking up another piece, he unwrapped a woman carved in simple clothing. Next came a baby lying in a sort of trough. Then another sheep. Last, Nathaniel unwrapped a man holding a staff.

Delia surveyed the wooden figures. "They all belong together?"

"Yes. It's my family's nativity."

A sense of wonder enveloped Delia. She leaned closer to study one of the sheep. "These are beautiful, Mr. Hawkins. I've never seen a crèche."

He must have guessed Delia's desire to examine them. Nathaniel picked up the figure of Mary and held it out to her.

"Father made this one. The nativity began a few generations ago but remained unfinished. Father added most of the pieces, intending to pass it on to the next generation."

Emotion tightened Delia's throat. "I see the love etched in them. The detail is amazing." She lifted the baby's piece. "The story of Christ's birth displayed by your family is a treasure."

Shifting on his feet, Nathaniel said nothing.

After setting down Mary and the Christ child, she lifted the figure of the man. "Is this Joseph?"

"No, it's a shepherd." A pained expression furrowed Nathaniel's forehead. "When I was a child, Father started a carving of Joseph but decided instead to let me have the honor when he passed the set to me. It's there." He dipped his head toward the last wrapped, unfinished piece.

"He has given it to you to finish."

Nathaniel shook his head. "I can't."

"You can't or won't?"

Rather than answer, Nathaniel grabbed a cloth. Unable to squelch the quaking in his fingers, he wound it around the babe in the manger.

Delia pressed a restraining hand on his arm. "Please don't put them away. Wouldn't it be nice to set them out, especially at this time of year? You could work on Joseph. There's still time before Christmas."

Nathaniel froze. Scowling, he stared down at Delia's hand. With a sharp intake of breath, she snatched it back and twisted her fingers together.

"I'm sorry. I didn't mean to overstep. They're such lovely things that I—"

"I don't see why a woman like you would take interest in ..." Leaving the words unspoken, Nathaniel's heated glance seared the words into Delia's core.

She took a step backward. "In what? Religion, the Bible? Forgiveness?" Balling her hands into fists, she dug her fingernails into the palms of her hand. "No, indeed. Why would *such* a woman, like me?"

Gathering her skirts, she fled from the room. Up the stairs, she scrambled—away from Nathaniel's condemnation, tripping over the shattered fragments of her heart.

If only she could wrap them up and pack them away so easily.

Six

"What have I done?" Nathaniel shoved himself from the table and trudged to the window. After raising it, he pushed open the shutters, allowing the cold air to slap his flaming cheeks.

He ground his teeth, loathing himself. He had wounded her. Badly. The harsh words had boiled up from within. Why?

An unbidden scripture flashed through his mind. *For out of the abundance of the heart the mouth speaks. A good man out of the good treasure of his heart brings forth good things, and an evil man out of the evil treasure brings forth evil things.*

What lurked inside him? Nathaniel had condemned Delia without knowing anything about her. Of all people, he should've understood. The pain of condemnation, shame, and separation throbbed with every beat of his heart.

Delia was a woman of conscience. Her words and actions testified clearly. He remembered her prayer before the meal, her delight in the Bible. Also, the way she admired the Nativity reached deeper than mere curiosity. In the little time they had spent together, the abundance of her spirit shone clearly.

Yet he had lashed out in anger.

Nathaniel splayed his hands on each side of the window

frame and leaned into the breeze. He filled his lungs, hoping to displace the ache in his chest. He closed his eyes, ignoring the yearning of his soul for his heavenly Father.

In his hour of need, the One he needed most had failed to shield him. His capture and imprisonment had provoked nothing but silence from heaven.

> Behold, I go forward, but he is not there; and
>> backward, but I cannot perceive him:
> On the left hand, where he doth work, but I
>> cannot behold him: he hideth himself on the
>> right hand, that I cannot see him ...

Opening his eyes, Nathaniel scanned the fading blue horizon of the sunset. Perhaps he had been too full of anger to listen. What did the Word say about bitter and sweet fountains?

Indeed, the waters of his soul were bitter.

Nathaniel straightened. Lowering the window, he turned back to the hushed room, listening for any sounds upstairs. None came. His guilt swelled.

On the table, the nativity figures lay disheveled, neglected fragments of a story separated by time, waiting for its conclusion. Nathaniel couldn't think of anyone else less qualified than him to leave his mark on the collection.

The flames crackled in the fireplace, an enticing invitation to cast every single reminder of his faith into the amber blaze. He flexed his fingers. How easy it would be.

But the absence of those things wouldn't purge them from his memory.

The invisible weight on his soul pressed harder. He neared the table and reached inside the trunk. One unwrapped figure still lay within the stable. Nathaniel removed the cloth to examine the unfinished carving. Joseph.

Father had barely started it before deciding to leave it for him. Turning the carving over in his palm, Nathaniel envisioned the finished work from its sandals to its facial expression.

How had Joseph coped with his circumstances?

Nathaniel reviewed the few details of the silent character who helped shape the boy Jesus. Life had etched certain traits in Joseph.

Faithful. He obeyed God without question, without hesitation.

At one time, Nathaniel did the same, but tragedy had come of it.

Honorable. Though Joseph initially doubted Mary's story, he listened to God's command and honored his commitment to her. Nowhere did he reproach or shame his wife.

Humble. No matter the dangers, regardless of the separation in Egypt from their people, Joseph kept the faith. He prevailed.

Nathaniel, on the other hand, had failed.

Rubbing his thumb across the wood, he sighed. Time behind bars couldn't rectify the past. If it had, he could live with it. But someone else had died because of his mistake. He was forever shackled to the reality. Waking or sleeping, it dogged him, dangling peace outside his grasp.

Carving a figure of Joseph would be a mockery. Neither Father nor Delia understood.

Nathaniel strained his ears for any sound upstairs but nothing moved. He rewrapped the piece of wood and laid it aside. Time to focus on other pressing matters. Sighing, he headed to the pantry to retrieve the bed warmer.

After scooping a heap of glowing embers into the brass warmer and securing its lid, he set it carefully aside. Next, he dipped the remaining stew into a bowl. Grasping it in one hand, Nathaniel picked up the bed warmer.

Time to reckon with at least one of his wrongs.

Shadows lengthened throughout the house as it welcomed dusk. The stairs creaked beneath Nathaniel's feet, fracturing the heavy silence as he neared the upstairs landing. His pulse ticked up a notch.

Several more steps brought him to Delia's door. Because of his laden hands, he lightly tapped it with the toe of his boot.

"Miss Evans? Might I have a word?" He cleared his hoarse throat.

"Say on." Her strained voice slipped under the closed door.

"Could you please open the door?" Nathaniel hoped his benign tone put her at ease.

The rustle of her skirts answered him. A second later, the door inched open, and Delia's glance swept over him. Her eyes widened.

For emphasis, Nathaniel lifted the bowl in one hand and the bed warmer in the other. "May I bring these inside?"

Delia bit her lip, hesitating several heartbeats before stepping aside to widen the gap enough for him to enter.

"Thank you." Nathaniel lowered the bedwarmer onto the hearth, where the morning's embers flickered. "I brought stew. Figured you might be hungry." He set the bowl on the bureau, noticing he had forgotten a spoon.

He braved a look at her. With crossed arms, she hugged her body as though shielding herself from him. An unexpected pang jabbed his gut.

"I forgot something. Excuse me." His lame words dangled in the air between them as he hurried to get a spoon from downstairs. When he returned, Nathaniel found Delia standing in the same position, frozen.

The spoon clinked too loudly as he laid it in the bowl, charging the atmosphere even further. From the corner of his eyes, he saw her flinch.

Now to face her.

"Miss Evans, I did a grave wrong earlier. I hurt you without cause." Nathaniel's voice crackled like sandpaper. "You didn't deserve it, and I'm ... I'm sorry."

He spied Delia's red-rimmed eyes and traces of tears on her swollen cheeks. What an utter fool he was.

Shock passed over her face, slackening her jaw. Her reply came hardly louder than a whisper. "I'm not used to apologies, Mr. Hawkins. I'm not sure of what to say except ... thank you."

Her kindness astounded Nathaniel. "You owe me no thanks." Striving to keep the sudden tremor out of his knees, he crossed to the fireplace and stoked the flames after adding the wood he chopped that morning.

Delia watched his every movement, the weight of her stare burning into the back of his broad shoulders. Standing, Nathaniel dusted his hands on his pants and gestured to the bed warmer. "It will stay hot as long as it's near the fire. I've already put embers inside, so you need only to pass it between the covers to warm the bed."

"It will help greatly." She unfolded her arms, her rigid stance relaxing slightly.

Nathaniel stepped toward the doorway. "If you need anything else, please tell me."

Swallowing, Delia nodded.

Closing the door behind him, Nathaniel stepped onto the landing and released a pent-up breath.

Seven

Despite a troubled spirit, Delia slept like one who might never wake, dreamless and deep. Early the next morning, while the sunrise splayed rays along the bedroom's walls and furniture, she sat on the edge of the bed and unbraided her hair.

All the while, she thought of Nathaniel.

What a strange man of contradictions. Never had anyone apologized to her, especially a man. Other than her mother, who had died when Delia was fourteen, no one had bothered looking after her needs. Her father had been too consumed with his own.

She pulled a comb through her long, chestnut tresses, puzzling over a man who showed remorse for hurting her. Like waves undulating along a shoreline, Nathaniel's words surged through her mind again and again.

I hurt you without cause.

A foreign sensation hummed within her. Try as she might, she couldn't name it. Laying aside the comb on the dresser, she tugged the ribbon from her skirt pocket and tied back her hair. Perhaps Mrs. Hawkins might lend her a few hairpins. In her hasty departure during the night from her home, Delia had forgotten hers.

You didn't deserve it, and I'm ... I'm sorry.

Nathaniel's sorrowful apology warmed something frozen surrounding Delia's heart. A piece of it crumbled, yet she didn't feel vulnerable like a caged animal.

Instead, Delia tasted freedom, albeit carefully. How strange. His words and deeds unshackled her spirit, even from wrongs not of his doing.

"Lord," she murmured, "show me how I can help Mr. Hawkins. Underneath his hardness, I believe there's something good."

The Bible and the nativity pointed to a background of faith, but Nathaniel resisted it. Delia recalled the haunted expression on his face as he showed her the figures and shared their history. The raw anger in his eyes when she had touched his arm and encouraged him to finish Joseph.

Then she understood. His outburst had nothing to do with her presence or her condition. Nathaniel was warring against himself and the God of his fathers. Whatever had driven him to prison still held him captive.

Closing her fingers around the door latch, Delia braced herself for whatever the day held in store. Sunlight spilled into the downstairs. Nathaniel must have opened all the shutters. What a difference it made to the shrouded, cheerless rooms. Delia dragged in a shuddering breath and crept down the steps.

She stuttered to a stop on the threshold, the sight in the parlor stunning her.

Standing hunched in front of a mirrored washstand, Nathaniel poised a pair of scissors over the top of his head while grasping a clump of his sandy hair in his other hand.

Delia held out her hand. "Wait. Don't do it."

Startled, Nathaniel jerked upright and lowered his arms. "I'm about to cut my hair."

"From what I saw, you're about to butcher it."

Nathaniel shrugged in frustration. "What else can I do? I can stand it no longer."

Sympathy tugged at Delia. What a picture he had made, slouched over the washstand, wearing a fresh change of homespun clothes brought by his mother while the rest of him remained unkempt. Like a bushy scrub oak in the fall.

Turning his attention back to the mirror, Nathaniel lifted the scissors. Delia hurried across the room, her tone insistent. "I'll do it."

Nathaniel's reflection frowned, unsure. "I can manage."

"I daresay you can't." Delia shook her head. "I've cut my father's hair plenty of times. I'm fairly adept."

"But I'm not your father."

For a moment, Delia's gaze faltered beneath his steady one. Cutting Nathaniel's hair would bring her far too close for comfort. Could she trust him?

She lifted her eyes and found his blue ones studying her with a bemused twinkle. Her spine stiffened with resolve. Surely, if she could stand to cut her father's hair, she should have no trouble clipping Nathaniel's.

Braving a few steps closer, she stretched out her palm. "Nor am I your mother. The scissors, please."

Nathaniel grunted but handed them to her along with a comb. After dragging the nearest chair to the washstand, he sat.

While Delia began her task, the silence crowded around them, thickening the air. Delia's tongue clung to the roof of her mouth. Should she focus solely on Nathaniel's mess of hair or make conversation?

Nathaniel's throat bobbed. "Did you rest?"

"Yes. The bed warmer helped."

"Good."

Petitioning a silent prayer for courage, Delia willed herself to remain steady. "Mr. Hawkins, I'd like to explain why I'm here."

"You don't owe me any explanation."

Delia nodded. "Yes, I do. It's hard to speak of, but I'll do my best."

Nathaniel averted his glance, focusing on another spot in the room as if to give her a little space. Delia continued working while gathering the right words.

"My mother died after I turned fourteen. She taught me her love for God. I gave my life to Him when I was still a child. My father had no use for our faith. He cared for his way, especially his whiskey."

Nathaniel's shoulders grew rigid.

"We have a neighbor, Clive Royce, who is a friend of Father's. He owns a local tavern, you see. He asked Father for my hand in marriage, but I refused."

"Might I ask why?"

Delia's skin pebbled while memories assaulted her. "He's a bad man. Greedy like Father, refusing to stop until he gets exactly what he wants. So he offered Father money to marry me. Twenty dollars."

"That's quite a sum." Nathaniel curled his fingers around the arms of the chair, his knuckles whitening.

"Father accepted the terms, but I still refused. He raved at me, said I'd marry Clive or else. A few evenings later, Clive came calling. I was alone." Delia's heart thrashed against her ribcage. "I know Father left me there on purpose."

The rest of the story lodged itself in her throat. Shame and rage coursed through her veins. Blinking away hot tears, Delia snapped the scissors through a shock of sandy hair.

Nathaniel hissed, "Are you saying Clive took advantage of you?"

Her watery rasp answered him.

To her surprise, he sprang from the seat, his glare murderous. "Where is the man?"

Delia's knees trembled. "No, Mr. Hawkins. It's better this way. I can't speak of the weeks afterward, especially when I discovered I was ... with child. They thought I'd be shamed into marrying, so they waited, believing I'd give in. I almost did." Tears severed the rest of her words.

A hint of compassion softened the hardness in Nathaniel's face. "So you ran away instead."

Nodding, Delia brushed her sleeve across her eyes. "In the dead of night. Father had been drinking, which meant he'd sleep most of the next day. I took his horse and some provisions."

"Where do you come from?"

"Near Lewisburg."

She watched him mentally calculate the distance. He blew out a breath. "You traveled a bit over two hundred miles."

"I avoided the roads when possible. Hid mostly during the day, moved at night. About fifteen miles from here, I sold the horse to a man traveling to Pennsylvania. I needed the money for food."

"The dried peaches?" Nathaniel crinkled his brow.

Delia grimaced. "I was down to the last bit of food when you showed up. I'd stopped at a store and bought turnips and potatoes along with them. I walked the rest of the way, till I could go no farther. When I found this house, I thought surely God had directed my path." Delia grimaced and shuffled her feet. "I told your father I'd committed no crime, but I did take my father's horse."

Nathaniel shook his head and appraised Delia as though seeing her for the first time. Something akin to respect warmed his gaze. "You did a courageous thing, Miss Evans. I'll do all in my power to protect you and the child."

His assurance washed over her wounded spirit like warm, healing waters. No matter his past, she sensed the truth in his demeanor.

"I won't stay a moment longer than necessary."

Nathaniel lowered himself in the chair once more and glanced at Delia through the mirror's reflection. "Looking too far ahead is troublesome." His voice roughened like gravel. "I'm glad you told me."

A bit of the shame and disgrace lifted from her soul. "Thank you for understanding." Delia raised the scissors and focused on

Nathaniel's hair while he stared at a nondescript point in the mirror.

What on earth was he thinking?

~

NATHANIEL PATTED his bare face with the towel and gawked at himself, grateful Delia had retired upstairs to take a nap and give him privacy.

The absence of a beard had erased ten years from his appearance. A distinct line divided his face between the pale skin long hidden by the thick scruff and his weathered complexion. The shoulder-length, scraggly hair was cropped short, revealing the soft waves he'd forgotten. Delia's work was more than fairly adept. He didn't recognize himself.

Though, inside, he still felt the same. A groan bubbled up his throat.

From outside, a muffled "Halloo!" scattered Nathaniel's thoughts. Snatching his coat from the peg, he shrugged into it and opened the door. A horse, carrying a lady riding sidesaddle, stomped its hoofs while standing in place.

The woman loosened the scarf around her face. A bright, rosy flush tinged her cheeks and the tip of her nose. Crossing the threshold, Nathaniel clenched his jaw. How many times had she haunted his dreams, the expression on her face identical to the one present now—taut, arrogant, and remorseless? Carrie Kimball had ruined him.

As she dipped her head in greeting, her gaze scraped over him. "Mr. Hawkins."

Nathaniel didn't return the gesture. "Missus ..." He left the question suspended, unsure of the answer.

"Mrs. Hampton." Not a flicker of the past softened her features.

Of course. Made perfect sense. Mr. Kimball had always favored a match between William Hampton and Carrie.

Nathaniel leaned against the porch post. "What do you want here? You've strayed a bit too far from home."

She ignored the bite in his words. "It's not for myself, I assure you. I've come to ask your assistance."

Nathaniel's brows arched. "To what do I owe this honor?"

Carrie's façade cracked. Squirming in the saddle, she steeled her tone. "Adam ran away yesterday."

Nathaniel recalled the Kimball slave, a good man, faithful to their family. He narrowed his eyes. "You've come to the wrong place."

Crimping her lips together, Carrie shook her head. "That's not why I'm here. Father and several others went after him. Late last night, they returned without Adam or Father. In the confusion after nightfall, my father became separated from his men. Another round of snowfall didn't help matters."

"It's foolhardy to go on a manhunt this time of year."

"I'm aware." She gripped the pommel of the saddle. "The men have searched all day but have found no trace of either of them."

Nathaniel scanned the gray horizon. "I don't imagine. More snow is coming."

A bit of desperation threaded Carrie's words. "You are the best tracker in the area. You know every nook and cranny of these parts better than most. If anyone can find Father, you can."

Heat seared down Nathaniel's spine. He shoved himself away from the porch post and glowered at the woman he once loved. "You're asking a lot of me."

Carrie's lips quivered. "I'm prepared to pay you for your trouble."

A mirthless laugh escaped him. "Pay me? You have your nerve, showing your face here, asking me to risk my life to find your father."

"Will you do it?"

"No."

She struck the saddle's pommel with her fist. "But he may die!"

"So may Adam, but he's not your concern. So might I, but that's irrelevant."

"Adam is probably far safer wherever he is than Father." Carrie's chin wobbled. "I can't believe you would let him—or any man—die if you could save him."

The utter gall of the woman. Nathaniel ground his teeth. "I tried to save a man once. Your father hunted us down. Thanks to you, a good man died."

Her mouth gaped. For once, he'd rendered her speechless. A biting gust of wind sliced between them, moaning through the bare tree branches. Nathaniel turned toward the door without a backward glance.

"You'd best hurry home, Mrs. Hampton, before the snow overtakes you."

Eight

Leaning over the table, Delia added vegetables into an iron pot prepared for stew. Before her nap, she had cleaned and pared the vittles.

Nathaniel thrust the door shut, returning inside. Jerking off his coat, he tossed it on the peg. When he swung toward her, she gasped, covering her mouth with her hand.

"Your face."

Nathaniel grazed his hand across the bare skin, the scowl receding from his features. "I shaved," he said absently.

A nervous laugh lifted the corners of her mouth. "So you have. You look human." In reality, his pleasing face possessed an earnest, straightforward quality. Cheekbones set not too high, a firm jaw, and a cleft chin. World-weary eyes pierced her, driving a sharp ache deep within her soul.

"Do I?" He growled, the blistering question twisting the ache further still. The hidden inquiry begged to be answered.

Delia weighed her response carefully. "What happened outside just now, did it set you free?"

"How much did you hear?"

"Before my nap, I cracked my window for fresh air. When I first heard her calling, I nearly jumped off the bed. The conversation wasn't hard to hear." She didn't bother adding she'd gone downstairs, listened at the door, and scrambled to add vegetables to the waiting pot when Nathaniel's footsteps neared.

"Eavesdropping, I see."

"I can't deny it." She'd even pressed her ear against the crack of the door. She braced herself for a possible outburst.

Instead, Nathaniel trudged to the nearby chair and slumped down onto it. Resting his elbows on his knees, he buried his face in his hands.

Delia swallowed in surprise. Eruptions of anger were commonplace in her life. Dealing with its absence swept her out of her element.

While the silence lengthened, she poured water from a stoneware pitcher into the pot, then added salt. The spoon scraped while she stirred. Potatoes, carrots, onions, garlic, and herbs—courtesy of Nathaniel's folks—swirled in the liquid, the colors reminiscent of a stained-glass window.

"There's more between you and the lady, I gather. Two people can't speak such words, otherwise."

"At one time, yes."

Delia dropped several strips of dried beef into the mixture. "Mr. Hawkins, I shared my story with you earlier. It was one of the hardest things I've ever done. I'd appreciate the same in kind."

Lifting his head, Nathaniel scrutinized her, his stare assessing whether or not he could trust her. Finally, he pulled in a lungful of air and then released it slowly.

"We were engaged to be married."

Somehow, the truth twisted her insides, even though she'd suspected they had been sweethearts. Delia composed her face to betray nothing. He was barely more than a stranger, after all. "I'm listening."

"A slave farther south had run away. I found him hiding early one morning in my barn. He was frightened and hungry. Lost. I assured him he was safe. Franklin was his name." Memories dimmed Nathaniel's gaze. "He told me where he was heading. While he rested for a few days, I discretely asked a few of Mr. Kimball's servants if they knew someone who could help.

"No one would talk, but one of them came to me around midnight. He told me where to take Franklin. Another servant told Carrie—Mrs. Hampton." Nathaniel clenched his hands together until the blood fled from his knuckles. "In turn, she told her father."

"How horrible." Outrage burned Delia's chest.

Nathaniel clamped his eyelids shut. "We were almost to safety when Kimball and his men caught up with us. We were no match for their hounds." Emotion rippled across his face. "They shot me through the shoulder. But they murdered Franklin."

The spoon in Delia's fingers clattered onto the table. For several minutes, the crackling fire and whistling wind filled the empty spaces of their thoughts.

"I should be dead, not Franklin," he whispered at last.

"I have no words. To be betrayed in such a way by ..." Delia bit her lower lip to quell sharp tears. "So that's why you went to prison."

Nathaniel bolted from the chair, almost knocking it over. "Now she comes asking *me* to track her father." His fingers kneaded the back of his neck.

The tortured look on his face knotted Delia's stomach. She, too, grappled with conscience and the will. She rounded the table, drawing closer to him. A decent man like Nathaniel must never put his honor to death. If he refused to help, he would never be free of his bitterness.

"Can you live with knowing you could've saved Kimball's life, regardless of his deeds? Is it possible, Mr. Hawkins?"

"If someone asked you to save Clive from death, would you?"

The question speared her soul, laying it bare. Quivering, Delia risked stoking his anger by laying her hand on his arm, but she needed to somehow reach him. She met his challenging stare.

"May God forgive me, but I would not."

The inner storm driving Nathaniel collapsed beneath the honesty of her reply. His shoulders drooped. Tears brightened his intent stare.

Then he did the unexpected.

He grazed his hand across hers.

A few hours later, the roughened warmth of his palm still radiated along Delia's knuckles, even after she had retired for the evening.

Though his touch lasted only a second, it mended a sore spot in her soul. She had hastily excused herself while Nathaniel had set the pot of stew over the fire. Afterward, she had failed to taste one drop of stew.

No man had ever touched her in such a gentle manner. Delia tugged the quilts halfway over her head and shifted to her side. A dull pain tightened the span of her waist. She massaged the taut muscles, a surge of apprehension prickling her skin. Soon, the babe would come.

Would she love this child born of force?

"Please, Lord, help me love this little one. It cannot help what happened." Long minutes passed, the firelight flickering along the walls, and the muscles relaxed. Her thoughts, however, tangled together like a knotted skein of yarn.

How would she provide for her child? The responsible thing would be to give the baby to a good family. Moisture stung Delia's eyes. Everything within her rebelled at the notion. Though the way would be clear for both of them, could she bear to give up this part of herself?

Her empty arms ached. Perhaps she did love this child.

Yet she saw no other way forward.

Stretching his legs, Nathaniel eyed the family trunk he'd shoved into the corner the night he humiliated Delia. Regret gnawed at him.

She embraced courage, fleeing a long distance from a hopeless future—all to protect herself and her unborn child. She placed her dubious trust in him—a stranger, a criminal in the eyes of the law. A man.

Delia had suffered at the hands of his kind. Yet she exhibited bravery when questioning his conscience. Her tremulous approach shook him when she touched his arm. No doubt she had been remembering his previous heated response. The memory twisted like a knife in his chest. Still, she had risked stoking his bitterness to expose his turmoil, the feud between right and wrong.

Her honesty had obliterated all of his defenses.

Did he possess the same kind of courage?

Standing, Nathaniel flexed his fingers. He needed to do something to settle his emotions and clarify his thoughts. From its corner, the trunk invited him to rediscover past hopes, dreams, and faith.

Faith. Somehow Delia believed he could find the strength to help Kimball. Lifting the trunk's lid, Nathaniel peered down at the very things symbolizing his family's struggles. Yet each carving also testified of their victories. What did the way forward hold for him?

He lifted out the unfinished figure of Joseph, wondering if this man had ever grappled with loss.

> Behold, I go forward, but he is not there; and
> backward, but I cannot perceive him ...

Laying aside the piece, Nathaniel removed the box of tools and then opened it. The adze, mallet, and carving tools beckoned, but would retracing the stories bring more pain? Could he endure the confrontation?

> On the left hand, where he doth work, but I
> cannot behold him …

After unwrapping Joseph, Nathaniel gathered the carving tools, the heavy weight foreign in his hands. He laid the tools on the table and then sat, turning the wood over in his palm, thoughts of Father filling him.

Hard times often shrouded God from view, yet he was never hidden from God. How many times had Father reminded Nathaniel of this? The crack of gunfire and Franklin's lifeless blood had driven him into darkness. Twenty-four months behind bars deepened it.

> He hideth himself on the right hand, that I cannot
> see him …

"Where were You, Lord?"

The shutters rattled against the frosted windows. Somewhere out there, the cold, pitiless storm trapped Kimball in its frigid grasp, perhaps forever. Yet it failed to satisfy Nathaniel.

Reaching over, he poised a carving knife in his hand while examining the figure his Father had begun. For now, he needed to calm his racing thoughts while the storm moaned around the house.

Nathaniel laid the blade on the wood then swiped it across the surface. Slowly, one stroke followed another, each growing more methodical.

Into the night, sleep eluded him, but the passage of time faded while the wood took shape between his fingers. The faith of his family and Joseph, though separated over a thousand years, spoke of God's everlasting faithfulness.

They overcame loss, dangers, poverty, and uncertainty. No matter where the journey had taken them, it always led to Him.

But he knoweth the way that I take: when he hath
tried me, I shall come forth as gold.

Mid-stroke, Nathaniel paused, awe thrumming around his soul. How had he forgotten the next part of the passage? Straightening his back, he rolled his stiff shoulders, suddenly shaken awake.

Though hardship had obscured Nathaniel's way, the Lord had never lost sight of the path. Nor had He removed His hand from shaping it. All the while, Nathaniel had withdrawn his hold from the Savior.

Puffing out a breath, he set aside everything. With his fingertips, he kneaded his eyelids.

"Forgive me, Lord Jesus."

Time passed while he poured out everything to God—his grief, anger, and confusion. For the first time, he held back nothing. He laid bare the most secret parts of himself.

When he finally lifted his head, a peaceful quiet filled every corner of the house. The sweetness permeated his soul. Then he realized a wonderous thing.

Outside, the storm had ceased.

Nine

"Are you going to look for Mr. Kimball?" After coming downstairs, Delia surveyed the two cloth sacks Nathaniel stuffed with dried provisions. Beside them lay two leather canteens, a bundle of kindling, a muzzle-loading rifle, a shovel, and snowshoes.

Nathaniel tied the bundles shut. "Yes."

"What changed your mind?"

Instead of a frown, a smile twitched Nathaniel's lips. "The Lord and I had a talk."

"Oh." She studied his face, noting the placid features void of misery. A wave of relief unfurled within Delia, startling her. How, in such a short time, had his peace become important to her?

With the canteens in hand, Nathaniel paused to observe her. "You look exhausted."

Honestly, she had tossed most of the night. Trying not to squirm under his steady gaze, Delia smoothed her skirt. "I had a difficult time sleeping. My back and side hurt at times."

His glance flicked to her stomach then returned to her face. "I'm going to my folks' for a pair of mules. I'll send Mother and Father to stay with you in case the baby comes while I'm gone."

"Thank you. I hate to be a nuisance, but it greatly eases my mind."

Nathaniel gave her a full smile that reached his eyes. "It's no bother." He held up the canteens. "I'll fill these at the well before setting off."

The first rays of sunlight glittered across the snowy yard while Nathaniel trudged to the well. Delia rubbed her arms. Would it be too late to save Mr. Kimball? Had he found a safe place during the storm?

Something near the fireplace caught the corner of Delia's eye. On the floor, sitting beside the hearth, was the nativity.

"Oh." She whisked over and knelt to inspect the figures. The stable sheltered the sheep, shepherd, Mary, and the baby Jesus, but another carving stood beside the mother. Tears pooled in her eyes, blurring the scene.

Delia picked up Joseph and traced her fingers along the planes of his face and robe—the woodwork intricate, each detail revealing the depth of Nathaniel's skill.

His footsteps thumped the porch as he stomped the snow from his boots. After entering, Nathaniel closed the door and caught Delia's gaze.

"I see you found them."

"These are beautiful. I can tell each one has been made with much thought and love." She held up Joseph. "Did you finish this last night?"

Nathaniel laid the leather canteens on the table and nodded. "It gave me plenty of time to think and pray."

Delia lowered the figure to its rightful place beside Mary. "You do excellent work. I'll spend many hours finding joy in this."

A flush crept up his neck, but he looked pleased. "In that case, it was worth the sleepless night."

Warmth bloomed into her cheeks. Clearing her throat, Delia rose from the floor and dusted off her hands. "I'll be praying for your and Mr. Kimball's safe return."

Nathaniel glanced out the window and scanned the sky. "I appreciate it. The weather will be favorable, I believe." He swung his gaze back to her. "I'm heading to my folks' now. I'll be back in a while with the mules."

After fastening the snowshoes to his boots, Nathaniel covered his head with a hat and wrapped his face in a thick scarf. With a wave, he closed the door behind him.

Delia watched him leave, his smooth strides clipping through the snow while the sun illuminated an azure, rosy sky.

"I SEE you've returned to the land of the livin'." A toothless smile cracked the lips of the aged Black woman as she beckoned Nathaniel inside her cabin. "I'll pour you a bit of coffee."

"I'm much obliged, Aunt Hester." Nathaniel inhaled the scent of salt pork and dried herbs as the warmth of the simple room embraced him. He unfastened his snowshoes and set them aside.

Hester Simms, a free woman known by all as Aunt Hester, lived on the edge of the forestland where, years before, a Quaker family had allotted a small corner of their farm to her.

Runaway slaves often fled through the forest on their way to freedom.

Though no one could prove it, many suspected Aunt Hester of helping the runaways.

"Here ya go." Hester handed Nathaniel a cup.

The heat from its sides drove the ache from Nathaniel's fingers. "Thank you." He lowered himself onto a crude bench and stretched his legs in front of the fireplace. "This is the best coffee I've had in a long time."

Chuckling, Hester poured herself a cup and sat in a chair opposite Nathaniel. "That ain't saying much, considerin' where you've been."

A quiet laugh rumbled in his chest. "No matter, it's still the best."

Hester sipped the liquid. "Thank the Good Lord you're rid of prison. Nasty business. What brings you here? I know it's not my coffee."

Steam curled around the tip of Nathaniel's nose as he lowered the cup from his mouth. "Mr. Kimball has gone missing while looking for his foreman. Adam ran away." He waited for Aunt Hester's reaction.

A steely glint entered her murky eyes. She probed him with her measured stare, weighing his words and countenance. Her jaw tightened.

Nathaniel met her perusal undaunted. "Is Adam safe?"

"You ain't lookin' for him, are you?"

"I'm searching for Mr. Kimball. Unless Adam needs help first."

Aunt Hester tapped the side of her cup with a forefinger. "Didn't Mr. Kimball turn you in? Why would you help the likes of him?"

Nathaniel rubbed his jaw and sighed. "His daughter asked for help. I refused at first but thought better of it later. The Lord has been merciful to me. Would it do me any good to refuse mercy, even to my enemy?"

The lines around Aunt Hester's eyes relaxed. "How often I've faced this struggle. I believe youse a honorable man, or I'd tell you nothin'."

"I'd die before telling."

Lifting the cup, she took another slow sip and swallowed. "Adam is safe. It's all you need to know."

God be praised. A bit of tension eased from the muscles on the back of Nathaniel's neck. He grazed the spot with his hand. "Good. Can you tell me anything to help find Mr. Kimball?"

"He be a wicked man," Aunt Hester huffed, rolling her eyes heavenward. "If it weren't for the Good Book, I'd ..." She chewed her lip. "Head northeast from here, toward the river. If he has any sense left that God gave 'im, he ought to be sheltered under one of the outcroppings near the bank."

"It will be a good start. I'm obliged, Aunt Hester." Nathaniel stood and set the cup on the mantel.

Rising, she grimaced. "Maybe the Good Lord will forgive me now and ease my conscience. Yesterday morning, his men came by, and I sent them on a wild-goose chase."

A broad grin almost crinkled Nathaniel's eyes shut as he shot a glance in her direction. "I reckon I can trust you."

Aunt Hester swatted his shoulder and shooed him toward the door. "With your life, young Hawkins. Godspeed."

Nathaniel mounted the lead mule. From the cloudless sky, sunlight glared across the snow, the bright reflection stinging his eyes. With an urgent kick, he nudged the animal forward toward the shade of the forest.

The Potomac River was a short distance away, just a few miles. Nathaniel's pulse kept time with the mules' rhythm. Every step carried him closer to the spot plaguing his memory. His stomach clenched.

Echoes of the hounds reverberated in his brain—the howls and barks, their crashing through the brush. The shouts of Kimball and his men close behind.

The blood careened through his veins like the unrestrained, rampaging waters of a creek after a downpour. Even in the snow, Nathaniel recognized the spot where everything unraveled two years ago. He closed his eyes, but it did little to obliterate the scenes.

Terrified and unwilling to be captured, Franklin had bolted as though deaf to the screams to halt. Nathaniel sprinted after him, but gunshots fractured the air, a bullet tearing through his shoulder while another one struck the center of Franklin's back.

Minutes later, the man lay dead.

"No!"

Nathaniel lurched in the saddle, his eyes flying open when he realized he'd shouted, just as he had on that awful day. The mules halted. The silence of the forest swallowed the abrupt sound.

He brushed a quivering arm over the sweat pebbling his forehead, his temples thundering. Bile gushed up his throat, and he had no choice but to empty the contents of his stomach into the snow.

How could he see this through?

"It's too much, Lord," he gasped. "I cannot go farther."

Swiveling in the saddle, he reached into one of the sacks and withdrew the Bible. Perhaps this was why he'd felt compelled to bring it. He opened it, and a passage in Jeremiah drew his attention.

> Is there no balm in Gilead; is there no physician
> there ... Oh that I had in the wilderness a
> lodging place of wayfaring men; that I might
> leave my people, and go from them ... an
> assembly of treacherous men ... trust ye not in
> any brother ...

Nathaniel thumbed through the pages, hungry for more.

> Fear thou not, O Jacob my servant, saith the Lord:
> for I am with thee.

The strange mixture of words radiated peace and buoyed his spirit. God had been there before and would be there moving forward. Returning the Bible to its place, Nathaniel murmured a prayer of gratitude.

If Kimball still lived, he was ready to face him.

Ten

"Try not to worry, Miss Evans. My Maggie will get you through."

Daniel Hawkins's encouragement belied his concerned expression while he cut a sideways glance at his wife. Mrs. Hawkins, however, looked placid, as though delivering babies occurred every day.

"With the Good Lord's help, I certainly will." She patted the side of Delia's clammy cheek, her fingers gentle and cool.

"I don't know what to do." Delia rubbed her side while the muscles hardened under another spasm.

"For now, we let time and nature take its course. I'll tell you when it's time to push. Daniel, I'll need your help getting everything ready."

Sending her encouraging smiles, the couple headed downstairs to prepare for the baby's arrival. Feeling helpless, Delia had no choice but to remain abed, sitting up. She leaned against the headboard and stared at the ceiling.

Earlier, after Nathaniel's departure, the pain in Delia's back had grown sharper. By the time his parents arrived, her waters had broken. They found her huddled by the fireplace, weeping.

Mrs. Hawkins had immediately taken the situation in hand,

her assurances stemming Delia's panic. The kind lady had brought several items of Nathaniel's baby clothes, including cloth napkins for the newborn. The personal gesture soothed Delia and quelled her tears.

Embarrassment burned her cheeks. She rarely lost her composure. Living with her father taught Delia to squelch her feelings, to pass over them and get on with whatever task lay at hand.

She relaxed her grasp on the quilt as the spasm receded, her mind swelling with another worry.

"Lord, what will I do about this child? I must find a decent home for him or her." Sweat prickled her neck and forehead. "Lead me. I want to do right."

Straightening her spine and rolling her shoulders, Delia craned her neck to look out the window. The early afternoon sun brightened the white fields and trees with blinding clarity. The shadows in her room shrank farther into the corners.

How does Nathaniel fare? Thank heaven for decent weather. She prayed no snowstorms would interfere with his search. "Father, help him to find Mr. Kimball."

While the physical tension drained from Delia's body, her thoughts lingered on Nathaniel. His courage won her respect, but his humility breached places she had locked away forever. Even from herself.

Though the sensation bewildered her, she refused to banish it, welcoming it instead, like the dawn. Like awakening after a long, merciless dream. Delia filled her lungs. "No matter where I go after this, Lord, I'll always be grateful for these folks. For Nathaniel."

WITH A LOW GROWL, Nathaniel brushed a sleeve across his forehead then cinched the shovel onto the mule. After spending the better part of two hours scouring beneath the outcroppings near the riverbank, he'd found no sign of Kimball.

Frustration coiled within him. Surely Aunt Hester hadn't misled him too. Nathaniel scanned the area, allowing his body to adjust to the frigid, damp air. Earlier, he shucked his heavy coat onto the saddle while he dug a path down to the river's edge. Better to avoid sweating, rather than catching a chill.

Now, what to do? For several minutes, his thoughts recounted every meticulous step. Rushed thinking wouldn't help him find anything. Maybe Kimball didn't reach the Potomac's edge.

Nathaniel ran his fingers over the mule's soft winter fur. "Looks like we'll retrace our path farther back to search along the upper bank." He donned his coat and scarf before mounting. He grasped the reins. "Father, I need Your help."

They made the slow climb to the crest, where Nathaniel turned the mules east. The storm had swept in from the northwest, possibly driving Kimball eastward.

Plodding through the drifts, Nathaniel skimmed the woods for signs of anything unusual, pointing to life. The next half mile dragged like agony, everything concealed.

After loosening a canteen, he swallowed a few mouthfuls of water and noted the shadows of the trees in the afternoon sun. He'd search until the shade stretched long, then make camp.

When he secured the canteen, several large branches low to the ground caught his glance about a hundred yards to his right. Nathaniel squinted. They leaned against a large oak like a makeshift lean-to.

He tightened his legs, urging the mule to quicken his steps. The branches rounded part of the tree, covered partly with brush on their sides, disappearing into the snow.

The clouds of vapor from his mouth quickened with his breathing. There *was* a shelter, buried three-quarters of the way in snow.

Nathaniel reined in the mule and then hopped to the ground.

A hole, no larger than his fist, gaped from one side. He knelt and peered down into it. Something lay there, large but difficult to identify.

"Mr. Kimball?"

No answer.

His chest heaved. With deft strokes, Nathaniel dragged handfuls of snow on either side of himself. He prayed he wasn't too late.

Moments later, his gloved fingers brushed a horse's hair. The animal lay on its side, unmoving. No. No. Heart hammering against his ribcage, Nathaniel scooped faster into the pocket of air until his fingers brushed the saddle blanket, which no longer covered the horse.

"Mr. Kimball." Nathaniel yanked away the cover to find the man underneath, huddled against his steed. Plain as plain, the animal was dead.

Clenching his teeth, Nathaniel whipped off a glove and pressed two fingers against Kimball's neck. Relief washed through him. The pulse beat steady, though weak.

Nathaniel called his name louder as he shoved away more snow. Ironically, the frigid tomb had held enough warmth to keep Kimball alive. He shook the older gentleman roughly.

"You must wake up, sir."

When Kimball didn't stir, Nathaniel shook him again, raising his voice even more. At last, a groan parted Kimball's lips, his eyelids flickering open.

"I've come to take you home." In a few strides, Nathaniel retrieved his second canteen and brought it back to the man. He held it to Kimball's chapped lips. "Here. Take a few sips of water."

Gray, hazy eyes fastened on him. Kimball worked his jaw. "What?" he rasped.

When the drops of water touched his mouth, he blinked. Clutching the canteen, Kimball took a few long draughts before Nathaniel withdrew it.

"Sir, the afternoon will soon be gone. We must leave now."

The words roused Kimball. Pushing himself to sit up, he glanced at his horse. "Baron is dead."

Nathaniel stood and reached down to grasp Kimball's elbow. "It's a shame."

"Am I dreaming?"

"No." Grunting, Nathaniel pulled Kimball to his feet. The older man cried out, his face contorting in pain.

Grasping him, Nathaniel braced himself against the man's weight. "Keep standing. You've almost frozen to death. When you feel you can walk, I'll help you mount my mule."

A judder raced through Kimball. "You are Nathaniel Hawkins?"

The frailty kindled compassion inside him. "Yes."

No words passed between them until Nathaniel helped him mount one of the mules. "Can you hold yourself up?"

Mr. Kimball curled stiff fingers around the rise at the front of the saddle. "I think so."

Satisfied, Nathaniel mounted the other mule and turned in the direction of Taylorstown while leading Kimball's mount. He sent up a prayer of thanksgiving for God's mercy. If Mr. Kimball had remained missing one more night, he would've perished.

As they traversed the forest, the crunching of hooves punctured the stillness. The silhouettes of the trees yawned farther in spots where sunlight spilled. Nathaniel glanced over his shoulder. Though wobbling, Mr. Kimball remained upright, clinging to the saddle's pommel.

Ahead, voices drifted to them. The mules pricked their ears. A group of riders rounded a tall hedge, their horses shuffling around the larger drifts.

"Hallo!" Nathaniel raised his arm in a wide arc.

In accord, the men spurred their mounts forward while Nathaniel reined his to a stop. When they neared, the leader stopped his horse and jumped from the saddle. He raced to Kimball's side.

"Thank God. We thought you'd be dead." The leader was none other than Kimball's son-in-law, William Hampton. Stunned, he turned to Nathaniel. "You found him, then?"

"I did, on the rise. He'd built a shelter. His horse was dead, and he wasn't far from dying either."

"I see you had a change of heart."

"I take no credit for it."

One by one, Nathaniel studied the men. Most of them had pursued him and Franklin with Kimball two years earlier. Shock muted their hard scrutiny. Which one had pulled the trigger on Franklin? On him?

The answer lay with God and conscience.

At last, Nathaniel could be at peace with it.

William approached, holding out a hand. "I'm grateful to you, Mr. Hawkins. I'm certain we wouldn't have found him in time."

Nathaniel accepted the handshake and passed the lead rope to William. "There's water and provisions in the bag, if Mr. Kimball needs them on the way. Return the mule to my father whenever it's convenient. I'll be on my way."

"Wait," Mr. Kimball croaked, holding up a hand. Nathaniel relaxed the reins.

The man's face crumpled as emotion rippled over it. His throat bobbed. "I ... I thank you for ..." A sheen glistened in Mr. Kimball's faltering gaze.

"It's all right, sir. I wish you well." Squeezing the mule with his legs, Nathaniel urged the animal forward, away from the riders, their watchful gazes probing as he passed.

When he finally reached the clearing, he realized an amazing truth. His answer to Kimball had been genuine.

Only God had made it possible.

Eleven

Lavender-gray clouds trailed Nathaniel on the way home, gliding over the sun and fanning out wispy fingers across the sky. A sign of another incoming blizzard.

Shaking away images of Kimball and his horse under the snow, he focused on the home lights ahead. His farmhouse. Someone had set the lantern in the window to guide him.

Was Delia ill? Her wan face after a restless night concerned him. Drawing near, Nathaniel spied his father standing on the porch, crutch under one arm. He waved.

"Did you find Kimball?"

"I did, buried under the snow in a shelter. His horse is dead." Nathaniel dismounted. "I met his men later, and they took him home. Someone will return your mule."

"I suppose they were a bit surprised to see you."

A slow, incredulous smile spread across Nathaniel's face. "I'm sure you can imagine. How's Delia?"

Raising his eyebrows, Father glanced upward, toward the upstairs. "Her pains have come. It's time. Mother is helping all she can, but it looks like it's going to be a long wait."

Nathaniel felt the color flee his face. "I'll be there directly."

After tending the mule in the barn, he dashed to the house, the first snowflakes brushing his forehead.

The parlor's warmth enveloped him and expelled the weariness from his limbs. He rushed upstairs, nervousness spreading in his chest. From behind the closed bedroom door, murmuring sounds spilled onto the landing.

Gathering courage, Nathaniel knocked.

Mother answered without opening it. "Yes?"

"Might I come in?"

Shuffling sounds scurried along the floor. Mother was most likely drawing the bedcovers over Delia. A few moments later, she allowed him inside.

"You can't stay long, son. This isn't the place for menfolk."

The bed swallowed Delia's slight frame. A clammy sheen bathed her face. Wisps of chestnut hair clung to her ivory skin. Nathaniel's heart lurched when he met her wide, brown eyes. Suppose she died? Or the baby? Perhaps both? The thoughts stole his breath like a fist blow to the stomach.

"I'm stronger than I look, Mr. Hawkins."

Blinking, Nathaniel realized he hadn't spoken, but instead stood like a stone. What a dolt he was. She had seen clear through him.

He cleared his throat. "Excuse me. Are you comfortable?" A useless question.

"Not exactly. Your mother says the first baby often takes the longest to come." She fumbled with the quilt. "I'm told you found Mr. Kimball."

"By God's grace, yes." While he ransacked his mind for something to say, Mother gripped his elbow with a tug.

"Time for you to go downstairs. Her pains will be returning soon, and she needs rest in between."

Part of Nathaniel hated to leave, but the other part wished to bolt for the doorway. He patted Delia's shoulder awkwardly. "I'll be praying."

A tremulous smile curved Delia's lips. "See that you do."

Without a backward glance, he left the women to their work. Once downstairs, he slumped into the chair and scrubbed his hands over his face.

Father stirred the fire. "There's soup and bread on the table. You look famished."

"Truthfully, I haven't thought of food." Thoughts of Delia or the babe perishing drove away all appetite. "I don't think I can eat right now."

"I understand the feeling." Father picked up a piece of wood from atop the mantel. "I hewed this today, removed the bark. It's ready for you." He handed it to Nathaniel.

Shaking his head, Nathaniel said, "You'll have to forgive my blurry thinking. Ready for what?" He inspected the surface.

"You've added Joseph to the nativity. He's a fine piece, son." The deep creases on Father's face crinkled with his proud smile. "Why not add something else?"

Nathaniel tilted his head, cutting a sideways glance at Father. "At a time like this?"

"Especially at a time like this." Father clasped Nathaniel's shoulder. "Better to keep the hands and mind busy."

"I have no idea what to make next."

"Sometimes all you have to do is start carving. Let it come to you."

While Father sat in the opposite chair, Nathaniel turned the wood over, grappling for an idea to compliment the manger scene. Overhead, Mother's footsteps padded the floor in Delia's room.

Father is right. I need to be busy.

The hours stretched past midnight while Nathaniel carved, and Delia strove to bring her child into the world. At times, Father murmured prayers with him. The nondescript wood gradually took shape. As Father said, the figure emerged between imagination and his hands.

Near the break of day, Delia cried out, the sound piercing Nathaniel's soul. A baby's wail split the air a few moments later.

"God be praised." Father raised a hand heavenward, the heavy fatigue weighing on his brow.

~

"You have a fine-looking son." After washing and swaddling the babe, Mrs. Hawkins handed him to Delia. "He's a strong one. A blessing, for sure."

A beautiful mixture of joy and love blossomed within Delia as her gaze roved over the little one's features. Such purity she'd never beheld in another. In an instant, she glimpsed how much the Lord loved all His creation.

"I had no idea it would feel like this," she whispered.

"There's no other feeling like it." Leaning over them, Mrs. Hawkins brushed back Delia's hair to dab her face with a cool cloth. Delia had long missed such gentleness. How she ached for her mother.

Footsteps thumped up the stairs. Straightening, Mrs. Hawkins laid aside the cloth on the washstand. A grin quirked the corner of her mouth. "The men can wait no longer."

Opening the door, she beckoned them inside. Nathaniel and Mr. Hawkins almost tiptoed to the bedside, the sight amusing Delia. Silently, they both peered at her, then the baby.

"Mother and son are both healthy." Mrs. Hawkins sidled next to her husband.

"A boy? I pray God's blessings on you both, my dear." Mr. Hawkins brushed a hand across the baby's forehead, making him squirm under the touch. Everyone laughed.

"What is his name?" Nathaniel asked.

An invisible sword plunged through Delia. The happiness radiating in her veins evaporated. She raised her gaze to their expectant faces, a sharp breath catching in her throat.

"I can't name him." Sudden grief choked her.

"Whyever not?" Confusion narrowed Nathaniel's eyes.

Against her will, tears erupted, snatching away her answer

while the others helplessly stared. After the space of a few heartbeats, Nathaniel took charge.

"Mother, Father, I need to speak with Delia alone."

When they were gone, he turned to her. "Tell me why. Please."

Delia gulped air. "I must find him a good home, the quicker the better."

"What?"

"Don't you understand?" Delia sobbed, turning her head away from Nathaniel. "If I name him, I won't be able to give him up."

A suffocating pause stretched between them. "How can you consider it?" Nathaniel shook his head, stunned.

"How can I not?" Her shoulders quaked. "I'll bring him poverty. I must find him a good, stable home with a family who will love and take care of him."

His silence chafed worse than a reprimand. Delia braved a glance.

Nathaniel had stepped to the window, his hands clasped behind his back while he stared at a blushing sky.

"You've found one. Here."

"Though I admire your folks, it's too much to ask of them."

"That's not what I meant." Turning, he faced her. "Miss Evans, I've no reputation to speak of, but I'm a hard worker. I'll provide for you and the babe. I'll be good to you both."

The words, spoken soberly, stilled Delia's tears. She sat up straighter. "What are you saying? I can't just stay here indefinitely."

"I'm asking you to marry me."

His serious expression sparked hope inside Delia, but she squelched it. Instead, she forced herself to keep a level head, considering his welfare as he likewise thought of hers.

"You're very kind, but I can't accept. You have a future to consider. We would only burden it. I thank you for the offer." There. She severed any obligation weighing on him. They could walk away free.

In reality, she would never be free. Her love for her son would always haunt her.

Nathaniel frowned. "If prison taught me anything, it's to live in the present. The future is fleeting. God's hands hold it. I think we'd make a decent match. I don't promise instant love, nor do I expect it. But I believe we'd grow into it if you'd give it a chance." He eased closer to her bedside, his gaze earnest. "You're an honorable woman, very brave, wise, and resourceful. I have everything to gain from a marriage to you. I promise you have nothing to fear from me. Please reconsider."

Peace, not of herself, settled over Delia's spirit while she contemplated Nathaniel's words. "I believe you're a man of integrity. Since coming here, I've been safe. I hope someday I can live up to your kindness to us."

An unsure grin crinkled the corners of Nathaniel's eyes. "Are you accepting my offer?"

"Yes, Mr. Hawkins." Her shy smile matched his.

Self-consciously, he rubbed the back of his neck and expelled a long breath. "I'd say it's high time we used our Christian names, don't you think?"

She'd not admit to already thinking of him in those terms. "I think so, Nathaniel." The word slid from her lips with ease.

He nodded, pleased. "Now, what do you plan on calling our boy, Delia?"

Our boy. Delia. The words rang true, anchoring themselves in her soul. She dropped her gaze to the sweet bundle sleeping in her arms. Though unaware of the momentous change in their lives, he would learn the story someday.

Delia stroked the baby's cheek with her fingertip. "He is Henry James." Had she not known his name for weeks but dared not utter it even in her dreams?

Nathaniel held out his hands. "May I hold him?"

She shifted Henry into Nathaniel's arms. Lifting him closer to his chest, Nathaniel studied Henry's face, wonderment brightening his expression. "Welcome to our family. I pray we do right by you."

Without looking at her, Nathaniel fished a kerchief from his pocket and handed it to Delia. "See, Henry, I'm already learning your mother's ways."

Despite her flowing emotions, Delia chuckled into the folds of the cloth.

Epilogue

One Week Later

Though Christmas was still a week hence, a festive mood raced through Nathaniel's veins, perhaps due to his marriage.

Riding in the sleigh beside him, tucked in heavy fur blankets, Delia retied her wool bonnet under her chin. Then her gloved hands flitted at the edges of the fur. *Is she nervous?*

Half an hour ago, they'd pledged themselves to each other. The license crackled in Nathaniel's pocket with every movement, seeming louder than normal. The same anxious tremor in Delia's hands settled in his knees, making them weak.

Nathaniel cleared his throat to ease the tension. "Delia, nothing needs to change. Let's take it day by day."

"But there will be changes."

"Most certainly, but with time. I'll confess something, though."

She whipped her head around, a suspicious frown puckering the skin between her brows. "Such as?"

"I don't believe I've ever been as sure about a decision in my life."

Delia relaxed, stilling her fingers. "You know, I feel the same. Strange, isn't it?"

"Whatever it is, I won't doubt it." Nathaniel reined the horse to a stop while Delia eyed him curiously. He reached into his coat pocket and pulled out something wrapped in a cloth. "Consider this an early Christmas present—for both you and Henry."

Her rosy lips parted. "But I have nothing to give to you."

"Let's agree it will be your turn next Christmas." He nudged the gift into her hands.

"Very well." A hint of girlish excitement twinkled in her eyes while she untied the cloth. When she unfolded it, she stared in shock, one hand pressed against her chest. "An angel. You made this?"

Nathaniel nodded, heat rushing up his neck. "The night you were having Henry. Father suggested I do something to ease my mind. Now, you have a part in our nativity."

For a long minute, she soaked in the details before flinging her arms around his neck in an embrace.

"Thank you for this, Nathaniel. I've never had anything so beautiful."

Hastily, Delia released him, skittering her glance to the angel. A bright glow blossomed in her cheeks.

Flicking the reins, Nathaniel urged the horse into a trot. The feeling of rightness strengthened. Between them, the promise of love took root. In the brisk air, happiness swirled a silent dance.

Gathering a bit of courage, Nathaniel stretched his arm across the back of the seat and around Delia's shoulders.

To his delight, she inched closer.

THE END

Discussion Questions

1. How did Delia's and Nathaniel's story impact you?
2. Does your family have a treasured heirloom? Has it impacted your life or beliefs?
3. What are your feelings on Nathaniel's decision to help Mr. Kimball despite his betrayal?
4. Have you ever been in a place where God seemed far away or absent? How did you deal with it?

Acknowledgments

It had been an honor and joy to work with Cynthia, Elaine, and Kelly on this project. Thank you, ladies, for your support, encouragement, input, and your friendship. Each of you have blessed me!

About the Author

Candace West was born in the Mississippi delta to a young minister and his wife. She grew up in small-town Arkansas and graduated from the University of Arkansas at Monticello. At twelve years old, she wrote her first story, "Following Prairie River." In 2018, she published her debut novel *Lane Steen*. By weaving entertaining, hope-filled stories, Candace shares the Gospel and encourages her readers. She currently lives in Arkansas with her husband and their son along with two dogs and three bossy cats.

THE *Christmas Carving*

Kelly Goshorn

To Debb Hackett.
Thank you for showing me how to be the hands and feet of Jesus.
Writing may have brought us together in friendship, but the Lord has
made you a sister of my heart.

"When they saw the star, they rejoiced with exceeding great joy."
-Matthew 2:10

One

Loudoun County, Virginia
December 1867

P ine boughs dotted with red bows draped the windows of the Taylorstown mercantile. Madelyn Cunningham's lips curved upward. She loved everything about Christmas —the festive decorations, special foods, and cherished celebrations all designed to point a weary heart toward a King born a babe so long ago. After so many years of hardship during and following the war, Madelyn was pleased to see that perhaps folks were finally ready to put differences behind them and make merry again.

Nearly three years had passed since she'd observed Christmas here in the community where she'd grown up. She hadn't wanted to leave then. She'd wanted to stay, hold her chin high, and help bring reconciliation to the town she loved. However, a broken engagement and no source of income meant she had little choice but to follow her father when he picked up stakes and moved to Leesburg.

It had been a cowardly response. After all, *they* hadn't done anything wrong. Her eldest brother's hotheaded inability to see reason, to see those who were still friends beneath their Federal uniforms, *that* was to blame.

Madelyn leaned forward and peered inside the shop. Her frosty breath fogged the glass, and she swiped at the condensation with her gloved hand. She squinted into the dim interior. A few lanterns were strung overhead, and the shelves were stocked fuller than she'd seen in a long while. Mr. Sullivan chatted with someone in a side aisle. Otherwise, the place appeared deserted. Just as she'd hoped.

She gently fingered the back of her chignon. The eleven-mile ride from Leesburg hadn't done too much damage. She reached for the doorknob. The little bell above the door jingled cheerily as she stepped inside.

"Good evening, miss. May I help you?"

The storekeeper's cheery greeting faded, along with the light in his eyes, when Madelyn stepped from the shadows. "Good eve to you as well, Mr. Sullivan."

He scowled. "It's been a while since we've seen a Cunningham in these parts."

Madelyn's gaze darted to the well-dressed woman beside the shopkeeper. Her eyes pinched closed.

Amelia Jackson.

Of all the luck. In town less than an hour, and she'd already crossed paths with her worst detractor—the one who'd turned Wyatt against her. Though they'd known each other since childhood, she and Amelia had always been more enemies than friends.

Madelyn lifted her chin, determined not to let the past dictate the future. "Yes, well, I think it's about time to change that, and Christmas is the perfect opportunity to—"

"Christmas is what sent you and yours packing."

Amelia's curt tone reminded Madelyn she'd need more than her spunky Christmas spirit to turn things around in Taylorstown. She'd need divine intervention.

"Maddy Cunningham. Well, aren't you a sight for sore eyes?" Olivia Sullivan rounded the corner and grasped Madelyn's hands. "It's been too long," she said after placing a delicate kiss on each of Madelyn's cheeks.

"Not long enough," her husband mumbled.

"Oh, hush, Gideon. It's time to put the past to rest—time to build a bridge to the future." She looped Madelyn's arm and tugged her toward the display window. "And Christmas is the perfect time to let forgiveness reign in our hearts again," she called over her shoulder.

Mrs. Sullivan paused in front of the intricately carved nativity scene—the same one that had been in the Hawkins family for generations. The one Madelyn had looked forward to displaying in her and Wyatt's home before he'd broken their engagement, adding to her own family's plummeting reputation in the community.

"I ... I can't believe Wyatt is selling this."

"I couldn't agree more." Mrs. Sullivan made a tsking sound as she shook her head. "My brother Nathaniel would roll over in his grave. But my nephew is not the same man you knew. Joy has fled his soul. Bitterness is choking him to death from the inside out."

A chill snaked down Madelyn's spine. She couldn't imagine Wyatt as anything other than content and gentle spirited, his deep green eyes twinkling when he teased his younger siblings.

Madelyn lifted one of the shepherds and examined the meticulous detail. The thin staff, the folds of his clothing, and the expression of awe chiseled on the man's face all spoke to the love that had been poured into the carvings over the generations. If Wyatt was willing to part with the treasured heirloom, then nothing his Aunt Olivia had written in her missive begging Madelyn to come had been an exaggeration.

"I'm not sure anything I have to say will be able to change that, Mrs. Sullivan. In fact, there's a real possibility my presence will only make matters worse."

"Nonsense child. I don't care what Wyatt says, he's never stopped loving you."

"Olivia. Customer," Mr. Sullivan called, exasperation garnishing his voice.

"Be right there." Mrs. Sullivan tugged her arm free and turned her dark brown eyes on Madelyn. "I think you're just what Wyatt and this entire community need to find their Christmas spirit again."

Had three years been enough for some of the wounds to heal? Madelyn didn't know, but if things for Wyatt were as bad as his aunt had described, then she needed to see him. See if any part of his heart would respond to her. She owed him that much, didn't she?

And maybe, just maybe, the spirit of Christmas would bring hope and healing to weary souls once more.

WYATT HAWKINS GLARED at the pine garland draping the iron fence and shook his head. Here, of all places. But it shouldn't surprise him, not really. Holiday decorations were popping up all over Taylorstown for the first time since that wretched Christmas Eve. The entire town seemed ready to move on—to let what Josiah Cunningham did slip from their memory.

But not Wyatt. He'd never forget, and as such, Christmas would forever be tarnished.

He lifted the latch. The rusty iron gate creaked on its hinges as it swung wide, granting him entrance. Hard-packed snow crunched beneath his boots. Wyatt shivered and hunched his shoulders against the cold. Avoiding this place hadn't made the pain of that night any less, nor had it granted him a lick of peace.

Reaching the spot where his friend slumbered eternally, he removed his hat. The chilly December breeze nipped at his bare ears. He stooped and dusted the snow from the face of the jagged stone.

Sgt. F. B. Anderson
Co. A, VA Volunteers
Loudoun Independent Rangers
April 17, 1843 - Dec. 24, 1864

Wyatt glanced over his shoulder. Seeing no one, he brought his fist to his mouth and cleared his throat. "Been busy helping your ma with the farm and making repairs to her house. She and Mollie are doing just fine. I promised I'd look out for them, and I've been keepin' my word. Your family will want for nothing."

He crumpled the brim of his hat between his palms. "It's probably silly for me to talk to you. It's not like you can help me sort things out. The preacher reminds me you're not here, not really. That you're in heaven with the Lord, but it still eats at me —your body lyin' here. It's just not right."

Tears stung the backs of his eyes. "I know you'd be the first person telling me to forgive, but I can't help believin' it should be that scum, Josiah Cunningham, in the ground instead of you."

His cold fingers traced the shape of the cross engraved above his friend's name. Three years, and he still hadn't any peace—not with himself, or Maddy, and certainly not with God. The emptiness inside gnawed at him, devouring him like a cankerworm feasting on the tender leaves of spring. He'd not only lost his best friend, but he'd also shoved the woman he loved away. If there was any sense to be made from this tragedy, Maddy would've been the only person who could've helped him find it.

However, Maddy had seen it all unfold that night. Seen the small band of Confederates rush into the family Christmas gathering and take their revenge on Flemon. Had seen their friend mortally wounded and die in his mother's arms. And saw her betrothed frozen in shock and fear, unable to use his sidearm or saber to protect Flemon from armed intruders in the Andersons' own home.

But it was the way she'd looked at Wyatt that night, as if she saw right through him, to the coward he really was. How could she ever depend on him to keep her and any children they might have safe? If he couldn't protect Flemon with two weapons at his disposal, how could he protect the woman he loved from the countless hardships and trials life would thrust at them?

No, he'd done the right thing in insisting she leave with her father. Maddy Cunningham deserved better than the likes of him.

Wyatt scraped a hand over his beard. This was exactly why he avoided coming here more often. Visiting made every detail of that awful night burrow deeper in his memory while doing little to ease his guilt.

"Hello, Wyatt."

He stiffened. *Madelyn?* What was she doing here? He'd been lost in thought and hadn't heard her approach.

She stooped beside him and laid a bouquet of pine boughs and winterberries at the foot of Flemon's gravestone before placing her gloved hand on his forearm. "It's been a long time. How've you been?"

His muscles tensed at her touch. Three years later and the woman's presence still sent his pulse careening through his veins. "About the same." He fought to keep his tone even, as if seeing her here was exactly what he'd expected.

"I couldn't stay away any longer. It's time to let the wounds heal."

He gave no response, just fixed his gaze on her simple, yet elegant, offering of remembrance. She'd taken care to wrap the stems in a burlap bow. It was so like Maddy to pay attention to every detail.

She rose to her full height. "I'm staying in town through the New Year."

Great. Wyatt exhaled, his breath crystalizing when it met cold air. He supposed it was a bit ungentlemanly to ignore her, but what was he supposed to say? *Nice to see you again, Maddy, but you remind me of the worst day of my life?*

Who was he fooling? He'd never had trouble talking to Maddy. Truth was, he rarely had to say what was on his mind. Somehow, she always knew. The real problem was how to avoid looking into those chicory blue eyes of hers when he spoke to her.

He shoved to his feet. "What are you really doing here?"

"Spreading a little Christmas cheer. You look like you could use some."

Her brows lifted in conjunction with the corner of her lips. Was she trying to elicit a smile from him? If you could store Christmas cheer in a well, then Wyatt's would be bone dry. He had no more use for Christmas than he did a ruffled petticoat.

"Not sure that's a good idea, Maddy." Something tightened in his chest when he'd spoken her name. "There are still a lot of folks around who remember what your brother did and won't be happy to see a Cunningham."

"Does that include you?"

He met her inquiry with silence and what he hoped was a penetrating glare. "I mean it, Maddy. There's no need to come back here stirring up trouble."

"I didn't pull the trigger, Wyatt."

"And you're not the one lying in that grave." He flinched at the harshness in his voice.

Maddy eyed him. "Neither are you. Leastwise, not your body."

Bullseye.

Right to the heart of the matter. How'd she do that? It was like the woman had a special gift to see inside his deepest thoughts.

"I should head back to town. I'll stop by your shop tomorrow. I have a favor to ask you." She dipped her chin and stepped onto the shoveled path that led toward the rickety gate.

Wyatt watched her slim figure disappear around a bend. He couldn't imagine what favor a sensible woman like Maddy needed that would bring her back to a town that no longer welcomed her, or to a man who'd sent her packing. But he had a feeling whatever it was, he wasn't going to like it.

Madelyn scribbled her ideas on the tablet Olivia Sullivan provided—*string popcorn, candies, and cranberries, ask Pastor Carmichael to speak to congregation following Sunday services, wool, ask Wyatt to read the nativity story.* She tapped the pencil against her cheek then added, *find women to knit scarves and mittens for the children.*

"You're up early. You sleep all right?"

Mrs. Sullivan's cheerful greeting warmed Madelyn's heart. So unlike Wyatt's frosty welcome the previous day. A shiver prickled her spine. At least one person in Taylorstown had been happy to see her. "I didn't sleep well, but I have so many things on my mind."

"Was one of them Wyatt, by any chance?" Mrs. Sullivan's brows tented.

Wyatt Hawkins wasn't *one* of the things stealing her sleep. He was the *only* one. She'd tossed and turned, rehashing their cemetery encounter earlier that day. He'd been terse and not nearly as flustered as she'd been by their first meeting in three years. She'd told herself that time had eased her longing for the man, but that malarky had dissipated the moment she'd laid eyes on him. Why, she'd nearly come undone when he'd spoken her name. Though she had no intention of sharing that truth with his aunt.

She offered a weak smile. "Thank you again for the use of Emily's old room. I know Mr. Sullivan isn't keen on my returning home, let alone staying here." Emily had been Madelyn's closest friend growing up. She wrote her friend's name on her agenda, *The more allies the better.*

Mrs. Sullivan waved a dismissive hand. "Don't pay Gideon any mind. He's a pussycat beneath that gruff exterior."

Pussycat? Madelyn thought a mountain lion might be a more apt analogy.

"If it wasn't Wyatt, and I'm not convinced you're being completely forthcoming on the matter," she said while pouring a mug of coffee, "then what has you up and dressed so early this morning?"

Heat flashed in Madelyn's cheeks. Was she that obvious? "Um, I ... uh, I have much to accomplish for the children's charity party and Christmas is only four weeks away. I wanted to jot down the biggest tasks and recruit volunteers to set them in motion. I'm hoping you might have a few suggestions." She added *advertisement*, to her lengthening inventory of assignments.

Mrs. Sullivan scanned the list over Madelyn's shoulder. Her finger tapped the top of the paper. "The mercantile will donate the wool for the children's scarves and mittens, as well as the cranberries for the garland. Gideon is picking up our order from Baltimore tomorrow. You may have first pick."

"First pick of what?" Mr. Sullivan stood in the kitchen doorway, his stony gaze fixed on Madelyn.

Mrs. Sullivan offered him her mug of coffee. "I'm donating some of our holiday shipment to Maddy for her project."

His bushy brows nearly melded into one long, hairy line above his narrowed eyes. "What project?"

"Maddy's organizing a benefit for the children of war veterans."

"*Which* war veterans?" he asked, his glare bouncing between the two women.

Mrs. Sullivan set the coffee on the table. "Sit down while I make you some eggs and toast."

"Olivia?"

"Hmm?" With her back to her husband, Mrs. Sullivan set about heating the large cast iron skillet.

"*Which* war veterans, Olivia?" he repeated, this time his voice resembling a growl.

Madelyn's pulse kicked up a notch. She hated to be the cause of strife between the Sullivans.

"Union veterans of course." Olivia dropped a dollop of lard into the pan. "And Confederates, too, I suppose, if we have any hope of reuniting the town."

Mr. Sullivan shook his slender finger at Madelyn. "You're going to stir up trouble if you even suggest bringing Union and Confederate veterans together, especially at Christmas. People are trying to put the past to rest. Mark my words, this will reignite anger and resentment in the community. Besides," he said, shifting his gaze to Mrs. Sullivan, who now stood with arms akimbo, challenge lighting her eyes, "it will be bad for business to sponsor this project of hers."

Maddy pursed her lips and said a quick prayer that Mr. Sullivan wouldn't persuade his wife to drop the whole affair. Mrs. Sullivan was her only supporter. After all, it had been her idea to fetch Madelyn back to Taylorstown in the first place.

Mrs. Sullivan added several sausage links to the skillet, then wiped her hands on her apron and stood beside Madelyn. "I know it's risky, Gideon, but it's time we try. Maddy's idea is a good one." Her eyes softened, reminding Maddy of the doleful look her hound had perfected when begging for table scraps. "So many children are suffering and living in near poverty along with their widowed mothers. This charity party is something the town can get behind."

He stroked his sagging jowls and heaved a sigh. "I want it

noted that I'm opposed to the idea. Anger and hostility run deep on both sides, but"—he paused—"I'll not stand in your way."

"I knew you'd see to reason." Mrs. Sullivan kissed her husband's cheek. "I best get cooking your eggs."

"Thank you, Mr. Sullivan. I appreciate—"

"Don't thank me yet. And you need to tread lightly." His tone matched the intensity of his gaze as it bore into Madelyn. "If folks don't come along beside you, you need to rethink the matter. We don't need more disagreements or more reasons to distrust our neighbors. Understood?"

Madelyn nodded. But deep down she knew before you made a cake, you needed to crack a few eggs.

Wyatt slid the plane over the small piece of wood and watched another pine curl float to the floor of his workshop. His fingers traced the smooth surface. *Perfect.*

The design was simple enough that he planned to make several of them during the slow periods of the coming year. By next Christmas, he'd have a half dozen ready to sell. The partnership with his Aunt Olivia to stock his hand-carved toys in the mercantile had already paid dividends with his farm and circus animals nearly selling out.

Surveying the collection of finished pieces made Wyatt's chest expand. Carving ran in the Hawkins family, a proud tradition passed from one generation to the next, and Wyatt anticipated teaching his own son some day—a son he thought he'd be raising with Madelyn. But that was not to be.

He retrieved a cloth and chased the sawdust from the rocking horse.

"That's lovely. May I take a closer look?"

Wyatt startled at the sound of Maddy's voice. The squawk of the shop door's rusty hinge usually alerted him to customers. That was the second time in two days she'd managed to sneak up on him. She'd promised to stop by to ask a favor of some sort and all Wyatt had to do was say no.

Remember to be strong. Let her down gently.

Without waiting for his response, she stepped closer to the toy positioned on the work bench. "Did you design this yourself?"

Wyatt nodded.

"You're still sketching?"

"In the evenings mostly. Whenever something comes to mind, I try to make a rendering before I forget."

"What color will you paint it?"

"I figured on white for the horse and rungs, and black for the mane, tail, eyes, and seat."

"Hmm," she said, angling her head and examining the rocking horse. "Want to know my opinion?"

Wyatt doubted anything he could say would stop Maddy Cunningham from sharing her assessment. He stuffed his hands in the pockets of his dungarees. "Certainly."

"You should paint the seat red. The bright color will make the saddle stand out."

Wyatt scratched his beard. The coarse hair needed trimming. Why hadn't he taken the time to groom himself properly this morning? He'd known she planned to come by today. *Because you're not trying to impress Madelyn Cunningham, that's why.*

"What do you think?"

Her idea had merit, and true to Maddy's knack for detail, changing the color could make a difference when selling the final product. "You may be right."

She dipped her chin. "We always did make a great team."

Yes, they had. But not any longer. He cleared his throat. "Yesterday you mentioned needing a favor. Thing is, Maddy, I'm pretty busy with the shop, and—"

"But you don't even know what I'm planning to ask."

"Sorry, Maddy, it's just …"

Her hands flew to her hips. "You could at least hear me out, Wyatt Hawkins, before burrowing in and telling me no."

Sass flashed in her eyes.

Heaven help him. The woman was even more fetching when her dander was up. "You're right, go ahead." *Don't look at her. Stay focused on … on what?* He spied the broom propped against the wall and began sweeping wood shavings toward the larger pile in the corner.

"I'm organizing a holiday celebration for the children of Confederate and Union war dead and—"

His head snapped in her direction as quickly as her palm rose shoulder high, halting the words on his tongue before he uttered a sound.

Wyatt listened while Maddy explained her plans. With her painstaking attention to detail, the woman was a natural leader. And clever, too. While the party would most likely be sparsely attended, and no doubt stir up strife best left forgotten, *if* there was anything that could unite the community, it would be a gathering for the children of fallen soldiers. How would he refuse her?

"You'll face some opposition, but your idea has potential."

A wide grin parted her lips. "I'm glad to hear you say that because I want you to read the Christmas story to the children during the party."

Why had he looked at her? The hopeful sparkle in her eyes would disappear with his next few words. "I can't help you."

"Can't or won't?" she asked, keeping her voice even, though his answer must have disappointed her.

"Can't. Christmas and I parted ways three years ago. You'll need to ask someone else."

"I remember the many Christmases at your parents' home, listening to your father read the biblical account of Jesus's birth using your family's nativity to make the story come alive." She paused and seemed to chew over her next few words. "I know you're trying to sell the heirloom. I saw it in the mercantile."

Wyatt tightened his grip on the broom. He didn't need another lecture on the intrinsic value of the nativity. What was done, was done.

"It's not too late," she said, eyes brightening. "You could get it back before it's sold."

The pleading tone in her voice pricked his heart. "Sorry, Maddy, I can't. Aunt Olivia stopped by earlier this morning and told me she has a potential buyer if I'm willing to finish the set. I agreed."

"That nativity has been in your family for generations. How could you let it go?"

He paused his sweeping and clamped his eyes closed. No one understood the hollowness, the ache inside that never ceased. He'd failed his best friend when Flemon had needed him most. Pushing out a heavy breath, he glared at her. "Like I said, I parted ways with Christmas. I have no use for it."

"No use for Christmas? It's not a commodity like a rocking horse or a pair of shoes you might outgrow. It's quite the opposite. A person grows into Christmas as their relationship with the Savior deepens."

"Well, the Almighty and I haven't been on the best of terms since Flemon died."

He grabbed a metal dustpan and scooped shavings into a barrel. These he could sell as packing material. He kept his back to her. "Look, Maddy, I wish you the best with your party, but I'm not the person you're looking for."

She reached for his arm, and a lightning bolt burst through him. Why'd she insist on doing that?

"I'm not giving up on you. Despite what you think, you *are* what this celebration needs, and truthfully, Wyatt, you need this celebration." With a firm set to her jaw, she gave him a tight nod. "I'll be back in a few days to see if you've changed your mind."

"I'm not gonna change my mind."

"We'll see," she said, pivoting on her heel and exiting the shop.

Wyatt deposited the dustpan and broom in the corner. Of all people, he thought Maddy would understand. All these years later, Flemon's death was still raw. Besides, he harbored too much anger toward God to read the Bible and encourage the little ones to believe something he doubted himself.

Nope. She could come back as many times as she wanted, but ice would freeze in summer before he'd agree to partake in Maddy Cunningham's futile effort to revive Christmas in their splintered community.

Three

Wyatt stomped his boots and swiped snow dust from his jacket before entering the door to his aunt and uncle's private quarters above the mercantile. The spicy scent of sausage gravy greeted him, and his stomach rumbled. His breakfast had consisted of coffee he'd reheated from the day before, a hard-boiled egg, and a slice of bread from which he'd cut the moldy crust.

"Aunt Olivia," he called, removing his hat.

His aunt rounded the corner, wiping her hands on the gingham apron circling her waist. "Wyatt, what a wonderful surprise. What brings you by this morning?"

He bit back a grin. Without a doubt, his aunt knew exactly why he'd stopped by. Three or four times a week, Wyatt showed up unannounced around mealtime to see if the older couple needed anything. His aunt would assure them they were fine and graciously invite Wyatt to stay and eat with them. They'd been playing this game for a few years now. Aunt Olivia loved cooking for him, and their unspoken understanding not only kept Wyatt's pride intact but kept him from withering away to skin and bones.

"Just stoppin' by to see how my favorite aunt and uncle are

gettin' along."

She planted her hands on her hips and cast a knowing look his way. "Well, I'd hope so, considering we're your only aunt and uncle." Her shoulders jiggled. "As usual, I've made more than we can eat. I just can't get used to cooking for fewer people now that your cousins are grown. Please stay and join us."

He hung his coat and hat on the hall tree, all the while licking his lips in anticipation of thick gravy laden with spicy sausage piled atop two of his aunt's flaky biscuits. "I wouldn't want to see your good cookin' go to waste."

He followed his aunt into the kitchen and jerked to a stop.

"Good morning, Wyatt. Sounds like you'll be joining us for breakfast."

"Maddy?" She sat at the kitchen table, papers sprawled in front of her. Several wisps of light brown hair framed her lovely face, and his chest constricted. How long before he could see her without the sharp ache rising in his chest? "I ... uh ... didn't expect to find you here."

Something flashed in her eyes. "Oh, didn't I tell you? Your Aunt Olivia graciously offered me Emily's old room while I'm in town."

"That's a bit surprising, considering Uncle Gideon's opinion of your family." He winced. Why had he gone and said that? Even from this distance, he could see the light in Maddy's eyes dim. While the statement might be true enough, Maddy was more than likely aware of Uncle Gideon's opinions. All he'd done was rub salt in her wounds.

"I'm sorry, Maddy. I shouldn't have—"

"No, it's fine." She waved a hand to dismiss his concerns. "While it may be unpleasant to hear, nothing you said was either new or untrue."

She'd always been a gracious woman, and he'd always been a stupid clod who stuck his foot in his mouth.

He tugged the bench from beneath the pine table and sat across from Maddy, who'd returned her attention to the papers in front of her. She angled her head to the side, and the tip of her tongue poked between her lips as she examined her work.

"I can't get the proportions quite right, but this will have to do."

Aunt Olivia stepped behind her, a large platter of biscuits in hand. "Mmm, yes, I see what you mean. Your garland looks a bit like a snake." She patted Maddy's shoulder and then set the biscuits on the table. "You're aiming to excite the children, not frighten them. Perhaps try Father Christmas."

Maddy shuffled through the stack, holding one up for Aunt Olivia. "I did." Her shoulders sagged. "He looks sickly and unappealing."

Wyatt smothered a grin. "What are you working on?"

"I'm designing a flyer to advertise the children's Christmas party, but so far, my ideas greatly exceed my talent for rendering."

"You were able to find some volunteers?" Although Wyatt had no plans to participate, even his calloused heart couldn't withstand seeing her efforts fail.

"Not yet." She looked him in the eye and forced a smile. "But there's still time."

"Perhaps if no one is getting behind the idea, Maddy, you should give it up."

"If it's the Father's will, He'll make a way."

How many times had he heard Maddy say that when she rallied volunteers for the knitting brigade, or the church social, or when they needed teachers for Sunday school. Ever the eternal optimist, not even having her family driven from town could dampen her spirits. He admired her pluck. That had been the quality he most loved about her.

"Drawing, however, has never been a strength I possess." She turned her doe eyes on Wyatt. "Fortunately, I know someone who has a fine hand for sketching."

He'd always enjoyed penciling the projects he would eventually bring to life in maple, pine, or walnut. It was his favorite part of the process. He could imagine the design in his mind's eye, but until he sketched it on paper, he'd have no luck getting the proportions right, no matter how many times he measured.

Although he should probably listen to the voice in his head imploring him to let Maddy sort out her own troubles, he convinced himself that helping her with the handbill wasn't the same as being actively involved in the event. After all, what harm could it do to offer a few suggestions?

"Let me see it." He extended his hand.

"Thank you, Wyatt." Her voice brightened. Clutching her papers, she scurried around the table and before he knew it, Maddy occupied the bench beside him. The enticing scent of rosewater frazzled his concentration.

"Which of those ideas do you think works best?" Her blue eyes fixed on him in a most serious fashion.

Wyatt cleared his throat while he searched his memory. Hadn't she said something about holly berries and peppermint sticks? Utterly clueless and unwilling to admit her feminine soaps had been a distraction, he grabbed a clean sheet of paper and began sketching. A few minutes later, garland draped and looped along the edges, creating a festive design for her advertisement but leaving plenty of room for copy. He sat up straight and studied the design. Satisfied, he offered it to Maddy.

She clasped her hands. "It's perfect. Thank you. I'll just write the text on a separate sheet, then I'm off to the printer."

Aunt Olivia set a steaming bowl of sausage gravy on the table. "I wish you'd take my advice and not return until the morning. I don't like the idea of you traveling at night."

"You're traveling to the printer in Leesburg and back today?"

"I don't have much choice. That's the closest printer. If I'm to have them to hand out after Sunday services, I need to take them today."

"You can't just show up and wait for them, Maddy. The printer will need a few days at least to fill your order."

"Thomas Appleton is a friend of my brother Jo ... anyway, his family prints a small circular each week, and I'm confident I can persuade him to rush my advertisement."

Thomas Appleton. There was a name he hadn't heard in a while. Thomas had served in Colonel White's Commanches with her brother Josiah and shown a great deal of interest in Maddy. Was something going on between the two of them? Not that it was any of his business, but she did seem convinced that he'd acquiesce to her request.

"I think you should stay the night at your parents' place," Aunt Olivia said. "It's just not safe for you to make the trip by yourself."

Maddy shook her head. "That's another three miles south of Leesburg. I'd rather put that time into traveling back to Taylorstown."

"What about The Leesburg Inn?" Wyatt asked. "You can get a good night's rest and head out early in the morning."

"Or you could accompany Maddy," Aunt Olivia said, "so she's safe and won't have the extra expense."

Silence filled the empty space between him and the conspiring womenfolk.

He needed to politely decline. If he didn't come up with a good reason why he couldn't accompany Maddy—and quick— he'd find himself alone with her for the entire day. Not that he'd mind bearing that burden, but it would only increase his longing for something that could never be.

"I suppose I can give you a ride."

What had his traitorous tongue just said? Was he completely daft? He wanted to give himself a solid *thunk* on the forehead. He'd been determined to say no, kindly, and leave. Now he'd spend the remainder of the day, some of it well past sunset, in the presence of Madeline Cunningham and her fancy rosewater-scented perfume.

And if Wyatt wasn't careful, the ever-present wound from her absence in his life would rip wide open.

~

RIDING beside Wyatt to and from Leesburg was the last thing Madelyn had expected to be doing today. She was glad for the turn of events, but the reticence stretching between them pinched her heart. The pair had never known such an awkward silence. Friends since childhood, and a couple since the day she turned sixteen, they'd always had things to talk about. On those rare occasions when nothing came to mind, the quiet was easy, like slipping into her favorite chair beside the fireplace.

During the years they'd been separated, Wyatt had never left her heart. Deep in her soul, in the crevices that only God and Wyatt had ever penetrated, she believed he still loved her.

She thought it completely reasonable that Wyatt would be hurt and angry over Flemon's death. That kind of loss took a heap of time and love to overcome. Because he'd been unable to help his friend, she suspected his pride may also play a role in why they'd never talked about that night and put matters to rights.

The discomfort that fought to redefine their relationship and keep them apart clawed at her. But what could she say when what needed to be spoken of was the one thing Wyatt would definitely not be amenable to? She tipped her head back, allowing the sun's rays to warm her face, and lifted a silent prayer for heavenly wisdom and patience.

Although she detested small talk, especially with Wyatt, she knew no other way to breach the increasing disquietude between them. Anything would be better than riding in complete and utter silence. "How are your mother and sister getting on?"

"Fine."

"Seems like the carpentry shop is doing well."

"Yep."

If all Wyatt was willing to give were one-word answers, this would be a long ride. She searched the corners of her mind, trying to find a topic that would encourage him to converse with her. "The rocking horse you made is lovely. When did you start making toys?"

He shrugged. "About two years ago. My brother, Henry, and his wife wanted a cradle for their baby, and it just grew from there. I mostly get orders at Christmas."

Again, the uncomfortable silence sat heavily between them, reminding her they'd been more strangers than friends in the last few years. At least this time he'd offered an entire sentence or two. "Do you still enjoy whittling?"

"Yep."

Back to one word. *Lord, give me patience.* This wasn't going as well as she'd hoped. Although she hadn't believed their romance would reignite, perhaps she'd been too naive to think that they'd fall back into their prior comradery. At least his affinity for carving hadn't changed. He'd always said it gave him time to process the day. How many times had she sat beside him stitching curtains or tying rag rugs for her hope chest? Other times she'd read to him while he carved.

"Any new orders?"

"I've made some farm and circus animals that seem to sell well year-round. Aunt Olivia wants me to make a dollhouse and furniture." He rubbed his chin. "Do you think they will sell?"

"A dollhouse is a grand idea. Perhaps something small, with only a couple of rooms."

Leaving one hand on the reins, he used the other to scratch his reddish-brown beard. "I'm concerned that making miniature furniture is going to be time-consuming work for the profit I'm likely to see."

"Carving the family is much more important than the furnishings. Let the little girl imagine what the inside looks like. Why, she could even find things in her own home to pretend are the tables, chairs, and beds. Perhaps she'll use odds and ends of fabric for curtains, rugs, and blankets. That way she can make it her own."

He stared at her for a moment, then shook his head before

turning his attention to the narrowing path across a one-lane bridge.

"What?"

"Nothin'."

Was he biting back a grin? Of all the nerve. She stiffened her spine. "It's fine by me if you don't like my ideas, Wyatt Hawkins, but you don't need to snicker. Just keep your criticisms to yourself."

"Whoa, girls," he called to the team, tugging their leads till they halted. "I like your ideas just fine, Maddy. Always have. That's not why I ... it just ... oh, never mind.'"

She coupled her hands in her lap. "I'm sorry if I jumped to the wrong conclusion, Wyatt. Please tell me what you were gonna say."

"You have a good head for business, Maddy. You offered a practical solution to my problem. I'm appreciative, is all."

Madelyn thanked him for the compliment but secretly doubted that was what he'd been about to say. She'd seen the tips of his ears redden beneath his hat—a telltale sign that whatever he'd been about to share had embarrassed him. But she decided to let it go. No sense pressing him.

With a flick of the reins, the horses began trotting again. In the distance, Madelyn could see the courthouse belfry rising above the town's rooflines. Only another mile or so until they reached the printer's shop.

"Do you have any thoughts on what pieces you'll add to finish the nativity for the new owner?"

"I'm gonna tell Aunt Olivia I've changed my mind. The set sells as is. I'm not interested in carving any more pieces. It's just a reminder of all that's changed."

He mumbled that last part, but Madelyn had heard it nonetheless, every syllable pricking her heart. Seeing him downcast and hearing him so plainly express his disbelief troubled her spirit. How much of her thoughts should she relay? Would anything she said help Wyatt, or merely push him further away from both her and God? While she didn't relish the thought of her life without Wyatt if they couldn't find a way to reconcile, if she managed to make his heart harder toward God, she'd never forgive herself.

"I understand you feel this way now, but in time you may regret letting such a precious heirloom leave your family."

"If I thought that were possible, Maddy, I'd have kept it."

"But, Wyatt—"

"Look, Maddy, God wasn't there for Flemon when he was attacked. He was an honorable man, one of the best I've ever known. If someone like Flemon can't count on God, how am I supposed to?"

She flinched at the harshness in his tone. "God doesn't promise us a long life or a life with no sorrow or pain. He doesn't even promise us happiness. Scripture tells us there will be trouble and strife on this earth, but that we can find strength and hope in the One who has overcome the world."

Wyatt muttered something under his breath, and Madelyn wasn't sure she wanted to know what it was. Instead, she eyed the store windows as the wagon made its way down King Street. A child clutching a peppermint stick in one hand held fast to his mother with the other as the pair exited the confectioner's shop. Most of the shopkeepers had festively decorated their windows, and the courthouse had evergreen swags topped with red bows hanging on its front doors.

She'd never known Wyatt to be so out of sorts with God or to set his mind in a certain direction so doggedly. But it wasn't her job to change his way of thinking, it was God's. All Madelyn had to do was pray and look for the opportunities God would provide for the Holy Spirit to work in Wyatt's life. Because whether Wyatt Hawkins liked it or not, she and the Almighty were on a joint mission to turn his heart toward his heavenly home.

Four

As the congregation began the last stanza of "O Come, All Ye Faithful," Madelyn closed her hymnal, deposited the book on top of the stack at the end of the pew, and slipped into the aisle. Pastor Kent had granted permission for her to pass out the handbills about the children's party following services, and she intended to position herself at the bottom of the stairs before the congregation was dismissed. She'd gone all the way to Leesburg and back with the taciturn Wyatt, and she had no intention of these advertisements going to waste.

She tucked the flyers beneath her arm and hurried down the stairs. The double doors opened, and the first congregants exited the church. Unfortunately for Maddy, she received more stony looks and upturned noses than interest in aiding the children of deceased or disabled veterans. Refusing to be deterred, she forged ahead with her efforts.

"Children's Christmas party," she called, offering the flyer to a woman cradling an infant. "Volunteers needed."

"I got no inclination to aid the sister of a murderer whilst my own babies need washed and fed."

Maddy nodded solemnly and tried again. "Children's Christmas party. Songs. Games. Presents."

A tall, thin man descended the stairs with the aid of a roughly-hewn crutch. He accepted the advertisement she offered and then scanned the paper. "How much?"

"How much?"

"The paper don't say what it costs for the littl'uns to come to the party."

"It's free, sir. Everything is donated."

He smoothed the wiry beard that hung several inches beyond his chin. "I'll think about it."

"Sir, if your wife knits, we sure could use her help making gifts for the children. We'll be here every day this week."

"You'll have to ask her. She's mighty busy with the young'uns."

"I understand, and I wouldn't ask for myself. It's for the children. If you tell me where you live, I'll bring her the yarn, and she can knit at home and drop off the items at the church when they're finished."

"Name's Talbot. We live just beyond the fork by the large oak tree west of town. Stay on Market Street. First lane on the left will lead you right to us."

"I'll be by this afternoon."

A young girl tugged on her skirt. "Can I come to yer party?"

"I don't see why not."

"Well, I's a Rockford. And some people don't like us Rockfords, cause my daddy wore the gray uniform instead of the blue one. He died fightin' at Manassas second time 'round." She dragged the toe of her scuffed boot through a small patch of snow. "If'n you's sure, I'll ask Mama if my brothers and sister and I can come. We's never been to a party 'fore, and I think yers sounds pretty fine."

"I'm sure. Your entire family is welcome." Madelyn handed the girl one of the advertisements. "Take this to your mother."

"Won't do no good. She can't read." The girl ran off toward a wagon with at least six other children in the bed. "But I'll tell her all 'bout it, especially the presents," she called as she wedged herself between her siblings.

The tension in Madelyn's shoulders eased a bit. At least someone was excited about her idea. Her contentment ended when her gaze snagged on Amelia's. *Give me grace, Lord.* To Madelyn's way of thinking, some people required a little more grace than others, and Amelia Jackson definitely fit into this category.

Amelia twisted a lock of chestnut hair around her finger. "Poor, Maddy. Looks like no one wants to come to a party hosted by Josiah Cunningham's sister?"

"I'm optimistic. After all, it's the first anyone's heard of the celebration. I'm sure folks will need time to consider if they're able to attend. I plan to distribute advertisements around town —the mercantile and hardware store windows, outside the livery, and a few obliging tree trunks in the town square."

"Well, I'm not fooled. I see right through this deceptive party you're organizing."

"What's that supposed to mean?"

"It means if you've come back here to wiggle yourself into Wyatt's good graces again, it won't work. You're wasting your time."

Wyatt's good graces? Why had she mentioned that? Was Wyatt paying calls on Amelia? If that were true, he'd drifted even further from the man she'd once known than she'd realized. "Wyatt and I are just friends."

Amelia lifted her chin and brushed past Madelyn. Her elbow collided with Maddy's, causing the handbills to slip from her hand. "Oh, I'm sorry." Amelia's eyes widened in a way Madelyn considered a fraudulent display of surprise. "Did I do that when I bumped you?" Her booted foot came to rest on a few of the bulletins that had fallen in the dirt. "Let me help you."

"I'm fine." Madelyn bent to retrieve the flyers. "I can manage quite nicely, especially if you remove your shoe from atop this pile."

"I insist." Putting her full body weight forward, Amelia rotated her foot, tearing the advertisements. "And if I see you making eyes at Wyatt, you'll have more than a poorly attended party to regret." She marched off, one of Madelyn's circulars impaled on her heel.

~

WYATT STARED at the blank sheet of paper. He usually had no trouble sketching ideas for projects but this one stymied him. Most likely because adding pieces to his family's nativity set held no interest for him. When Aunt Olivia told him the buyer would pay double if he finished the set, he couldn't resist. She'd also mentioned the new owner had been emphatic that Wyatt include a star that could be affixed to the top of the stable.

A star? Of all things. Seemed a bit simplistic, but if that's what the customer wanted, that's what the customer would get. His gaze drifted back to the pristine tablet. *Concentrate, Wyatt.*

A hammer pounded outside, drawing his attention to the window. A woman in a dark coat bashed a nail into the trunk of a smallish maple tree in the town square. Although her bonnet blocked his view of her face, he recognized the clothing and the shapely curves of the woman who wore them. *Madelyn Cunningham.* She'd been wearing the same coat when they'd spoken in the cemetery.

He watched as she moved to a second tree, this one with a sturdier trunk. Maddy pulled a nail from between her teeth and tapped its head. By the way she waved her hand, she must have missed and whacked her thumb instead. Wyatt winced. *I bet that smarts.*

Since the sketching wasn't coming along, perhaps he'd see if she needed any help before both thumbs weren't fit to knit the gifts she hoped to make for the children. He grabbed his hat and slipped into his heavy coat before joining her.

"Mind if I give you a hand, Maddy? It'd be a shame if you had to bandage both your thumbs."

She pulled the injured appendage from her lips. "You saw that, huh?"

"Maybe."

She swatted his arm. "I'll take you up on that offer."

Wyatt gave the nail a few strong taps and then turned to Maddy. "Where next, boss?"

"I thought to hang one on the door to the school and your Aunt Olivia's shop."

Fifteen minutes later they'd hung the last handbill on the schoolhouse door. Maddy shivered. "Thanks for helping me, Wyatt. I finished a lot sooner than I expected."

"You're welcome." He rubbed the back of his neck. "You wanna come inside the shop and have some coffee?"

She pursed her lips. Her gaze darted toward the open field next to the school.

"It's already hot. I won't keep you long." Why had he said that? He sounded desperate. What happened to his plan to keep his guard up? To maintain distance between them?

"It's not that. It's just ... well, what about Amelia? I don't think she's taking too kindly to our renewed friendship."

Wyatt's head jerked. "Amelia? What's she got to do with anything?"

"She seems awfully ... protective of you." Maddy squared her shoulders and forced herself to swallow like she had something important to say. "If you enjoy her company, then I'm happy for you, Wyatt."

He narrowed his eyes. "I'm not pursuing Amelia Jackson. Since her father and brothers didn't survive the war, I help out at the farm when I can. But we're *not* a couple—no matter what she or her mother says about it. Truth is, she remains as disagreeable as ever."

Maddy lifted a hand to her mouth, but it did little to conceal the grin Wyatt saw peeking around the edge of her fingertips.

And nothing to hide the spark that flashed in those bright blue eyes. "Then I accept your invitation."

Out of courtesy, Wyatt offered his arm. At least that's what he told himself as they strode toward his carpentry shop. Funny how such a small thing like Maddy's hand nestled close to his side could make him feel complete. If only they could find a way to ... No, they weren't a couple, and they had no future together. At least that's what he kept telling himself. Besides, he'd shoved her away. She wouldn't trust him again too easily.

Once inside, he led Maddy toward his small living quarters in the back of the shop. He tugged a chair from a small table and motioned for her to be seated. He glanced at his meager possessions—a small stove, a straw ticking in the corner, and a shelf that held exactly two plates, one bowl, and a couple of chipped mugs. The place was bare bones. No bright, frilly curtains hung at the windows and no hand-tied rag rugs lined the floorboards. No one would mistake this place for anything other than what it was—the home of a lonely curmudgeon who'd shut himself off from everything he once loved.

He set two mugs on the table. "If I remember right, you take some sugar in your coffee, but I'm out at the moment."

She stared at him.

"What?" he asked, unsure what he'd said to elicit such an intense gaze.

"You remembered how I take my coffee."

He shrugged and took the seat across from her. "Sure. It's hard to forget how the bitterness makes your lips purse."

She raised the mug and inhaled deeply before taking a sip. "Sorry to disappoint, but I've grown used to the strong taste. Sugar is a luxury Pa can't afford." Maddy glanced toward the open sketchbook. "Are you planning a new design?"

"I'm trying to decide what pieces to sketch to complete the Nativity set. The three wise men are an obvious consideration, or I could build a new stable."

"All good choices, but I'm surprised the buyer offered you no direction."

"They only requested a star, but that seems sort of ... dull and uninspired. I'd like to give them more than that."

"I don't know, Wyatt, I think the star is very inspiring."

"How do you figure that?"

"Remember now, it wasn't just any old star dotting the night sky. Its brilliance caught the attention of the Magi, and they were curious to see where it led them. Because they pursued God's heavenly sign, they found the Christ child." Her smile broadened. "It must've been a wonder to behold."

"Huh," was the only response he could muster. He rubbed his chin. Her words made sense.

Maddy slid her hand atop his, and there was no denying the jolt that followed escalated his pulse. "People tend to overlook what's most important because it seems too simple." She squeezed his hand. "Even when it's right in front of them."

Madelyn glanced at her watch pin, the one Wyatt had given her for her eighteenth birthday, then quickened her pace. She didn't want any volunteers leaving because she'd arrived too late to open the church social hall. Usually one to be on time, it seemed that since she'd returned to Taylorstown, she was more apt to be tardy than punctual.

With a mile-long to-do list and only two weeks until the party, she'd been rising an hour earlier each morning in a feeble attempt to squeeze more time into her day. But whenever she scratched a task off her list, she added another.

She halted by the maple tree in the town square. Where was the sign Wyatt had hung just two days prior? Come to think of it, she didn't recall one on the mercantile door either. Perhaps the overnight wind had been gustier than she'd thought. She made a mental note to replace it later that afternoon.

Smoke billowed from the chimney as she rounded the corner. While appreciative that someone had shown the initiative to start a fire in the potbelly stove, it was another reminder of her tardiness. However, a lit fire meant volunteers were present, and her censure quickly abated. *Thank you, Lord.*

She scurried up the stairs and stepped inside only to have her spirits dashed when her gaze landed on Mrs. Kent—the only person inside.

The Reverend's wife glanced over her spectacles. "Hello, dear."

"Good morning." Where the older woman's greeting had been strong and cheerful, her own sounded weak and hopeless. A difference Mrs. Kent must have noted as the gentle woman placed her knitting on the empty seat beside her and moved closer to Madelyn. "Let's not worry, shall we?"

Not worry? How on earth were the two of them to knit enough gifts for all the children? Would any even be allowed to come?

A heavy breath escaped her lips. For the first time since returning to her hometown, she doubted her decision to organize the children's Christmas party. Perhaps healing the division brought by four years of war and strife festered too deep for her meager attempt at reconciliation. Hadn't that been what everyone had warned her about?

"Looks like it may just be the two of us this time, but don't fret," Mrs. Kent said, patting Madelyn's hand. "Folks will come 'round to the idea. They just need a little more time."

Madelyn's shoulders sagged along with her resolve. "Unfortunately, with the party only two weeks away there isn't a great deal of time to accommodate their hesitation."

Mrs. Kent returned to her chair nearest the stove and her fingers adeptly renewed wrapping the dark wool around her knitting needles. "All you can do is spread the word. He will raise the workers."

Madelyn inhaled and slowly let the air seep from her lungs. "You're right." She nodded for emphasis and secretly hoped the gesture would fortify her dwindling determination. She unbuttoned her cape and took a seat beside Mrs. Kent. Within minutes, a simple red chain trailed from Madelyn's needles.

Just because God had given her a burden for this community,

and for Wyatt, didn't mean it was going to be easy. Still, she wouldn't argue if an abundance of workers had shown up and she didn't have to wait until the last second for God to fulfill His plan. She supposed that scenario wouldn't grow her faith as much, but she wouldn't mind giving it a go at least once.

As the two women worked, they prayed for the children who would receive these gifts, for the ladies in the different churches to step up and volunteer, for those who may be knitting at home, and for the Lord to bring healing to their town and neighboring farms.

After a solid "amen" that warmed Madelyn's heart, Mrs. Kent smiled and lifted the project she'd been working on. "I started this black scarf for my husband. Although he appreciated the kindness, he insisted his blue one would be fine for one more winter and suggested I donate it for the children."

Next to Olivia Sullivan, Reverend Kent's support couldn't be underestimated. Not only had he agreed the knitting brigade could use the church social hall, he'd made a donation to cover the cost of the handbills, and accompanied her to every church in Taylorstown, Waterford, and Lovettsville. The Quakers were the most supportive, which did Madelyn's heart good, seeing as how they'd been the driving force behind the Loudoun Independent Rangers, Flemon and Wyatt's unit. And therefore, the most aggrieved by her brother's horrendous act.

She'd always thought it a most unlikely circumstance that Quakers, known for their traditional stance as pacifists, would pick up arms. But when their farms and mills were constantly threatened, they raised a local militia to combat the guerilla raids by Colonel White and his men. Now they'd joined the effort to bring reconciliation to this part of the county.

"What are your plans for the party, dear?"

"Caroling and games with the children. The Sullivans are providing cider, popcorn, and cranberries for stringing, as well as wool for the gifts. Emily is coming for a visit to help me bake cookies."

"And Gideon Sullivan has agreed to all of this?"

Madelyn paused her knitting. "I'm not certain. But most of it was Mrs. Sullivan's idea, so I imagine she'll persuade him."

"So, the temperature is still a bit frosty where Wyatt's uncle is concerned?"

"I'm afraid so. Sometimes I wonder why God placed any of this on my heart. I'd like nothing more than to pack my bags, hug Mrs. Sullivan and Emily goodbye, and return home. But I know that's not what God wants."

"I don't think it's what God wanted three years ago when your family left Taylorstown."

Madelyn's stomach knotted tighter than a ball of yarn after the barn cats were finished batting at it. Something that happened every time she thought about her father's decision to pull up stakes and leave town. "I don't think so either."

"I'm sure your father did what he thought was best to keep his family safe."

"There may be some truth to that, but mostly I think Papa was ashamed of what Josiah had done and that Colonel White had given him immunity. Papa told Josiah that none of it was an honorable way for a soldier to conduct himself."

She resumed her knitting, and the two women worked in silence for a few minutes. "Sometimes I wonder if the town would have been forced to heal a lot sooner if my family never left."

Mrs. Kent shook her head. "We'll never know about that, but He's surely placed you right here, right now, 'for such a time as this.'"

The tension in Madelyn's neck and shoulders eased. "Thank you, Mrs. Kent. I needed to hear that."

The latch clicked, and Amelia Jackson entered the room. Madelyn stood. "Please come in. I ... uh ... wasn't expecting you to join us today."

Her narrowed gaze scanned the room. "I will not. I have no

intention of supporting this feeble attempt to clear your family's name."

Not this again. Madelyn had little patience for Amelia's antics. "If you've not come to help, then why are you here?"

"I've come to return these." She opened a small paper sack, flipping it upside down. Shredded paper drifted on to the floorboards between them.

Recognizing the garland border Wyatt had so generously designed for her, Madelyn stooped and swept bits of the torn advertisement into her hand. So, it hadn't been the wind after all. "Why would you do this?"

Amelia's chin jutted toward the air. "I'll never let Wyatt, or anyone else, forget what White's men did to Taylorstown, this part of the county, or to Flemon."

Wyatt? Why had she mentioned him? He'd assured her only two days before that he and Amelia were only friends.

Amelia's lips slithered into a smirk that Madelyn wanted to remove with a smack to her adversary's cheek. Instead, she folded her arms tightly across her chest and asked the Lord for an extra measure of grace. She seemed to be repeating that request every time the disagreeable woman came near.

"I shouldn't keep Wyatt waiting any longer." She spun on her heel and left with the same overwhelming flourish with which she'd arrived only minutes earlier.

Heart hammering in her chest, Madelyn moved to the window as Wyatt assisted her rival into his wagon.

Rival? Was that how she viewed Amelia? She needed to keep her emotions in check. Wyatt was not *hers* any longer, no matter how much she may wish it.

The surly woman looped her arm through Wyatt's. Madelyn stepped back when he glanced her way so he wouldn't think she was prying, even though that was exactly what she'd been doing.

They certainly appeared cozy. Perhaps Wyatt's heart belonged to Amelia after all. If that were true, why hadn't he just said so the day before? She'd never known him to be untruthful.

Had God brought her back home to help Wyatt heal only to become Amelia's husband? The notion roiled her stomach.

Although her mission hadn't been to rekindle their relationship, deep down in places she barely voiced in prayer, she hoped their time together might awaken old feelings. Feelings she'd not extinguished even though it now appeared Wyatt had.

This revelation was a searing reminder of all she'd lost. Her breath hitched, and a deep ache rose from the pit of her stomach, leaving her hollow inside. What if her own heart never healed? How would she go through life feeling like a part of her was missing?

Mrs. Kent's shaky hand offered Madelyn a handkerchief then gently guided her to an empty seat. Unable to contain the emotions she'd locked up inside her, she sank onto the chair and wept.

Wyatt waited outside the church for Amelia. He had no idea what errand would take her to the social hall in the middle of the day. She'd offered no details, and Wyatt didn't feel the need to ask any questions. As soon as she returned, he'd take her home and help set up the Christmas tree he'd chopped down earlier that morning, just as he'd done for other widows in the area for the past couple of years.

He might not have any use for Christmas, but many folks still seemed to find peace and healing this time of year. Christmas just dredged up memories he'd rather keep buried. Besides, he had a soft spot for the widows and orphans which made it increasingly difficult to resist assisting Maddy with her party.

Amelia trotted down the stairs. Wyatt assisted her into the wagon and then climbed in beside her. She slipped her arm inside his and glanced over her shoulder. "I'm ready to go."

Wyatt followed her gaze. A woman watched from the front

window. Was that Maddy? He raised a hand to wave, but the figure stepped away.

He untethered himself from Amelia's arm. "What was that all about?"

"I'm not sure what you mean," she said, fluttering her eyelashes like a hummingbird hovering above a patch of morning glories.

"Oh, I think you do. You don't need to be unkind toward Maddy, Amelia. She's not staying, and we're not a couple." He flicked the reins, steering the horses toward the road leading to Amelia's home. "And, neither are we."

"I know. You've made that painfully clear."

"Then why are you cozying up to me?"

"To make her jealous." Amelia straightened her shoulders. "She still loves you, and it annoys me beyond reason that she can waltz back into town and think everyone will forget what her brother did." She knotted her hands in her lap. "Well, I won't forget, and I won't let anyone else forget either."

Amelia had practically hissed the last few words and the venom in her tone made Wyatt shudder. Is that how he sounded when he talked about the injustice done to Flemon? Were his words filled with the same vitriolic inflections?

"Her family didn't kill Flemon. Only Josiah did." A bell rang in Wyatt's head and reverberated clear to his heart. Madelyn hadn't known what her brother was about, nor had she ever made excuses for his actions. And Flemon, the man her brother murdered, had been Maddy's friend too.

Amelia's head snapped in his direction.

"What?" he asked.

"She's wormed her way back into your good graces, hasn't she?"

"We're not together, nor are we likely to be. I already told you that."

"Perhaps, but you've always held the entire Cunningham clan

accountable. That's why you broke your engagement and sent her away with her family."

A tight pinch at the back of his throat, accompanied by a similar, more painful feeling in his chest, made it a bit difficult to breathe. Amelia had spoken the truth, and while he'd known what he'd done, in his grief it all made sense. Her bitterness mirrored his own and nauseated him.

"You're right. In the past, I've held the entire family to account for the actions of only one of its members," he said. "That was wrong of me. But that's not why I broke our engagement."

"Then why did you?"

"That's none of your concern."

He wasn't about to confess that he'd sent Maddy away because he was a coward. A coward who wouldn't pull his saber to defend Flemon, the Andersons, or his fiancée. In the frenzied attack, all he'd seen was Josiah Cunningham, his childhood friend and brother of the woman he loved. He could no more pull a weapon against him than he could draw his sword against his own mother.

Clinging to his anger and resentfulness for the last few years was the only way he'd known to close the gaping wound seared into his soul when he sent Maddy away. But all that had done was to leave him as cynical and disagreeable as Amelia. A thought he found particularly distasteful.

He tugged the reins to a halt outside her home.

"But—"

"Let it go. Some things are better left unsaid."

Although Wyatt knew his revelations needed sharing, he had no idea if the woman he yearned to tell would listen.

Six

Resembling a deer caught unaware in the forest, Mr. Sullivan darted his gaze nervously between Madelyn and his wife. No doubt he'd noticed Madelyn's swollen, puffy eyes, a direct result of her ardent display of emotion earlier that afternoon in front of Mrs. Kent.

She stared at the chunks of venison and carrots on her plate and sighed. Between the ripped flyers and only one volunteer attending the knitting brigade, her spirits had taken a hit. Observing Amelia smugly secured on Wyatt's arm had nearly broken her.

If it weren't for disappointing the children, she'd toss her hands in the air and leave Taylorstown tonight.

Why did it bother her to see Wyatt parading about town with another woman? Three years had passed since he'd broken her heart, so why couldn't she put him and the hope of any future together behind her? If Wyatt was ready to move on, then she would wish only the best for him, but Amelia? How was that possible? And why hadn't he just admitted to there was more to their relationship when she'd seen him a few days ago, instead of denying it?

Mrs. Sullivan nudged her wrist. "You haven't eaten a bite of your supper."

"I'm sure it's delicious. I suppose I don't have much of an appetite tonight." She slumped forward, both elbows on the table, and rested her chin on her curled fists. "I might've underestimated how difficult it would be to rally the town in support of the war orphans. Perhaps people aren't as willing to reconcile as I'd hoped."

Mrs. Sullivan reached for her hand. "One day doesn't make or break the party. There's still plenty of time. I'm sure, after a good night's rest, you'll have a better perspective on the whole event."

Not wishing her gloomy mood to cloud the Sullivans, she nodded in agreement. "Do you mind if I excuse myself? I'm not hungry. I think I'll go to my room and knit a pair of mittens."

"Perhaps we could do that together in the parlor. I might even persuade Gideon to play the piano for us."

Madelyn had many fond memories of Christmases past when Emily would invite her friends to the Sullivans' for caroling around the piano and making ornaments for the town tree. The same tree that had remained unadorned since the war began. "Would you, Mr. Sullivan? I think singing might be just what I need to shake these doldrums."

"Certainly."

"I have an idea," she said, her voice already sounding lighter. "Rather than decorating a small tree in the church social hall, the children will trim the large evergreen in the town square. Then we'll sing carols, just like we used to." She leaned closer to Mrs. Sullivan. "Doesn't that sound marvelous?"

Mr. Sullivan's fork clanked against his plate. "Look, Maddy, I can see how much you want things around here to be like they were, but too much has happened, too many people have been hurt. The war has changed folks and it's not easy to undo such a thing." He sprinkled pepper over his stew. "I'm doubtful anyone will come."

"I understand, but if it's only me and a few children, it will be worth it." Her heart thrummed in her chest. This was the perfect idea, and God had chosen to reveal His plan when her discouragement had reached its zenith and she was about to abandon her mission.

"I'll be right back. And, I think my appetite has returned," she called over her shoulder as she disappeared into the hallway.

She retrieved the small tablet where she'd been recording her ideas and making lists for the party then returned to the table and ate two quick bites of stew. "We'll need some volunteers to string the berries and pop the corn." She tapped the pencil against the side of her cheek. "We'll need some needles and thread too."

"I'm sorry, dear, but we weren't able to secure the order of cranberries as I'd thought," Mrs. Sullivan said.

"Oh, well, then we'll make do with only popcorn, but I'll need to double the amount." She jotted that note on her tablet. "The children can congregate first at the social hall to make the garland and paper ornaments and play party games. After that, we'll parade to the town square singing carols. It's bound to draw a few people from their homes, don't you think?"

When her gaze snagged on Mr. Sullivan's, he shook his head. Now what? She'd finally found her enthusiasm again and didn't need any more discouraging insights, even if they were most likely true. "Something wrong?"

"You're really not here to restore your family's name or even your relationship with Wyatt, are you?"

"No, sir. I came because ..." She glanced at Mrs. Sullivan who gave her permission to continue with a tight nod of her head. "I came because Mrs. Sullivan wrote me about how bitter Wyatt had become. Through our letters, I learned it wasn't only Wyatt clinging to past injustices, but most of the community as well. When she shared that Wyatt was thinking about selling his family's heirloom nativity, I knew I had to come and at least try to make a difference—for everyone. However, I won't deny that if folks regained their favorable opinion of my family, I wouldn't be displeased."

Fingers intertwined against his flat stomach, Mr. Sullivan rocked back on the hind legs of his chair. "And you and Wyatt are—"

"Only friends, sir." She tried to mask the disappointment in her voice when she mentioned her relationship with Wyatt, but the deepening ache in her chest every time she spoke his name made it an arduous task.

She tossed a questioning look at Mrs. Sullivan. "I just wish I'd been told beforehand about his interest in Amelia Jackson. I still would've come, of course, but I'd have prepared my heart to see him showing interest in another woman."

"Wyatt and Amelia? That's unlikely."

"He told me the same a few days ago but this morning I saw them cozied up snug as you please on his wagon seat."

"I'm not sure what you saw, but there is no way in heaven my nephew would court Amelia."

She wanted to believe Mrs. Sullivan's words. After all, she was Wyatt's aunt. Madelyn recalled her conversation with Wyatt. Hadn't he said, *no matter what she or her mother said about it?*

That dirty, rotten ... Amelia flaunted a phony relationship with Wyatt just to taunt her, and she'd gobbled it up faster than a garter snake swallowed a field mouse.

WYATT RAPPED his knuckles against the door. Was Uncle Gideon playing the piano? He hadn't heard his aunt and uncle singing carols since the year Flemon died.

The door swung open. Aunt Olivia stood on the threshold, one hand on her hip and the other motioning for him to enter. "Are you going to stand out there and freeze to death or are you coming in?"

He kissed her cheek and stepped inside.

"What brings you out on this cold night?" she asked.

"Uncle ..." His gaze immediately went to Maddy. It never mattered how many people were present. If she was nearby, he sensed her. Then, without any conscious thought on his part, he just knew where to find her. Even now when she had tucked herself in a corner almost out of his line of sight.

The knot that had been twisting in his gut ever since she'd returned to Taylorstown tightened when he laid eyes on her. When she left in January, he'd have a heap of sorrow to tangle with all over again.

"Wyatt?"

"Huh? Oh, Uncle Gideon asked me to come over and settle some of the accounts for the items you've sold for me in the shop."

"I thought I'd given you the money for the rocking horse and farm animals already. Did I miscount?"

"No," he mumbled. "It's for the sale of the nativity." Finalizing the sale was proving a bit more difficult than he'd expected, but it was too late to reconsider his decision. He'd given his word. Backing out now would reflect poorly on his aunt and uncle.

He lifted a burlap sack. "I've completed the last few pieces." He tugged on the drawstring and retrieved a bundle of tissue paper. Setting the bag aside, he carefully unwrapped the first item.

Aunt Olivia gasped. "Wyatt, this is beautiful."

Uncle Gideon examined the wise man in his wife's hands. "I've never seen such precision, son." He patted Wyatt's back. "This is as fine a whittling as I've seen. Nathaniel would be proud."

Although they were only words, his uncle's remark made Wyatt feel a bit taller than normal. He'd always enjoyed carving alongside his dad. Making furniture and repairing an occasional wagon provided a living, but whittling was a passion he shared with a father taken way too soon.

Would he be proud of the man Wyatt had become? Or only the work of his son's hands? More than likely, he'd be ashamed that Wyatt had turned away from the faith he'd so lovingly taught all his children.

Guilt niggled at Wyatt's conscience. What would his father think of his decision to sell the family heirloom? Not wanting to ponder that question, he quickly shoved his father's imagined rebuke from his mind.

Maddy touched his arm, jolting him from his thoughts. "May I?"

Uncle Gideon handed her the wise man. Her fingers traced the folds of his clothing and the intricately carved gift in his outstretched hands. She stared at Wyatt, jaw slightly unhinged. "It's lovely."

The richness of her tone made his heart tick a bit quicker. "I have two more." He removed each of the remaining Magi from their tissue paper nest. His smile broadened as Madelyn and his family fussed over the subtle details of his work.

Maddy glanced toward the burlap sack at his feet. "Is the star still inside the bag?"

"I know the buyer requested one, but I couldn't imagine a design that intrigued me enough to carve it. Hopefully, these will more than make up for not having a star."

Aunt Olivia shook her head. "I don't think the buyers will be disappointed with your creations, but I'm afraid they were emphatic about the star. They didn't ask for any flourishes, just a simple, five-point star. Can you have that to me by the beginning of next week? They plan to pick it up on Christmas Eve."

He scratched the coarse hair of his beard. "All right. I'm not too excited about the project, but if you're sure that's what the buyer wants . . ."

"Perhaps reading the account of Jesus's birth in Matthew will provide the inspiration you're lacking?" Maddy shifted her attention to Aunt Olivia. "I'll put the kettle on. Any chance we can persuade you to share some of those oatmeal raisin cookies?"

He followed Uncle Gideon and the ladies to the kitchen, but Wyatt hadn't missed the gleam in Maddy's eye when she'd suggested he read the Bible. The woman was relentless.

"Maddy has a new idea for the children's party," Uncle Gideon said.

Wyatt snagged a cookie from the plate Maddy had placed on the table. "Thought you weren't supporting her endeavors."

Uncle Gideon tipped his head in Maddy's direction. "She's finally convinced me that her heart is in the right place. Still not sure folks around here will be receptive to the idea of veterans' children from the Rangers and Comanches mixing at the same party, but she's been working real hard to make this gathering a success. I've decided to help her any way I can."

Maddy pivoted toward the table. "You have?"

"I have."

Maddy hugged Wyatt's uncle.

"And I'd like you to do the same, Wyatt," Gideon said. "I believe she still needs someone to read the story of Christ's birth. As I recall, you're her first choice."

Wyatt waved his hands. "Sorry to disappoint you both, but I can't read from a book I'm not sure I believe in any longer."

She placed a mug in front of Wyatt and then sat across from him. "I understand."

He narrowed his gaze. "You do?"

She tugged her bottom lip between her teeth. "I could use your help with an equally important but potentially more difficult task."

Wyatt dragged a hand over his chin. "Look, Maddy, I'd like to give you a hand—"

"That's great, Wyatt. I knew you wouldn't let me down."

Uncle Gideon snickered.

Wyatt glared at his uncle. "You're not making things any easier."

"Sorry, son. You might as well tell the lady yes. I don't think you have it in you to deny her twice."

Truer words had never been spoken. Recognizing defeat when it slammed into him, Wyatt shoved a weighted breath from his lungs. "What do you need?"

$Seven$

Madelyn could hardly believe her ears. Wyatt had finally agreed to assist her with the children's Christmas gathering. Although he had no idea that she was about to ask him to escort her into the proverbial lion's den.

Visiting Flemon's mother was a task she'd put off long enough. She needed to seek reconciliation with his family for her own sake and the sake of their entire town.

Mr. Sullivan shoved his chair from the table. "I think we should take our tea to our room, dear. Perhaps you could read a little more of that Dickens novel, *Bleak House*. I'm curious to know if Honoria will be found out."

"What of the dishes?"

Madelyn poured the remainder of the coffee into Wyatt's mug. "I'll be certain to wash and dry them all before I come to bed."

"And you won't forget the candles in the other room?"

"No, ma'am."

"Or to lock up after my nephew leaves?"

Mr. Sullivan clasped his wife's hand. "Come dear. Maddy isn't a child. I'm sure she knows what's to be done before she retires for the evening."

Madelyn waited until she heard the click of the Sullivans' bedroom door before glancing at Wyatt. He'd relaxed in his chair and now sat with his hands interlocked over his mid-section and his long legs stretched before him. He raised his brows in question, no doubt curious as to what she would ask him.

When she didn't reply to his silent inquiry, he grinned, and Madelyn's stomach somersaulted, leaving her both giddy and anxious. The same emotions had warred within her as a child when she and Wyatt would pass a lazy Sunday afternoon tumbling down the steep hill behind the apple orchard. *Oh, how she loved this man.*

"This must be a mighty big favor."

"What makes you say that?"

"I've known you all my life, Maddy, and the only time I can recall you being at a loss for words was the night Flemon died."

He stood and grabbed his coffee. "C'mon," he said, gently cupping her elbow. "Let's go sit by the fire in the parlor. I can tell from the look on your face, this isn't gonna be a short conversation."

She allowed him to lead her to the pair of rocking chairs positioned on either side of the hearth. His touch, both familiar and foreign, made her yearn for a future with Wyatt and reminded her of the distance still lingering between them.

Wyatt poked at the smoldering logs, and soon gentle flames licked at the wood they consumed. He settled into the rocker opposite her and waited for Madelyn to find her words. No fingers drumming on the armrest or feet bobbing against the floorboard. He merely pumped his rocker in a steady, rhythmic fashion as if he had all night for her to find the mettle to speak her mind. She'd always admired his fortitude.

Hoping to convey an air of confidence, she lifted her chin. "I plan to pay a call on Mrs. Anderson, and I'd like you to escort me there."

He didn't respond immediately, but she'd noticed the slightest jerk of his head and suspected her request had surprised him. "She must've heard by now that I'm in town, and I think it only proper that I inquire after her—let her know how much I regret Josiah's actions, and hopefully set our relationship to rights."

He leaned forward, elbows resting on his knees and fingers steepled. The old Wyatt would've been asking God's direction, but she wasn't sure how this Wyatt went about making decisions.

"Before I agree, I need to know why you want to pay her a visit. It's been three years. Don't you think it might be best to let the past stay in the past? We can't fence time, Maddy. Nobody can."

"I don't want to dredge up bad memories, assign blame, or persuade her to change her opinion of me or my family. I want her to know that despite all that's happened between us, I do care about her."

He scratched his beard. "It's that important to you?"

"It's why I came back. We are friends and neighbors with a shared history—one we all need to make amends with. How can I ask others to lay their grievances aside and settle their accounts with one another if I haven't even attempted to do so myself?"

MADELYN CLUNG to the pinecone and winterberry wreath she'd made for Mrs. Anderson and stepped through the open wrought iron gate Wyatt held for her. The Anderson's three-story home looked exactly as Madelyn remembered. Brown, twiggy stems that would burst into beautiful shades of violet when the wisteria bloomed in late spring clung to the stone edifice. Harrison, the family's orange tabby cat, scurried beneath the porch as the pair climbed the stairs.

"Ready?" Wyatt asked.

She offered a quick prayer beseeching God to allow her visit to be an instrument of His healing in the community—one of many she'd prayed on the two-mile walk from the Sullivan's store. Hoping to project more confidence than she felt, she squared her shoulders. "Ready."

Wyatt lifted the brass knocker. A few moments later, the Andersons' servant opened the door. "Mr. Hawkins. What brings you 'round today?"

Like so many others in and around Taylorstown, Gemma's expression soured when her gaze landed on Madelyn. "Not sure the Missus will want to receive you, Miss Cunningham."

She should be accustomed to this reaction by now, but it still stung. Would she or her family ever escape the scourge of Josiah's actions?

"Please let Mrs. Anderson know that Miss Cunningham is with me, and we've come to pay a social call."

"Certainly." She stepped back and motioned for them to come inside. "You know Mrs. Anderson is always pleased to see *you*, Mr. Hawkins. Please wait here while I see if she's inclined toward visitors this mornin'."

Gemma disappeared down the corridor that led to Mrs. Anderson's fancy parlor. With marble-topped tables, burgundy striped cushions, and velvet curtains, Madelyn had always thought it the most handsome room in Taylorstown. She recalled many fond memories of dances and celebrations held in the Andersons' spacious home.

She stared at the large, empty space where the mahogany stairs bent before continuing their ascent to the second floor. A lump formed in her throat. Normally, a tall evergreen would be positioned in the two-story foyer to greet holiday visitors.

While many of the German families in the area waited until Christmas Eve to adorn their trees, the Andersons had always held an annual tree-trimming party about two weeks prior. The community-wide gathering brought rich and poor together for a celebration of Christ's birth. The family often gave the local children sweets and simple toys, rather than the more practical gifts given by their parents. The tree's absence was another reminder of the damage Josiah's reckless act had left in its wake.

The padding of Gemma's footsteps dragged her from her reminiscences. "Follow me, please. Mrs. Anderson will receive you now."

Mrs. Anderson sat near the fire on an upholstered wingback chair, similar to the one that had snagged Flemon's sword, preventing his escape the night he died.

When Maddy and Wyatt entered the parlor, Flemon's mother closed the book she'd been reading and removed her wire spectacles. "It's always good to see you, Wyatt. Miss Cunningham."

While she'd kept the same pleasant tone when addressing Madelyn as she'd done with Wyatt, the absence of Madelyn's Christian name from Mrs. Anderson's greeting hadn't gone unnoticed. Still, she had agreed to the visit. That was what Madelyn needed to focus on.

"Good day, Mrs. Anderson." Maddy forced herself to relax her grip on the wreath she'd brought. "My apologies for not coming sooner. I've not been back for a visit since ..."

Brilliant, Madelyn. In the door less than five minutes, and you've already referenced the worst day of the woman's life. She swallowed, but the former lump in her throat now felt like a boulder. Unsure how to proceed, she shot a gaze at Wyatt.

"Don't you have a gift for Mrs. Anderson, Maddy?"

That's right, I do. She'd have to thank Wyatt later for rescuing her. She offered the wreath to Mrs. Anderson, who examined it for a moment before smiling her thanks.

"It's fairly simple," Maddy said, "but it reminded me of the wreaths and garland we made years ago to decorate the church cemetery."

Mrs. Anderson's face paled. She removed a handkerchief from her sleeve and dabbed her eyes.

Wyatt's chin dropped to his chest, and he cut Madelyn a stern glare.

"Uh ... I didn't mean to say ... to cause you any pain." What was the matter with her? Normally, Madelyn advised others what to say in tricky situations. Problem was, she'd never known a circumstance as difficult, or so painfully self-inflicted, as this one was becoming. If she could remove that boulder from her throat, she'd insert her foot. It seemed to enjoy living there.

"I'm so sorry, Mrs. Anderson. I shouldn't have come." Retreat her only option, Madelyn spun on her heel and charged toward the foyer.

"Madelyn." Mrs. Anderson's genteel voice drifted across the parlor, bidding Maddy to halt her exodus. "Other than bringing me this lovely wreath, why did you come to see me today?"

Madelyn gnawed on her lower lip. Perhaps all was not lost. Slowly she faced Flemon's mother. "I wanted you to know that you've been in my thoughts and prayers. And that I'll always be grateful for the many kindnesses you've shown me over the years."

Mrs. Anderson tapped her finger against her lips, her dark eyes taking a long measure.

Madelyn resisted the urge to shift her weight from one foot to the other under the older woman's scrutiny. Instead, she forced herself to stand erect.

"That's kind of you, all things considered."

"I hope my presence won't intensify your grief."

"I'll always miss Flemon, but I've not been in the throes of grief for quite some time."

Madelyn nodded. "That's good to hear. Flemon would not want us living bitter lives." She glanced at Wyatt and thought she saw him squirm a bit.

"I've heard tell you're planning a Christmas party for the children of disabled or deceased war veterans."

Madelyn swallowed hard. She'd hoped against all odds to

avoid breaching this topic with Mrs. Anderson. "Yes, ma'am," she said, voice cracking.

"And you think it wise for the opposing sides to come together in this fashion?"

She glanced at Wyatt. The tight nod of his head encouraged her to speak her mind. If Madelyn believed in this party, she needed to find her fortitude, which had been sorely lacking of late. She raised her chin. "I do. What better occasion to cast one's differences aside than Christmas?"

"Indeed."

Mrs. Anderson's agreement emboldened her. "If I may," Maddy said, "you're the inspiration behind my efforts."

"Me?" Mrs. Anderson covered her parted lips with her fingers.

"The party you held each Christmas was the focal point of the holiday season. I couldn't think of anything better that might entice our neighbors to attempt reconciliation."

"She's been doing nearly everything for the party herself," Wyatt said.

Was that a hint of pride she'd detected in his voice? Perhaps he was finally warming to the idea.

"That's not entirely true. Wyatt designed a handbill to let people know about the event and the Sullivans have donated wool, for volunteers to knit into scarves and mittens for the children. And Emily is coming later this week to pop the corn for the garland. Even Mr. Sullivan has said he'll help us trim the large tree in the town square."

"How can I help?"

Madelyn blinked. "Oh, Mrs. Anderson, I did not come here to enlist your help, but merely to mend any broken fences that needed repairing."

"Let us consider them all mended."

The weight Maddy had been carrying since that awful night lifted. With one hand pressed to her heart, she bit back the tears pricking behind her eyes. "I'd like that as well."

Gemma returned, carrying a silver tea service. "Excuse me, ma'am. I brought both coffee and tea." She set the tray on the cherry sideboard. "I'll be back shortly with biscuits and honey."

Mrs. Anderson thanked Gemma and then returned to her earlier conversation with Madelyn. "If the Anderson family Christmas gathering was the inspiration for your party, then I'd like to help. How can I be of use to you?"

Receiving Mrs. Anderson's forgiveness was more than Madelyn had hoped for, and now she had her support as well. "Would you attend? If you, who were most grieved by the incident three years ago, would give your blessing, others may begin to put their anger, bitterness, and grief aside as well. Perhaps it will be the first step toward reconnecting with our neighbors."

"Consider it done."

Mrs. Anderson's generous offer to attach her name to the party was a godsend. Why had Madelyn doubted His prompting to return to Taylorstown?

"What of a practical nature can I assist with? Do you have sweets for the children?"

"There will be cookies and cider at the gathering."

She waved her hand. "That will never do. It's Christmas." Mrs. Anderson set her determined gaze on Wyatt. "It might be too late to acquire enough toys, but perhaps I can persuade you to make a trip to Leesburg to purchase peppermint sticks, walnuts, and oranges if you can find them."

Wyatt nodded. "Maddy's been after me to be more useful, so this is the perfect task for me."

Poor man. First, his uncle had prodded him to volunteer, and now he'd been enlisted by Flemon's mother. And he'd never tell her no, even if it meant walking to Leesburg and back. He'd wanted to avoid helping with the celebration, but it seemed God might have other plans for Wyatt. Plans that went far beyond assisting with a children's party.

Eight

Wyatt slowed his gait to match Madelyn's. Although their visit to the Andersons' home had been a successful one, they'd spent most of the return journey in silence. Too many conflicting thoughts crowded his mind, and he needed to sort them.

He admired Madelyn's determination to set her relationship with Flemon's mother to rights. That couldn't have been easy for her. If he acted as boldly, was there any hope of true reconciliation with Maddy? One that would include a future together? Or would the truth of why he'd broken their engagement, and the subsequent pain he'd caused her, remain a wedge between them forever?

He'd tried denying his feelings for her, but it was a lost cause. For three silent years, he'd not allowed himself to love this woman or receive her love in return—the only atonement he could offer for allowing his best friend to perish. But now she was right here beside him, and the powerful longing he'd suppressed came hurling forward, crushing his resolve.

The Sullivans' store came into view. *Great.* They'd be parting ways in just a few minutes. *C'mon man, where's your gumption?*

She paused and faced him. "What's the matter, Wyatt? You've barely said a word since we left Mrs. Anderson."

He inhaled deeply, letting the chilly December air bite at his lungs before exhaling. What did he have to lose? "If you're not in a hurry, could I come in? There are some things I need to say."

Worry lines creased her beautiful brow, but she didn't voice a sound. She simply nodded and followed the path to the stairs behind the store that led to his aunt and uncle's private residence.

Once inside, Wyatt started a fire. Maddy settled into one of the rocking chairs beside the hearth.

She cleared her throat. "I understand that you're not inclined to help with the party, Wyatt. You have a business to run, for pity's sake. Please don't feel obligated to travel to Leesburg before the festivities on Tuesday. We'll manage just fine without sweets for the children."

He returned the poker to the hook on the stone hearth. "It's a tad inconvenient on such short notice, but I don't mind being of use to you. Not anymore. Besides, I can't deny Mrs. Anderson's request. You know that. But that's not what I wanted to speak to you about."

He exhaled again, but it did little to relieve the heavy weight of guilt pressing on his chest, making it difficult to breathe. "I owe you an apology, Maddy. I never should've pushed you away after Flemon died. I know I hurt you, and—"

"You did more than push me away, Wyatt." Her voice warbled. "You made me equally complicit in his death. But what I don't understand is why. You know Flemon was like a brother to me."

Hands clasped behind his back, he stared at the flames. Anywhere but her face. "Because it was easier to blame you, to make you at fault, than look inside myself and admit the truth. Flemon is dead because I'm a yellow belly."

She sprung to his side. "You are *not* a coward, Wyatt Hawkins."

A burning pain pinched his throat. "I told Flemon to run."

"Are you forgetting how outnumbered you were? Twelve armed soldiers stormed the Anderson home that night. Twelve."

"And I never drew my weapon. Not even when your brother aimed his revolver at Flemon."

He rested his palm on the mantel. "Truth is, I didn't see Josiah as a threat. Despite all the skirmishes between the Rangers and Colonel White's marauding band of Comanches, I didn't see his gray uniform—only *him*. My childhood friend and brother of the woman I loved. I could no more draw my saber on him than I could run through my own mother."

Wyatt shook his head. "The fault is mine. I never thought Josiah would actually pull the trigger. The Rangers and Comanches tussled all the time. I thought he'd arrest us, hold us for a few days, and then negotiate a prisoner swap with Captain Grubb."

He slumped onto the rocker and raked his fingers through his hair. "How'd I make such a colossal mistake?"

Madelyn knelt beside him and wove her fingers between his. "You didn't. Like any good soldier, you assessed the situation and made a decision. You chose to shove Mrs. Anderson to the ground and shield her with *your* body. Standing next to Flemon as she was, she'd most likely be dead if it weren't for you."

"But Flemon was my best friend."

"And you saved his mother. If we could relive that ill-fated night, do you think Flemon would ask you to save him instead?"

"No. But—"

She silenced him with a tap of her finger against his lips. "Flemon's death wasn't your fault any more than it was mine or my family's. You've got to forgive yourself, Wyatt. That's the only way to pick up the pieces and rebuild your life."

He gazed into her beautiful, familiar blue eyes. Did she really not believe him to be the coward he saw every time he looked in a mirror? "How am I supposed to do that?"

~

EVERYTHING MADE sense to Madelyn now. Wyatt had never truly blamed her. Attaching the burden of Flemon's death to her and her family had merely been a tool he'd used to deal with his own misplaced guilt.

Lord, please help Wyatt find his way back to You. I can't heal the wounds he's carrying. Only You can do that. But if You'll allow it, I'll be right here beside him, pointing the way back to You.

She glanced at Wyatt's hand, laced together with her own. "We're stronger together than we are apart."

For the first time in three years, she allowed her gaze to linger on his face. She traced the outline of his beard with her thumb. Did he not understand the depth of her unconditional love for him? A love only God could design.

She leaned forward and touched her temple with his. "With God's help, we'll do it together."

~

WYATT TUGGED the collar of his winter jacket higher on his neck and shoved his gloved hands into his pockets. He'd always enjoyed looking at the night sky. He'd been hoping for some motivation to complete the last piece of the nativity set, but he was having an awful time thinking about anything but his conversation with Maddy a few days earlier.

She was right, they were stronger together than they were apart. Why hadn't he told her that he'd not stopped loving her? That he longed to spend forever together?

Because deep inside, he knew Maddy Cunningham would never have him until he made himself right with the Almighty— no matter how much she might love him. And lovin' a woman was no reason to pretend he understood anything God had done since the moment Josiah pulled the trigger.

Focus, Wyatt. Finish the nativity set.

The buyer had explicitly requested a simple star. Where was the creativity in that? He'd made a rudimentary sketch, something any seven-year-old could do, then measured all the angles so his finished product would be in proportion. Carving the star, however, held little interest for him.

An infinite number of stars twinkled back at Wyatt from the night sky, but none shone brighter than any other. Why would God choose something so familiar to announce the birth of His Son? To Wyatt's way of thinking, he'd want to create something different, something unique. Like the new table design he'd been contemplating. One that would expand to reveal a hinged central leaf that would unfold and increase the number of people that could be seated.

However, as a businessman, he always aimed to please his customer. If the nativity's new owner wanted a plain old ordinary star, that's what they'd get.

Maddy seemed to think it was a promising idea, and she usually had good instincts. Maybe she was right. Maybe people did tend to overlook the most important things, even when they were right in front of them.

He doubted it could be that straightforward. If only a body could find the road to peace and contentment so easily. Why didn't God put miraculous signs in the paths of His faithful today? That sure would be a whole lot less complicated.

Wyatt grabbed the lantern he'd placed on the barrel outside his workshop. He could at least add dimension to his star, couldn't he?

With a bit of renewed vision, he stepped inside and fetched the box that housed his small hand tools from the shelf beneath his workbench. His fingers traced the roughly hewn H carved into the lid. Wyatt not only treasured these woodworking tools, but the craftsmanship that had been passed from father to son over the generations. Most of the Hawkins men had been farmers by day and whittlers by night. Like his grandfather,

Daniel, Wyatt had been one of the few to make his living as a carpenter.

He removed his chisel, knife, and gouge from the box. The sooner he completed the star, the sooner he could finalize the sale. A sale he was regretting more with each passing day. There was nothing to be done about that now. Perhaps, someday, if he and Maddy did settle down like he hoped, he could begin the tradition of a Hawkins family nativity all over again.

He selected a piece of pine about three-eighths of an inch thick, squaring the board to four and a half inches. Using a medium-sized plane, Wyatt slid the tool along the grain. Before long, thin shavings curled away from the plank's surface and fell beside his boots.

Next to designing, this was Wyatt's favorite part of woodworking. The steady, rote strokes of planing allowed his thoughts to wander with little or no risk of injury. He just couldn't wrap his mind around why that particular item would be so important to the buyer that she'd insist one be included or they'd void the sale. His curiosity piqued, Wyatt set the plane on his workbench, grabbed his lantern, and sought out the only place he might be able to find the answer.

He rifled in the trunk at the foot of his pallet. The same trunk that had once housed his family's heirloom nativity. Beneath a shirt that needed mending lay his Bible, a gift from his parents when he'd turned thirteen. He hesitated as if touching the Holy Book in his doubt-filled state would sear his skin. When he finally grasped the soft leather Bible in his hands, he had to admit it felt good, like greeting an old friend he hadn't seen in a while.

Once seated at the table, he opened the cover and stared at the inscription written in his father's hand. *Wyatt, when you feel lost, lean on His Word. It will be a light unto your path. Pa*

For the first time since Flemon died, he bowed his head and talked with the Almighty. "As you know, I haven't been in Your Word or even talked to You since Flemon passed. So, if there's somethin' in here You wanna show me about why the star is so important, then I'd appreciate it if You'd make it clear because I'd like to know the answer."

He flipped to the book of Matthew and read the account of Jesus's birth and the wise men who'd come from the East. Huh. No train whistles blared, or bells rang pointing to a new insight. He'd acquired no more understanding than before he'd reread the passages.

Wyatt slid the Book away and stared at the ceiling. "Do You want me to understand or not?"

He glanced at his sketchbook. What if he approached this as he would designing a new piece of furniture or repairing a wagon? Instead of drawing a sketch, he'd take notes. Although the hour was late, he doubted he'd sleep unless he at least attempted to unlock the mystery of the star.

Invigorated, Wyatt fired up the stove and made a fresh pot of coffee. He gathered his sketchbook, pen, and inkwell then settled in at the table again. As he read, he jotted down every reference to the Magi's quest for the Christmas star he could find in Scripture.

1. They followed the star.
2. They knew the prophecy and anticipated his arrival.
3. They asked for the King of the Jews, whose star they'd seen.
4. They rejoiced when they saw the star.

He read the notes he'd taken many times over. Still uncertain, he circled each action the Magi had taken to answer their questions about the star.

God had used a heavenly luminary to lead the Magi to His Son, but *they'd* made the choice to follow it. They must have faced hardships on such a long journey but that didn't deter them. They were committed to their mission to find the Christ child that had been foretold in Scripture and worship Him.

Wyatt, on the other hand, had cast his faith aside when he'd needed it most. Nearly two thousand years later, could the star of Christmas be leading him down a similar path? A path that would renew his relationship with the Almighty and restore peace and contentment in life?

"Followed, knew, anticipated, asked, and rejoiced." He covered a yawn and then repeated the words again and again until his eyelids grew heavy.

If he truly wanted to restore peace and contentment in his life, he'd have to make a choice too. And his would require humbling himself at the foot of the cross once again.

Nine

Madelyn knocked on the door to Wyatt's shop a second time. Still no answer. She glanced at her watch pin. Five minutes after nine. His shop should be open for business by now. Where could he be?

Concerned, she walked around the side of the building and peered in the window. What on earth? Wyatt sat at his kitchen table, his chest and arms sprawled over a book and sketch pad.

If she didn't know better, she'd think him passed out, but she'd never known Wyatt to drink spirits.

She tapped on the glass. He lifted his head about an inch off the table, and a page from the book clung to his cheek. Without acknowledging her presence, he returned to his slumber.

"Wyatt," she called, tapping on the glass again. "Are you all right?"

He sat up this time, wincing when the morning sun hit his eyes. "Maddy?"

"Yes. Out here. Can I come in?"

He glanced toward the window. "Coming." Or at least that's what it sounded like through his half-yawned words.

Wyatt stumbled toward her and grunted when he lifted the

343

crossbar. He opened the door and covered another yawn. "What brings you by so early?"

"Early? It's well after nine and your shop isn't open."

"I overslept," he said, scratching his beard. I was up late working on ... a project."

She narrowed her gaze and studied him head to toe. His sandy brown hair stood at attention, and his clothes were less than fresh. She leaned closer and sniffed.

"What are you doing?"

Madelyn stepped back, but not before waving a hand in front of her face. His breath smelled like yesterday's coffee. She was pleased he didn't reek like the bottom of a liquor bottle, and he'd obviously not used his tooth powder that morning. He'd always been a well-disciplined, stick-to-the-schedule sort of man. What else could account for his odd behavior if not alcohol?

"I have a favor to ask you, Wyatt, but I grew concerned when I found your shop closed. Then to find you sleeping ... at your table, no less ... I—"

"You're worried about me?" He inched closer. "I like that."

Heat crept up her neck. There was no denying how adorable he looked, all rumpled in the morning, but responding to his flirtations would only tease her lovelorn heart.

She whisked by him and stood beside the table. "My favor concerns the party. Don't worry, I'm not here to badger you about reading the Bible story to the children. I'll do that. But Your Uncle Gideon hurt his back last night, unloading a shipment for the store. He was going to fill the coal bins in the church social hall from the supply in the cellar. I was hoping you might take on the task before the party tomorrow."

"Sure, I'd be happy to help."

"Thank you," she said. "I knew I could count on you."

She glanced at the items strewn over his table. His Bible lay open to the book of Matthew. She tugged his sketch pad free from beneath the Holy Book and scanned his list. Tears pricked the corners of her eyes. He'd been studying God's Word? She searched his face. "Wyatt?"

He stuffed his hands in his pockets. "I've been thinking on what you said about the star. I thought it might be a good idea to read about it for myself. Make my own decision about whether I'm gonna follow the path that leads to the Almighty, like the Magi did, or whether I'm gonna keep on doin' things my own way."

A frisson of excitement swept over Madelyn. She could barely believe the words he'd spoken. Why had she ever doubted? Wasn't this why God had brought her to Taylorstown for Christmas? To help steer Wyatt back to his heavenly Father. And if God was anything, He was true to His Word. "What did you decide?"

He dragged a hand over the back of his neck. "I've been miserable since Flemon passed, and I'm thinkin' I want to make things right between me and God again."

"That's wonderful, Wyatt, but what's holding you back?"

Eyes bright, Wyatt straightened. "Nothin', Maddy. Nothin' at all."

WYATT TOOK the church stairs by twos. He gulped for breath as the cold December air nipped at his lungs. Reaching for the latch, he recoiled. He hadn't been here since Flemon's funeral. What if he took this step and nothing changed?

Strains of "Silent Night" echoed through his memory, quieting his fears. No, it was time. He'd stayed away long enough.

Grasping the latch a second time, he pushed open the door and stepped inside the vestibule. He slid his hand over the maple pew, its finish worn from decades of the faithful worshipping God in this place.

He stared at the simple wooden cross hanging on the wall

behind the altar. Maddy had been right about the star all along. The same celestial sign that had led the Magi to the Christ child foretold in Scripture had prompted Wyatt to humble himself at the cross where that babe would later lay down his life for mankind.

Could a simple act of repentance tonight begin a chain of reconciliation that would mend the wounds inflicted by a war that had pitted neighbor against neighbor, friend against friend, and at least one foolish man against his God? Maddy thought so, and he was inclined to agree.

There were no guarantees. Wyatt understood that now. But as Maddy said, allowing God back in his life was the only way for the healing to begin. Letting go of the anger and bitterness that had been his constant companions for the past three years wouldn't be easy, but change didn't have to come overnight—it just had to come.

With that thought in mind, Wyatt bowed his head and made peace with his God.

Ten

Madelyn adjusted the red and green table covering Mrs. Anderson had loaned them for the party.

When she'd arrived at the social hall to decorate, Flemon's mother had been waiting for her with candles, greenery, and holly snips to give the church social hall a festive appearance. She'd also brought three platters of cookies, which made the children's eyes nearly bulge from their sockets.

Susan Rockford's laughter drew Maddy's attention. Mrs. Sullivan and Mrs. Anderson sat with the children in a large circle, showing them how to string popcorn to make a garland for the tree. Susan had accurately predicted few others would attend if the children of a Confederate came. Peter Talbot and his boys, Isaac and Elijah, were the only exception. Mr. Talbot had fought alongside Flemon and Wyatt in the Loudoun Rangers. That made twelve guests, if you didn't include friends who were helping with the celebration. Not the numbers she'd hoped for, but it was a start.

Maddy dipped a ladle into Mrs. Anderson's crystal punch bowl, making sure to avoid scooping the orange slices floating in the cider. She offered the drink to Mr. Talbot. He leaned his worn crutch against the wall and accepted the cup. Maddy scooted a chair beside him.

"I'm a bit surprised to see Flemon's mother, especially with 'em Rockfords here."

Wyatt had told her that Peter had taken a bullet in his hip the first time the Rangers and Comanches had sparred in nearby Waterford.

"No more surprising than seeing you, here, Mr. Talbot."

He shrugged. "Blasted Comanches didn't kill *my* son. Besides, my hurts don't need to be those of my children. Seeing as how we aren't likely to go anywhere, and neither are 'em Rockfords, I figure we should all try to find a way to at least live peaceably together." He sipped his cider. "Ain't that the point of this party?"

"Most certainly." His words soothed her worry over the poor attendance. A spark of healing had to begin somewhere. She trusted God knew best how to fan that spark into a roaring blaze.

Mr. Talbot nodded toward the rear door. "He's a good man."

Madelyn followed the wounded soldier's gaze. Wyatt slowly turned one of the blindfolded Rockford children in a circle. She had no idea where he'd disappeared to after she'd woken him from his slumber on the kitchen table yesterday. However, the image of the Holy Scripture stuck to his cheek made her smother a grin.

"I probably shouldn't be telling you this," Mr. Talbot said, "seein' how we barely know each other." He leaned forward on his elbows. "But that fella sure did pine after you when you left town. Wyatt and I were never close like, but you only needed eyes to see how miserable he was without you."

A blush heated Madelyn's cheeks. She rarely mentioned her relationship with Wyatt to others. Having someone she barely knew speak of it made her squirm in her chair.

"Hi, Peter. Maddy."

The deep timbre of Wyatt's voice gave rise to gooseflesh that skipped along her skin. His mere presence made her heart thrum quicker.

Wyatt shook Mr. Talbot's hand and then pulled a chair beside his friend. The two began conversing about Flemon and their days serving in the Union Army.

Mr. Sullivan crossed the room, his gait slower than usual, and conversed with his wife.

"Excuse me," Maddy said. "I'll be right back."

Madelyn joined the Sullivans in the rear corner of the room. The older woman balled a few of the children's coats and stuffed them behind her husband's back. "Comfortable, dear?"

He squeezed his wife's hand. "Yes, thank you."

"I'm surprised to see you here, Mr. Sullivan," Maddy said. "Are you sure your back is well enough?"

"Don't mind me. I'm perfectly fine to sit here in this chair and read the story of Christ's birth, if you'll have me?"

She blinked. "Of course I'll have you."

"It's no secret I wasn't fond of you returning to Taylorstown and I certainly had more than a few doubts about this party. But you've proven this old fool wrong." He paused then swallowed hard before speaking again. "I'm sorry, Maddy. I hope you'll forgive me."

Madelyn sucked in a quick breath, then covered her mouth. *Would wonders never cease?* She stooped beside Mr. Sullivan and kissed his cheek.

Perhaps it had been naive for her to believe that one party, one Christmas, could bring reconciliation. But as she glanced around the room, she heard the flicker of hope in the laughter of Confederate and Union children playing blind man's bluff with Wyatt. Perhaps other hearts, like Amelia's, weren't ready yet. But some were, and if they allowed, God would show them the path to forgiveness.

～

WYATT LIFTED Jeb Rockford onto his shoulders. The child grasped his collar and giggled as Wyatt trotted toward the refreshment table. He handed the little fella a cookie. Jeb snatched the treat. Seconds later, cookie crumbs tumbled down Wyatt's nose. It was a good thing he'd decided not to offer the boy cider.

He grabbed two more cookies and scanned the room for Maddy. She and Uncle Gideon were chatting. His heart thrummed a bit harder when she kissed his uncle's cheek. He hoped the pair were putting any remaining strife between them to rest.

When he'd left the church earlier that morning, he'd stopped by the mercantile and made a special purchase. Aunt Olivia had been all a flutter and he'd sworn her to secrecy. As near as he could tell, his aunt had been true to her word.

"Circle round, children," Maddy called. "I have a peppermint stick for each of you and you may eat it while Mrs. Anderson reads 'A Visit from St. Nicholas.' Then we'll sing Christmas carols and conclude our party with Mr. Sullivan reading you the story of Jesus's birth."

"Peppermint stick." Jeb yanked on Wyatt's collar again. His small feet knocked into Wyatt's chest as if he were a pack mule the boy wanted to move faster.

The promise of candy sparked the children to hurry and seat themselves on the floor in front of Mrs. Anderson.

Finally, an opportunity to speak to Maddy privately. There was so much he wanted to tell her. So much he wanted to discuss, like the matter of their future.

He lowered little Jeb into the circle as Mrs. Anderson began reading. Maddy slipped a peppermint stick into Jeb's waiting hand and nudged him a little closer to his big sister.

"C'mon," Wyatt said, nodding toward the door. "I need to tell you something."

"Perhaps we should wait till after the party? I might be needed to assist with the children."

Wyatt rocked back on his heels. He couldn't contain the grin he felt inching across his face. "I've waited long enough."

"All right, but we'll need to be quick. I have a surprise for you, and I don't want you to miss it."

He helped Maddy into her coat then shoved his arms into the sleeves of his own before ushering her outside. He guided her to a bench under a winter canopy of barren oak trees.

"First, I wanted to apologize for tearing out of the shop yesterday like a swarm of bees was chasin' me. Sometimes you just know what you need to do, and there's no sense waitin' any longer to get it done."

Tiny little lines etched her forehead. The same ones that showed up every time he didn't make a lick of sense.

"You asked me what was holding me back. Remember?"

She nodded, but the creases hadn't disappeared yet. He hoped if he just plowed ahead, it would all make sense in the end. "When I didn't have a good reason, I realized the only thing holding me back was me."

Finally, the wrinkles disappeared from her brow and her eyes brightened. "Wyatt, are you saying—"

"I've made my peace with the Almighty. I'm pleased to tell you that He and I are on speaking terms again. I know it's gonna take some work for my hard heart to soften in some areas but I'm promisin' you that I'm committed to letting go of the past."

Tears pooled in her eyes. Was she gonna cry? Hadn't she been encouraging him to do just this?

In a very un-Madelyn-like display of public affection, she lunged toward him and wrapped her arms around his neck. He grabbed the back of the bench and anchored himself firmly on the seat. Unflustered, Maddy's ardent grasp never faltered. Confident they wouldn't tumble onto the melting snow, he tugged on her wrists. "Let go, Maddy ... before you strangle me to death."

She reclined against the bench. "This is the best Christmas gift you could've given me, Wyatt." She fished a handkerchief from her coat pocket and dabbed her eyes. "This is an answer to my prayers. I know it's why God brought me home this Christmas."

He swiped a tear from her cheek. "I hope it's not the only reason."

She twisted the handkerchief between her fingers and looked away.

With his index finger, he gently turned her chin toward him. "Is that the only reason you came home?"

She pursed her lips. A sharp pain stabbed his gut. Had his inability to put the past behind him sooner cost him the only woman he'd ever loved? Would his newly revived faith survive if she left again?

"It's not the only reason," she whispered.

Her breathy voice made Wyatt's pulse stammer. He stroked her cheek with his thumb, and she nestled into his palm. He didn't deserve this woman but if she'd found a way to love him again after all he'd put her through, he didn't plan to question his good fortune.

He dug a small velvet bag from his pocket, loosened the drawstring, and emptied the contents into his palm. A single gold band shone in the winter sun.

"Maddy, I've loved you since we were kids. I was a fool to deny that and chase you away. I never want to know the pain and agony of spending another day without you by my side until the Good Lord takes one of us home. Please say you'll spend forever with me."

A WAVE of gooseflesh rippled over Madelyn's skin as a sultry grin eased over Wyatt's lips. She traced the outline of his beard with her finger. "Forever will do just fine."

"That's mighty good to hear, because I'm not planning on you being anywhere but at my side ever again."

His strong hands encircled her waist, and he tugged her close. She breathed in the heady scent of bay rum and spice, and her eyes fluttered closed. Her heart hammered in her ears as his lips sketched a slow, tender path from her jaw to the corner of her mouth, eliciting a soft moan.

He paused and met her gaze. "I love you, Maddy, like I've never loved another."

"And I love you, Wyatt Hawkins. I always have, and I always will." The pain and heartache of the last three years faded to a distant memory. She was her beloved's, and he was hers.

Without thought to who might glance through the window, she slid her arms around his neck and returned his kiss, allowing every ounce of suppressed longing to voice what her words could not.

ALTHOUGH HE'D BE QUITE content to kiss her a spell longer, Susan's voice calling for Miss Cunningham bade Wyatt to soften his mouth against Maddy's. He brushed his lips against her temple and stepped back. "I look forward to a lifetime of sharing kisses like that, once I make you my wife."

"Miss Cunningham," Susan called again before rounding the corner of the building. "Mrs. Sullivan sent me to fetch ya. Her husband is startin' the Bible story."

Maddy nodded, and Susan started toward the front of the church then turned back. "He's got an angel, and a shepherd, and even a tiny baby Jesus, all carved outta wood. I ain't never seen anything like it afore."

Wyatt snapped his gaze toward Maddy. "You don't think ..."

She lifted her hands, palms up. "Let's go find out."

Once inside, they stood behind the children as his uncle positioned Joseph and Mary inside the Hawkins family crèche.

Wyatt massaged his temple. "How can this be? When I

dropped off the star earlier today, Uncle Gideon indicated the buyer would pick it up this afternoon."

Something twinkled in Maddy's eyes. "She did. I was there when she picked it up."

"Mrs. Anderson ... bought my nativity set?"

She entwined her fingers with his. "No. I did."

His head jerked slightly. "You?" He tapped his fist against his mouth. "I thought it was gone ... forever," he said, his voice choked with emotion.

Warmth spread through Wyatt. He loved this woman. How could he have ever jeopardized that by hanging on to past hurts? With God's help, he'd show her how much he cherished her until his last breath.

Wyatt slipped his arm around her waist and pulled her tight beside him. He'd been given so many gifts—the restoration of his relationship with the Almighty, the love of a good woman, and now, the deep and abiding connection with the generations of Hawkins men who'd carved that precious heirloom.

She tucked her hand inside his. "I couldn't bear to think of the nativity set leaving your family. I thought in time you'd have regrets, so I decided to hold on to it until you were ready to embrace its worth."

"Thank you," he whispered before letting her go.

"Wyatt." Uncle Gideon beckoned for him to come to the front. "I think you should have the honors," he said, holding up the star. "The wise men have found the Christ child."

Wyatt slid the star onto the small nail attached at the top of the stable's slanted roof then returned to his spot beside Maddy. He never could have imagined carving a star for his family's nativity would guide him back to his Savior, or the woman he loved.

Perhaps the heirloom wasn't the intricately chiseled pieces of the nativity, or even the manger itself. The heirloom was the legacy of faith passed from one generation to another. The faith he saw in the woman standing beside him.

Treasured gifts he'd never abandon again all reflected in one simple sculpted piece of wood—a star carved for Christmas.

355

Epilogue

Three Years Later
December 1870

Wyatt lifted two-year-old Flemon from his shoulders and settled him into the wagon next to his mother.

Maddy tugged the boy's knit cap over his ears. "Come snuggle next to Mama," she said, opening the quilt wide so he could scoot beside her. Once he nuzzled close, she tucked the blanket around his shoulders and legs.

"Did we forget anything?" Wyatt asked, stepping up on the wagon wheel beside her.

"I don't think so." Maddy stifled a yawn. "It's late, and we should get Flemon home. Besides, we'll be back to visit the Andersons again soon and can get anything we left behind."

"You'd better stay awake, Mrs. Hawkins," he said, waggling his brows. He planted a modest kiss on her lips. "We made a deal earlier. And, seeing how I'm a man of my word, I intend to keep it. *After* we get the littl'un to sleep."

"You're incorrigible."

The moonlight shone bright enough that he noticed her cheeks blush, and Wyatt's heartbeat ramped up a notch or two. Whether the pink that bloomed resulted from his kiss, the frosty December air, or the promise of what the evening might bring, he couldn't tell. But every time those chicory blue eyes landed on him, Wyatt was reminded how much he loved her. And, how close he'd come to losing her and this life they'd made for each other.

He pecked her cheek then climbed into the seat beside her.

"Oh, good, you're still here." Mrs. Anderson hurried toward them. "You nearly left the ginger root tea behind. Now, mind what I tell you. The herbalist in Baltimore assured me this would help assuage the nausea you're having this time around."

Maddy placed the jar of loose-leaf tea in her lap and squeezed Mrs. Anderson's hand. "Thank you. That was such a thoughtful gift."

"You're welcome, dear. Merry Christmas."

"Merry Christmas."

Wyatt slapped the reins, and the wagon lurched forward. The horses' hooves crunched against the packed snow, and an owl hooted in the distance. They'd not even traveled a mile before Maddy's head bobbed. "Tired sweetheart?"

She yawned again. "I'm not sure, but it seems like I had my stamina back at this point when I was carrying Flemon."

Wyatt shifted the leads to his left hand. "How about if you put Flemon on your lap and cozy up to me? You can put your head on my shoulder."

She nestled close against him, and Wyatt inhaled deeply. He had everything he ever wanted right here. Before long, Maddy's soft breathing told him she'd fallen asleep.

He steered the team onto the road that would eventually lead them to their small stone cabin. The night sky twinkled brilliantly, and Wyatt once again considered the star of Christmas.

What a sight to behold.

How radiant it must have been to stand out among such a luminous display on a night like this.

Only three years ago, he'd told Maddy he had "no more use for Christmas than a ruffled petticoat."

Wyatt scoffed at his own folly. He couldn't have been more wrong.

People *did* grow into Christmas as their love for the Almighty flourished inside them. It was that love for mankind that inspired Him to send His Son at Christmas for all to find ... if they were willing to follow His star.

THE END

<h1 style="text-align: center; font-style: italic;">A Note from the Author</h1>

As a long-time resident of Loudoun County, Virginia, I'm fascinated with our county's rich history. I first learned about the tragic events of Christmas Eve, 1864, when I attended a presentation given by local author, historian, and playwright, Meredith Bean McMath, *Seldom Heard Stories from Loudoun Civil War History*. Meredith also pointed me to my primary source for this story, *History of the Independent Loudoun Rangers, U.S. vol. cav. (scouts) 1862-65* by Briscoe Goodhart, who served with the Loudoun Rangers.

The Loudoun Independent Rangers, of which Sergeant Flemon B. Anderson and my fictional hero, Wyatt Hawkins were members, was an independent Calvary unit formed from the largely Quaker and German communities of Northern Loudoun County, Virginia. Although known for their pacifist beliefs, Virginia Quakers enlisted in both the Union and Confederate armies.

The Loudoun Rangers, as they were more commonly referred to, were formed in June 1862, by Samuel Means, a Quaker who owned one of the county's largest mills. Farmers and business owners with Union sympathies, like Means, were often targets of guerilla-style attacks. One such band of marauders, "White's Comanches," led by Lt. Col. Elijah V. "Lige" White (35th Battalion, Virginia Cavalry), would become the archnemesis of Loudoun's Rangers.

What's most interesting to me is the familiarity these soldiers had with one another. Not only were both units recruited in the same portion of the county, but the same surnames appear on the muster rolls for both the Rangers and the Comanches. Men who'd been raised side-by-side, attended the same churches and schools, knew where one another lived and the names of their intended, now picked up arms and violently clashed on the same land where they'd spent their childhood together. Over time, their frequent skirmishes began resembling the notorious feuds of the Hatfields and McCoys and embedded themselves in Loudoun's folklore.

This is the backdrop for the tragic events of Christmas Eve, 1864, when Sergeant Flemon B. Anderson brought a few of his fellow soldiers, and lifelong friends, to his Taylorstown home to celebrate the Christmas holiday. Tragedy struck at 9 p.m. when twelve Confederates, largely from White's Comanches, stormed the Anderson home and fired upon Flemon as he attempted to flee for his life. When his saber caught on a wing back chair in his family's parlor, the fatal bullet struck his head. He died moments later in his mother's arms, his sweetheart looking on.

From here, I created my fictional cast with only Mrs. Anderson being a real historical figure. It was widely known that Mrs. Anderson enjoyed entertaining and held many social events, including a Christmas Eve gathering each year. I took liberty to make her party a community wide event emphasizing charity toward those in need.

While not in the story, two other historical characters are referenced, Mollie Anderson, Flemon's sister, and Col. Elijah V. "Lige" White, whose men led the raid on the Anderson home. There is no evidence that White issued any orders to storm the Anderson home, or even knew what his men were planning, as the unit had ceased operations for the winter.

In *The Christmas Carving*, I wanted to explore how the events of Christmas Eve, 1864, may have affected those who witnessed them firsthand, as well as the ripple effect they would have throughout the tight knit community of Taylorstown. How do you love your neighbor as yourself in the face of such an abhorrent act? Would they choose to forgive or remain shackled to bitterness and anger?

It is my hope that after reading *The Christmas Carving* you will come away more determined to lay grievances at the foot of the cross choosing instead reconciliation over bitterness, kindness over animosity.

Thank you for reading Wyatt and Maddy's story.

Blessings,
Kelly

Discussion Questions

1. Maddy arrives in Taylorstown with a mission to turn Wyatt's heart back to God and bring healing to her war-torn community. Describe a time in your life when you felt a strong God-given purpose in your life?

2. At the beginning of the story, Wyatt tells Maddy he has "no more use for Christmas than a ruffled petticoat." Why did he feel that way? What did you think of Maddy's response? How would you respond to a friend or family member who found Christmas to be a difficult time of year?

3. Wyatt has let bitterness steal everything dear to him. What do you think of the way Maddy helped him see past his hurt? Can you think of someone who's hurting that you could show the love of Christ to this week? Brainstorm ways to be the hands and feet of Jesus in the situations described.

4. In spite of all the obstacles in Maddy's way, she is generally resilient and determined to bring about change? What is the source of her fortitude? What Scriptures can you recall that inspire perseverance?

5. Forgiveness and reconciliation are underlying themes of *The Christmas Carving*. Have you ever found it hard to forgive someone who has hurt you? Have you ever sought forgiveness only to have it denied? How did the situation resolve itself?

6. Maddy hoped to facilitate reconciliation between the Union and Confederate families in Taylorstown. Although she is initially disappointed with the poor attendance for the Christmas party, she eventually concludes that some hearts weren't ready to let go of their past hurts and differences. Other than Maddy and Wyatt, what characters were ready to embrace change by the end of the story? Which were not? Would you have chosen a different outcome? Why or why not?

7. When Wyatt is finally ready to forgive himself and let go of the anger and bitterness he'd been clinging to since Flemon's death, he recognizes that "change doesn't have to come over night, it just has to come." Do you find it easier to forgive others than yourself? Why or why not?

8. The Merriam-Webster Dictionary defines an heirloom as "something of special value handed down from one generation to the next." Besides the nativity set, what other items were passed from one generation of Hawkins men to the next? Which did Wyatt conclude held the most value? What heirlooms do you hold most dear?

9. The Hawkins' family nativity is more than a holiday decoration, it's an heirloom that Wyatt and Maddy both cherish as a symbol of faith and family. Do you have any Christmas heirlooms or traditions you enjoy displaying each year? Why are they special to you? Have you considered starting a new tradition with

your family or friends? If so, consider sharing it with
the group.

365

Acknowledgments

I'm so grateful for all those who have come alongside me to bring *The Christmas Carving* to life. None more so than my Heavenly Father who graciously allows me to co-create with Him, and my sweet hubby, Mike Goshorn, who prays me through each and every deadline.

To local historian, author, and playwright, Meredith Bean McMath, for bringing the tragic events of Christmas Eve, 1864, to my attention during her presentation, *Seldom Told Stories from Loudoun Civil War History,* and for pointing me to my primary source for this work.

Many thanks to Cynthia Roemer for inviting me to join this collection and to my fellow authors, and new friends with whom to share the writing journey, Elaine Cooper and Candace West. It has been a joy working with you all.

To my critique partners Lori Altebaumer, Cynthia Roemer, and Debb "The Slasher" Hackett for your invaluable input and encouragement. Debb, thank you for your faithfulness to read, reread, and brainstorm this story in the midst of your own deadlines.

To my Darling sisters who were always willing to Zoom-write, trouble shoot, and brainstorm this project with me—Lisa Kelley, Dani Pettrey, Crystal Sandow, and Stephanne Smith. Thank you for cheering me across the finish line, ladies. I love you all.

Heartfelt gratitude to my sweet friend and agent, Cynthia

Ruchti. I appreciate your insight, wisdom, and suggestions. I've learned so much from you already and we're just getting started.

And finally, to Linda Fulkerson and all those behind the scenes at Scrivenings Press who worked tirelessly to bring the *Chiseled on the Heart: A Christmas Legacy Novella Collection* to print.

About the Author

Kelly Goshorn weaves her affinity for history and her passion for God into inspiring stories of love, faith, and family set in America's vibrant past. Her debut novel, *A Love Restored*, won the Director's Choice Award for Adult/YA fiction at the Blue Ridge Mountain Christian Writers Conference in 2019 and earned recognition as both a Selah Award finalist in the Historical Romance category and as a Maggie Award Finalist for Inspirational Fiction.

She earned her B.A. in Social Studies Education from Messiah College and her M.Ed. in History from The Pennsylvania State University. Kelly is an active member of ACFW Virginia where she currently serves as the Conference

Coordinator for the chapter's popular virtual Royal Writers Conference.

Kelly has been enjoying her own happily-ever-after with her husband and best friend, Mike, for 33 years. When she is not writing, Kelly enjoys binge-watching BBC period dramas, board-gaming with family and friends, exploring historical sights, and spoiling her Welsh corgi, Levi.

Reflecting on Christmas Past:

31 Daily Devotions with Annual Reflection and Journaling Pages

by Heather Greer

Each December starts with hope. This year the peace and joy promised in every Christmas song will finally be ours throughout the season.

By mid-December, we're worn out, weighed down by our to-do lists. Decorating the tree was rushed, crammed between baking and visiting relatives. Our card list grew. So did the gift list. Now that the kids (or grandkids) are all in school, we have more than one Christmas program to attend. We can't skip the office party. Oh, and did we forget caroling again?

Wouldn't it be wonderful to slow down and focus on the traditions that make Christmas meaningful to us? Wouldn't it be nice if we could remember what those are?

With thirty-one devotions and ample space for reflection and memories, we can enter each Christmas season with renewed focus on what matters most to us and leave behind the extras that usher in disappointment and fatigue. Ending this holiday season with the same hope, love, and joy we entered it with is what Reflecting on Christmas Past is all about.

Release date: October 10, 2023

https://scrivenings.link/reflectingonchristmaspast

~

Mama Dated Santa

Contemporary Romance by Amy R. Anguish

Trudy McNamara doesn't do Christmas anymore. But she will do anything for her nephew Mark, even take him to visit Santa. After Dad died and the holiday bucket lists stopped, December hasn't been the same. But Trudy finds herself tangled up with the toy store Santa and Christmas when she discovers her mom ... dated Santa.

Nick Russo, manager of Russos' Toy Emporium, is at a loss as to how to save his family's store. When Uncle Paul, the Santa and part-owner, hires Trudy to revamp their store, Nick's life turns upside down. He's been so focused on the numbers, the Christmas season has become nothing more than one last drive for sales. But Trudy makes him re-evaluate his attitude as well as want to help hers.

Release date: October 17, 2023

https://scrivenings.link/mamadatedsanta

~

True Blue Christmas

Mystery by Susan Page Davis

New neighbors, cryptic Christmas cards, and jury duty. What next? Campbell McBride is juggling her new role as a private investigator with her slightly wacky personal life. Can she and her dad figure out who stashed a valuable painting in their client's attic? And is the murder of an egocentric landlord somehow connected?

Release date: November 7, 2023

https://scrivenings.link/truebluechristmas

~

12 Days of Mandy Reno

Contemporary Romance Novella by Regina Rudd Merrick

Law student Amanda Reno is stuck in her tiny hometown in Kentucky to complete her studies virtually and work part-time at the Clementville Café. Her parents are stuck in Brazil, leaving Mandy to celebrate Christmas without them.

Young Sheriff Clay Lacey takes matters into his own hands, devising a plan to take Mandy's mind off her crushed expectations. She is no longer his classmate's tagalong kid sister, but a young woman he is increasingly attracted to.

How will Mandy react when she finds out Clay is the one working to make sure she has a memorable Christmas? Will she be pleased? Or will she cringe as she thanks the man who may be falling in love with her?

Release date: November 14, 2023

https://scrivenings.link/12daysofmandyreno

Stay up-to-date on your favorite books and authors with our free e-newsletters.

ScriveningsPress.com